Undone

Carly Phillips

Donna Kauffman
Candace Schuler

Undone

HARLEQUIN®

TORONTO • NEW YORK • LONDON
AMSTERDAM • PARIS • SYDNEY • HAMBURG
STOCKHOLM • ATHENS • TOKYO • MILAN • MADRID
PRAGUE • WARSAW • BUDAPEST • AUCKLAND

ISBN 0-373-83680-5

UNDONE

CONTENTS

GOING ALL THE WAY
Carly Phillips

Chapter One

REGAN DAVIS glanced around Divine Events one last time. The hottest party-planning business in Chicago earned its name, but since she'd been dumped, Regan had no more use for their specialty skills.

She paused at the table in the reception area and took in the large Grecian urn she'd seen many times before. Filled with bird-of-paradise, hyacinth, hydrangea and lush greenery, the flowers created a canopy over the table. Gliding her hand over a set of white photo albums—portfolios of Divine Events' creations—her hand skipped from book to book until she reached a red leather-bound volume. The draping flowers had hidden the album from view until now and she paused, intrigued.

A few feet away, the doorway, fresh air and a new life beckoned to her. Beside her, a crystal bowl full of candy sat available for picking. But not even the gourmet chocolates or the taste of freedom tempted Regan as much as that book.

Why? Why did that single volume entice her so?

Because her life was in the dumps and she was ready for something, anything, to turn it around, spice it up, make it what she wanted it to be. And the scarlet book just oozed scandal and sin. As she remained alone in the room, there seemed to be no reason not to peek, so she sat on the couch, then reached for the heavy book. No title and the leather turned out to be a protective covering for an oversize paperback. She tried to flip through but each page had been sealed, a fact that further heightened her piquing curiosity. She bit down on her lower lip and opened the front of the book in search of the title page.

Sexcapades: Secret Games and Wild Adventures for Uninhibited Lovers. Oh, my.

She slammed the book closed. She was certain a furious blush now covered her cheeks, but her southern breeding took over. She glanced around through lowered lashes. Though voices buzzed from the back fitting rooms and other areas of the shop, no one was in the reception area or entryway. Because she was alone, Regan indulged herself further. Her heart beat out a rapid rhythm and her mouth grew dry as she looked at the first sealed section. "Tie Him Up in Knots: For Women Who Like Being in Control."

An erotic tingling heightened her senses, but she acknowledged that the words on the page hit her on another level. It had been a long time since Regan had been in charge of anything, especially her life. Yes, she'd made a start, but it was long overdue.

Prior to her trip to Divine Events to cancel her wedding plans, Regan had stopped in at Victoria's Secret and purchased the most naughty, racy, sexy nighties she could find. Clothes had to come next. She pulled at the silk blouse buttoned to the top that was making her perspire. No, darn it, the blouse was making her *sweat.* She snorted aloud, disgusted. Her southern manners and refinements were so ingrained, even losing them took premeditated thought.

From being the dutiful daughter to almost becoming the obedient wife, she'd lived her life by the rules indoctrinated in her and her sisters since birth. Her parents already had a banker and two attorneys as sons-in-law, and Regan was to have added a third lawyer to the *perfect* family tree. Regan would have finally become the perfect daughter, not the disappointment. Not the daughter who did things her own way.

Her daddy, the judge, had been thrilled and her mama would have been, if Regan had planned to hold the wedding at the country club in Savannah. That had been a huge disappointment for the Davis family.

Her move to Chicago one month ago was another, but her fiancé had insisted they marry here, in the city where they'd relocated thanks to his being named head partner of the new office. Regan had been too happy to go along. Anything to escape the restrictions she'd grown up with. And now she had to deliver the third blow. She shook her head, unable to stifle a laugh because, before today, Atlanta burning had been the darkest day in the history of the Davis family.

A proper southern belle, born and bred, Regan had been groomed to be a blushing bride. Instead she was a jilted one. Which didn't bother her as much as it should have, considering her life's mission would now be classified as a failure by her loved ones. Her mother would be particularly disappointed. Kate Davis was at her best as a parent when her daughters complied with her southern expectations. Defy them and Kate withdrew, turning into a stranger instead of a mom.

With this broken engagement, Regan's family would be devastated, but Regan was grateful to be liberated from the shackles of propriety and from the fiancé who'd been yet another concession to expectations.

Regan should be desolate. Instead, with her wedding canceled and her fiancé gone from their shared apartment in the Chicago high-rise, she felt relieved—despite Darren's betrayal. They'd used each other—she accepted that now. She'd chosen him to please her family, never mind all the things lacking in their relationship. And he'd picked her because of her daddy's standing in the legal community. Still, Darren had walked out on her first. She was almost tempted to applaud his courage.

And wouldn't her parents be shocked to find out that Darren had grown tired of the proper southern manners schooled into Regan since before her coming out? What a laughable irony. He preferred the loud, tacky, foul-mouthed legal associate he'd hired to work beside him. Regan shook her head. She had no business thinking evil thoughts about a woman who was bold enough to wear miniskirts and dark, sexy-looking lipstick, and to speak in a manner that demanded a man's respect. Not when Regan wanted to be more like her and always had.

She wanted to be free. Free to wear clothing she liked, not clothing society, or her mother, deemed proper. Free to channel her public relations abilities into a career beyond charity work. And free to choose a sexy guy without checking his credentials or pedigree. Heck, at this point she'd settle for being able to think for herself. Living in Savannah had stifled her and she hadn't realized it until she'd moved to Chicago one short month ago—and she hadn't accepted it until now.

But her life could start fresh. New. Now. Darren, the no-good cheating rat, had given her that chance—if she had the nerve to reach out and grab the opportunity.

Sexcapades. She ran her hand over the soft red leather. The scarlet covering. How apropos, Regan thought, and after a quick glance around to make sure she was still alone, she defiantly undid the first few buttons on her silk blouse, giving an unobstructed view of a matching pink lace bra and, she thought proudly, the ample cleavage her sisters envied.

She ran a hand through her carefully set curls, creating what she hoped was the disheveled, come-hither look her mother associated with bimbos and tainted women. A quick peek in her compact mirror proved her right. Her cheeks were flushed pink and a quick swipe of lipstick added a sultry appeal. Talk about making do with the bare minimum essentials, Regan thought. But it'd have to do, at least until she could shop for hot, skimpy new clothes to go with her bold new outlook and attitude.

The more she removed the external shackles in her mind and the external ones she put on each morning, the more

Regan's courage grew. She glanced down. The directions inside the book were clear, instructing readers to tear out a section that sparked their interest, then live and love!

Her palms grew damp and her hands shook, her gaze returning again to the "Tie Him Up in Knots" section. Oh, yes, she'd like to tie a man up in knots, to see a spark of desire light in his eyes and know his need was for her and her alone. And, suddenly, she didn't want to wait for the right man to come along sometime in her future. She wanted to grab control now. Before she informed her family about the broken engagement, Regan wanted to take that first step and establish her independence. Starting with a no-strings-attached affair.

At that heady, seductive thought, liquid desire flowed through her veins, pulsing, pounding, assuring her she'd chosen the right course. And she'd start with picking her fantasy. Despite her resolve, southern breeding took over, and her gaze circled the shop to see if anyone would catch her stealing a page. No, she was still alone. She reminded herself that, after today, she'd never see this place or anyone in here again, then she mustered her courage and ripped out the page.

The tearing sound echoed loud and clear in the empty reception area. Regan winced, but when no one came by to chastise her, she folded the paper and slipped it into her purse. Mission accomplished, she thought with pride.

Now she just needed a man.

THE THINGS a guy put up with for his friends, Sam Daniels thought wryly. He stepped out of the fitting room in Divine Events, leaving the monkey suit and the rest of his best-man trappings behind—at least until tomorrow's ceremony. Tonight was the rehearsal dinner and, thank goodness, the bride and groom had opted for casual clothing.

He swiped a hand over his eyes but the bleariness remained. Well, what did he expect after taking a late-night flight out of San Francisco? Before coming home, he'd been on a prolonged trip, as he usually was in his job as a corporate pilot for Connectivity Industries, a large computer company. His most recent stint had been taking the CFO and some underlings to Paris, which had entailed a stay at the Ritz and assorted other perks. Man he loved his job.

After growing up in a hellhole in San Francisco, he'd promised himself he'd get out and stay out. And he had. Sam had a condo in a high-rise in the Embarcadero with a view of the Bay Bridge. Overlooking the city reminded him of how far he'd come. Thanks to his hard work, he'd landed a job that took him all over the world and paid extremely well. The luxuries associated with his career weren't bad either.

The only downside was jet lag and Sam suffered the bone-weary feeling now. He was in no mood for his newest obligation, but, as best man, Sam was duty bound to do right by his good friend, a guy he'd met in flight school. Bill had decided to give up flying and settle down with his soon-to-be wife. Sam snorted, disappointed with his friend's choice, but determined to respect it nonetheless.

Like Sam's mother, Bill's fiancée didn't want a man who wasn't home, one who traveled for a living. Sam just hoped that unlike his old man, Bill didn't wither into a shell of a human being as a result. Sam shrugged. Bill was a grown man and knew what he was getting himself into. But no woman would get Sam tied up in knots, in matrimony or in anything else besides a sizzling-hot affair.

And it had been too damn long since he'd indulged in one of those. Mostly because women claimed they could handle one night—just like they claimed they could cope with his lifestyle—then, before he blinked, they were trying to change him. To convince him what he really wanted was to leave the friendly skies behind in favor of hearth and home.

Like hell.

Despite his personal feelings on the subject, he'd rearranged his schedule in order to hit Chicago a few days before the wedding, but he wanted out of *this* place now. All the flowers and white accessories screamed *wedding* and that made Sam shudder.

He tucked his T-shirt into his jeans and strode through the hall and into the reception area. Only the sun could reflect brighter than all these damn mirrors surrounding him. He squinted his eyes as he set foot in the entryway. Then he froze, mesmerized.

She was a blonde and he'd always been a sucker for blondes. She wore silk, a fabric that reminded him of the feel of a woman's skin. And her fingers glided over a red book in a delicate, erotic way, adding to the intensity that had begun throbbing through his body. And he hadn't even seen her face.

Not that it mattered. If she was in Divine Events, she was either about to be married, a maid of honor or a bridesmaid, which in Sam's book usually meant she was waiting to catch the bouquet and be next in line to tie the knot. At least that's what his sisters and their friends claimed and Sam refused to be trapped. He shook his head and laughed.

At the sound, she looked up, wide-eyed, and met his gaze. Stunned and obviously embarrassed, judging by her pink cheeks, she slid the book off her lap and back onto the table.

He didn't know what intrigued him more, the scarlet book, the pink cheeks…or her. She had large blue eyes with a hint of sadness and secrets, porcelain skin and the most gorgeous bone structure he'd ever seen. And she couldn't tear her eyes from his.

It'd been a long time since he'd experienced such a strong, reciprocal visceral reaction to a woman. Long enough that he decided it was worth exploring further.

He strode to the couch and settled in beside her, laying one arm behind her head. "Hi," he said and leaned close. A floral scent assaulted his senses and inside his jeans he grew hard. Talk about instant attraction. He hadn't been so immediately horny since he was a kid.

She inclined her head so blond strands brushed her shoulder. "Hi, yourself." Her eyelashes fluttered in a move unpracticed yet seductive at the same time. Added to the sultry southern accent, the gesture caused desire to rush through him at Mach speed.

He let his gaze travel over her hands, which remained splayed on her thighs. No rings adorned any finger, just an intriguing tan line on the ring finger of her left hand. From looks alone, she appeared single.

Score one for him, he thought. "So what's a nice girl like you doing in a place like this?" He chose the worst, most obvious pickup line he could think of.

As he'd hoped, she rolled her eyes and laughed, a light flirtatious sound he enjoyed.

When she didn't answer immediately, he questioned her further. "Bridesmaid fitting, maid of honor or planning your wedding?" He ticked off each possibility on one finger.

She exhaled a long sigh. "Try, canceling one."

"A fitting?" he asked.

"My wedding," she replied, her gaze darting from his.

That took him off guard and explained the hint of sadness he'd glimpsed in her eyes. "I sure as hell hope it was your choice or else your fiancé's got rocks in his head." And in his pants. Sam might not be into commitment but what kind of guy walked away from a woman like this?

"I think I'll take that as a compliment," she said.

"I think you should."

Her gaze jerked toward his. For the first time since he'd sat down, her smile reached her eyes. No pain, no sadness, no vulnerability remained. Just pure seductive woman.

Acting on impulse, he reached for her hand, threading his fingers through hers. Her lids opened wide with surprise, her thick lashes fluttering over her huge and—if he wasn't mistaken—hungry eyes. Her shock gone, she obviously liked his touch as much as he enjoyed hers.

And he did enjoy. Her skin was as soft as her voice, as hot

as the need gliding through him and telling him not to let this woman walk away just yet. "Was it your idea or his? To call things off, I mean."

"His." She shrugged, managing to give even that everyday gesture a delicate bent. "But he did us both a favor. Even if he is a cheatin' son of a bitch," she muttered under her breath.

But not low enough. "Sounds to me like you're better off without him."

"Tell me something I don't know." She turned towards him. "So what's a nice guy like you doing in a place like this?" A quirky grin pulled at her lips. "Are you the groom, best man or usher?" she asked.

"Best man."

Her gaze boldly traveled over him, from the tips of his old sneakers to the top of his head. "Now *that* I can believe."

"I think I'll take that as a compliment."

She laughed. "I think you should. I also think you need to tell me what you're after," she said, glancing down at their still intertwined hands.

Once again, she'd stumped him. Normally a take-charge guy, he didn't know what to say now. He was attracted to her. Sexually, he desired her. That had been the start. But now he realized she was hurting and, though it shocked him, he wanted to take away her pain. To hear her laugh again. To know when he flew home on Sunday, he'd leave her happier and with good memories to take away the bad.

But there was no other way to describe what he wanted other than a no-strings-attached affair. His body was primed and ready since laying eyes on her. Problem was, she was vulnerable and he didn't want to cause her any more pain. The choice had to be hers.

Regan looked into the eyes of this gloriously sexy, raven-haired stranger and she melted like chocolate in the hot sun. His face was scruffy from needing a shave and his green eyes glittered with desire. Exactly the type of guy she'd fantasized about when deciding to exert her independence.

Yet, as interested as he'd initially appeared, as bold as he'd been in taking her hand, he seemed hesitant now. "Let me make this easy for you," she said to him, leaning closer. Then she drew a deep, shaky breath. After all, she'd never propositioned a man before and this was all so sudden. As much as she intended to turn off those ingrained expectations, some old-fashioned honesty would come in handy now.

"Obviously I'm coming off a bad situation, so I'm not looking for anything long-term. But I want to take charge of my life and I want to begin now." She paused, meeting his gaze. Her heart pounded from just looking at him, and her breath caught when desire flared in the depths of his intense eyes. "And I want to start with you."

Lifting her hands to his mouth, he pressed his lips against her knuckles. Moist heat licked at her skin and her breath caught in a hitch.

"I'm listening," he said, obviously interested.

If he was this good with his mouth on her hand, she wondered just how good he'd be with his tongue and lips on certain other body parts.

She couldn't believe she was having these thoughts about a man she'd just met, any more than she could believe she was having this conversation with him. But she'd wanted to start *now* and fate had sent him her way. She wasn't about to turn him away. "I have this one weekend before I have to go home to Georgia and break the news to my family about the engagement."

He nodded, light dancing in his eyes. "What a coincidence. I have this one weekend before I return to California. Minus a wedding appointment or two, I can be all yours. What did you have in mind?"

Regan clenched her free hand around the handle of her purse. Inside sat the folded page from *Sexcapades*. Was this man up for bondage games?

Was she? "I'm tired of being a good girl and doing the proper thing."

"You want to be bad."

She nodded. "Wickedly bad." With trembling hands, she opened her bag and pulled out the sheet of paper that had started her on this insane course, and handed it to... Regan blinked in surprise. "I just realized I don't even know your name."

His gaze darted to the page, then back to her, those green eyes filled with intrigue and hunger. "Well, if you're going to be tying me up, I'd say introductions are in order."

Chapter Two

"REGAN DAVIS." She held out her hand for a shake, which felt ridiculous considering his mouth had already brushed over her skin. Considering her nipples had already puckered into her flimsy bra and even less substantial silk blouse.

"Sam Daniels," he said, his lips twisting in an amused grin. "Seems silly to shake on a deal as intimate as this one, don't you think?"

He'd read her mind. And, yes, she thought it was ridiculous. But proper introductions demanded a proper handshake and Regan Davis had been raised a proper woman. "Damn," she said, forcing the profanity from the back of her throat.

He lifted an eyebrow in question and Regan sighed. "You see, I'm a southern lady, born and raised." She deliberately added to her drawl. "And I want to leave that upbringing in the dust, but if I keep falling back on proper behavior, I'll never have the adventure I want." She'd never make it past Divine Events' threshold with this man, and that would never do because she wanted to end up in his bed!

"Yes, Regan, you will." He pulled her to her feet.

She shivered at the seductive way her name sounded rolling off his lips.

"Just remember we're way past the handshake stage and you'll be fine," he said, twirling the *Sexcapades* page in front of her eyes before folding it and placing it in the back pocket of his jeans. Which, she noted, molded to a perfectly defined behind. She shook her head. Which molded to a perfect male *butt,* she silently amended.

He patted his rear with one hand where he'd tucked in the page. "If you want it, you're going to have to come get it," he said with a suggestive grin.

Now that was an intriguing idea, but before she could respond, they were interrupted.

"Hello, folks." Cecily Divine, owner of Divine Events, strolled into the reception area. "Can I get you two anything?"

"No, thank you, we were just leaving," Regan said, taking charge of the decision for both herself and Sam.

Cecily nodded. "Okay. It's started to rain. Need me to call you a cab?"

If Cecily thought that anything about Regan having met or hooked up with Sam was odd, she didn't show it.

"Regan?" Sam asked, leaving the choice of transportation up to her.

"Actually we can take the el. My apartment is in Lincoln Park, right near the DePaul stop." And one of her resolutions was to become more worldly and stop taking taxis when she could commute by the el.

Cecily shrugged. "Okay, then. I'll leave you two alone and bother some other customers." She walked over to give Regan a quick hug. "You take care, okay?" Stepping back, she then shook Sam's hand. "I'll see you tonight at the rehearsal dinner." Like the efficient whirlwind she was, Cecily disappeared as quickly as she'd come, leaving Sam and Regan alone again.

"Ready?" she asked him.

"Born ready. Since I came straight from the airport, my duffel bag's in the coat closet." He headed to retrieve his things, apparently not the least bit hesitant about leaving with her.

She wasn't unsure either. Still, she swallowed hard.

He returned, duffel in hand and together they started for the exit. He swung the door wide, holding it for her. "Lead the way."

"What a mass of contradictions," she said, laughing. "Who are you, really? The gentleman holding the door or the one willing to give me control?"

He cocked his head to one side and self-assured sexiness oozed from him in waves. "Damned if I know myself, but one thing's for sure—thanks to that fantasy of yours, by the time the day's over, we're going to know a helluva lot more about each other."

And, Regan had a hunch, she'd learn even more about herself.

SAM WALKED into the entryway of a glass-and-chrome apartment building, took in the obviously expensive decor and let out a long, slow whistle. "These are swanky digs."

Regan waited until they'd reached the elevators and pushed the button before she turned to face him. "According to the real estate agent, Lincoln Park has more restaurants per capita than almost any other neighborhood in the city. I can make reservations every night of the week and never duplicate a meal for a good long time."

"Sounds like a working woman's dream."

She glanced up at him through wide blue eyes. "Not being a working woman, I wouldn't know."

They walked into the waiting elevator and the doors closed behind them. He propped a hand against the mirrored wall and anchored her body between himself and the back corner.

So she didn't work. "What do you do?" he asked.

She lifted one shoulder in a dainty shrug. "I chair committees and benefits, raise money for charity and the right causes. Anything that made my family and fiancé happy, I took on. And, in turn, they made sure I was treated like a princess. Until Darren took on that old double standard.

The one my mama accepted from my daddy." She pursed her lips in disgust, making him wonder what she'd reveal next. "You see, cheatin's okay as long as he treats her right." She shook her head. "What do you think of that code of ethics?"

"Cheating's never all right," he said, vehemently. No man should make a vow and deliberately break it. It went against everything Sam believed in. One thing he knew for damn sure—if this woman belonged to him, he'd never stray.

"Are you trying to tell me you're a one-woman man?" She made light of his words, but her expression was one of gratitude.

"I'm telling you if I'm with you, you can be sure there's no one else to worry about." He brushed a strand of hair, damp from the rain, off her forehead.

"Well, good." Her lashes fluttered down in obvious relief. He wasn't surprised his southern beauty was raised in luxury, a far cry from the way he'd grown up. Nor was he shocked she was a kept woman, either by her ex-fiancé or her family. Old southern traditions were hard to break. He didn't hold it against her since she'd as much as told him she'd never known any other way.

But she was fighting her way out now and he admired her for it. He was actually thankful he was able to play a part in her belated attempt at joining the women's revolution. Even if it was just a sexual part. Especially if it was a sexual part. Hell, sex was a great start to a new life and he intended to give her a night she'd never forget.

"An affair's one thing, but I don't want to live a double standard and take someone else's man."

Knowing how solitary his life had been lately, he chuckled. "I can promise you, you're not poaching on anyone else's territory."

She raised her gaze. "What's wrong with the women in... where did you say you were from?" she asked.

"I didn't. But I'm from California, and there's nothing

wrong with the women there except for the fact that, like most women I've encountered, they're looking for commitment."

She rested a shoulder against the elevator wall. "And you're gun-shy?"

"I wouldn't say that. I just like my life the way it is. I'm a pilot and my job takes me around the world." He shrugged. "Being confined isn't my thing. Unless it's like this. With you." He stroked a hand down her cheek and watched as her pupils dilated at his not-so-innocent touch.

He let his lips hover over hers, the desire to taste her strong. But not stronger than the need to learn more about her. In the background, the elevator hummed, a metronomic accompaniment to the passion beating through him. Any second now, they'd reach her floor. He turned away long enough to hit the stop button on the elevator.

If she was surprised by his action, she didn't react. "I'm glad to know you're not the cheating kind." She ran her tongue over her lower lip.

Unintentional or deliberately sultry, the result was the same—an electrical current rushing straight to his groin. "I'd never do such a despicable thing," he said, intent on distinguishing himself from not only her ex, but the so-called acceptable traditions of her past.

"Not all men think that way and, damn it, they should," she said, punctuating her statement with a stamp of her foot.

She pursed her lips again and it was all he could do not to kiss her senseless. But he wasn't ready. Time would build their need and make anything between them even more spectacular. "Anyone ever tell you that your southern accent comes out when you're mad?"

She blushed. "Another thing I need to overcome."

"Not in my book. That drawl of yours turns me on." He stepped closer, until he felt her pert nipples through his light cotton shirt.

"*You* turn me on," she said in the most obvious and deliberate *sexy* southern drawl he'd ever heard.

She wrapped her arms around his waist at the same time she let out long a breath, which ended on a thick, sultry moan. His groin, already full to bursting, lodged a protest at being confined in his jeans. He gritted his teeth, because no matter how much he wanted her, an elevator wasn't the place.

"You know what else?" she asked, talking when he wanted to do anything but.

"What?" he managed to ask.

Her fingers tangled in the back of his hair, her nails grazing the sensitive skin on his neck, tugging at his scalp and arousing him in ways he'd never known he could be aroused. Then her hand slipped downward around his ass, teasing him with alternately firm, then gentle gropes.

"When I told you I needed to be in control, I meant it." Without warning, she stepped aside, dangling the white *Sexcapades* paper in front of him, just as he'd done to her earlier.

He'd been had.

And damned if it didn't make him want her more.

REGAN LED THE WAY into her apartment. Lordy, she was warm and it wasn't because of the summer heat. The things Sam could do to her body with a look or a simple touch defied logic. But then logic had nothing to do with chemistry. He wasn't into commitment or women who wanted anything from him other than sex. And that was all she needed from Mr. Sam Daniels, pilot from California, who'd be making his trip home and out of her life come Sunday.

A brief glance at the clock in the hall as she tossed her keys onto the counter told her it was quickly approaching dinner time. "Can I get you something to eat or drink?" She turned and was stunned to find him not just behind her, but extremely close.

"You sure can." He bracketed one hand above her head, pinioning her body between his and the wall, much as he'd done in the elevator. Only this time, they were in the privacy of her apartment. No door would be opening, nor would anyone be interrupting them anytime soon.

With his free hand, he tilted her chin upward and his lips hovered over hers. "I've been dying to taste you since the moment we met."

"I don't see what's stopping you now." And then, because she'd promised herself she'd maintain control, she cupped his face in her hands and brought his mouth down hard on hers.

For two strangers, they fit together perfectly, Regan thought. He kissed her with an intensity that backed up his earlier words. She'd wanted a man whose eyes flared with desire only for her, whose kisses made her tremble and whose body wracked with a need she inspired. She'd found him.

He made kissing into an art form, his lips creating exquisite texture, his tongue finding a home inside her mouth. He tasted like mint and sexy, seductive man, and a ripple of heat seared straight through to her core. Her breasts grew heavy, her nipples tight, and between her legs, a trickle of moisture that was so very welcome settled there.

Her fingers traveled from his stubbled cheeks to the back of his head where they tangled in his hair. She discovered that if she massaged his neck in a certain spot, he groaned and pressed her more fully against the wall, letting her feel his hard body intimately against hers. And she learned that when he nibbled, suctioning her lower lip into his mouth, her back arched and her breasts pushed harder into his strong chest.

She didn't know how long she stood, back against the wall, lost in the pure pleasure of a kiss, but the erotic sensations continued to build inside her, creating a cascading whirlpool of cavernous need. And by the time he broke the kiss, she'd come to the conclusion that with this man, there would be no being in control. She'd just have to jump without a parachute and hope the glorious ride was worth the potential danger.

He leaned his head against hers, his breathing harsh and ragged. "I think I'll take that drink now."

She forced a deep breath into her lungs. "Sure thing. Let me see what I've got." Ducking beneath his arm, she headed for the kitchen and a brief escape to collect herself. If such a thing were possible.

The man could definitely kiss.

Opening the refrigerator, she scanned the meager contents. She was due for a grocery trip. "I can offer you a glass of white wine," she said, looking at the top shelf. "Or..." she knelt on her knees to scan the bottom, "there's a six-pack of beer my ex left behind."

"Beer sounds good. And don't bother with a glass. We're going to rough it," he said, his dual meaning clear.

When they came together, they were combustible and there'd be nothing genteel or civilized about where they were headed. Regan was glad. Her heart pounded in her chest and she wanted this one experience to prove what kind of woman she could really be.

She pulled out two bottles. "Make yourself at home," she called to him. Knowing he liked her accent allowed her to use it shamelessly.

"I'm one step ahead of you," he said from the other room.

Bottles in hand, she walked around the corner and headed into the living room. He'd already settled himself on the leather couch. He'd kicked his shoes off and left them in the hall and the television remote control was in his hand.

"Looks like the VCR was left on," he said. "Anything worth watching in here?"

She shook her head. "I wouldn't know. I usually watch TV in the bedroom, but Darren used to watch movies with his friends when I'd be out at a charity event." Which was fairly often.

Soon after their arrival in Chicago, her fiancé had handed her a list of organizations his law firm planned to help pro bono, and suggested she start her fund-raising campaigns immediately. Though he couched his reasoning in the fact that it'd help her make friends, she realized now that he'd pro-

vided himself with many free evenings to play with his female coworker when Regan wasn't around. She shrugged,
pushing the memory back into the past where it belonged in
favor of joining her soon-to-be weekend lover on the couch.

She perched herself a respectable distance away. Before she
could think about her next move, he grabbed her hand and
hauled her beside him. "Next time don't wait for me to ask,"
he said gruffly, his eyes twinkling as he made his demand.

He wanted her close, she realized and warmth settled in
her chest. Because she'd been thinking of Darren, she'd re-
verted to her formal, let-the-man-be-in-charge attitude. This
was Sam and he liked her more forward.

"What kind of charities do you work for?" he asked, hitting the rewind button on the remote.

She curled her legs up on the couch and leaned against his
chest. "I wouldn't want to bore you with details."

He shot her an aggravated glance. "If I didn't want to
know, I wouldn't have asked."

She nodded, accepting his point. "Darren's law firm pro-
vides free legal work for a woman's shelter and many of their
residents. I use my people skills to raise money for the cause.
That's one type of work I'd done back home that I wanted
to continue here. Same with some of the local youth centers."

A warm, approving smile settled on his lips. "I'd already
guessed you had a big heart. I'm glad you proved me right."

"Flattery will get you nowhere." She didn't want lies or
even flirtatious, overblown compliments to come between
them. What she liked best about Sam so far was his down-
to-earth style. She didn't need him praising her as if she was
his well-trained dog. As Darren had done.

"I'm already where I want to be—with you. And your
choices please me. You have no idea how much people like
that need your skills."

She rolled her eyes. "Of course I know or I wouldn't
waste my time raising money for them," she said, tired of
the same old words Darren had used to push her buttons

and steer her towards his choice of charities—the ones that benefitted his firm first and foremost. But Regan hadn't given a fig about whether his law firm benefitted from her effort or whether it helped push Darren up the partnership ladder. She might have been guided by her family and taken the expected path, but she'd stood firm and chosen those most in need of her help.

"I didn't mean that literally," he said his voice taking on a hurt tone. "And when I say those women or kids need you, I'm telling you from firsthand experience. A youth center I used to hang out in when I was a kid was shut down for lack of funds. No one gave a damn that the kids they turned out into the street ended up doing drugs or stealing as an after-school activity."

His revelation stunned her, because she knew only the self-confident, self-assured man before her. She knew nothing about his childhood or upbringing and was glad he'd offered some insight.

Beside her, his body tensed, putting a barrier between them and guilt settled on her shoulders for misjudging him. "I'm sorry. I'm just touchy about my lack of real work experience. I thought you were patronizing me like…"

"I'm nothing like Darren," he said, reminding her about something she already knew.

She sighed, hoping she hadn't blown her chance with him before she'd even had one. "Can we rewind and start over?" She wanted to get back to the easy camaraderie and sexual sparks that had come so naturally before they'd begun inadvertently pushing each other's hot buttons.

He chuckled, breaking the tension, and she let out a relieved breath.

"I'm already there," he said. Then, as if to prove his point, he pointed the remote at the large-screen TV and hit Play. "Let's see what movie Dagwood left for us to watch."

She chuckled at his chosen nickname. "I'm a fan of the old *Bewitched* television shows myself."

He grinned. "If this Darren's anything like that Darren, then Endora had herself a point. And based on everything you've told me, *Dagwood* seems to fit the jerk."

Regan bit the inside of her cheek to keep from laughing aloud. Sam seemed to have her ex-fiancé pegged. As for the movie, she hadn't any idea what kind of movie Darren would have chosen. She didn't even know anything about his taste in television shows, she realized. She knew he preferred dry wine to fruity, and champagne most of all. So much about their relationship had been based on the superficial. She shook her head. She was lucky to be out and on her own now. Luckier still to be with Sam.

She snuggled into him and he wrapped an arm around her, placing the remote on the table and exchanging it for a beer. From the TV, music she didn't recognize began to play, credits she wasn't paying attention to flashed across the screen.

"Want a sip?" he asked.

"Sure." She started to reach for her own bottle but instead he held out his.

She placed her mouth over the opening of the long neck and let him tip the contents so the beer began a slow trickle into her mouth and down her throat. The rim was warm from Sam's mouth and the malty taste was what she could only describe as down-home good, the combination making for a delicious yet erotic taste. Without warning, the brew dripped down her chin and he had to pull the bottle away so she could swallow faster.

She laughed at the mess and lifted her hand to wipe her face, a southern no-no she would definitely enjoy, but he stopped her hand in midair. Taking her off guard, he leaned forward and kissed her, running his tongue deliberately around her mouth, lapping up the beer and arousing her at the same time.

Regan couldn't remember the last time she'd played while fooling around with a guy and the enjoyment hit her from all sides. Easing herself forward, she came down on top of him, her body prone along the length of his. The reminder of how much she wanted to be in control ran through her mind at the same time the *Sexcapades* article taunted her with naughty possibilities.

He threaded his hands through her hair and a low growl of desire rumbled from his chest, reverberating through her, turning her nipples into tight, aching peaks. She needed him to touch her, to feel the weight of his hands surrounding and massaging her breasts. She'd never asked a man for what she wanted, never had the nerve to verbalize her desires. Perhaps it was time.

"Give it to me, baby." A husky female voice mimicked Regan's thoughts.

"Who said that?" Regan lifted her head and met Sam's amused gaze.

"Apparently Dagwood was into porn." He gestured to the television.

Regan blinked, surprised. "I had no idea."

She turned in time to see a couple lying together on a couch. The similarities to Regan and Sam were strong, from the man's jet-black hair to the woman's blond tresses. But unlike Sam and Regan, the couple was completely naked and unlike Regan, this woman wasn't intimidated by her sexuality or need. Nor was the man.

"Ever watch one of these before?" Sam's arms wrapped around her, his hands splayed beneath her shirt against her back.

She shook her head, unsure if she was more embarrassed, startled...or secretly intrigued by this turn of events.

"Want me to turn it off?" he asked, probably in deference to her more delicate sensibilities.

"No," she said softly. Because Regan was coming to realize she didn't have as many sensibilities as she'd once thought.

After all, she'd brought Sam back to her apartment and now she was watching in awe as the woman on the small screen acted out Regan's own fantasies. The woman was taking control by orchestrating their movements and positions, her goal obviously to maximize her own pleasure. Regan's surprise at her ex's movie choice took a back seat to her astonishment over the fact that this enactment actually turned her on.

Chapter Three

HIS SOUTHERN BELLE was turned on. Oh, she'd been hot for him before the movie but now… Now she was watching a couple go at it on the television while lying on top of him and, no doubt about it, she was squirming. Sam grinned.

His jet lag had all but disappeared, especially since she'd maneuvered to a sitting position, her mound nestled firmly over his aching groin. He might not know her well, but he understood that this entire experience was new to her. He'd go as slowly as she needed, but his gut told him that once she got going, Regan and her *Sexcapades* page wouldn't need slow.

He lifted her top and slid his hands around her waist, letting his callused fingers glide against her soft skin. But she hadn't met his gaze since she'd realized what was showing on the screen. "There's nothing wrong with being aroused by a movie."

"I never thought it was proper."

There it was again, that thicker-than-normal southern accent because she was nervous. He chuckled. "Neither is picking up a man in a wedding shop, sweetheart, but here we are. Might as well enjoy it, don't you think?"

"Yeah, I do." Her stare drifted to his, the blue irises slumberous, her lashes heavy and her smile widening.

Now this was the woman he'd come home with. "So let's

leave proper at the door." To punctuate his point, he gripped her tighter, thrust his pelvis upward and rolled his hips, maximizing not just contact but pure enjoyment.

His body was already hard and aching and the sultry moans and groans emanating from the television only served to inflame his need. And when Regan added to the chorus with a long drawl of delight, he nearly came in his jeans.

"That wasn't proper, darlin'" he said, mimicking her accent and treating her to a wicked wink.

She shook her head and her blond mane tousled around her flushed face. "I do think I like being bad." Desire darkened her eyes and, taking him by surprise, she hooked her fingers into the belt loops of his pants, locking their bodies tightly together. He didn't have to touch her to know that if he drove inside her, she'd be slick, hot and wet—just for him. Just as he was rock-hard for her.

The friction of denim rubbing against his erection wasn't easing his need but heightening it and driving him crazy. Above him, his sexy vixen rode him, capturing his cock between her thighs and driving both herself and him to insane heights.

His breath came in shallow gasps and wave after wave of intense ecstasy pummeled his body relentlessly, taking him closer and closer to the edge. He was beyond thought and nearly beyond reason, but he gritted his teeth and managed to hang on, letting her climax hit. And when it did, he forced his eyes open and watched as she came, her face flushed, eyes closed in sheer rapture and bliss.

Her body shuddered and her thighs squeezed tight, her hips gyrating, her pelvis straining against his erection, milking him and enjoying every last spasm until she was sated. Nearly boneless, she splayed on top of him, collapsing against his chest.

Her breathing came in ragged gasps. "Lordy, Sam, that was awesome."

"There's something to be said for being in control, huh?" He ran his hands through the tangled strands of her hair.

"Oh, yes," she said, her breath hot against his neck. "And there's something to be said for losing it, too."

He agreed wholeheartedly. He clenched his jaw against the unrelieved ache in his jeans. "Think you're ready for more?"

She raised her heavy-lidded gaze and smiled. "Can't see why not." Then without warning, she rolled off him. "Be right back." She disappeared into another room and returned in seconds, a foil packet in her hand. "Darren believed in bein' prepared," she explained, tossing the condom onto his chest. "Of course, I never thought they'd come in handy once he was gone. Then again…" She pursed her lips in obvious thought.

"What?" he asked, curiosity overriding desire, at least for a moment.

"Then again they didn't come in handy that often when he lived here, seein' as how he was always so tired." She frowned. "Which I suppose is what happens when you're expending energy on another woman." She placed her hands on her hips, which had the effect of pushing out her breasts and making her nipples point through her silk shirt.

"Come here." He crooked a finger and she jumped back onto his lap, assuming her former position.

He'd been planning on dropping his pants and driving into her, anything to slake the need racing through him still. But now that he had her here, he wanted more.

Wanted to taste and devour. He'd propped himself up against the arm of the sofa and she sat astride him. Taking advantage, he levered himself up and pulled her by her blouse, bringing her close. His gaze never left hers, but his intentions were clear as his lips hovered over one full breast. She had time to object, and when she didn't, he closed his lips around her distended nipple, suckling her through the silk.

She let out a soft moan. "You're killin' me."

"I sure as hell hope not," he murmured, then nipped her with his teeth before grabbing the lapels of her shirt and pulling them apart, ripping the buttons and flimsy fabric, and exposing her lace-covered breasts for his view.

At his dominant behavior, Regan sucked in a startled breath, shocked, yes, but also thrilled at the turn this was taking. She'd wanted a man wild for her and now it seemed she had one.

"Don't be afraid of me," he said, his voice rough and gravelly, the desire she'd so wanted obvious in his gaze.

She shook her head. "I'm not. I'm..."

"Excited?" he asked, a wry but pleased smile on his lips.

Regan nodded. "That's one word. But don't forget this is my fantasy," she said, reminding him of her *Sexcapades* paper. "My show." But even as she spoke, she knew bondage games could wait. She'd let herself experience his idea of control, then she'd take over, in all her dominant glory.

Meanwhile, his hands remained at his sides and she had to do something about that. Feeling bolder by the minute, she unhooked the front clasp on her bra and pushed the cups aside, baring her breasts to the cool air and his hotter gaze. She grabbed his wrists and placed his palms on her breasts. On the first feel of his strong, heated hands on her softer flesh, her nipples puckered into tight peaks and liquid desire trickled between her thighs, the swirling need building all over again. Lordy, but this man did something to her she'd never experienced before.

He shut his eyes and a low growl rumbled from his throat, but he made no other move to touch her.

"What are you waiting for?" she asked, frustrated.

"Instructions, sweetheart. You said this is your show."

So she had, but she liked his aggressive side. Meanwhile the condom lay on his chest where she'd tossed it earlier.

"I changed my mind. This time," she said, making sure he understood her rules, "I want—" She paused, uncertain how to express her sexual needs as she'd never done so before.

He arched an eyebrow. "Just say it," he urged her. "Whatever you want, tell me." His eyes darkened and, beneath her, his body was rigid and hard, solidly male, just waiting for her okay.

"I want you to take charge."

"And?"

"I want to feel all that power you've been restraining and I want to feel it inside me." Having said that, she expelled a long breath of air, but before she could register whether she was more relieved or more proud of herself, Sam dislodged her from her position on top.

She didn't know how he managed it so quickly, but in the blink of an eye, she lay prone, while above her, he stripped, pulling off his shirt and tossing it on the floor, then getting to work on his jeans.

Regan wasn't about to waste time either. She sat up and let her torn shirt and open bra fall off her shoulders, before swallowing any embarrassment and taking her pants off next. When she finally stopped her frenzied actions, she glanced up to see Sam, condom in hand, staring at her naked body. But she couldn't worry about being modest because her focus was *him*. Long, thick and hard.

"Oh, my." She licked her lips and forced herself to meet his gaze.

That was one way of putting it, Sam thought. He'd never been so damn hard in his life, and the woman who was the cause sat naked in front of him. He'd never seen such a mass of contradictions bundled in one delectable, desirable package. Southern and shy one minute, aggressive and dominant the next, willing not just to indulge in what she wanted, but to let him take control as well. Which was the real Regan?

And why did he want so badly to find out?

He moved over her, straddling her until his erection touched her downy thatch of hair and her damp desire moistened his skin. He shut his eyes, absorbing the incredible feeling of this moment—the moment just prior to when he'd slide inside and feel all that slick heat meant just for him. Without warning, she plucked the foil packet from his hands and he opened his eyes as she ripped it open and tossed the wrapper somewhere on the floor.

"May I?" she asked, holding the condom in her delicate hands.

He chuckled at that. "You most certainly may." Hell, she could do anything she wanted to him and more, with his permission, without his permission, it didn't matter, he was so wild with wanting her.

Determination etched her features as she placed the condom on the head of his penis and rolled the latex over his straining shaft. Only determination, and the knowledge that he'd rather be inside her body, kept him from pumping into her hand and coming right then.

"I do believe I got it right," she said, a satisfied yet wicked grin on her face.

His vixen was enjoying this and he couldn't be more pleased. But now it was his turn to control the show. "Raise your hands."

Her eyes opened wide with curiosity. "Why?"

"Because you wanted me to take over and I'm doing it," he said, his voice gruff with the force of his restraint.

Without another question, she raised her hands over her head. Leaning forward, he rained hot, devouring kisses on her uplifted breasts, then switched to hot strokes of his tongue, working his way upward to her lips. He could kiss this woman forever, but more urgent needs beckoned, and, breaking contact, he lifted his body, splayed his hands on her thighs and waited until her gaze met his.

Never breaking eye contact, he slipped his finger inside her, parting her feminine folds. He told himself he wanted to make sure she was ready for him this first time, but he knew better. He wanted to feel her. Now he lubricated the condom with his finger, rubbing her slick essence over the head of his shaft, her eyes eagerly following his movements, her arms still over her head. Apparently not only did she like being in control, she followed orders equally well.

She was delicate and rare and he promised himself he'd take things slowly as he nudged the head of his penis inside her. She let out a long, satisfied moan and slow was no longer an option. Nor, he sensed, as she bent her knees, deliberately pulling him deeper, did she want it to be, and he thrust inside her with a hard, fast, penetrating thrust.

"Wow," Regan said, her voice causing him to focus.

"Hell yeah," Sam muttered, agreeing. He'd found heaven on earth, he thought and clenched his jaw tight, savoring the sensations rippling through him.

But he wanted her to savor them too, and there was only one way to guarantee such tight, intimate contact throughout. He needed to be able to thrust as hard and deep as she wanted, as he needed. "Hold your knees," he told her with a wink. "It's going to be a bumpy ride."

She grinned. "Whatever you say, Sam. After all, you're the pilot." Lowering her arms, she grasped her knees with her hands, holding her legs open wide, giving him leverage, providing him complete access and affording him ultimate trust.

As for Sam, he was lost in her slick, wet heat and the friction of their bodies as they found a perfect rhythm. While he braced his arms on either side of her head, he pumped into her, harder and faster with each successive thrust. Regan met him with her body, accepting him deeper, her pelvis grinding in a circular motion. From her soft moans and frantic movements, her release was obviously close.

So was his and when it came at the same moment she did, Sam let go as he hadn't done with any woman. Ever.

Chapter Four

REGAN PULLED the sash of her silk robe around her waist and tied it into a bow, then, drawing a deep breath, she joined the man she'd left in the next room. When she stepped into the den, Sam sat on the couch, wearing jeans and nothing else. He'd shut off the television and the shocking movie they'd found in the VCR. She was still surprised, not just at the porno movie, but at her reaction to it and the resulting shedding of inhibitions that had followed.

Feeling her body begin to heat all over again, she pulled her lapels closer.

"It's a little late for modesty, babe." Sam crooked a finger her way.

"You've got a point," she said, joining him on the sofa. "I was thinking you must be hungry."

He leaned his arm over the back cushion and shot her his most wicked grin. "You could say I worked up an appetite."

She laughed. "Are you always so incorrigible?"

"Only when I have the perfect audience."

She rolled her eyes. "Well, Chicago has the best deep-dish pizza ever created. We can go out if you like." Regan didn't know what else to offer this man who she'd been intimate with yet still didn't know well enough. And she wanted to know more.

"I'd rather bring in. We have such a short time together."

He was right. It was late Friday afternoon leading into evening and he was gone on Sunday. Before she could reply, he continued.

"And I'd rather not share you with anyone, including a waiter." His fingers dipped into her robe, reached under the silk and tickled her shoulder.

His words pleased her as much as his caress. "That sounds perfect to me, as long as it's not really an excuse to avoid being seen with me in public," she said, jokingly. She'd love more intimate time with him here.

"As if. Any guy who lays eyes on you, I'd have to consider competition and I'm really not in a dueling mood." His eyes danced with laughter, but there was a hint of possessiveness in his tone she enjoyed, too.

"I'll get a menu." Rising, she headed for the kitchen drawer, where she kept her stash of take-out menus, when the doorbell rang. "I don't know who that could be."

She glanced through the peephole, saw her ex-fiancé and groaned. "This is trouble."

Sam came up behind her. "What kind of trouble?" he asked.

"Trouble named Darren."

"Want me to wait in the other room?" His voice left no doubt he'd rather not disappear.

But he'd obviously respect her choice and she appreciated the offer. "Don't worry about it. He's probably here to pick up some things he left behind."

"Like his tape?" Sam asked wryly.

"Oh, Lordy, no. I doubt he'd have the nerve to ask for that."

"Then why don't we just offer it to him?"

She turned around to smack him lightly for his joke, but he grabbed her instead and pulled her into a ravishing kiss. A mind-blowing, tongue-tangling, arousing kiss. One that seemed to go on and on, until the doorbell and persistent knocking interrupted them.

"Open up, Regan. The doorman said you were home," Darren called impatiently.

And he should have called up for permission instead of giving Darren entry privileges, Regan thought.

"Go on and let him in," Sam suggested. "Now that you look well and thoroughly kissed."

A heated flush rose to her cheeks, but she had to admit an ornery part of herself, a part previously ignored in favor of proper behavior, relished the thought of being caught in her apartment with a sexy man—after they'd made love.

Regan opened the door to an irate ex-fiancé. Darren's face had turned red and his hand was in the air to knock again. "It took you long enough."

"I didn't know I had to operate on your timetable anymore," she told him. "What are you doing here?"

"I left some things." He stepped inside without being invited.

"And I told you to call first." But apparently he was only worried about manners when it came to his fellow partners and friends, not her.

"I was in the neighborhood." He started for the den, and when Regan turned around, she realized Sam had disappeared into another room.

She sighed. Well kissed or not, it didn't matter, since Darren hadn't spared her a second glance. His only concern was his box of things, which he apparently thought she'd left in the hall closet since he'd stopped in front of it, ready to rummage through.

She perched her hands on her hips, piqued he'd treat her as if she were invisible in her own home. "Darren, you don't live here anymore, so it's rude of you to come stomping in as if you own the place, don't you think?"

"Last I heard, my firm's still footing the bill. Now where are my things?"

She clenched her teeth. "I hardly think that excuse would hold up in a court of law."

Ignoring her, he opened the closet door, only to have a large hand slam it shut.

"You heard the lady," Sam said, obviously having decided to take control.

At the sound of a male voice, Darren turned fast. "Who are you?"

Sam, still dressed in jeans and nothing else, stood with his arms folded over his broad chest and stared at Darren. "I'm the man who's been invited here." He looked Darren over. "Unlike you."

Regan bit the inside of her cheek, enjoying this display of testosterone.

Darren turned toward her. "Regan, I realize I hurt you but picking up a stranger...that's beneath you. And your parents would die of humiliation."

At his words, Regan cringed, and knowing he'd intentionally gone for her weak spot didn't help soften the blow. After all, her folks had barely accepted her living with Darren. They'd only allowed it because they favored him as their soon-to-be son-in-law and he'd done an admirable job of sweet-talking them into accepting the arrangement. If they knew she was having a weekend affair, her mother would probably take to her room with a migraine and her father would... Well, it didn't bear thinking about, she thought with a shudder.

But before she could reply to Darren, Sam grabbed her hand, caressing the inside of her palm with his thumb, reminding her of all the positives in their relationship. Brief or not.

"Look, Dagwood, you have no idea how long I've known Regan or what's between us." Sam leaned closer to her ex-fiancé. "And between us guys? You don't want to know." He squeezed Regan's hand in a gesture of support she appreciated.

Darren scowled. "I want my things."

Regan shrugged. "Well, I could have saved you a trip if you'd called like I asked. I put them in storage. I didn't want them cluttering the apartment."

"But you knew I was coming by for them," he said, a man used to her doing his bidding.

"And you knew you were engaged, but that didn't stop you from relegating me to the basement, so to speak. I'd say we're even." She rubbed her hands together. She was embarrassed to admit revenge felt good.

Especially with Sam by her side.

"You've changed, Regan." Darren shook his head slowly back and forth, in a gesture she found more irritating than she remembered. "And your parents won't be pleased," he added.

"Then don't tell them," Sam suggested.

"They'll find out we're finished regardless of who tells them," Regan said. "And you're right. I've changed—enough not to care if they're disappointed about any choices I make," she told Darren, proud of every word she spoke. And meaning it despite the obvious repercussions.

Sam grinned at her, obviously pleased as well. Then he prodded Darren towards the front door.

She watched, mesmerized. Sam was a gentleman in more ways than a man like Darren could understand, or even her parents could for all their so-called social graces. Sam was a gentleman in his heart, where it counted. Breeding couldn't create a decent human being. Sam won on the inside.

And on the outside, there was no comparison between Sam and Darren, at least none that Darren could win. He was slighter and paler than Sam, and Savannah's Golden Boy looked lost beside Regan's pilot.

Her pilot had, in one short afternoon, brought out her naughty side and taught her she had more courage and self-confidence than she'd imagined. Enough to stand up to the disappointment sure to come from her family once they learned of her broken engagement and subsequent affair. But was she now brave enough to stand on her own?

"Darren, wait!" Regan called out, before Sam could shut the door behind him.

"I'm sorry, but you can't talk me out of it, Regan. I have to talk to Kate and Ethan," Darren said, speaking of her parents. "They'll want to know you've fallen into a downward spiral. They'll bring you home. Or send you on vacation and hide the embarrassment until this blows over," he said.

"No, you twit," Regan heard herself say. "You forgot your tape," she said, ejecting the porno video and running to hand it to Darren with a bow and much fanfare.

Red-faced, he snatched the tape and stormed out.

Sam slammed the door closed behind him. "Jackass," he muttered.

"Well said." Regan grinned. "I didn't think I'd feel like celebrating after Darren left, but that was amazing." She laughed and spread her arms in the air and spun around.

Freedom had never felt so good.

"Enjoyed that?" Sam asked, flipping the dead bolt closed.

"Heck, yeah! I got to him." She shook her head, amazed. "It's not that Darren cared that I was with anyone else—I mean, he dumped me first—but the look on his face when he saw you, and then when I handed him the tape, it was priceless."

Sam's eyes sparkled with laughter and innate understanding. "You humiliated him in front of another guy. That's as good as trumping his cheating ass, that much is for sure." He pulled her into his arms. "Stand proud, Regan. You showed him he didn't defeat you."

"I did, didn't I?" She laughed. "I also worked up an appetite." Pulling him toward the room where she'd left the menus, they agreed on a vegetarian deep-dish pizza and Regan called to place the order.

Forty-five minutes later, they were eating a late meal at her small kitchen table. Sam had to leave in a few hours—for a while, at least—but she refused to think about that now. Not when she was more relaxed than she'd ever remembered being, including at meals with her family and during those alone with Darren. Sam didn't watch which fork she picked up first, or if she even used a fork or placed the napkin in her lap. Little by little, she was shedding the burden of the rules by which she'd lived her life and they were taking on less importance.

Sam had come along at the most opportune time and she'd never forget him or this life-altering weekend he'd given her.

SAM WATCHED as Regan devoured her pizza with gusto, delicately licking sauce off her fingers before moving on to the next bite. The episode with her ex had revved her up and the resulting adrenaline rush was inspiring to watch.

Pushing the pizza box out of the way, he leaned forward on his elbows. "Tell me about your family. Why Dagwood used them as leverage to hurt you," he asked, violating his cardinal rule by asking about her personal life.

An affair ought to be just that, simple and easy to walk away from, but he was too drawn to this woman to leave things between them purely physical. Not that the physical wasn't spectacular—it certainly was. Unfortunately it wasn't enough for him.

"Honestly, you don't want to know." She met his gaze through lowered lashes, obviously embarrassed by his question.

"Honestly, I do." He held out his hand and waited until she joined her palm against his. "I want to know what brought you to this point. What brought us together."

She bit her lower lip before speaking. "Well, as you might imagine, I have a controlling family. Certain…expectations. And I was supposed to fulfill them. My sisters already had. My folks had no trouble with them." Regan's eyes glazed over as she remembered. "But in here I didn't want to be like my mother or sisters." She tapped her heart. "So instead of marrying young and the person handpicked by my father, I found something wrong with every man he chose. Disappointing them at every turn."

Sam shook his head. "This all sounds so antiquated."

She laughed. "You just described my family. And all my parents' friends' families. It's real debutante society where we're from. And as much as I told myself I accepted it, I really rebelled. I rejected everyone they pranced in front of me. They called me picky. I called it being selective." She rose and began cleaning up the remnants of dinner.

Without thought, he stood and helped. "Personally I don't think you should have to marry someone to make your family happy. And your family shouldn't expect you to conform if it makes you unhappy." He folded the empty pizza box in half and stuffed it into the garbage bag she held out. "Let me throw this in the incinerator and we'll finish talking."

As he took the garbage down the hall, for the first time, he allowed himself to think about the man Regan had been engaged to. An obviously born-to-money guy with an attitude to match. A guy who'd grown up with everything Sam had lacked, but one who had no character, who didn't take responsibility for his own actions, who would humiliate a woman if it made himself look better in the eyes of her family and the people back home.

He was unworthy of a woman like Regan and Sam was glad she'd gotten out, even if she had been hurt in the process.

She was obviously pleased too, which made their joining even better. She might have turned to him on the rebound, and he might have accepted a stranger's invitation to have sex, but in a few short hours, they'd progressed way beyond that.

He stepped back into the apartment and closed the door, locking it behind him. Regan had finished cleaning and shut off the lights. Only the soft glow from a lamp lit his way. As he entered the family room, he found the silk robe that Regan had been wearing. He took it as an invitation and when he bent to retrieve the garment he paused, bringing the soft silk to his face. He inhaled Regan's fragrant scent, letting his body become fully aroused, before heading for the bedroom he hadn't yet seen. He hung the robe on the doorknob and, strung tight, he stepped over the threshold.

"Regan?" he called out.

"I'm here." One hand on the wall, she stepped out from a doorway, a vision in a black silk teddy.

The outfit was an incredible contrast to her light blond hair and fair skin, a complex contraption that teased him with possibilities. Straps crisscrossed her shoulders. Sheer lace covered her breasts and revealed her pert nipples and luscious flesh. His gaze traveled lower. Her stomach was uncovered, her belly button tempting him and making his mouth water with the urge to lick, suckle and taste. And lower, lace covered her feminine secrets, but the triangle of blond hair was visible beneath the sheer material, making him harder. And he hadn't thought that was possible.

His mouth watered at the sight, but, at the same time, he knew they hadn't finished their discussion and there was so much about this woman and her facets he wanted to know about.

He stepped forward. "You don't look like any spinster I ever met."

"Why thank you, Sam."

"You're welcome."

She crooked her finger his way, mimicking his gesture earlier. Desire glittered in her eyes and an invitation was clear in her body language.

"How'd you end up in Chicago?" Talk about fitting everything into a short amount of time, he thought wryly, asking the question as he started toward her, intending to accept her invitation with a resounding yes.

Regan sat on the bed, her movements orchestrated and seductive as she crawled over the cream-colored comforter and stretched out on top. Waiting for him.

"Darren's a lawyer," she explained, crossing one leg over the other, teasing him for a second with the hint of exposed flesh. "He was put in charge of a new Chicago office, so we settled here. The wedding was to have been here, too."

"And your family accepted that?" He unzipped his fly and pulled down his jeans.

Regan nodded. "Mama was so happy I'd finally landed

myself a man, she was even willing to accept a northern wedding." She patted the mattress beside her.

Kicking his jeans to the floor, he eased himself onto the bed, the comforter as cool as his body was hot. "How old are you, that they had you pegged a spinster?" An outdated word if he'd ever heard one, but then most of her family's values seemed antiquated to him.

"How old do I look?" A grin lifted the corners of her mouth.

He chuckled. "That's a loaded question, sweetheart. And one I refuse to answer on the grounds I might get myself in trouble."

She pulled open the nightstand drawer and, leaning over, she reached inside. He figured she was getting a condom and with the view of flimsy lace barely covering her backside, man was he ever ready.

"I'm twenty-five," she said at the same time she turned back towards him, a sash from her robe in her hand.

He raised an eyebrow, fairly certain of what she had planned, which made keeping his mind on conversation extremely difficult. "And at the ripe old age of twenty-five, if your parents thought you were having an affair, would they really worry about scandal?"

"Oh, yes." She nodded seriously. "If my mama even found out I wasn't a virgin, she'd have sent my daddy after poor Robby Jones with a shotgun."

"But wouldn't that have caused a scandal?" he asked.

"An acceptable scandal as long as it ended in marriage." She crinkled her nose in disgust. "It's hard to explain the way my parents think if you haven't lived it." She sighed dramatically.

She was right about that. Since he came from a neighborhood that *was* a scandal, Sam couldn't understand it.

"What if they disapproved of the man in question? Would your father actually use the shotgun?" Sam laughed but behind the joke, he was serious. After meeting Dagwood, he could envision Regan's parents going ballistic if they thought a man was beneath their daughter.

A scenario he'd never have to deal with since he was heading back to California on Sunday. Less than two days. So why did the thought of that disapproval eat at his gut?

She pulled the ends of the sash, the snapping sound drawing his attention away from his thoughts. "Don't worry, Sam. My daddy's not coming after you to force you into marriage."

"Because I wouldn't meet their expectations?"

She glanced at him, obviously as surprised as he was by his question. It had been years since his background had bothered him and it shocked the hell out of him that it did so now. And because of a woman.

This woman.

"Sam?" Regan asked, suddenly realizing she had to tread cautiously because she was dealing with his feelings. She didn't know enough about him, but was grateful to learn his vulnerabilities. Grateful for the chance to prove he could trust her with them.

"What is it?" he asked gruffly.

"You meet every expectation I ever had," she said, her smile widening as she spoke the truth.

When she'd turned down various men, each man that her parents had pushed her way, she'd always kept in mind that, as a husband, she'd have to look at this man across from her in bed every day. And southern propriety be damned, she'd at least wanted him to make her hot. Darren had been good-looking, but he'd fallen short. The sex hadn't been spectacular nor had he made her feel desirable. Still, she'd given in to her family's haranguing and accepted Darren's proposal. She'd been a fool, she realized now.

"And just what are those expectations?" he asked. "Just what am I?"

"You're kind and chivalrous." He'd exhibited those qualities tonight, both before Darren's arrival and during. Regan rose to her knees in front of Sam, wanting him to hear how special he was. "Not to mention you're handsome as sin, sexy and you turn me on. And if that's not enough, you know how to follow orders. Raise your hands," she instructed.

His sensual gaze never leaving hers, he did as she asked, never once questioning her command.

Once she had his hands positioned by the iron headboard, she tied the sash around his wrists and shackled him. Regan knew, as did Sam, he could break his bindings easily.

But what fun would that be?

Chapter Five

REGAN HAD HIM just where she wanted him and damned if Sam didn't like it there. He enjoyed the look of determination in her eyes and the way she took control of their situation. Of course, he stopped being amused when she turned hot and predatory and all he could think of was what she intended to do to him.

"You've been really good to me, Sam. From just being kind, to helping when I stood up to Darren, to just being you." Her smile reached her eyes and, in doing so, touched his heart.

Just as quickly, she moved to straddle his legs, settling herself on his thighs, the only thing between them his aching member.

He swallowed hard. "Being good to you is easy, sweetheart."

"So is returning the favor." At that moment, she wrapped her hands around him and he clenched his jaw, trying to concentrate instead of giving up to sensation. Not yet.

He'd learned much about her today, and he'd shared more with Regan than any woman before. But because Dagwood had hurt her so badly and because he'd driven her to this ultimate act of rebellion against her past, Regan wasn't thinking about Sam as anything more than a weekend fling. Perhaps it was that very fact that made him think this was the first woman who could make him want more.

And, to start, he'd prefer any favors she returned to be based on more than physical need. But when she began to pick up a persistent rhythm, running her palm up and down his straining shaft, he knew any more thinking would have to wait. She let her hand glide up, then down, the friction intense and hot, increasing with each successive slide of skin against skin.

He swallowed a groan, lifting his hips and thrusting himself harder and faster, wanting to complement her rhythm but with his wrists bound his movements weren't anchored and he was unable to accomplish much.

"Relax," she said softly. "And I promise to make you feel so good."

She was an angel, but one dressed for sin as she tossed her blond hair in a seductive movement and lowered her head, closer and closer to his erection until he had no doubt what she intended.

He gritted his teeth, knowing that if she touched him, he wouldn't be able to stand it for long. When her lips caressed the head of his shaft, he knew he was right. He expelled a long hiss of breath, but she showed him no mercy as her lips opened over him and, using her tongue, she drew him into her mouth.

"God," he muttered as her tongue swept over his tip and down his straining shaft.

From there, physical sensation took over and he gripped the headboard as she worked him with her mouth, then, without warning, added her hands. Using the moisture she'd created with her lips, she glided her palms up and down, bringing him closer and closer to release. His hips bucked, his body strained and finally he came, a tidal wave of utter completion overtaking him.

When he came back to reality, his breathing still labored, Regan was untying his hands. "You could have released yourself anytime, but you didn't," she said, surprised.

"I knew you wanted to be in control."

She tossed the sash to the end of the bed. "I knew you'd follow orders well."

"And, man, was I rewarded." He leaned his head against the headboard and looked at her.

When she met his gaze, her eyes were wide, her expression honest. "I've never done that before," she admitted.

She'd taken him off guard. Twice. Because when she'd initiated bondage games, he'd assumed she wanted to be in control of her pleasure. Instead she'd commandeered his.

And now this. "Never?" he asked.

She shook her head.

"Not even with—"

"Nope." She looked at him, her tousled hair falling over her cheeks. "Could you tell?" she asked, and lowered her lashes.

Like a bombshell hitting him in the gut, he knew he'd fallen hard for this woman in a way that exceeded anything he'd felt before or had even considered possible. "No, babe, I couldn't tell. You were incredible."

"Well, that's good to know." She flipped her hair off her face and began massaging his wrists, obviously keeping herself busy so she wouldn't have to face him or her embarrassment.

Her sudden shyness was completely at odds with the sexy vixen in the silk teddy. Her contradictions intrigued him and he knew he could never be bored with this woman.

Sam sure as hell had never thought he'd buy into love at first sight, but he believed in it now. She'd blown him away the minute he'd seen her at Divine Events and everything he'd seen and learned since then had only cemented his first impression and growing feelings.

He grabbed her hands, stopping her from continuing her soft massage of his wrists. "Do you know what I want?" he asked her.

"No." She bit down on her lower lip.

"I want to pleasure you. I want to strip you out of that skimpy outfit and devour you until you scream, and then I want to make love to you until you scream some more. Oh, and did I mention, I want you tied up when I do?" He raised an eyebrow, waiting for a response, even as he knew what it would be. After all, she'd proven herself up for a challenge.

"I like the sound of that," she said, in her husky southern voice.

She was eager and willing. As proof, she picked up the silk sash and draped it across his chest, making contact with his nipples—on purpose, he was sure, and then she held her hands out toward him, palms up. "So what are you waiting for?" she asked. "Go for it."

He grinned and began tying up his angel. Sam had never thought much about love, only about maintaining the life of travel that meant so much to him, the life he'd seen his father give up. He'd never wanted to be stifled in that same way. Women had always signaled trouble to him. To him, women meant staying at home and giving up your dreams.

At first glance, Regan seemed the kind of female who'd demand just such a thing, but she was deep, thoughtful and understanding. He wondered if he'd finally found someone who could accept and understand his needs, his dreams. He wondered too if she'd even want to.

A glance at the clock told him he didn't have much time left in which to find out. But his gut told him all things were possible and he trusted his instincts. After all, he was beginning to know her well.

Now it was time she learned more about him. Just as soon as he returned the favor and took Regan where she'd just taken him. To heaven and back.

REGAN SAT cross-legged on the bed, her light robe all she had wrapped around her to keep her warm. With Sam showering and getting ready to leave, she was more chilled than she had a right to be. And that scared her considering she'd only known him a couple of hours.

He stepped out of the steam-filled bathroom, a pair of

boxers on his hips as he ran a towel over his damp hair. Her gaze traveled the length of him, appreciating his masculine physique all over again.

"If you keep looking at me like that, you'll be flat on your back and I'll miss the rehearsal dinner," he said, shooting her a wink.

"Now that's something I wouldn't mind." She let out an exaggerated sigh. "But they'd miss you at the dinner." Just as she'd miss him when he left. "So tell me about this friend of yours who's getting married." She tried to keep conversation casual and not let on about the inner turmoil roiling inside her.

"Bill?" Sam asked, leaning down to pull clothes from his duffel bag. "We were buddies in flight school. Two cocky kids who couldn't wait to fly." He stood, clothes in hand. "Of course for me, flying meant freedom. I worked my ass off to pay for college, juggling as many jobs as I could handle and still get through school. I was determined to have an education in case being a pilot didn't pan out. Then I worked on getting my certification." He shrugged. "That's when I met Bill. We bonded instantly. First off, we both came from working-class backgrounds and things hadn't been handed to us." He winced, instantly catching his mistake. "That didn't come out right."

She laughed though, not at all insulted. "Just go on, sugar. I know who and what I am." And she was fascinated by this insight into him.

He grinned sheepishly. "Well, anyway, my dad was a trucker who loved being on the road, but my mother hated not seeing him, so he gave up his freedom in exchange for a desk job with the same corporation who'd employed him as a driver." Sam lowered himself to the edge of the bed as he continued to tell his story. "It nearly killed my father to stay in one place, and as much as he loved his family, he resented us for tying him down."

"That must've been hard for you."

He inclined his head. "It was. And I guess I decided young that I wouldn't be tied down, too." He paused and met her gaze, heat flaring between them. "Unless it's by a beautiful woman with only seduction in mind," he said, his voice taking on a husky undertone.

She laughed at his double entendre, but his words stayed with her and she glanced out the window, wondering what Sam saw from his perspective as he flew a plane. The lure of that kind of freedom must be potent. After years of feeling constricted by others, she understood his needs and what drove him. "So you equated flying with freedom."

He nodded. "I thought Bill did, too. Apparently I was wrong, since he quit his job as a corporate pilot and is settling in Chicago with his soon-to-be wife."

"To each his own, I guess." She looked at the clock and realized she was keeping him talking when he needed to finish up and move on. "You should get dressed."

"I will, but I wanted to talk to you about something first. This rehearsal tonight, it's casual and informal." He pointed to the pair of khaki-colored chinos and the burgundy polo shirt in his hand.

She leaned back into the pillows. "Sounds nice," she murmured inanely, not sure what else to say.

"It should be, but I won't know many people there and..." His voice trailed off. "Come with me," he said at last, taking her completely by surprise.

She ran a hand through her mussed hair. "I...wasn't invited," she said, falling back on her southern proprieties as an excuse.

"*I'm* inviting you. Bill said to bring a guest if I was seeing anyone. At the time I wasn't, but now I am." He raised his shoulders as if things between them were that simple. His eyes twinkled with possibilities and, damn him, hope.

She didn't want to dash his expectations, but this was all too much, too fast. She was scared to death of what she was feeling for this man so quickly. Coming off a broken engagement she hadn't even told her family about yet, she was falling for a sexy stranger she'd picked up in the wedding planner's, of all places.

Talk about reasons for mortification! Yet she wasn't ashamed of Sam. Only afraid of her own feelings. She met his gaze. "I wish I could but—"

He leaned closer, placing his hand on her leg. Fiery darts of heat immediately set off in her body, her breasts peaking and dewy dampness settling between her thighs. That easily, he turned her on. That quickly, he'd touched her heart.

"Come on, Regan. It's not like we'll have that much time together this weekend, so why not make the most of what we do have?" he asked, giving it one last shot.

"I wish I could." She curled her legs, wrapping her arms around her knees. The effect was to pull away from his touch and, as much as it hurt her, shut him out. "But...I can't." She forced the words from the back of her throat.

"You mean you won't." He straightened, then rose from the bed. "What the hell. It was only supposed to be a quick fling, right? It was stupid of me to push for anything more." He closed himself in the bathroom to get dressed.

Regan swallowed hard, pain rippling through her chest and throat. It wasn't supposed to be like this. Yet here she was filled with more conflicting emotion than she had been when Darren had broken their engagement and admitted he'd been fooling around. She wrapped her fingers around the comforter and shut her eyes tight.

She kept them closed until the bathroom door opened and Sam walked out, dressed to kill in his casual outfit, smelling of his sexy cologne, a cool, disappointed look in his eyes. A look she had never seen before, since, from the moment they met, his gaze had been heated, warm and welcoming. She hated the change, yet acknowledged she was the cause.

"Time for me to go." Duffel in hand, he strode toward the bed and leaned close. "It's been fun, darling." Without asking, he closed the distance and sealed his lips over hers, kissing her long and hard.

She had no right, but she parted her lips anyway, deepening the kiss and the connection, so that when he finally pulled away, his breathing was labored. "You're a mass of contradictions, but I do understand," he said.

She raised her eyebrows. "You do?"

He nodded. "I'm the one who's always been looking for freedom, remember?"

She forced a smile. "Yes, I believe I do." She also realized he was letting her off the hook for her decision, for which she was grateful. "Have fun tonight."

"I will." He rose to his full height.

"Where are you staying? Because if you don't have a hotel reservation, this side of the bed is yours," she said, patting the free end and setting herself up for the same rejection she'd just given him.

He chuckled. "Now who doesn't want to be seen in public with whom?" he asked, teasing her with her own words from earlier in the day.

She shook her head in denial. "I promise you, that's not it." She just wasn't ready to admit a more intimate connection between them. Sex was one thing, she told herself; attending a wedding as a couple was something else entirely. But she was lying to herself. Because the truth was she felt too overwhelmed to deal with her emotions. She hoped a little breathing room would help her figure out her feelings.

"I know." He took two steps, then turned back, meeting her gaze with his deep, compelling one. "Mind if I leave my bag?"

She exhaled a long sigh of relief that their time together wasn't over yet. But when he walked out the door, her keys in hand, leaving her alone with her thoughts, he left her completely alone in a way even Darren hadn't.

Lordy, she was a mess, but she'd better get her act together fast. She needed to find out who she was before she could allow herself to get involved with another man. But as the long, solitary night ticked away, she was forced to admit she was already involved. Deeper than she'd have believed possible.

Chapter Six

SAM LET HIMSELF into Regan's apartment way after midnight. The rehearsal dinner had run long, the guests only too happy to party, drink and have fun. Then, after Bill had walked his fiancée, Cynthia, to her car, he'd insisted they go out for a drink. Sam couldn't deny his friend on his last night of bachelorhood, so they'd hit a local bar, where Bill had indulged and Sam had nursed a beer and thought about the woman he'd left behind.

He stripped off his clothes, including his boxers, and slipped into bed beside her, immediately pulling her close.

"Sam?" she murmured drowsily.

"Mm-hmm." He took it as a good sign that even in sleep she recognized him and didn't mistake him for Dagwood. Obviously her ex played no part in whatever fears or reservations she held about her and Sam. "It's me," he told her. "Go back to sleep."

"'Kay." She wiggled closer, her behind snuggled into his groin, her body fitting perfectly with his.

He buried his face in her hair, letting her fragrant scent surround and soothe him. Arouse him, too, but amazingly that wasn't what he needed from her now.

Sam might not choose to give up his career as Bill had done, but damned if watching the soon-to-be bride and groom together hadn't made him long for the closeness they

shared, and the knowledge that they'd face the future together. Sam wanted those things with one woman only, and
she lay sleeping in his arms now.

True, he hadn't known Regan long enough to ask that of
her, but he wanted the opportunity to see where things could
lead, and he doubted they'd stand a chance if she remained
in Chicago. He was based in San Francisco as was Connectivity Industries. He had to be available at a moment's notice and be willing to travel when the need arose. Sam still
needed the sense of freedom flying gave him. He just wanted
to know Regan would be there when he came home.

And from the reactions of most women, he knew how big
a sacrifice he'd be asking of her. Not only would she be moving to a new state with no family or friends, but he wouldn't
always be there to ease the transition.

If he thought asking her to go to a rehearsal dinner had
been a shaky proposition, he couldn't imagine her reaction
to this particular question. But by the time Saturday night
or Sunday morning arrived, he'd have no choice but to
broach the subject—or head home alone.

REGAN AWOKE to a warm body covering hers. She couldn't
say she minded the delicious feeling; in fact, she savored it.
She'd heard Sam come back last night and, if she were completely honest, she hadn't fallen into a deep sleep until she'd
known he'd returned.

Now she lay on her stomach with Sam above her, cradling
her in masculine heat. "What are you doing?" she asked.

"Waking you up." He brushed her hair off her cheek and
began kissing her neck, grazing softly with his teeth and
then stroking her with warm laps of his tongue.

She shivered at the sensual assault and her body arched,
her pelvis accidentally rubbing against the mattress, the contact having the erotic effect of arousing her even more.
"Mmm. You're going to make me immune to alarm clocks,"
she murmured.

"If that means you need me to wake up in the morning, that's fine with me."

Before she could tense at his words, he began a slow nibbling on her earlobe, certainly meant to distract her. It worked. She let her lashes flutter closed and allowed him to arouse her with his mouth, his tongue, teeth and oh-so-able hands, knowing all along this might be their last time together.

He worked his way down from her earlobe to her neck, pausing to kiss, caress and touch every part of her back. All the while, her body writhed and her feminine mound ground into the mattress, her climax closer and closer with each rotation of her hips. Her breathing came faster and a soft moan rose from her throat.

Without warning, she felt his hands clamp down on her thighs and she stiffened, startled.

"I want you to trust me, sweetheart." His breath rushed over her neck; her skin tingled with heated awareness.

"I do." She swallowed hard. She trusted him with much more than just the use of her body, she thought, her heart thumping hard in her chest.

His touch gentled as he spread her legs wide. Her adrenaline picked up speed as his fingers dipped between her legs, moistening her with her own juices, and then she felt him beginning to ease himself inside her.

She shut her eyes and let out a slow moan, he felt so amazing.

"Are you okay?" he asked.

"I'm go-oo-d," she said, drawing out the word. Very good, she thought. How could she not be when his big body surrounded her in warmth and he was so excruciatingly gentle inside her?

He brushed her hair off one side of her face and nuzzled her cheek. "I want you better than good, babe," he said, taking himself deeper still.

She clenched her thighs tighter around him, letting the

swirling vortex of desire inside her build. With every slow, careful push he made, he brought her closer to the breaking point. She needed him to move, to thrust inside her hard and fast. Her body shook, trembling with unslaked need and she dipped her head into the mattress to keep from crying out.

"Tell me what you want." Sam's husky voice reverberated in her ear. "You told me you need to be in control of your life. You can have that with me. So tell me what it is you need."

No man had ever given her that right, that freedom, and suddenly she understood how he felt when he was flying. She fully comprehended *why* he needed that freedom. And the fact that he was offering it to her now made her want to cry, even though she didn't know if she could make herself utter the words out loud.

Between her thighs, she felt him pulsing inside her, his own body shaking with the force of his own restraint. He understood her in ways no man had before and she needed him in ways she'd never needed another man. And silently, only to herself, she could admit it wasn't just sex between them, even if, at the moment, that's all her body cared about.

He seemed to understand that fact as he slipped his hand around her, cupping her breast in his hand and taking hold of her nipple, rolling it between his fingers gently but persistently until desire mixed with the pain of need.

"Trust me enough to tell me what you want, Regan, or what do we really have between us?" he asked.

She swallowed hard, knowing he was right. Hadn't she just admitted it to herself? "I need you. Hard and fast," she said, a tear dripping down her face and her voice breaking, so great was her need.

"Finally." The word came out on a groan as he thrust into her all the way.

He was big and solid and this position allowed him to fill her in a completely different way. She *felt* him, she thought. Because she wasn't focused on his face. Because after thrusting deeply once, he'd paused, and she'd really felt the connection of their bodies. And the longer he waited, the more she contracted around him and the more intense the swirling sensations of desire became.

He did as she asked and started to move, showing her no mercy as he began thrusting hard and fast, his body joined with hers. Between the slick movement of his penis inside her, and the rhythmic contact of her mound against the mattress, climax soon beckoned. Shocking herself, she cried out, feeling the unreal sensations build higher and higher until they peaked, taking her over the edge and into blessed oblivion. All the while, he continued his relentless movements until she was sated, her climax ended, all but the contractions still pulsing around him.

She'd come, but Sam wasn't done. Not by a longshot. He had so little time to bind this woman to him and though he knew he'd made a huge leap just now, he wasn't finished. And he wasn't just talking about his own release, which somehow he'd managed to contain.

He pulled out of her just long enough to roll her boneless body onto her back.

She opened her still-glazed eyes and met his gaze. "You didn't come yet, Sam."

He grinned. "You noticed."

"Everything about you," she admitted.

He withheld a grateful sound. "How are you feeling?" he asked instead.

"Amazing." She'd obviously learned her lesson about the too-bland word *good*.

He leaned down and kissed her on the lips as he'd been dying to do the entire time they were making love. For the first time, Sam refused to think of it as just sex.

Taking him by surprise, she grabbed his hips. "Let's go, lover boy," she said in a teasing, sultry southern voice. "It's your turn."

He chuckled. "If you think you can handle me again."

"Anywhere, anytime." Her voice turned intensely serious.

Good, he thought. He'd gotten to her. Now to make it last. "Want to know why I didn't come earlier?" he asked her.

She nodded.

"Because I wanted to see your face when I come. Because I wanted you to see mine." He rose over her. "And because I never want you to forget," he said, joining their bodies again, feeling every slick, moist inch of her.

And from her wide-eyed stare, she felt him as well. Satisfied he'd accomplished his goal, he began to take them both over the edge, doing as he'd promised. He watched her as she came, and he noted with satisfaction she also watched him.

But that didn't mean he'd made the progress with her that he wanted. In fact, he had no idea what Regan wanted from him, and after turning down his invitation to a simple party and after he'd pretty much bared his soul while making love, Sam decided the ball was now in her court.

If she wanted more, she'd have to come to him.

REGAN WAS ALONE again and she hated it. She paced the bedroom, trying in vain to ignore the rumpled sheets on her bed, the duffel bag in the corner, and the potent scent of Sam's cologne that remained. It wasn't as if she didn't know how to be alone, or as if she couldn't function as a single person. After all, she'd been on her own for years, even if she had been bowing to convention. But the simple fact remained, she missed Sam.

A not-so-smart realization, considering the man was leaving in the morning. And though he'd hinted that more existed between them than just sex, she would be dreaming if she allowed herself to believe him or believe that his words would last beyond their affair. First off, they'd just met. What could they really know about one another or have in common? Second, they lived miles apart. And third, he didn't want to be tied down as his father had been. As his best friend would soon be.

Her heart rebelled against her objections, but, before she

could think things through more clearly, her thoughts were cut off by the jarring ring of the phone. With a groan, she picked up the receiver. "Hello?"

"Regan, darling, I'm worried sick. Please tell me Darren's hallucinating and you aren't consortin' with a man who isn't your fiancé." Her mother's pleading voice sounded on the other end of the phone. "Please tell me the wedding's going on as planned." Kate sounded near hysteria and from the slanted viewpoint she'd obviously gotten from Darren, in her mind she had good reason.

Her mother would believe Darren, if only because Regan had consistently disappointed her—unlike her other daughters who'd always done the right thing, in the right time frame. Regan had come close to pleasing her family, but she was about to destroy any last illusion they might have held about her finally falling in line as the perfect daughter.

Unless Kate could see past social standards and understand what was in Regan's heart, she and her daughter were destined for a rift that would be difficult to breach. As much as Regan longed for a mother who would console, she didn't hold out much hope. Just enough to make her hold her breath.

But Darren had set the stage for disaster, and if he were standing in front of her, Regan would throttle him without second thought. "Mama, listen, things aren't what they seem," she said, hoping to explain Darren's mass of lies.

Kate exhaled a loud breath of air. "Thank goodness. You mean you aren't sleepin' with a strange man?"

Regan shook her head and leaned against the kitchen counter for support, having the distinct feeling she was going to need it. "Mama, I'm twenty-five years old. I—"

"I'll take that as a yes," Kate said, her wail of despair cutting off Regan's next words. "Oh, I knew I never should have agreed to let you go to Chicago before the wedding. If you'd just been home, where we could keep an eye on you, none of this would have happened."

Since Regan had already pointed out her age, she figured reminding her mother was a futile point.

"Don't you realize poor Darren's beside himself with worry?" Kate asked. "And your father, well, I haven't figured out how to break the news to him. You finally found yourself a good man but you couldn't hold onto him, could you?" Kate asked, full of reproach. Full of disappointment that, thanks to Regan, she'd have to be embarrassed in front of her friends. Yet again.

Regan opened her mouth to argue, but realized she'd be fighting an old battle, one she couldn't win. It reminded her of the time she'd refused to attend a country club gala with her father's best friend's son because the last time she'd been alone with him, he'd tried to force himself on her. Her parents hadn't believed her then, instead opting to think she was being typically picky, obstinate and stubborn, defying them on purpose. There was no way her mother would believe her now. No way she'd even try.

Kate had always loved the idea of having daughters she could parade in front of her country club friends, during their coming outs, their engagements, their weddings, all on schedule, *just like her friends' daughters*. But when Regan had turned out to be an individual with her own likes and needs, Kate hadn't known what to do with her. She hadn't ever tried to figure Regan out. And since her father had relegated raising the girls to Kate, neither had he.

Still, they were at a crossroads now and Regan couldn't allow Darren's view to stand. Regan intended to start with the truth. "Mama, listen to me," she said, patiently, wanting her mother to see her point of view. "Darren broke up with me over the weekend. He was cheating on me with—"

"One of his associates," Kate said, taking Regan by surprise. "I already know. Darren warned us you'd be defensive and come up with a story like that to blame him. He said you've been that way since the move to Chicago. He's had to work long hours to establish the new office, but you didn't understand. You've been cold and distant and turned to another man for attention."

Regan leaned back, deliberately knocking her head against the cabinet, but it didn't cause her to mercifully black out or make her mother's ridiculous faith in Darren disappear.

"I have a plan," Kate said.

Regan rolled her eyes. "I really don't want to know."

"Of course you do. Your daddy can talk to Darren and I'm sure he'll take you back."

She shook her head. "I don't want Darren back even if he would take me, which he wouldn't. Didn't you hear what I said? Darren was cheating on *me*. He doesn't love me and—"

Her mother let out an exasperated sigh. "Love's got nothing to do with a good marriage, Regan Ann Davis. The point is to marry someone of equal stature and live the life you were meant to have. End of story."

End of story for Kate, maybe, but not for Regan. "Don't you care that Darren's been unfaithful?" she asked, hating the little-girl voice that begged for her mother's approval.

But whatever Regan needed from Kate, she'd never get it. Not when Kate accepted so much less for herself than she deserved. But not Regan. Not anymore. And no more pretense, either. She was through trying to be someone she wasn't or couching the truth to avoid hurting her parents' feelings.

"I suppose I should have spoken to you about men and their needs long before this," Kate said, resigned. "Men cheat. It's their way. But if you accept it, you'll have everything you ever want in life. Everything you deserve."

Regan twisted the phone cord around her finger as her mother spoke. "What things are those? Money? A big, cold, lonely house? Is that what I deserve?" Is that what Kate thought *she* deserved?

Tears welled in Regan's eyes as her childhood came back to haunt her. Memories of her mother crying in her bedroom when her father failed to come home; memories of Regan and her sisters singing lullabies to each other, each one louder than the last in order to drown out the sound.

Well, Regan wanted more for *her* children. She wanted more for herself.

"Those are important considerations, honey-child," Kate said, calling Regan by her childhood nickname. "Just what are you without them? Who are you without money? Stature? Standing in the community, and your good name?"

Regan swallowed hard, the answer coming to her without thought. "I'm me," she said in a soft but determined voice. "I'm Regan Davis." And that was good enough for her.

It was also good enough for her pilot. In one short week-end she'd gone down a road of discovery, learning her inner strength and her true desires.

She'd been on her way since her trip to Victoria's Secret and her subsequent discovery of the *Sexcapades* book in Di-vine Events' lobby.

But it had taken Sam and his quiet acceptance for her to complete her quest for self-discovery—Regan liked the per-son she was. She liked the woman with fewer inhibitions who didn't worry about what people thought and who acted on her baser instincts.

Regan had thought she had to find herself and figure out who she was and what she wanted in life, but she had already known. All she had to do was be willing to step outside the protective cocoon created by her family then maintained by Darren, and venture into the big, bad world by herself.

And once she did, once she established her own identity, maybe her parents would see her differently. Maybe not. But at least Regan would be happy within herself. No matter how sad she was now.

"Regan are you listening to me?" Her mother's shrill voice traveled through the phone line and forced her to focus. "I said you need us and you need Darren. Call him and apologize. I'm certain with some smooth talking by your father, Darren will take you back."

"No." Regan verbalized her defiance for the first time, despite knowing that being proudly independent would never be something that would draw out her mother's love and approval. Nothing would, short of caving in. And that Regan wouldn't do.

"Excuse me?" Kate asked.

Regan imagined her mother straightening her spine and taking on her haughty air. "I said no. I won't apologize. I don't want Darren back, even if he did want me. Which by the way, he doesn't."

"Nonsense."

"Try asking him next time he calls to snitch on me, okay? He broke up with me." And, boy, was Regan glad. "But at least it made me realize that I have more self-respect than to settle for a man who doesn't want me. Doesn't love me. And certainly doesn't respect me."

She swallowed a laugh since Darren certainly wasn't banging down her door begging for a second chance. But her parents didn't realize that. They were too intent on finding fault with their daughter, while Darren played into their fears. He knew them well enough to play the game his way—and win.

"If you refuse to cooperate now, I'm not going to be able to bail you out of this," her mother warned.

Regan straightened her own shoulders. "I'm not asking you to." She swallowed hard, accepting her mother for who she was and hoping that one day her mother would do the same for her.

Silence descended for a few moments before Kate resorted to sniffles and probably tears. "You're going to disappoint your daddy, Regan, and I won't be able to hold my head up at the country club." Kate wasn't threatening, she was stating bald fact, and Regan understood how disappointing and devastating her act of rebellion was for Kate.

Once Regan hung up, there'd be no turning back unless

she crawled. And *that* day would never come. She blotted tears from her eyes. "I'm sorry, Mama."

Not for becoming her own person, but for the pain she was inflicting on her parents who knew and understood no other way to live.

The click and resulting dial tone on the other end confirmed Regan's hunch of how the conversation would end. She hung up the phone, her hands shaking, then hopped up and sat on the kitchen counter.

Though she was well and truly alone now, as a result of taking a stand she no longer felt bereft or empty. She had herself. And she would survive without her family's support or her fiancé's money. She had enough PR background to finagle a job somewhere and she could talk circles around anyone to raise money. Regan had faith in herself, she realized for the first time.

And she had Sam to thank for helping her to come to that realization. Sam Daniels, a man who allowed her to be herself—and loved her anyway. She'd bet her life on it because she loved him. Her mouth grew dry and her heart pounded in her chest as she allowed herself to think the words for the first time.

She loved Sam. And she did believe he loved her, in his own way. Not that she deluded herself into thinking that love changed who or what he was—her pilot who needed his freedom in order to survive. As much as he accepted her, she also accepted him.

She wondered if his solitary view of the world left any room for her. For them. And she realized there was only one way to find out.

Chapter Seven

AS SAM FINISHED his toast to the bride and groom, he raised his glass. "And here's to a lifetime of health, happiness and kids who look like Cynthia," he said, ribbing Bill. "Cheers."

The crowd broke out in applause and Bill stepped away from his bride long enough to give Sam a warm hug and pat on the back.

"Be happy," Sam told his friend. Not only did he mean it from the heart, he finally understood how such a thing as "happily ever after" was possible.

For years Sam had believed commitment, marriage and even a woman's desires would never mesh with his own. He thought his parents' situation was a living, breathing example and the women he'd come into contact with had never proved him wrong. Until now.

In his male arrogance, Sam had figured he'd never be the one with anticipation and nerves churning his gut. Had never thought he'd want a woman so badly, he'd be willing to do almost anything to keep her in his life.

He'd just never met the right woman.

Now he had, and he wasn't worth shit without her. Hell, he'd been propositioned by one bridesmaid and felt up by another and, though both were attractive, neither had interested him. Not even for prolonged conversation. Sam knew he'd spend a damn long time trying to get over Regan, his "one-night stand."

He made his way to the bar, ordered a Scotch, then headed for the front entryway to get away from the noise of the band and the throngs of people. He stood, shoulder propped against the wall, and watched from the doorway of the Grand Ballroom as the bride and groom danced to a slow song.

"Funny, but I would have pegged you as the type of guy who'd be in the middle of a party, not hanging out on the sidelines."

Regan's voice took him by surprise, and he figured he must have wanted her so bad, he was hallucinating now. He turned to see her standing behind him wearing a knee-skimming black dress with a shawl collar, a full face of makeup she didn't need, and her hair pulled back into a twist, looking like a million bucks.

"What are you doing here?" he asked, still shocked and not daring to hope for anything.

She shrugged, her fingers curled tight around a small black purse. "I'm looking for you."

The ballroom doors swung open, interrupting them. He grabbed her hand and pulled her toward the back hall where the restrooms and pay phones were, so they could be alone.

"So, how'd you find me?" he asked, because they'd never discussed where the wedding was being held.

She let out a long, feigned sigh. "Sadly, I resorted to snooping through your bag. How else would I find the invitation and information?" She shook her head in a dramatic fashion. "Oh, the shame."

He chuckled. "And what made you decide to come looking in the first place?" After she'd turned down his request to accompany him to the rehearsal dinner, he deliberately hadn't invited her to the wedding.

Bill had laced into him for that omission the entire time they were changing into their tuxedos earlier. Because Sam had been dumb enough and drunk enough to spill his guts to his friend over drinks the night before, he'd set himself up for a lecture today. Never mind that he probably deserved one for taking the risk of losing her, Sam believed the next move had to be Regan's.

And he hoped like hell she was making it now.

He placed a hand beneath her chin and raised her head until their gazes met and locked. "I forgive you for snooping."

"Whew." She lay a hand across her forehead in Scarlett O'Hara fashion. "I thought I might have to work a little harder for that one." She smiled at him, but the gesture didn't match what he saw inside.

He raised an eyebrow, not trusting her light tone and flippant demeanor. Not when up close her eyes were red and puffy beneath the makeup and her voice shook beneath the brave exterior. "What's going on, babe?"

Her shoulders lowered and she let out a long breath. "I'm not pulling this off, am I?"

"Depends. You found me and I'm glad. But something's wrong and I want to know what it is." With his plane leaving in the morning, Sam knew they had no time for games.

A group of women shuffled out of the ladies' room, giggling and making too much noise. "So much for privacy," he muttered. "Follow me." Taking her hand again, he led her into the bride's room and locked the door behind him.

They might be surrounded by stray panty hose, hair spray and things, but they were finally, blessedly alone. He sat on a bench, then pushed a pile of clothing onto the floor and patted the space beside him.

Regan joined him. "My mother called," she said as soon as she was seated.

"Darren let her in on his version of events, huh?" It wasn't hard to hazard the guess.

She nodded. "He made it sound like he was the wounded party, and I'd caused the breakup because he found me with another man. The nerve of the louse!"

Sam had to agree and waited for her to go on.

"Mama suggested I go crawling back and apologize." She snorted, rolling her eyes. "As if I ever would."

No, Sam didn't see Regan crawling back to any man, but she *had* come looking for him and, despite his best efforts, hope expanded in his chest. "What happened next?"

"Well, Mama wasn't much interested in my version of events. She said even if they were true—as if I'd lie—that men cheat. That it's their way." Regan narrowed her gaze, then leaned closer until they were mere millimeters apart. "Which brings me to my question." She pursed her lips.

Luscious lips coated with shimmery gloss. She also smelled delicious and he got a damn hard-on just being near her. He figured he'd be eighty and still get horny anytime she came near.

"What are you laughin' at?" she asked him, kicking his shin with her foot.

Damn it, was it his fault the woman made him happy?

"There's nothin' funny about this," she said, furious with him and so very southern in her anger.

He stroked a finger down her cheek, trying to calm her and ignore the throbbing in his shin and the growing need filling certain other body parts. "You make me smile, Regan. There's nothing I can do about that, but if you're going to injure me every time I do, we're going to have a problem."

She dipped her head. "Sorry."

He chuckled. "Apology accepted. Now, what did you want to ask me?"

She clasped her hands behind her. "I wanted to know…" Her voice trailed off, her face flushed pink. "You're either going to laugh or think I've gone plum crazy."

"I promise I'll do neither." They'd obviously reached a crossroads and he wasn't about to blow it. "Go on," he said in a gruff voice.

"If you were mine…I mean, if I was yours… If we belonged to each other, would you find cheatin' acceptable? Necessary? A man's way?"

Through her rambling and obvious embarrassment, he understood how serious she was with her question. She wasn't just asking his opinion on cheating, because they'd covered that topic already, but she was trying to find out, in her adorable, roundabout way, whether he wanted more with her than the weekend they'd shared.

He already knew his answer. Sam's perspective had changed enormously since flying into Chicago yesterday morning and this bundle of nerves questioning him now was the reason.

For both of their sakes, he decided to tackle things head-on. "From the day I laid eyes on you, you spoiled me for anyone else. That's the way it's supposed to be between a man and a woman." He cupped her cheeks between his hand. "Between a couple. I never knew it before, but once I met you, it all became clear."

Her eyes grew wider. "So me and only me would be enough for you?"

"That goes both ways. I wouldn't expect anything less from you."

"I can live with that." She nodded, her big eyes solemn and serious, a happy smile pulling at her lips. "You spoiled me for any other man, too."

"Good. Now I have a question of my own." A huge question, one that had been niggling at him for a while now. "What happens if your parents' disapproval becomes too much? Have you thought through what you want out of life?" He was who he was, after all—a pilot from the wrong side of the tracks. He wanted her to know the obstacles up front.

She glanced down at her hands. "My parents have never cared about what I want, only what they think is right. It took me leavin' Atlanta to realize it, so I can thank Darren for that, at least." She ran her tongue over her glossed lips. "But I'm finished livin' life for anyone but me."

"And what about what *you* want?" He grasped her hands in his, knowing they'd come to the crux of things. "I can't give up flying—"

"Who asked you to?" she said, sounding offended at the prospect.

He swallowed hard, daring to believe at last that this woman really did understand and accept him. "I can't leave California, either. The corporation I work for is based there. And I know it's a lot to ask after just one weekend, but if you're willing to move to San Francisco, I believe we have a chance."

She rolled her eyes again. "So do I or I wouldn't be here."

He wanted to grin, to laugh, to kiss her senseless, but he couldn't. There was more. "I can take you with me on certain trips. It's allowed and this way we wouldn't be apart for long. Still, you'll be alone a lot when I'm gone, no friends—at least at first," he warned her. "But my family's there and they'll really like you. My sister will make you feel at home, and—"

"I'm a big girl, Sam." She wrapped her hands around his neck, her fingers tangling in his hair. "I know how to make friends and I can occupy myself easily. I know what I'd be getting myself into."

"It can get lonely," he said, repeating the words he'd heard his mother utter often enough.

"I like my own company." She straightened her shoulders and met his gaze. "Sam, are you trying to scare me off?"

He shook his head. "But if you're going to walk away or make demands, better now than later."

"Silly man." She caressed his cheek, holding his face in her hand. "There'll be no later. I love you. I told you I believe we can make this work and I meant it."

"Well, hell." What else could he say?

She smiled wide. "I want you to know, I don't expect you to support me. I'll get a job. I've got great PR skills. I know how to raise money and—"

"Do you want to work?" he asked. "Or do you want to keep doing your fund-raising? Because I can afford to support you. Hell, I want to support you. So if that's what you want, I can hook you up with the right charities. And that way when this thing between us works out like we know it will, you can have my kids and not have to worry about giving up a job—"

"Who'd have believed Sam Daniels is rambling? We have so many decisions to make, but the important ones are ironed out. Right?" she asked.

"Right."

"So do you have anything else to add?" she asked, laughing and happy. "Because it seems to me the most important thing's gone unsaid." Her eyes glittered with ultimate happiness and certainty, and though he hadn't told her yet, she obviously already knew.

"I love you," he said, his words the most serious he'd ever spoken.

He didn't think it was possible, but her smile grew wider. "I love you too, Sam."

He pulled her towards him until he captured her mouth, parting his lips and making her his with the deepest, most intimate, primal kiss he could manage. After all, he was sealing the most important bargain of his life.

Later, when he finally broke for air, Regan said, breathlessly, "Now do you want to know why else I came looking for you?"

Sam stroked her hair, dying to undo the knot, but knowing if she was going to meet his friends, she'd want to look her most southern perfect. "I want to know anything that's important to you."

She glanced at him with those huge eyes. "I want you to make me a member of the mile-high club," she explained.

He groaned. One thing he knew for sure. With Regan in his life, she'd keep him on his toes and he'd never be bored.

He held her hands in his and promised. "Babe, you have got yourself a deal."

HER SECRET THRILL
Donna Kauffman

To my Lawman.

Chapter One

WHERE HAD LIZA DISAPPEARED TO?

Natalie Holcomb pasted a smile on her face and said good-night to another cluster of Liza's glitzy guests as they left the penthouse suite. She closed the door behind them, wishing like hell she could slip out of these heels and go soak in that Olympic-size sunken tub she knew awaited her in her private bath.

She couldn't deny Liza knew how to throw a party...and where to throw one. The Maxi was the newest hotel in New York City and Liza had reserved the entire penthouse level for her latest bash. Typical overindulgence—Natalie went for elegance over opulence—but Liza could definitely afford it. Or, more correctly, her newest client could.

At twenty-nine, Liza was the crème de la crème of the young Turks invading the public relations business. Tonight's bash was a big coming-out party for the sexiest soap star to grace the set of the hottest soap, *Steam*. It was *the* party at which to see Conrad Jones, and to be seen by everyone else. Conrad's surgically perfected face and buffed action-figure body didn't do it for Natalie, but she'd quickly learned she was the only female under eighty who apparently felt that way. Then again, she didn't recognize anyone here, so what did she know?

"Where's Liza?"

Natalie spun around and automatically pasted on her hostess smile again. *Now I know how a beauty pageant director feels. Inferior, with a good case of lockjaw.*

"I'm not sure where she is at the moment," Natalie said graciously to the chic couple. "But I'll be certain to tell her you said goodbye. I know she was thrilled you could make it." *Whoever you are.*

They gave her the "yeah, whatever" nod that clearly stated they realized she was a nobody and therefore not worthy of more of their time. Natalie didn't stick her tongue out and slam the ten-foot-tall door behind them, but she thought about it. Which only went to show how late it really had gotten. She couldn't care less what these people thought of her. Glitz and glam was Liza's life. Corporate law was hers. She smiled, thinking it really wasn't much different. Sharks and barracudas abounded in both arenas. Liza just swam with better-looking sharks.

They'd shared a dorm at law school for four semesters before Liza had dropped out to head for the Big Apple to realize her own dream. That was six years ago. Natalie looked around and had to smile in approval. They'd both done pretty well. It was probably their drive to succeed that had kept them close despite their crazy schedules. Natalie lived in New York City but traveled all over the country. Liza worked out of L.A., but also traveled extensively. The only reason Natalie had come at all tonight was that they'd both been in the same town at the same time, and that happened all too rarely. She'd agreed to stay with her in the penthouse so they could spend some time together. Not, she thought as she looked through the rapidly thinning crowd, that she'd actually gotten to do much of that. She sighed but shrugged it off. Liza was... well, Liza.

NINETY MINUTES and a couple of dozen more locked-jaw goodbyes later, Natalie sank thankfully back against the double doors. "Finally." Liza had never surfaced. Knowing her, Natalie figured Liza had let Conrad talk her into hitting some hot club or another party. Liza was a slave to her career and loved every minute of it. Of course, Natalie thought with a private smile, Liza had probably let Conrad think *he* was her slave master. She shook her head and wandered to the oasis that was the kitchen, gathering up empty glasses as she went. She had let the bartending and wait staff go home at two. It was now almost three. She knew there would be a cleaning crew coming in the morning, so she'd just set these in the sink and head toward that sunken tub.

"Excuse me."

Natalie squealed and spun around. The deep voice belonged to a tall guy with dark-blond hair and amused-looking blue eyes, who quickly stepped forward to catch the crystal stemware she almost bobbled to the floor.

He rescued two of them, and Natalie managed to get the other three onto the counter intact.

"I'm sorry. I didn't mean to startle you."

She shook her head, willing her pounding heart out of her throat. "I—I thought I was alone." She meant to look away, regain her composure, but something about the direct, easy way he held her gaze prevented her from doing so. "Let me, uh, that is, I, um—" She broke off, suddenly feeling silly for being so tongue-tied. Like she hadn't seen a hundred gorgeous blondes tonight. It was just that he looked, well…real. It was simply a shock after all those capped teeth and spa-pumped pecs.

Taking a discreet, calming breath, she trotted out the pageant director smile one last time. "I'll show you to the door." She stepped forward, obviously expecting him to move back out of the doorway and follow her. Only, he didn't do as she expected.

She stopped, feeling the first tiny frisson of—well, not fear exactly, but definitely awareness that she was alone in this suite with a stranger. A stranger that had a good four inches and fifty or sixty pounds on her.

Projecting the calm, cool wherewithal that had gotten her farther inside the boardroom than most women her age— hell, twice her age—she gestured ahead of her. "This way, please."

She knew the look she was giving him made it perfectly clear she had no intention of playing any games. It was a look she'd perfected back in boarding school. Boys, especially rich ones, thought all a girl needed was a sharp smile and a fat bank account to fall thankfully on her back and spread her legs. Boys, rich or otherwise, learned quickly that Natalie Holcomb, of the Connecticut Holcombs, was not impressed with vast wealth, much less a hot bod.

As it turned out, men hadn't proven to be any different from boys.

By now the look was second nature to her. She didn't mind the ice princess reputation it had earned her, either. In fact, she took pride in it. At the end of the day, she knew— as did they—that she'd gotten where she was by working hard. With her knees firmly in the closed position.

She held his gaze evenly and motioned to the door.

He smiled at her. Totally unaffected by "the look." Before she could follow up with her patented verbal ice blast, he nodded to a point behind her.

"My jacket. It's in the other room."

Oh. Natalie simply refused to blush. Holcombs didn't. She'd learned at her father's knee to smooth over minor gaffes with unshakable calm. Therefore, the knowing twinkle in the man's eye meant less than nothing. Not even a ripple. Really.

"I'll meet you at the door, then," she said, all good grace and polished manners.

"No need to bother. I can show myself out," he said as he moved past her.

She swore she could feel the heat emanate from his body. Probably a flashback to the tightly pressed throng of bodies she'd been wedged into all night. Nothing more. She resisted the urge to fan her face. At least he wasn't doused in some designer scent. Whatever he was wearing was very subtle. And quite effective.

She refrained from sniffing the air behind him, but barely. Obviously she was far more tired than she'd thought. Good breeding—nothing else, certainly—sent her to the front door. She'd see him out simply to assure herself she was well and truly alone. No other reason.

"I have a problem."

She started at the sound of his voice. Damn him for doing that to her. Twice. She turned. "What problem?" She'd sounded sharper than she'd meant to, almost snappish. *Calm and controlled, Natalie.* Never snappish. That he had her reminding herself of things that were normally automatic responses only proved how overtired she really was.

She smoothed her features into a composed mask, although truthfully, she felt anything but. Certainly it was the fatigue, after all, it was after three in the morning—but there was no denying he unsettled her with that direct, amused gaze of his. What was it about this guy, anyway?

He was nice enough to look at, if you went for the earthy, muscular type. Actually, she wasn't sure what her type was. But it certainly wasn't mountain man here. Not that he was all that huge when you stopped and really looked him over. *Rugged.* Yes, rugged was the right way to describe him, now that she thought about it. He definitely filled out his black jeans and that amber knit pullover pretty damn convincingly—

Dear God, she was ogling. She jerked her gaze up to his face. He spared her the knowing smile, but somewhere behind those eyes of his she knew he was feeling smug.

"What is the problem?" she asked again, just wanting him gone. The hell with being polite. He'd found his jacket, so that wasn't it. The well-worn brown leather jacket made those shoulders look even wider, his arms bigger, his chest broader. Whoever created his look had definitely chosen well.

Liza had told her plenty of the stories about casting directors who discovered guys in the unlikeliest of places and, with a personal trainer, personal shopper and good dentist, turned them into daytime gods. Mechanic, she thought. Construction worker. UPS delivery guy.

"My wallet," he said, breaking into her reverie.

Caught again. What was wrong with her, anyway? Never mind the sunken bath, she was going right to bed.

"I gave it to Con to tip the limo guy." He shrugged and smiled. "Guy just signed a seven-figure contract but never has money on him." Those blue eyes twinkled quite charmingly. "Probably why he keeps me around."

"Con? As in Conrad Jones?" She groaned inwardly. She'd been ogling a groupie. At least she could have consoled herself if he was a working professional, instead of a…a sycophant, a hanger-on.

"We grew up together. Lamont, Wyoming."

A childhood groupie. Even worse. He'd made a life out of standing in his pal's spotlight. But this was none of her business. "Let me get my purse, I'll be glad to loan you—"

"I don't need the money," he said quickly. "It's just that Con—"

Right then, a loud thumping reverberated through the room at the end of the hallway, followed shortly thereafter by someone screaming, "God, yes!"

That someone sounded suspiciously like Liza.

"What the—?" Natalie went to move past him down the hallway.

The blond stranger reached for her arm. "You might not want to—"

His warning wasn't even completed before another, far more masculine, shout echoed around the room. "Ooooooooh, yessssss. I'm coming, baby!"

Natalie froze as an incredibly primitive and impossibly loud groan followed that pronouncement. Shrieks of undeniable rapture accompanied said groan. Liza's.

Well. Okay, then. Natalie was pretty sure that in her entire twenty-eight years she'd never once covered this particular social gaffe. At least she now knew where Liza had gotten off to, after all. *Gotten off.* Dear Lord. Her face flushed and no amount of social breeding was going to stop it.

"I'm sorry," he said from behind her.

She turned to face him. Best just to brazen it out. "Well, I guess I'm really not alone, after all." She wanted to smile brightly, make light of the whole thing, but she couldn't pull it off.

"Yeah." He did have the grace to look a little uncomfortable. "Listen, maybe I will just head downstairs and see if the bar is still open or…or something. I'm staying with Con and I don't have keys to his place," he added by way of explanation. Then he gave up and grinned. "This is really embarrassing, isn't it."

And just like that, she suddenly found the whole situation hilarious. She was already laughing even as she nodded in agreement. And once she started, she couldn't seem to stop. He joined in, and they were both leaning against the hallway walls by the time they managed to stop long enough to catch their breath.

"Um, just tell Con I'll be in the lobby. Or leave a note. Whatever."

"But what if— I mean, are you sure he'll be leaving?"

"If I had my wallet, I'd just get a room, but—"

Whatever she'd thought moments ago, right now Natalie felt a certain kinship with him. They were both being put in an incredibly awkward position by their friends. The least she could do was end it as gracefully and quickly as possible. "I know you'd rather handle this on your own, but I honestly don't mind reserving a room for you. You can always switch the charge to your card when you…um, get your wallet back." Laughter threatened to erupt again, but she tamped it down. She was so tired now that she knew the giggles were perilously close to the surface. Best to get him on his way so she could go bury herself in her room under a mound of covers and forget this whole episode.

She didn't give him a chance to refuse. She moved past him and went toward her bedroom, where she'd stashed her purse in a dresser drawer. "I'll be right back."

"Really, it's okay," he said, half following her down the hall. "You don't have to—"

And just then, the thumping started again.

Natalie stopped and whirled around. "Oh, for heaven's sake." She looked at the far wall, where the paintings already had shifted to an odd angle. Liza's bedroom was on the other side of that wall. The thumping increased. And there were groans now. "You've got to be kidding me," she muttered.

"I'm sorry, I don't know your name."

She looked at him. "Pardon?"

"Your name?"

It took her a moment to process the request and why it mattered. It was impossible to think with the sex marathon getting into full swing in the next room. She was fairly certain *swing* might be the operative word. "My name? Natalie," she said absently, trying hard to block out the escalating groans and *yeah, baby*s coming from the other room.

"I'm Jake. Listen, Natalie, why don't I get you out of here and buy us both a cup of coffee."

She looked at him as if he had just grown two heads. What was he saying? He was asking her out? "You don't have any money."

He grinned sheepishly. "Okay, well then, I'll let you buy me a cup of coffee."

"But I can't reserve you a hotel room? What, you have a limit on charitable donations?" This whole conversation was getting strange.

But then he stepped closer to her, and she found herself completely focusing on his blue eyes. She told herself it was the only way to block out at least some of the shrieks of ecstasy now coming from the other room.

"What kind of vitamins do they take, anyway?" he asked.

Then he grinned. It was the grin that did it. Or maybe Liza's noisy climax. She wasn't sure. All she knew was that she couldn't stay in this room one more second.

"Come on," he said again, as if sensing her shift. "Let's get out of here and leave them alone. Not that they seem to care, but I do."

Right at that moment, she couldn't find a hole in that logic. She ducked into her room, snatched her purse and headed to the front door, not even looking to see if he was following her. She'd buy them some coffee, talk him into letting her get a room for him, and hope that by then Liza and Con would have screwed themselves into unconsciousness—and she could crawl into her bed and sleep till noon.

Galvanized by the plan, she walked over to the elevator and punched the only button on it. Jake stepped out into the hall, Liza's shouted "Yes, right *there!*" following him through the open doorway.

They both stepped into the elevator, careful not to look at

each other. Or at the door to the penthouse. Natalie punched the lobby button.

"Going down," intoned a deep recorded voice.

They both glanced at each other. Jake snickered first. Natalie snorted. Then they collapsed in laughter that continued for the entire eighty-eight floors.

Chapter Two

NATALIE WAS SLIGHTLY overdressed in a gold-colored tunic—Liza's—over tight black silk pants. Also Liza's. She'd only caved to Liza's pleading and worn the slinky attire because she knew she'd be in the penthouse all night and not out in public. Well, she was out in public now. But after what she'd just been through upstairs, wearing pants that clung to her fanny and outlined her thighs like a second skin, along with a top that could only be worn with no bra, seemed like a cakewalk in terms of public discomfort.

They were in an all-night café several doors down from The Maxi. Jake motioned past the counter to a small booth. Thankful, she took him up on the offer. Not as much of her would show if she was tucked into a booth.

His hand brushed the bare skin of her back ever so slightly as she moved in front of him to slide into her seat. For whatever reason, that brief touch was like a hot jolt of electricity. Flustered and caught off guard by the heat of her reaction, she instantly opened the small menu in front of her, even though she had no intention of ordering more than one quick cup of coffee. She just didn't want him to notice the fact that her nipples had become little heat-seeking missiles.

Surely it was the atmosphere she'd just left that was making her body react that way. Mortifying as it had been, there was also no denying it had been just a little bit...well, arousing.

"Black, please," she mumbled to the waitress. *What was she doing here again?* Now that she'd escaped the sex-o-rama upstairs, she was having second thoughts.

"I'll have the same, please. But with cream." Jake smiled at the tired waitress. "Real cream if you have it."

The waitress actually smiled. "Sure thing, hon."

Natalie's eyebrows lifted. "I didn't think waitresses were allowed to smile in New York City. Isn't that a code violation or something?"

Jake grinned and shrugged out of his jacket. "Guess it's that Wyoming charm my mom pounded into me."

And damn if he didn't have it. In spades. She could keep on telling herself that it was the late hour and her obvious fatigue, but her life had stepped so far outside its neat little box in the past fifteen or so minutes, she decided to just say the hell with it and go with the flow. Tomorrow, life would resume. And boy, were she and Liza going to have a little talk.

But for now, she was drinking coffee at a quarter-to-four in the morning with a good-looking guy in the city that didn't sleep. Might as well enjoy the rare adventure.

"So, how long have you known Liza?"

Small talk. Small talk was safe enough. "Since law school." She smiled over his obvious surprise. "Liza dropped out. I didn't."

"What kind of law do you practice?"

"Corporate. Boring stuff." She loved her job but didn't want to talk about herself. She wanted to talk about him. He was the adventure, after all. "What do you do back in Wyoming?" Then she remembered. He was one of Con's followers. Oh well, she wouldn't let that dampen her newfound spirit of adventure. She could sustain her little thrill for at least as long as it took to have one cup of coffee.

"Cattle ranch."

She couldn't hide her surprise. "You work on a cattle ranch?" *Cowboy*. She should have guessed. Definitely more a cowboy type than a UPS guy. Although they both looked damn fine in brown. She felt that giggle rising in her throat again and took a sip of the coffee the waitress had set down.

"Actually, it's a family-run operation. I'm fourth generation. But I spend more time on airplanes than I do on the ranch."

"Ranching requires a lot of travel?"

"It's as much a corporation as it is a ranch. I handle the business end of things. We sell our stock worldwide."

"Wow, I never knew cows were in such demand."

"Cattle. And our breed is. We Lannisters have been selling cattle for as long as there's been cattle in the West. Or close enough, anyway," he added with a grin.

He lifted his cup, and she found herself studying his hands. They were big, with thick fingers that she could see were quite scarred. Apparently he hadn't spent his whole life in airplanes.

Echoes of Liza and Con rippled through her mind, and she couldn't help wondering what those rough hands of Jake's would feel like if he—

"Is this the first time Liza has ditched her hostessing duties on you?"

She jerked her gaze back to her own mug. "Actually, no. Most of the time, Liza goes where the evening leads her." She smiled dryly. "I just thought this time it led her out of the penthouse. I don't mind helping out. I know the party was important to her, business-wise." She stopped just then, remembering what "business" Liza had been engaged in.

She felt a little heat rise to her cheeks and covered it with another sip of coffee. It was one thing to laugh with a stranger when caught in an uncomfortable situation, but now that they were sitting in the relative quiet of a coffee shop, she couldn't simply discuss it as if it were an everyday topic.

"You said you knew Conrad as a child," she said, gamely moving the conversation along. "I guess you must be pretty proud of his success."

"I'm happy he's found something he likes. His family back home is soaking it all up, enjoying his celebrity status." Jake smiled. "Even if they are a bit uncomfortable with the show itself. Have you seen it?"

Natalie shook her head. "I've only heard what Liza told me. I guess a name like *Steam* sort of sums things up, though."

"Exactly. Con's parents aren't uptight, and neither is our town, really. But I have to admit the show was a lot more graphic than I'd ever thought. Especially right in the middle of the day."

"Not a soap fan, I take it," she said.

"No." He chuckled. "Although, I'm thinking about changing my mind. Beats CNN when you're on the road alone as much as I am."

He laughed, and so did Natalie, but she couldn't push the accompanying images out of her mind. Jake in all those hotel rooms, watching all those amorous couples on the television screen, feeling amorous himself, doing—

She cleared her throat. "I—I used to watch a couple of them. In college. Actually, it was Liza that got me watching. She has always loved the entertainment industry. I'm not at all surprised she's found her niche there. Things have really taken off for her."

"You sound like a good friend."

She smiled at that. "Thanks. I'm not so sure she'll agree after I have a little chat with her tomorrow, though."

He raised his eyebrows. "What are you going to say?"

"Well, just that I don't really appreciate her putting me in such an awkward position. Not the hostessing—I could do that in my sleep. But what if there had been more people still around when they started—you know."

His grin made his eyes twinkle. "Well, that could have been interesting. Maybe everyone would have loosened up a little."

Natalie's mouth dropped open, then snapped shut. What was he suggesting? An orgy?

As if sensing her thoughts, he added, "Well, you have to admit that was a pretty uptight group. Everyone was so concerned with who was talking to whom and what designer they were wearing. I've never seen so many self-involved people in my life. No disrespect to your friend. She wasn't like that at all."

Natalie blew out a breath and relaxed. "No, she's not, but I agree about the rest. Although you should mingle with the people in my firm trying to make partner. Talk about self-involved. Only, all the talk is about investment counselors, stock portfolios and real estate. The only designers they talk about are interior designers." She suddenly started laughing.

"What?"

She shook her head. "Nothing." But she couldn't stop grinning. "Okay, I was just picturing Liza pulling that stunt during one of *my* business parties." She rolled her eyes. "Although, I don't think even Liza and Con doing the wild thing right in the middle of the room would have loosened up any of them."

Jake shared her laugh. "Guess your world is pretty buttoned-up, huh?"

She considered that. "On the surface, certainly. Behind the scenes…well, let's just say the gossip mill doesn't suffer from lack of worthy grist to keep it going."

"I think people are all pretty much the same in that regard, once you get beneath the surface, don't you?"

"What do you mean?"

"I mean, no matter whether they are free spirits like Liza and Con, or a three-piece Suit whose daily routine is as predictable as the weather, underneath they are all still motivated by sex. Or their sexual nature, anyway. Suit might not ever do what Liza and Con did, but that doesn't mean he might not fantasize about it, or wish that he was bold enough to do it."

"I don't think that's the case at all. I mean, some people would be appalled publicly and feel exactly that same level of mortification personally."

He took a sip, considering, then held her gaze over the edge of his coffee cup. "Did you?"

She stilled. Or, at least, her heart felt as if it had. "I beg your pardon?"

But her attempt to make him reassess the conversational turn he'd taken didn't even make him blink. If anything, he looked even more determined. "I said, did you? You were definitely uncomfortable, so was I. I mean, it's an embarrassing situation, no question. Made more so by the fact that we were strangers to each other, but both knew the...well, them." He put his mug down. "But other than dealing with my presence while you were listening to them, were you really appalled *personally* by what they were doing in there?" He leaned closer. "If you'd been alone, what would you have done?"

His expression was daring her. She took him up on it. "I'd have gone into my room, closed the door and run a loud bath. I believe in giving people their privacy."

"Okay. So not appalled, then. You'd just remove yourself from the situation."

She thought for a moment, then nodded.

"So you're in the tub. Are you honestly not thinking about them then? Thinking about what you just heard?"

"Probably I'd be thinking about it, it'd be pretty hard to ignore. I mean, it's not a typical thing to be presented with."

"So you'd be thinking about it. Appalled? Or aroused?"

She wasn't liking where he was going, she'd come here to get away from this—not examine it. But his question intrigued her. Mostly because she was finding something out about herself that surprised her. And since it was only a harmless discussion, she saw no harm in sharing it.

"Maybe I'd be aroused. But not in a voyeuristic way. I can't say that element has ever remotely appealed to me. But in the earthy way it would make you think about sex in general, I suppose."

There, that was safe and analytical sounding. Never mind that she wanted to squirm in her seat and that the friction of her shirt against her nipples was driving her mad at the moment. He didn't have to know that.

Looking into those amusement-filled blue eyes of his, however, she had to wonder.

"So you see, we *are* all the same," he concluded. "In general, I mean. We might harbor different fantasies. You don't get into voyeurism. But you have other things that work for you. We all do. No matter how prim and proper we are on the surface, we are all basically driven by our sexual selves, don't you think?"

"Not to the exclusion of everything else, no."

"But you do agree that people who pretend they aren't sexual creatures, that they don't respond to some kind of stimuli, are fooling themselves? Even cheating themselves?"

Natalie thought about that. "Perhaps."

He grinned. "You don't look too convinced."

"I think maybe there are people who don't so much deny their sexuality and their needs, as ignore them." After all, that summed her up neatly. Not that she was going to share that. "People can have other priorities besides sex." She shot him a dry smile. "Well, women can, anyway."

He raised his hands. "Ha-ha. But I'll agree that men are a bit more sexually centered than women. In general."

"Now, there you have my complete agreement."

He grinned and finished off his coffee. "For someone who seems fairly at home with her sexuality, you appear to be pretty conscious of those who aren't. Are all the lawyers you work with that uptight?"

She was honestly surprised at his assessment. But the surprise and the late hour had her responding before she could stop. "What makes you think I'm at home, as you call it, with my sexuality?"

"The clothes you're wearing, for one." He shrugged off her expression with a smile. "I know I probably shouldn't judge you by your appearance, but I don't know much else about you. What I do know is that outfit is definitely not for the faint of heart. Or a person not completely at home with the fact that she's a woman."

She wouldn't squirm. She wouldn't. But damn if she didn't want to. She should have felt self-conscious about that description. And she did. But she also kind of...liked it. Still, she felt compelled to be honest. Besides, no way could she back up what this outfit promised.

"Thank you for the compliment. But in the spirit of full disclosure, I must admit that these clothes belong to Liza." She folded her arms on the table. "She didn't find my legal-eagle party clothes suitable for *her* party. Which basically just proves my point. Liza is sexually adventurous, and her wardrobe and lifestyle reflect that. But I'm not, and *my* wardrobe and lifestyle reflect *that*." There, now at least he'd know she wasn't advertising something she had no intention of putting on the market.

Although, she couldn't deny that the thought sent a brief thrill through her.

Jake seemed to think for a moment about what she'd said. "So which precludes which?"

Confused, she said, "What do you mean?"

"I mean, does the lifestyle and wardrobe follow the inherent nature of the woman? Or does the woman simply choose to bury her nature due to her lifestyle and accompanying wardrobe?"

Natalie had no answer for that. It was one thing to reveal that maybe, just maybe, she'd enjoyed daydreaming once in a while about having a wild fling after hearing one of Liza's tales. It was quite another admitting she was really more like Liza deep down, or would be if she allowed herself to be.

Was she? Had she really subverted her nature because of her family and her career?

"I guess a little of both," she answered as honestly as she could. "My family is not outward about stuff like that, but I can't say I share that. Not fully. I might not be comfortable with outward displays, but it doesn't mean I wouldn't enjoy them. Maybe. With the right person. I do enjoy my career, and it is my priority right now. I don't feel like I'm giving anything up for that." She shrugged. "But maybe I repress that side of me to some point. I don't think I deny I have it, however." She looked at him with a little grin. "I guess I haven't found an easy way to combine the two, so sex usually loses out."

Was she really sitting here having a frank talk about her sexual nature with a man she just met? But she couldn't deny it was the most stimulating thing she'd done in recent memory. Stimulating in several ways.

He didn't say anything, just responded with a little smile of his own.

She realized she was really enjoying herself. He was fun

to talk to, intriguing, thought-provoking. She was ashamed at her earlier assessment and rejection of him. Maybe she was guilty of categorizing men, making them less appealing to her so she didn't have to deal with them. Something else she'd have to think about. What was she afraid of, anyway?

Well, *that* she knew. Though it wasn't fear. Merely an intelligent assessment of past problems. Entanglements impeded her career. Right now, she was simply not up to dealing with all the baggage and emotional drain that inevitably came with building a long-term relationship.

He smiled at the waitress when she brought more coffee and cream. He waited for her to leave, then turned his full attention back to Natalie. "I can hear the wheels turning over there. What are you thinking?"

She lifted her shoulders and sipped at her coffee. "Nothing. Everything." She laughed lightly. "I'm not used to such deep philosophical conversations at—" she glanced at the wall clock and groaned "—four-thirty in the morning. My God, how did it get to be so late?"

"It was already 'so late' when we started this."

She looked at him then. And he was looking at her. *Really* looking at her. And it was as if the air stilled…or something. A certain kind of quiet descended between them, encompassed them. Her throat grew tight, as he continued to look at her.

"Started this?" she managed to say, hardly above a whisper.

He didn't shift so much as a hair. Didn't reach out to touch her or make any kind of calculated move. He simply held her gaze as easily as he had all night long and looked at her as if he knew exactly what she was thinking.

"Yeah," he said quietly. "This."

Natalie felt such a rush of arousal that she clutched her coffee mug like a lifeline. Amazing. No one had ever made her react like that. And other than that little brush of his fingertips, he hadn't even touched her since they walked in. And yet...she felt him.

She wanted to believe it was just the obvious stimulation of their conversation. But surprisingly, neither of them had been at all leering or suggestive the entire time they'd talked. Which made the way he was looking at her now all the more erotic.

Ridiculous. There was nothing here. It was simply an intriguing interlude with a stranger.

A stranger that was currently soaking her panties just by looking at her. And honestly, when was the last time that had ever happened to her? More honestly, when was the last time she'd ever have let anyone get close enough for her to find out?

And this little moment she thought they were sharing could be in her sleep-deprived head, too, she thought with a silent laugh. Or she could just come out and ask him what he meant by *this*. No. No, she couldn't. This was fun and even exciting. But no. She had a life to return to, a plane to catch late tomorrow. Later today, actually. And he had business. In Wyoming of all places. She was never in Wyoming—

Which suddenly made *this* sound perfect.

She was wanting. He looked to be willing.

She wanted to clamp a hand over her mouth. A one-night stand? Natalie Holcomb? But in the next breath, she thought, *and why the hell not?* Maybe she'd been repressing more than she thought. Because the idea scandalized her. And turned her on so much, she thought she might come just thinking about it.

Oh...my...God. She wouldn't. She couldn't.

Liza would.

She looked at him, then down at those hands of his. When she looked back up, that amused twinkle was back in his eyes.

"We're not— This is just—" She couldn't look away from his eyes. "Coffee," she finished, almost breathlessly.

He nodded. "Best coffee and conversation I can remember having. Maybe ever."

He glanced down at his coffee but it was the look in his eyes when he lifted his gaze back to hers that did it. Not smug, not aggressive, not pleading. Simply...honest.

"Would you like to extend this conversation?" he asked.

Her throat closed over. Her nipples were so tight now that they actually hurt. He wanted her. Right now. And there was no denying she wanted him. Right now.

And frankly, right now, that was all that mattered.

It was that simple. That thrilling.

"Yeah." She cleared her throat, her heart began to race. "I mean, yes. Yes, I believe I would like that. Very much."

"More coffee?"

Natalie jerked her gaze from Jake and looked up at the waitress. "Um, no. No thank you. Just the check."

The waitress laid the bill on the table. Natalie nervously fished out a ten and tossed it on the pile, not caring about the change.

Now what?

Chapter Three

IN THE MOVIES, this was where it always segued to the two lovers groping inside the private confines of their room. *Lovers.* She swallowed. The movies never dealt with that awkward transition sequence.

Then Jake was standing beside her holding out his hand, that charming grin crinkling the corners of his blue eyes. And it was as easy—and as hard—as just reaching out and taking that hand. She took it.

He let her hand go as soon as she stood, but there was that electric brushing of his warm hand on her bare lower back as he guided her to the front door and out into the New York sunrise.

She stopped and turned, an awkward laugh escaping her. "Um, I guess the standard 'your place or mine' is out of the question?" She wanted the adventure, but she wasn't taking him back to her place.

He laughed. "Yeah. I had forgotten about that."

Her heart was pounding, but Natalie relaxed a little. It was obvious that he wasn't used to this, nor had he planned it, any more than she had. That relieved her. And somehow made this all the more erotic and exciting.

"Maybe another room at The Maxi?" she offered.

"Actually, I know a place. Uptown. I've stayed there before. It's quiet, out of the way." He caught her gaze. "Private."

She liked the sound of that. "Okay." She stepped to the curb to whistle for a taxi. The streets were pretty quiet; only the early risers and workaholics were out.

He reached for her hand and tugged her back.

She whirled, liking the contact of his hand on hers. When he went to drop it, she instinctively tightened her grip. He paused, looked at her, then tightened his grip as well. She liked the assurance it gave her that they were both in this together.

"We have another stop to make first," he said, then nodded toward a drugstore on the corner.

Dear Lord, she was so far gone that she'd forgotten about all that.

"I wasn't exactly planning on meeting you," he said.

She liked how he said that. Not "I wasn't planning on having a night of wild sex." Just that he hadn't planned on her. Specifically her.

Careful, Natalie. Wild sex was exactly what all this was. Nothing personal, nothing lasting.

He tugged on her hand, and they walked to the corner. His hands were both smooth and rough. And warm. And big. His fingers were all but wedged between her slender ones. She shivered at the thought of where else they might wedge themselves.

"Cold?"

It was early fall, but even now there was a bit of summer in the air. Though that wasn't why she felt warm. She smiled at him and thought, *What the hell.* "Not hardly."

He grinned. "I think you ought to let Liza dress you more often. Brings out the wild side."

She laughed as they pushed into the drugstore. "Maybe it does."

What should have been an awkward errand surprised Natalie by turning into part of their foreplay.

Jake kept her hand firmly in his as he wound his way up and down the aisles, looking for condoms. He glanced over at her, that grin playing around the corners of his mouth. "Ribbed or smooth?"

She tried to play it cool, to keep her mouth from simply dropping open, but she couldn't.

He laughed. "I'll choose."

So much for abandoning all her staid principles. But he didn't make her feel self-conscious about it. In fact, she got the feeling he was rather enjoying teasing her. She was certain of it, when he stopped as they passed a refriger-ated unit.

"Hmm." He slid open one door and pulled out a slender canister. "Harbor any fantasies about whipped cream?"

She tilted her head as if to ponder the question, when the truth was she'd never once thought about sex with whipped cream on top. "Give me a few minutes," she finally said, when he raised his eyebrows.

He laughed outright but put the can back. She was almost disappointed. Almost. Right now she only wanted him. Unadulterated.

They made their way to the counter. She should have been uncomfortable, standing with him while he—or rather she—made such an obvious purchase, but instead she held the clerk's rather direct gaze with a direct one of her own. *Go ahead,* she thought, *judge me. But I'm going to be having a lot more fun in the next couple of hours than you will.* Right then, she began to see why Liza indulged in this side of life.

It *was* fun.

Jake got the taxi. He gave the cabbie directions, then leaned back. The radio was blasting and the traffic was steadily picking up. They were both silent, but Jake still held her hand. As they made their way uptown, he began to trace small patterns on her palm with his fingertip.

She didn't squirm. Or lunge at him. But she wanted to do both. She'd assumed people who did this would be groping and tearing at each other's clothes the whole way to their room. This wasn't at all how she would have pictured it. It seemed so sedate. Detached. And yet, it was anything but. Sitting silently next to him, feeling his fingers on her palm, was extremely sensitizing. It allowed her to think, to feel, to absorb. To imagine that fingertip brushing her in other places, slowly, lazily.

He made her feel that there was all the time in the world and he intended to make good use of each and every second.

Dear God, but she was dying to have him.

IT WASN'T AWKWARD at the hotel, either. They knew him there, but were discreet enough not raise an eyebrow when she slid her credit card across the desk. There was the briefest of moments when they asked about needing a bellman for their luggage, just enough to tell her that Jake didn't typically show up with a woman on his arm at the crack of dawn. Enough to make her feel better...but also just enough to make her feel naughty. In a sort of decadent, delicious way. *Was this really Natalie Holcomb?*

As he guided her across the thickly carpeted lobby, she decided she was glad they'd come here. The hotel was small, but intimate and modestly elegant. Apparently cowboys had style. She let Jake direct her to the elevator. They were the only two to step inside.

When the doors swished shut, Nat felt a tiny jolt of panic. Well, not panic, but...reality maybe.

"You okay?"

He was so aware of her. She liked it, rather than resented it. If he was that in tune to her, it could only mean good things later. Right? She tried not to gulp. She was really doing this. In broad daylight, even. Somehow that made it feel even more sinful.

She looked at him and he took her hand, that playful, sexy smile on his face.

Oh, yeah. She was definitely doing this.

"I'm nervous," she said honestly. "But very okay."

He smiled. "Me, too. On both counts."

She laughed suddenly. "I have to say it—I can't believe I'm doing this." Might as well get that out in the open.

"Me, either." He moved closer to her. "Although, I'm beginning to think I owe Con a thank-you."

He was so warm. So big.

She nodded. "I'm probably not going to be having that talk with Liza, after all."

The doors slid open, but they stood, mere inches apart, staring at each other.

"I need to ask you something," she said.

The doors started to slide shut, but Jake reached out and held the button. "Ask me anything."

"What is this—exactly?" She laughed a bit nervously at his confused expression. "I mean, I know what *this* is. But I'm catching a plane later today. And another one a few days after that. And so on. I wasn't planning on—"

He pressed one of those big, thick fingers against her lips. "This can just be...this. No strings. No tomorrow." He let his finger slide slowly off. "Is that what you wanted to hear?"

She was pretty sure that was exactly what she wanted to hear. She didn't dwell on anything beyond that. "Yes."

He let his finger off the button, and the doors shut. "Come here," he said softly, and pulled her into his arms.

She went into his arms as if she'd been there hundreds of times before. And yet it was an electrifyingly original experience.

He tipped her chin up and angled his head. "Let's taste each other. And go from there."

His kiss was tender but firm. His lips warm and dry...then quickly wetter. She slid her arms around his waist and smoothed her hands up his wide back. God, he was big. She'd never been with a man this...large. There was something deeply elemental about how overpowering he was compared to her shorter, slighter frame. But rather than be intimidated by it, she was secretly aroused by it.

In fact, as his wide hands moved up her back and cupped her head, moving it exactly where he wanted it, she felt an undeniable urge to have him move her whole body exactly how and where and whatever way he wanted it. She wanted him to be in control, to take her...and make her like everything he wanted to do to her.

She would have been shocked by the realization—she was definitely one for equal partnerships—but she was too busy reeling from the feel of his tongue invading her mouth.

He didn't push or shove. He enticed. Goaded. Teased. Twined. Made her want to do the same. So she did.

There was a sudden clearing of throats.

Natalie jerked her head up to find two elderly men staring at them. The lobby stretched out behind them. They'd apparently gone back down. She'd forgotten they were even in the elevator.

Her cheeks warmed. Jake caught her eye and winked, then tugged her out of the elevator. "You take this one, gentlemen. We'll catch another one."

Natalie was going to tell him that wasn't necessary. In fact, she might have enjoyed making the old codgers squirm a little bit on the ride back up. But the idea that maybe there was a little voyeur down deep inside her, after all, surprised her so much, she missed her chance.

Jake pushed the button on the opposite wall, got them into

that elevator and gently backed her to one side. "You stand here." He moved away, pushed for their floor and stood against the opposite wall. At her questioning look, he grinned and said, "Just ensuring we make it to the room this time."

She laughed, but as the elevator jolted upward, their smiles slowly faded. They stood on opposite sides of the small car, gazes fixed on each other.

Natalie felt her entire body come alive as he very deliberately let his gaze roam over her. When he met her eyes once again, she found herself slowly, shockingly, running her tongue over her lips. When she saw his throat visibly work, she grew bold enough to slowly allow her own gaze to travel over his wide shoulders, deep chest, narrower waist, down his long legs...and back up again. Stopping very deliberately for one extended moment at the juncture between them. Then she gazed directly at his eyes. And licked her lips again.

This time he was ready. His grin was slow, his eyes hot...and demanding. His hands had been pressed to the wall behind him, but now they slid over his thighs...and rested on the zipper of his pants.

Her eyes widened at the very primal, direct gesture, and her knees went a bit weak. She'd never thought about watching a man stroke himself. Ever. It simply wasn't part of her sexual experience. But damn if she didn't want to add it in. Right now.

She looked to his eyes and saw a taunting there. Was he daring her? Did he want her to ask him?

She looked back to his hands, but they just stayed there, resting over the bulge she knew very well was behind them.

The elevator stopped and the doors slid open. Her breath came out in one long sigh. But there was more frustration in it than relief.

He reached for her hand, she lifted hers to his. She was half wondering if he was going to direct it to his fly, but he folded his fingers between hers and pulled her out of the elevator into the hallway. He checked his room key, then the signs, and headed down the hall with her in tow.

She liked his long-legged stride, liked the way he kept looking down at her with such heat in his eyes.

Suddenly he tugged her against him and ducked into the little vending machine alcove.

"You're driving me crazy," he murmured against her mouth just before taking it again.

Natalie thrilled to the way he simply took her. But while his kiss was demanding, it was also generous. He gave... aggressively.

When he pulled back, they were both breathing heavily. "I could climb right out of my skin, I want you so badly."

The rush of pleasure his roughly spoken words sent through her was so intense, it was all she could do to nod in agreement.

He wrapped her against him, then finally swore and left the alcove. "I'm going to embarrass myself completely if I don't get you in that room right now."

Natalie decided right then that groping and tearing had its moments, too. She was itching to pull off every stitch he had on.

He fumbled the key card into the slot, repeating the motion three times before they finally got the door open.

Natalie didn't even pay attention to the lovely little room or the original antique furnishings. In fact, if he hadn't been as hot to get to her as she was to get to him, she'd have been appalled at her greedy behavior.

He slid off his jacket, yanking the bag from the drugstore out of the pocket and tossing it on the bed before tossing the jacket in the general vicinity of the closet. But just when Natalie thought—hoped—he'd drag her to him and thoroughly ravish her, he stilled, drew in a deep breath, then laughed lightly, rubbing a hand over his face.

"I wasn't like this even when I was sixteen." He looked at her with an adorably wry smile. "I guess my lack of finesse is showing here. Once a cowboy, always a cowboy."

"I'm not finding anything lacking." Natalie took a breath herself. "Except that we're still clothed."

He grinned. "Where have you been all my life?"

She laughed and let him guide her to the bed. She loved the heady mixture of laughter and passion that accompanied them so easily. Why wasn't it always this easy?

She knew why. Because there were no expectations here. No public aspect to this. Nothing to worry about beyond right this moment. She could be anyone. Do anything. And it would be just between them. No explanations. No apologies.

If she hadn't already been intoxicated by the possibilities, looking into his eyes now as he tugged his shirt out of his pants had her almost drunk and reeling with them. No apologies. No regrets.

She unhooked the neck of her tunic, let it fall to her waist and stood bare-breasted before him. She was not particularly well endowed, but she'd always thought that what she had measured up all right. The leap of desire she caught in his eyes erased any other concerns she might have had. The fact that she willingly stood there boldly before him was as arousing to her as it apparently was to him.

He removed his shirt, and she forgot all about her own nudity. Dear Lord, he was even more impressive than she'd imagined. His chest was broad and well muscled with a light swirl of hair across his pecs. His stomach was flat, his waist lean. She wanted to slide her hands in the waistband of his pants and shove them down. Her fingers curled inward against the need to follow through on that desire.

"What do you want?" He looked from her closed fists to her eyes.

He never missed anything. "I want to see the rest of you. You're truly beautiful."

Surprisingly, a little heat bloomed in his cheeks. She laughed. "Surely I'm not the first to tell you that. You do own a mirror or two."

He smiled and gave a disarming little shrug. "It wasn't what you said, it was how you said it." He lifted one of those fists, opened it and kissed her palm. "Thank you."

"You're welcome," she said, very unsteadily. He was simply too perfect. And he was hers. At least for the next couple of hours.

The grin was back, along with a wink as he placed her hand on his waistband. "You strike me as a woman who has no problem going after what she wants. So go ahead. Take what you want."

She looked into his eyes, saw that he was serious and said, "I think I just might do that."

"Please."

She grinned and flicked open the silver button of his jeans, then tugged down his zipper. It was a bit challenging as it was currently being stretched rather beyond its intended usage. She paused halfway down. "I don't want to— I'm afraid I'll—" She stopped, then laughed lightly when his hands covered hers. "So much for being the bold, daring, take-what-she-wants type."

"I thought you were doing just fine." His voice was hoarse and a little strained. Natalie looked up into his eyes and found such dark desire there, her smile faded away. He tugged on her hand, and she looked back down as he finished unzipping. He moved her hands to his hips, urging her to shove his pants down. She did. He kicked out of his shoes and socks, sending the pants after them.

"Briefs," she murmured. Black ones. Bikini style. She gulped as he took her hands again. She wasn't ready, not yet. Well, she was, she was all but salivating. But not yet. Instead she moved his hands to her hips.

It wasn't until he began peeling the skin-like pants off her that she remembered she had nothing on beneath. He didn't seem to mind. Neither did she, as it turned out.

She went to step out of her heels, but he said, "Leave them on."

She darted a look to his eyes, but complied. As it was, he was about four inches taller. Without the heels, it would be about half a foot difference. She figured it wouldn't hurt to minimize the difference, at least while they were standing.

Then he said, "Walk over to that chair." It wasn't a command, more a request.

Still, she was surprised by it. "Why?"

He smiled. "Because I asked nicely?"

Her thighs trembled a bit. Hadn't she fantasized about him calling the shots? The very idea made her even wetter. If possible. She felt her inner muscles clench hard as she turned and walked away from him across the room to a high-backed, Victorian-looking chair.

"Turn around."

She did. Very slowly. She didn't smile, nor did she look cool. She simply did as he asked until she faced him again. Then she waited.

"You are stunning."

Now she smiled. Felt her skin heat.

"Don't believe me? Turn to your right."

She did, and gasped. There was a full-length oval mirror tucked in the corner between the dresser and the chair.

"Look at yourself, Natalie."

She couldn't not. She looked…ripe. And those black,

razor-sharp heels were downright sex on stilts. She'd always thought herself passably attractive, basic beauty but no frills. Only, right now…dear God.

"Know what I see?" He moved behind her, so she could see him in the mirror. His body was wider than hers, taller than hers. He framed her entirely. His skin was darker, his look wilder, rougher. He made her look all the more refined, yet she didn't feel fragile.

He reached through her arms and gently cupped her breasts. She exhaled on a sharp gasp of pleasure, her knees giving slightly at the hot rush his touch set off.

"I see nipples that stand out for my attention." He slowly rubbed his thumbs over them, eliciting a moan from her she couldn't contain. She whimpered when his hands slid away, but moaned again as his flat palms smoothed over her abdomen, then spread downward.

She trembled hard as his fingertips brushed at the dark, downy curls at the apex of her thighs.

"I want to see what you have waiting for me here, Natalie," he said, his lips against the side of her neck.

It was impossibly arousing. She wanted to move his fingers lower, push them inside her. She stepped back, needing to feel his body touching hers, needing more than just his palms on her stomach, his fingers brushing her.

But he stepped back, then moved in front of her. He turned to face the mirror, almost entirely blocking her from view. "Turnabout is fair play, right?"

The muscles between her legs were tied in a knot of pleasure so tight she wanted to scream with the need to untie it. But she looked at him in the mirror and knew she wanted this even more.

She stood just to the side of him and pressed her hands to his hips, then slid his briefs all the way down his legs to the floor. She was almost kneeling. She placed her hands just above his knees, then slowly dragged them upward as she stood again. He gasped this time as she slid her fingers around his pelvis, almost brushing against his jutting erection...but not quite.

"Do you know what I see?"

"What?" The word sounded as if it had been ripped from him.

She looked to his face, which stood in chiseled relief as he clenched his jaw, straining for control.

"I see a man who can fill me like I've never been filled before."

He groaned but kept his hands at his side.

She remembered that moment in the elevator, when she'd fantasized about him stroking himself. She wanted to ask him to do it, even just once. She wanted to see his strong hand circle himself. He was so thick and rigid, and there was something so primal— But she couldn't.

"What is it, Natalie?"

Damn the man for being so focused. "Nothing. I—"

"Tell me." This time it was a command.

"I—I wondered what it would look like if you—" She darted her gaze from his in the mirror, downward...then back up again. She couldn't say it, so she showed him. She took his hand. Hers was shaking. And she moved it across his thigh...and upward. "I've never— I wanted to see what—"

And then he wrapped his big, wide hand around himself and stroked all the way to the tip and back again. "Is that what you wanted to see?"

She was panting. "Yes," she gasped. "God."

"Would you like to?"

She shook her head, but what she said was "Yes."

He took her hand and wrapped it around him. Again her knees buckled. He felt so intensely hard, and yet his skin was like velvet. Tightly ridged with veins that twitched beneath her touch. He groaned deep and long, as she slowly moved her hand down the full length of him.

Dear Lord, how she wanted to take him!

"Stop." The command was harsh and hoarsely spoken.

She dropped her hand. "I'm sorry."

He turned to her. "We were both going to be really sorry there in a second."

Amazingly, she smiled, even laughed. "Then, thank you for stopping me."

"I didn't want to." His gaze darkened. "Damn but you feel good on me, Natalie."

She swallowed. He was truly overwhelming to her in every way. It was a very heady thing to know she could affect him like this, too. It was that realization that gave her the boldness to look up at him and say, "I want to know how good you'll feel *in* me, Jake." She turned fully toward him so the tip of his erection brushed her belly. "Right now."

Chapter Four

JAKE HAD NO IDEA what he'd done to deserve this day, but he damn well wanted to find out so he could do it again.

Natalie was like no other woman he'd ever met. She was intelligent, witty, sharp and absolutely sexy. But she was also somewhat shy, or at least private. Definitely reserved when it came to sex. And yet she wanted so badly not to be. He was more than glad to help her out. In fact, it stunned him just what emotions and urges she brought out in him.

He had always firmly believed in seeing to his partner's pleasure as well as to his own. But something about Natalie brought out twin urges to protect...and to dominate. He wasn't all that surprised at the former. But the latter shocked him. He was definitely not that guy. And yet he'd never felt more natural than when he told her to walk across that room. Yes, he'd sensed she wanted direction, wanted to be absolved, at least a tiny bit, of the pressure of being in control.

But nothing had prepared him for the rush it had given him when she'd complied. Maybe it was because she'd done so with her head high. No meekness, definitely no submissiveness. It hadn't been about domination or even control. It had been... primal. Visceral. This need to push her. Push her toward discovering her own pleasure...and toward discovering his. Maybe it was because he knew she'd push back.

And the idea of that happening rocked him even harder.

"Now?" he answered her command. And yes, it had been a command. He had never been one for that, either, never desired women who almost liked to punish men for giving them pleasure. But this command, it was about mutual pleasure. He could definitely identify with that.

And maybe that was the real thrill here. That they would push and shove, command and demand the absolute greatest degree of pleasure from one another.

He grinned down at her, hoping they both survived the onslaught. She squealed when he suddenly stooped and scooped her into his arms, holding her tight against his chest. "Bed or wall?"

Her eyes popped wide. He loved that.

"I beg your pardon?"

"No begging. I'm too far gone. I promise to make you beg next time, however. If that's what you want."

Her eyebrows narrowed. He loved that, too.

Then the most devilish smile curved her lips. "We'll see who begs."

He swore his knees went a bit woozy. Certainly his heart skipped one or two beats.

"Bed," she said decisively. "Wall next time. If you're lucky."

"We'll see who feels lucky when I'm done with you."

He felt her squirm in his arms and knew he'd been right about the control issues. They would each test the other's limits. And have the best damn time of their lives doing it. He wondered how long he could keep her here in this room where they could do anything and everything. No strings attached.

He carried her to the bed, aching just to slide her body down and onto his. But the brown paper bag on the bed stopped him. Her gaze fell on it at the same time. "Do you want to do the honors? Or would you rather me?"

He could see her getting ready to say she'd rather let him, but after the slightest pause, she said, "I'll do it."

She truly intrigued him. He realized he was like some bold adventure to her, that it wasn't about him personally, but this secret thrill he'd come to represent to her. But rather than be insulted or offended by that, he had this undeniable urge simply to be the best damn adventure of her life. After all, it wasn't like he wouldn't be having a damn fine time, as well.

"I got several kinds."

She smiled. "I know."

"So just reach in and pick one. Unless you've decided you have a preference."

He let her slide to a stand, then turned to yank the covers off the bed, while she dumped the bag out on the sheets. He sprawled across the bed, then smiled and beckoned to her with a crooked finger. "And the lucky winner is?"

Me, he answered himself, as she crawled across the bed, purple foil packet in hand.

She was comfortable in her own skin, he noticed, but mostly when she wasn't thinking about the fact that she was naked in front of him. Part of him wanted to keep her distracted so she'd stay more at ease…and an equal part wanted to nudge her to confront it, to deal with it—and his part in it.

He rolled to his side, facing her. She didn't look at him as she struggled to tear the package open.

"You want help?" His offer only made her more determined. He'd remember that.

She finally looked right at him…and tore it open with her sharp white teeth.

He'd do well to remember that, too.

"Okay," she said, looking from the silky latex in her hand, to him. "Are you sure we got the right size?"

He couldn't help it. He laughed. "Yeah," he finally managed to say. "Here—" He held out his hand, but instead of taking the condom, he took her wrist and guided her hand to him. "Just put it like this." He showed her. "Then roll it down. It stretches."

He had planned on watching, but as soon as her slender fingers moved over him, pushing the latex down over his pulsing skin, he rolled to his back and groaned. He closed his eyes as she tugged and snugged it all the way to the base. He decided right then and there, he was never putting on his own condom again.

"Okay," she finally said.

He forced his eyes open. "Maybe you need more practice."

Her mouth dropped open, then snapped shut as she realized he was teasing. "You do have a whole bag full of them." She was taunting. Daring.

He reached out and tugged her across his body. She yelped as he rolled her swiftly under him, pinning her arms gently but very firmly over her head. His legs held hers to the bed with no room for movement. He'd meant to taunt her back, make some smart-ass comment about seeing how many they could use in the next couple of hours.

But everything had changed the moment he had her helpless. There was not a shred of fear in her eyes. No. Exactly the opposite. Excitement, anticipation and...outright need shone from her dark eyes.

She wasn't helpless, after all. She had him right where she wanted him.

"I'm going to take you, Natalie." He knew it was the right thing to say when her pupils all but exploded in their rush to expand. "I'm going to fill you, every inch of you." He nudged himself between her legs. "One...inch...at...a... time." With each word he nudged a little more deeply. "I'm going to make you scream, Natalie," he promised. She moaned softly, her hips pushing off the bed. He levered his body closer to hers, putting his mouth beside her ear. "With pleasure."

He pushed slowly into her, keeping her legs pressed to the bed so she could barely arch into him. It was excruciating torture for them both…and unbelievably arousing. She was so wet for him, his control slipped—and slipped badly.

"Scream for me, Natalie," he said hoarsely, and pushed all the way in, his hips coming down hard on hers.

She did scream, and bucked hard against him. He stilled, but only for a second.

"Again!" she rasped. "God, Jake. Do it again."

"Yeah." It was all he was capable of, and even that came out like a grunt. She was sweet and tight and goddamn if she didn't take all of him and beg for more.

He pushed into her, making the bed jerk against the wall. Again. And again. And if he slowed down even slightly, she demanded it from him.

"Faster," she gasped.

He kept her pinned. She writhed beneath him like a fury, but kept him locked so tightly inside her lean, little body, it might as well have been he who was pinned.

"Again, Jake. Deeper."

He growled, unable to stop now. His hips moved like pistons, plunging and withdrawing, only to plunge again. Again and again she took him, kept him, released him only to clutch at him again. He'd never been driven like this, mindless like this.

Then she turned her head and whispered, "Come for me, Jake. Come for me."

And now *he* screamed. His climax was instantaneous and all but ripped out of him. It kept rolling over him and through him for what seemed like an eternity. Afterward, he barely sustained his upper-body weight on his elbows to keep from crushing her altogether. He was still shuddering, and he felt so completely drained that he wasn't sure he'd ever be able to move again.

He pressed his face to the side of her neck. "You tricked me," he murmured.

"Tricked you?"

He finally managed to release her arms and roll to his side, pulling her with him. "I was going to take you to the very limits…and then you tricked me into coming."

"I didn't think of it that way. Are you complaining?"

No way was he that good an actor. "Dear God, no." He laughed when she grinned. "But I was sort of focused on doing that for you." At the desire that spiked in her drowsy, sexy eyes, he pushed her to her back. "Not that I can't take care of that now."

She opened her mouth, then shut it again.

"You're not going to argue, huh?"

She shook her head, laughter and need mingling in her dark brown eyes.

"Smart girl." He leaned down and kissed her. "I'll be right back."

She half sat up as he left the bed, but he waved her back. "Clean-up duty." While in the bathroom, he also turned on the warm water and soaked a washcloth with it. Making sure it wasn't too hot, he wrung out the excess water and returned to the bedroom.

She looked quizzically at the little white towel, but said nothing. He slid onto the queen-size bed and urged her to the middle. "Prop your head on the pillows." She tugged several beneath her head. "And hand me the other one." She looked at him, but said nothing and pushed the last one toward him.

He shifted between her legs, then began to tuck the pillow beneath her hips. Her eyes widened in that way they did, and he smiled. "Trust me."

She shot him a look, but relaxed back on the pillows again. He wondered that she'd never played around like this before. Her previous partners must have been lawyers, too, he surmised with a private smile.

Once her hips were gently lifted, he spread her legs more widely. "Keep them here." Before she could reply, he unfolded the warm towel and laid it right between her legs. She gasped and started to sit up, but before he could even say anything, she sighed and laid right back down.

"God, that feels really good."

"Close your eyes and just relax. And enjoy."

Even as she nodded, her eyes were drifting shut.

He let the warmth of the towel soak into her, soothing her where he'd so recently been roughly moving against that soft skin. She moaned softly as he gently pressed the heel of his hand down against the warm towel.

He maintained the pressure, then slowly moved his palm down, until one finger dragged slowly and gently in the crease between her legs. She gasped again, this time her hips moving up to push against his finger.

He stroked her again...and again, until she was moaning and reaching for his touch with her hips. The towel was becoming cool, so he slid it slowly off her, making sure it rubbed against her budded and highly sensitized clitoris before replacing it with his mouth.

She arched violently against his tongue as he invaded her. He lifted his head just enough to look up at her. "Reach up, Natalie. Hold on to the headboard."

She opened her eyes and looked dazedly down at him. "Don't stop," she said hoarsely.

He grinned. "I have no intention of stopping. Hold on to the headboard, Natalie," he repeated.

She reached blindly above her head as she continued to look at him.

"Hold on. Tight." And then he slid his finger into her and up over her, making her bow right off the bed. "Now, Natalie. You come for me. You come for me hard." And he kept his tongue right there, on her, at her, until she completely came apart over him.

He was so fully into her orgasm, it took him a moment to realize he was hard again, his hips pushing involuntarily against the bed. Blindly he groped for the condoms she'd poured on the bed, even as he watched her climb that peak again. She shattered again, screaming this time.

He reared up, all but ripped the condom out of the packet and yanked it over himself. Then he was pulling her hips right up off the bed and onto him. Her legs flew up and locked tightly behind him as he gripped her hips and pushed into her almost violently. He couldn't get deep enough, she couldn't push herself onto him hard enough.

He kept his eyes on hers and watched as she climbed again. He slid a hand from her driving hips and rubbed his finger over her, just above where he was buried so deeply. She shrieked as she came even harder than before. And his climax came thundering right after.

They both slumped to the bed in a tangled, moist heap, the room filled only with the sounds of their heavy breathing.

Finally Jake managed to move. He pulled a pillow under his head, grabbed another from where it had been shoved in the frenzy and tucked it under her head. Then he turned to his side, pulled her slick body against his, tucked her head beneath his chin and let himself fall blissfully asleep.

NATALIE WAS TRYING to slide quietly from the bed, when he finally woke up. "What time is it?" he murmured.

"Two. I have to catch a plane out of La Guardia in a couple of hours."

"Why are you whispering?"

She paused in gathering her clothes, then grinned. "Because you were sleeping," she said, still whispering.

He finally shoved the rest of the cobwebs aside and sat up. So, it was over. He felt as if it had just begun. "Let me grab a quick shower and I'll go to the airport with you."

That stopped her. She stood up, clutching her gold-colored silk top and impossibly spiky black heels. "I— I don't think we should. I mean, it's a long ride out, and I'm sure—" She gave a little self-conscious laugh. "Actually, I'm not sure of anything at the moment."

He slid off the bed and walked over to her. He tugged the shirt and heels out of her hands, glad when she didn't put up much of a struggle. He pulled her against him. "I'm sure of one thing."

She eyed him warily. "What is that?"

"I've never spent a more enjoyable morning in my entire life. Thank you for that, Natalie."

She smiled then, looking almost shy. "I can return the compliment."

"I know you want this to be a sort of once-in-a-lifetime adventure."

She tensed and started to pull away.

He tightened his hold just enough to keep her in his arms. "Hear me out." He waited until she nodded. "I know your career is your focus. Right now, I'm pretty busy in that regard, as well. We both travel a lot, and that makes relationships almost impossible."

She seemed to relax a bit.

He looked into her eyes, then took a breath and said, "So since we're both in the same boat, neither of us looking for something permanent, the kind of thing we'd have to share with the other parts of our lives...why don't we just share this."

"This?"

"Yeah." He motioned to the room around them. "This."

"You mean, like have an affair?"

"I don't know if it has a name." He touched her hair. "I think we both enjoyed some of the things we explored here today. It was good and fun. But it was also kind of safe."

"Safe?"

"Yeah. I knew you weren't looking for more than this, and you knew the same about me. It sort of frees us up to just relax and enjoy. And explore a little more than we otherwise would." He tilted her chin up, when she looked away. "Didn't you feel that, Natalie? A sort of secret thrill in getting to do things you wouldn't normally do?"

She looked at him for so long, he didn't think she was going to answer. He hadn't realized he'd been holding his breath, until she did finally speak.

"Yes. Yes, this was...exciting." She looked at him. "And no, I don't normally do this."

"Nor do I."

"So what are you proposing?"

"That we exchange travel itineraries. See where and when they might intersect. When they do, we can get together and...explore. Safely. No other strings."

"No intrusions into the other parts of our lives." She said this almost to herself.

He felt hope blossom in his chest. "Right. This is just for ourselves. No expectations other than that when we're alone together, we leave everything else outside the door and just enjoy each other. Maybe explore some of those other hidden desires and wants you've wondered about but haven't wanted to give your partner an insight into."

She pulled out of his arms. "I don't know, Jake. This was undeniably wonderful. But I don't know if I can just...I don't know...schedule something like this into my life. It seems so—"

"Perfect," he said, unwilling to give up. "I'm not seeing anyone seriously. You?"

She shook her head.

"Like I said. Perfect. Consider it an outlet. Something you give yourself, like a trip to the spa or something."

She laughed.

"Okay, okay, but you know what I mean. What's so wrong with that? No one has to know. And if we meet someone in our personal lives that we intend to get serious about, then that's it. No questions asked. Otherwise, it will last as long as we both want it to." He walked to her. "No intrusions into each other's lives. We control this. It is what we want it to be. Nothing more, nothing less."

She looked into his eyes again, then finally looked away. "I don't know." She pulled away again and went to the bathroom. "I just don't think I can do that. I'm sorry, Jake." She disappeared behind the bathroom door. He didn't pursue her.

What he did instead was to grab some hotel stationery and write down his itinerary for the next several months. He jotted down where he'd be, on what dates, and at what hotels. He tucked it into her purse for her to find later. Maybe by then she'd have a change of heart.

At the bottom of the note, he wrote, "Now you know where to find me." And he signed it "Your Secret Thrill."

Chapter Five

"LIZA, I CAN'T." Natalie tucked the phone against her shoulder and nodded to her assistant, Nancy, who had just layered her desk with another stack of files. She signed several forms, flipped the folder shut and handed it back to Nancy who silently mouthed that she was late for a meeting. Natalie made the okay sign and took hold of the phone. "No, Liza, there is no way I can fly out there this weekend. I've got two depositions to take, and a brief to write that will take a ton of research."

Besides, she knew Jake would be in California this weekend. In San Diego. Which was very close to L.A. Too close. "I promise I'll try next time. And it would help if I had more than three days' notice."

She was still laughing at Liza's less than politically correct response after she hung up. Her friend's sense of humor was just what she needed today. She looked at the mess in front of her and groaned. These past two weeks had been brutal, her workload doubled since her immediate supervisor had landed in the hospital with acute appendicitis.

More laughter was the least of what she needed. What she really needed was a break. Jake's sexy grin popped into her mind, along with the rest of his heart palpitation-inducing body—something that happened with alarming frequency these past two weeks. And as she had every time previously, she shut the image down directly. So what if she had to do that a dozen times a day, and sometimes that was before noon?

But today his image persisted. As did memories of that glorious morning she'd spent in bed with him. Surely she'd blown it totally out of proportion. If she ever saw him again—which she wouldn't—she would probably be forced to realize it had been average at best. Better to leave herself with glorious, if somewhat debatable, memories.

"Yeah," she said with a heartfelt sigh. "Thanks for the memories." Then she grabbed a small fraction of the mountain on her desk and headed out the door.

THREE HOURS LATER she returned to her desk with more work than when she had left. She felt numb with the kind of battle fatigue one could only feel after a long session with the partners.

Nancy popped in a moment later. "Your sister on line two."

"Which one?" Not that she was in the mood to hear from either of them. If she had to listen to them vent about the rigors of chairing yet another country club committee or charity drive, she'd surely lose it and say things that were never said in her family. But no one could keep her from feeling them, thank God.

She didn't wait for Nancy to reply, but punched the button and picked up. After the past three hours, dealing with either sister would be child's play. "What's up?"

"It's father. He's golfing." It was Sabrina, her oldest sister. The drama queen. *Great.*

Natalie sat back in her chair. "Horrors. Thank God you caught this aberrant behavior in time! Have him locked up immediately."

Sabrina also had no sense of humor—a Holcomb genetic trait that had somehow skipped over Natalie—as her long-suffering sigh indicated.

"Spare me your sarcasm today, Natalie. I have a brutal headache."

Sabrina had very convenient brutal headaches. "Fine. So Dad is golfing again. This is a problem, why?" *And why is it now my problem?* Although, she already knew the answer to that one. She was the only one of the four Holcomb children born with a backbone made of sterner stuff than a spaghetti noodle. Real genetic freak she was. Not for the first time she wondered if Mom had had a fling with the mailman or something.

"Natalie? Are you listening to me?"

No, not really. "Yes, yes."

There was an impatient huff, then Sabrina said, "You know perfectly well his cardiologist told him to take it easy after his last...episode."

"You mean heart attack." Natalie had zero patience for their New England, upper-crust doublespeak today. "He had a heart attack, Rina. An episode is something you watch on television."

"You know Daddy forbid us to use that term."

Yes, Natalie knew very well. Wouldn't look good on the company bio for the founder and CEO to be human. *Have to stay strong, never let them see you sweat.* Much less have a heart attack. They're hell on those stock options.

"So why are you calling me?" she asked needlessly.

There was a pause, and Natalie prepared for the sudden switch to Ms. Wheedling Sweet Voice.

"Nat, you know Daddy listens to you, honey. Why don't you call his caddy's cell phone and ask to speak to him."

"And say what? Leave the sixteenth hole immediately or else I'm telling on you?" Natalie didn't have the time, much less the patience, for this. "Honestly, Sabrina, he's a grown man. If he chooses not to listen to his doctor, then that's his business. We're not his keepers." Which wasn't precisely the truth.

Ever since her mother died, back when Natalie was still in boarding school, her two sisters and older brother had begun turning to her when things needed saying to their father. Said things usually having something to do with the family business, a.k.a. their livelihoods and source of the children's trust funds. Probably because she was the only one who didn't rely on Holcomb Industries for her daily bread.

She hated being the baby of the family.

"Just call him for us, Nat, okay? He listens to you."

When he feels like it, she thought. "I'm really busy. It's crazy here and—"

"You could stop all this nonsense of working in the city, Nat, and come home where you belong. I don't know why you think it's so important to establish yourself outside the family. After all, our father didn't slave all his life so that his children would have to start from scratch. It's almost insulting when you think about it. And before you lecture me on the importance of a career, keep in mind the charitable works Melissa and I provide to the underprivileged. You could always help us out, because, Lord knows, we are overburdened as it is. You can't believe the hours I've spent organizing this year's food drive. Of course, if you insist on using that law degree, Daddy will make a place for you at work and you can…"

Lose my freaking mind, along with what little privacy I've ever had, Natalie finished with a silent scream, tuning out the rest of the speech she'd heard a million times before. "I'll call him, okay?" she said, when Sabrina came up for oxygen. Anything to shut her up. "Give Reese and the boys a hug for me," she added quickly, before her sister could wind up again, and hung up.

Nancy popped in again. "Harwood on line three. He's not happy."

Natalie nodded, then let her forehead drop to the pile of folders on her desk. If she were a lesser woman, she'd throw a nice little tantrum. She sat up and pushed her hair back from her face. *But you're not a lesser anything, you're a Holcomb. God help me,* she added, then instructed Nancy to get her father's caddy on the phone before she picked up line three.

FIVE HOURS LATER Natalie whimpered into her loft, kicked off her heels and sank her grateful toes into the thick carpet. She set down the cardboard carton of work she'd toted home and ignored the blinking message light on her phone. Probably her brother Chuck or, worse, her other sister Melissa, calling to whine for something else.

"Well, I'm fresh out of tolerance tonight," she said aloud, and headed directly for the only wine she was still in the mood for. A nice, light sauvignon. Preferably chilled.

She'd barely taken the first sip, when her phone rang. She merely took another sip, deciding to let the machine take it. On her schedule was a long bath, followed by some Chinese takeout and at least three more hours of work. Whoever was on the line could wait their turn.

"Holcomb, this is Harwood. If you're there, please pick up."

Natalie groaned, and as she headed for the phone said several things no upper-crust, born-and-bred New Englander would ever say. Yes, the joys of being the family black sheep were small, but she took them where she could.

Harwood was her supervisor's boss, one of the newer partners in the firm. Newer and therefore frantic to do whatever he could to impress his new fellow partners, which was often at his subordinate's expense. But as a fellow ladder climber, she bowed and did as she was asked, all in the hope that one day she, too, could terrorize minions.

She snatched up the phone. Harwood talked right over her hello and kept on talking, until he finished and abruptly hung up ten minutes later.

"So nice talking to you, too, sir, Grand Pooh-Bah, sir," she said, making a face as she hung up. As the dial tone rang in her ear, right then and there she vowed never to abuse her minions. "If I ever have any." Which, of course, she would. She was a Holcomb. "And Holcombs always have minions. It's in section two, paragraph four of our genetic code."

But there was a silver lining to Harwood's latest edict. She swallowed the rest of her wine and picked up the phone again. With the time change, Liza would likely still be in her West Coast office.

"Guess what?" she asked in lieu of hello.

"You're coming?" Liza squealed. "Oh, this is great! But I thought you had depositions and briefs and research." The latter part had been said in her nasal, uptight lawyer voice, which somehow always made Nat laugh.

"Rescheduled. The Grand Poo-Bah has spoken. I take the red-eye tomorrow night and have meetings all day Thursday and Friday. I'll probably look like something the cat dragged in by Friday night, but if you still want me to come, I'll be there." Natalie ignored the fact that she'd still have all her own work to do, in addition to what had just been added to her schedule. But if they were going to drown her in legal briefs, then damn if she wasn't going to have at least an hour or two doing what she wanted.

Jake.

No. She resolutely would not go there. So what if he'd be in town at the same time. She'd already decided it had to be a one-time affair. She'd be too busy, anyway.

"I guess staying with me is out of the question."

"Too far," Natalie agreed. Harwood specialized in entertainment law. "I'll be out near Century City." She smiled. "Besides, having me there would sort of cramp your style. Isn't Conrad still staying with you?"

Liza laughed. "First of all, since when has having someone else around ever cramped anything of mine?"

Natalie knew that better than anyone. She could still hear the shrieks of ecstasy coming from Liza's bedroom at The Maxi.

She still hadn't told Liza about Jake. She'd wanted to, intended to, but somehow she'd ended up just telling her she'd gone out for coffee after the party. And since she'd never see him again, there was no point in telling Liza now. She'd only hound Natalie about seeing him again.

"As for Conrad, yeah, he's still around."

"Almost two weeks. A record for you, Liza," she teased. "Better watch out, you're rushing headlong into what others might actually describe as a relationship."

Liza wasn't offended. In fact, she laughed. "Never fear, honey. You know I get bored easily. And with all these luscious men out here? Why waste them on the young and naive, when I'm available?"

Natalie laughed along with her, but privately she felt the same twinge of worry she always did when her friend talked like that. Of course, since her morning with Jake, she had no right to talk. In fact, she'd privately wondered if maybe she shouldn't be more like her best friend, more cavalier about life and love and having a good time. After all, how many times had Liza tried to pound it into her that they were only young once? And Liza intended to stay that way as long as possible. Of course, the secret to her fountain of youth was usually about six-two and built like a billboard model. In fact, he usually *was* a model.

"I keep telling you to come out here and ply your legal-eagle trade. I could teach you how to have a good time."

Natalie had heard this too many times to count. But she liked the energy of New York. And, like it or not, being here made it easier to make the obligatory trips home when absolutely necessary. Which was far more often than she liked.

"Well, with the way you go through men, there's hardly any left for me, anyway," she joked.

"Oh, sweetie, they come in daily. By the busloads. Trust me. Hey! You want me to set you up for Friday?"

"No!" Natalie cleared her throat. "I mean, I'll be happy if I don't look like a whipped puppy. The pressure of a blind date would kill me. Okay?"

There was a telling pause.

"Promise me, Liza. If I even think you'll pull a fast one—"

Liza laughed gaily. "Oh, but, sweetie, the fast ones are the most fun!"

Natalie wondered what her friend would say if she told her just how fast she'd been at Liza's last party. "Thanks, but no thanks. Swear?"

"Swear. But all work and no play—"

"Makes Natalie a successful, if lonely, attorney. Now go play with Conrad, and I'll see you Friday."

She hung up smiling, glad she'd called. She was in a much better mood. She only whimpered a little when she looked at the cardboard box full of files she had to go through tonight. "All work and no play." She sighed. "That's me."

You could play with Jake. All day Saturday. Or whatever part of it he's free, her subconscious taunted her. *In a little more then seventy-two hours you could be sweaty, naked and having multiple orgasms.*

She resolutely ignored her body's lurching response to that idea and punched her speed dial for the nearby Chinese takeout. "I'll show them I know how to live." Tonight she'd order Peking duck instead of her usual moo-shu pork. With extra plum sauce. So there.

Coming, again and again, while he pounds into you like a—

And just for good measure, while she was out, maybe she'd better pick up some extra batteries for her vibrator.

Chapter Six

NATALIE STARED at the one outfit she'd brought for Liza's party and found herself wishing she'd opted for something less…clingy. She'd worn "clingy" the last time she'd gone to one of Liza's shindigs, and look where that had landed her.

She snatched the silky, ruby-red dress off the hanger and slid it over her head. It felt like sin sliding over her skin. She told herself it was the extreme fatigue that made her skin feel the way it did, overly sensitized to every little touch or caress. Well, anyone would be edgy after two days of brain-frying debate, she told herself. She allowed herself a private little victory smile as she stepped into her heels. Even Harwood would be impressed with the results she'd gotten today.

"Now it's time to party!" She ducked into the bathroom and checked her makeup one last time. Not her best, but at least two degrees better than the whipped-puppy look she'd been sporting earlier, so she was happy enough.

She managed to not think about Jake all the way to the lobby—only a five-minute trip total, but it was a start. Then she passed the concierge desk and paused. Again. As she had every time she'd passed it during her stay. And once again she wondered if she should leave a message at Jake's hotel. She'd resisted every other time. But now she was less than twenty-four hours from leaving the city. The city *he* was in. Who knew when their paths might cross again? Although, if by some miracle Liza kept seeing Conrad, it could happen, and when Natalie least expected it.

Maybe it was best if they met under her terms. With such a short time before her departure, it was unlikely he'd have time for anything more than coffee. And the more she thought about it, that might be the perfect end point for her little escapade with him.

If she saw him this one last time, she would be able to put this whole thing in its proper perspective and stop fantasizing about the guy every other minute. After all, the last time she had seen him he'd been sprawled in bed wearing nothing more than a sexy grin. Maybe she just needed to see him out in public, clothes on. Sexy grin optional.

So what if the one and only time she'd seen him they'd ended up having wild passionate sex…wild passionate sex he'd asked her to have again. Certainly she could manage one innocent little cup of closure coffee without succumbing to her baser urges again. Baser urges she hadn't even known she'd had until—

"Oh, for heaven's sake." She marched up to the concierge and snatched a piece of paper, scribbling her note before she lost her nerve.

Dear Jake. I'm in town briefly and wondered if you'd like to meet me for a quick hello and a cup of coffee at my hotel tomorrow afternoon. Best, Natalie

She folded the note, wrote the name of the hotel and his name on the front, and slid it across the counter. The concierge barely had his fingers on the edges when she slid it back again. "Wait a minute." She read the note over and wrote a new one, scratching out the word *quick*. Too close to *quickie*. She also changed the part about meeting at her hotel. Or any hotel. Best not to tempt fate by having available beds too close at hand. She ignored the fact that that hadn't stopped them last time, and shoved the new note across the desk. "Can you deliver this tonight?"

He nodded, and she slid him a tip for his trouble, then left the hotel with very damp palms and...well, damp everything. "It's only coffee," she murmured as she got into her cab. He might not even respond to her note.

"OH GOD," she whispered under her breath when she returned from Liza's several hours later to find the message light blinking on her phone. *Jake.* It had to be. She picked up the phone with shaky hands, then put it back down again. She wasn't sure she was ready to hear his voice. Even recorded. She didn't know what she'd expected. A note at the lobby desk? She wondered if *he'd* wondered why she hadn't called him directly. *Oh, this was ridiculous.* "Just pick it up and get his message already."

She stared at the blinking phone. What if he turned her down? Or worse, what if he sounded like a total dork or a jerk, and now she'd have to have coffee with him? Maybe it had been the night and the party and the wine she'd had that had made him seem so sexy and wonderful.

"Get over yourself and do this." She could always cancel, saying her flight had been moved up. Okay, she was ready now. Escape hatch firmly in place. Palms...and other parts damp, she picked up the receiver and punched in the numbers to get her messages. There was only one. She pushed the button to hear it.

"Natalie."

"Oh God." The first word, and she'd already clenched so hard she almost came right then. This was not a good sign.

"I've been thinking about you, hoping you'd find the nerve to call me."

She bristled. Both at the amused little note in his voice and the nerve *he* had in even suggesting, after what she'd done with him after only knowing him mere hours, that she lacked nerve of any kind. She conveniently ignored the fact that it had taken her two full days here to finally send the note at all.

"There's a little place off Melrose that makes the most incredible oatmeal."

"Oatmeal?" She laughed. "So much for a repeat of our last romantic rendezvous." Not that she'd wanted one, she quickly added. But oatmeal? No one planned a seduction with an invitation for oatmeal. She should be relieved. Despite his teasing, he'd apparently drawn the same conclusion she had. Once had been wild and crazy, twice would only be asking for trouble.

"I have a ten-thirty meeting, so if you don't mind an early hour, meet me at Aunt Sue's at eight. Just leave a message at the hotel if you can't make it."

There was a pause, and Natalie had her finger on the erase button...well, maybe it was hovering over the replay button—damn his voice was just as sexy as she remembered—but then he said something else and her hand fell limply back to her lap.

"If you have to turn me down, could you please leave a voice message?" A short pause followed by a self-deprecating chuckle, then, *"I just want to know for sure if you sound as good as I remember."*

Natalie sighed. The man gave good phone message, no doubt about it. Oatmeal and all.

"Don't chicken out."

She was still huffing in disbelief as the *click* ended the call and the message. Chicken out? She'd never once thought it.

Her escape plan had strictly been protection against discovering that her memory of him had been tainted by passion.

It hadn't been tainted.

"Chicken out," she grumbled. "I'm a Holcomb. We never chicken out."

AUNT SUE'S turned out to be a really tiny little restaurant crammed in between a bunch of tony shops just off Melrose. It was all white clapboard and gingerbread trim, but somehow managed to fit in. Very "Hansel and Gretel Do L.A.," she decided, then took a deep breath and went inside.

She had no idea if the storybook decor on the outside matched the inside. In fact, if asked her name that very moment, she'd likely have drawn a blank. *There he is* was all she could think. Only the back of his head was visible to her, but she knew that head. Intimately.

"Okay, no thinking about…you know," she schooled herself, as she had all the way there. It hadn't worked then and it sure as hell wasn't working now.

As if he sensed her arrival, he turned and saw her just as she…well, she certainly hadn't been turning back to the door. She'd merely been looking for a waitress…or something.

Then he stood and smiled, and she forgot what was left of everything she'd ever known.

"Natalie."

God, he was perfect. Gorgeous as all get-out—and that voice, that hint of a drawl. It was all good and just as she remembered it. Maybe even better.

"Jake." Damn, she sounded way too breathless. Not good. She held out her hand, just in case he was planning on hugging her. Hugging him would be total sensory overload. She wasn't even certain she'd make it through the handshake without a telltale little moan slipping past her lips.

She should never have done this. But then she caught the

twinkle in his eye, as if he'd noted her slight hesitation in actually taking his hand. *Don't chicken out.*

Hardly.

She took his hand in a firm shake, as she would that of any worthy boardroom opponent, and promptly let it go. Good, good. Except, just feeling those thick fingers brush over hers had soaked her panties. *Wham,* just like that.

She moved past, careful not to touch him, and slid into the booth. As he sat back down, she quickly opened her menu and glanced over the colorful words in front of her, not seeing any of them. Well, it wasn't every day she had breakfast with a guy she'd spent a wild night with. In fact, it wasn't *any* day she did this.

She smiled brightly, still not looking directly at him. She could pull this off. Then get the hell out of here before she did something really stupid. Like end up in bed with him again. Only problem was, at the moment she was hard-pressed to remember exactly why sex with this man—phenomenal sex, if memory served, and she knew damn well it did—was a stupid thing.

"So, they make great oatmeal here, huh?" She dared a quick glance. "Not exactly your normal business breakfast spot." Although a quick look around proved her wrong. The place was packed, and most of the men and women were in suits.

"I found this place a few years ago. I think a lot of us miss that good bowl of stick-to-your-ribs oatmeal our moms used to make us."

Natalie laughed. "My mother never made me a bowl of oatmeal." Her mother would have had the cook do it for her. Except, oatmeal would never have graced the Holcomb table when something more elegant would look ever so much lovelier in the everyday china. "The only time I had it was in boarding school, and then only when I had no choice."

"Well, you'll never think about oatmeal the same way after you taste this."

Natalie sighed in relief that he hadn't picked up on her unintentional revelation and questioned her about her family. Now she did focus on the menu. "Who knew there were so many varieties?"

Jake gently lowered her menu, forcing her to look at him. It wasn't hard at all. The problem was... stopping.

"I hope you don't mind, but I took the liberty of ordering for us."

A part of her was a bit put off by his take-charge action. But it was a really tiny part. She couldn't stop thinking about how he'd pinned her hands to the bed and taken charge of her then, how he'd made her hold onto the headboard while he took even more delicious charge of her.

"No." She had to stop and clear her suddenly dry throat. "I don't mind." Not then, not now.

Just then a waitress popped up and took her drink order, and was back in a blink with tea and juice. "Your tray should be out shortly." Jake smiled and winked at the older woman, who saucily winked right back at him. "I'll hurry it up, sugar," she said.

Natalie bit back a smile, but Jake caught it.

"What?"

"Nothing. Just leave it to you to find the one Southern belle in all of L.A."

His eyes widened. "What did I do?"

"You're a natural flirt."

His grin didn't deny the charge. "I'm just friendly."

Boy, are you ever, Natalie wanted to say.

"Besides, she's old enough to be my mother."

"I'm guessing here, but something tells me age is generally not a deterrent to you. Or to the women in question."

"Well, in general, you would be right." He glanced at the

waitress who was surreptitiously straightening her apron over her matronly girth. Jake nodded when she looked his way, sending a blush clear up to her teased-tight bun. He looked back to Natalie. "It's not about age, it's about attitude."

Natalie sipped her tea and thought about that. "I suppose you're right." She was attracted to good looks—who wouldn't be?—but she'd dated her fair share of average-looking men. Attitude did have a lot to do with attraction.

"Wheels are turning up there."

She laughed and put her mug down. "You make me think about things in ways I generally don't." *See, they could talk and it didn't have to be about sex.*

"If I recall, we both discovered some new things about ourselves the last time we saw each other."

Okay. So it was about sex. She was saved from responding by the arrival of their food.

"My God, Jake, how much did you order?"

The server, a young man this time, was steadily setting out bowls of various things. There was brown sugar, confectioner's sugar, raisins, dates, various nuts, fresh strawberries, shredded coconut, granola, blueberries, chocolate chips and...she lost track at that point. Their waitress followed with two flat bowls full of steaming, thick, creamy porridge.

"Enjoy," she said.

Natalie had to admit, it looked wonderful. "Thank you, I'm sure we will." Of course, the waitress wasn't looking at Natalie, but she nodded and sent an absent smile her way as she took one last longing look at Jake.

When they were alone, Natalie looked at the bounty before her and said, "I don't even know where to begin."

"I know. Amazing, isn't it."

"You know, if our family cook had known such a presentation could be made out of oatmeal, we might have served it, after all." She quickly clamped her mouth shut, but

Jake merely smiled at her and began sorting through dishes with the spoon provided in each one.

That made her pause. He didn't push her about her private life. Maybe he had no interest in it. Maybe he was only interested in her for one thing. She should be insulted. But she wasn't. She was relieved. Hadn't he said that if they were to continue doing…what they'd done before, that there would be no outside world intrusions? When they were together it would just be about them exploring each other, and themselves…and nothing else?

She was finding herself entranced with the very idea that she actually could do that. Actually take time away from everything and do this just for herself. No denying it was exciting, enticing even. But could they really sustain it?

She watched him pop a plump blueberry in his mouth and sigh as he ate it. *Yeah,* she thought, *I might be able to watch him eat for, oh, another ten or twenty years at least.*

Of course, he'd said nothing about his proposition. Maybe he'd changed his mind.

"Here—"

Her attention was jerked away from the bowl she'd been mindlessly stirring, her thoughts stirring right along with it. When she looked up, she found him offering her a strawberry.

She went to take it with her fingers, but he shook his head. "Wait." He rubbed it on his own lips, then dipped it in the confectioner's sugar. "Now taste it."

He held it closer, intending her to take it from his fingers right into her mouth. In the middle of a restaurant. Anyone watching this little interaction would assume they were not having a business breakfast.

The look in his eye was more a dare than a question. And she knew that if she took the strawberry, she was tacitly agreeing to his previous offer.

"Do you always debate taking something you know you want?"

She smiled at that. "How do you know I like strawberries?" She knew that wasn't what he meant, but he was fun to tease. And he returned it so well.

"Who could resist this one?"

A better woman than her, apparently.

Even as she leaned a fraction of an inch closer to take the fruit, he was already lightly rubbing it over her lips, coating them in white sugar and berry juice.

She quickly took the fruit, almost swallowing it whole and trying like hell to resist looking around her to see if anyone else was watching. She ducked her head and licked her lips, dabbing at them with her napkin.

"It bothers you, then?"

She looked back at him. "What?"

"That people might see me feeding you?"

Her face colored, and there was no way to stop it. "You offered me a piece of fruit and I took it. No big deal. People taste each other's meals all the time."

He merely smiled. "It bothers you."

"Okay, so I'm uncomfortable with being...I don't know— open about what we're doing."

Now he leaned forward, his gaze so intent she could feel herself respond by tightening up almost to the point of cramping.

"*What* are we doing, Natalie?"

"Having breakfast?" she said weakly.

He slowly shook his head. Then he picked up a small chunk of chocolate and wedged it in another strawberry before dipping the whole thing in granulated sugar. He held it out. "This isn't about breakfast."

She started to look around the room.

"Don't."

She stilled, then wondered why she listened to him. She'd look around if she damn well wanted to.

"Do you know any of these people?" he asked.

"I have no idea."

"Do you care what they think of how we choose to eat our meal?"

"I suppose not."

"And if they realize there is more going on at this table than merely breakfast between two business associates...do you care?"

She paused before answering that one. "I shouldn't."

"But you do?" He rolled the plump fruit between his thick fingers.

She shrugged lightly. "Habit, I suppose."

"Always have to be decorous, do you? Always put on the polished front?"

"Something like that."

"So what if you didn't? What do you think is going to happen?"

She thought about that. "Nothing, I guess."

"Then, take the fruit, Natalie. Take it like you want it. Enjoy it like you know you will. Don't hold back because someone else might be watching."

She took the fruit. The sweet of the chocolate exploded through the tart of the strawberry as it slid down her throat. Looking at him while she did it made her want to moan. Breakfast would never be the same again.

"People are looking at you," he said softly.

"I'm trying not to care."

A little grin quirked the corner of his mouth as he offered her a blueberry this time. She took it.

"Wonder what they're thinking?"

"No. I really don't want to know."

"What if this is turning them on?"

"What if it is?" she asked, working hard to stay in the moment and not let herself care that they were in a crowded restaurant.

"What if watching you eat fruit from my hand is the most erotic thing they've seen in years? What if it makes them leave here and go find their significant other and feed them some fruit?" He grinned now as he fed her another strawberry in powdered sugar. "Who knows, we could be personally responsible for an entire city ending up in bed today."

She'd just taken the fruit as he said that, and now laughed as she chewed and swallowed. "Yeah, that's me. A one-woman pied piper of sex."

Jake laughed, too. "There are worse things to be."

Natalie nodded, then stifled a sigh as Jake went back to his own oatmeal.

He was stirring some brown sugar into his bowl, not looking at her, when he said, "So, do I get to taste some of your food?"

She dropped the spoon she'd been balancing several blueberries on, but gamely recovered. "What, you think you can be a better pied piper than me?"

His eyes were twinkling, but only for her when he looked at her. "No. I just want to taste a strawberry that's been rubbed along those lips."

"Oh." She managed a shaky smile.

"Feed me, Natalie."

She didn't look around the room this time. She deliberately selected the fattest strawberry in the dish and ran it slowly over her bottom lip. She was going to dip it into the sugar, but Jake took hold of her wrist and guided the fruit to his mouth.

"Nothing can top the taste of you," he said quietly, holding her gaze as he took the strawberry between his white teeth, then sunk them slowly into it.

That did it. She clenched so hard she was pretty sure it counted as a minor orgasm. And minor just wasn't going to cut it. "Do we—" She cleared her throat. "Do you want any more of this?"

"Oh, I want a *lot* more of this."

"Here?"

Mercifully he shook his head and stood. But not before pocketing the rest of the fruit in one of the restaurant napkins. "Come on." He held out his hand. "Let's finish this meal in private."

Natalie paused only for a split second, then took his hand. "Yes. Let's."

Chapter Seven

JAKE RAN the sliced strawberry around Natalie's nipple, growing harder—if that were possible—at the way it peaked for him. She moaned under her breath, and he felt himself climb closer to the edge. The edge that had begun the moment he'd read her note.

He honestly hadn't expected to end up in his hotel with her today. But the moment he'd felt her standing behind him in the restaurant, he knew he wasn't going to let her run away again without a good reason. What they'd shared back in New York had been a memory that clung to him as resolutely as the scent of her had clung to his skin.

He'd sensed from the note and from the short time frame she'd allowed for them to meet that she was still undecided about his offer. But not so much so that she'd been able to resist contacting him.

He leaned down and licked the trail of sweet red juice he'd drizzled all over her breast. Now he was the one groaning, when she arched easily beneath him. It was as if they'd never left each other's arms.

And if he had his way, before they left here today, they would have a time and place where they could meet again.

She'd been so incredible in the restaurant. Worldly on the one hand, and yet sweetly insecure on the other.

He traced the strawberry to her other breast, following it with his tongue. He finally pressed the soft fruit down over her nipple, then sucked the whole thing into his mouth.

She groaned and arched violently.

"Do you think everyone in the restaurant is picturing us just like this, Natalie?" he murmured as he worked his tongue along her collar bone.

"I'm not thinking about anything except—" She gasped as he bit her earlobe at the same time as he gently rolled her nipple between his fingers.

"Except?" he urged, when she went breathlessly silent.

"This," she managed faintly. "Dear God, Jake."

His body twitched hard at the sound of his name, the way she said it, all needy and amazed.

He had thought a great deal about the things he learned about himself when he'd been with Natalie the first time. He'd promised himself that if he were ever fortunate enough to explore with her again, he'd push the boundaries and learn more about himself. And push her to learn more, too.

He wasn't an exhibitionist, had never once fantasized about people watching him in an intimate situation. Until today, when Natalie had blushed at the idea that he was feeding her in front of others. At the time, he'd been so focused on her that he'd forgotten all about where they were. But the instant she'd become aware, the idea of pushing that had been irresistible to him. He'd given her the option of backing away from it...but she hadn't. Which had told him she wanted to push some barriers, too.

And look where that had led them.

He pushed her blouse open farther. She immediately moved to take it off. "No, leave it on."

She lifted her head off the carpet. "I suppose asking to get off the floor and find something a bit softer is out of the question, too?"

He laughed, then licked at her nipple, making her gasp. "I was hungry. I never finished my breakfast."

"Haven't you ever heard of breakfast in bed?"

He rolled on top of her and pressed his hips into hers. "We'll get there." He shoved her skirt up. She shoved his pants down. He groaned as her hands skimmed his bare backside, then groaned in frustration when he realized one little thing they'd forgotten. "We missed a pit stop on the way here."

Her head was tilted back, her eyes shut as she ground her hips up into his. So it took her a second to respond. "Pit stop?"

Her hips tucked into his too damn well. "Condoms. We need some. Many. Now."

She laughed and groaned at the same time, as they both kept moving against each other, almost desperately. "It's okay."

"No, it's really not okay." He pushed her into the carpet, shoving her skirt higher, knowing he should be pulling it back down, instead.

"Oh God," she whimpered when his hands brushed over her silk panties.

"Exactly."

"Take them. Off." She arched into his probing fingers. "Now."

"But—"

She grabbed his face and kissed him, then whispered, "I'm on the Pill."

That stopped him. "Since when?"

Her cheeks bloomed and he grinned, knowing it was full of smugness, yet not caring. It brought the defensive, cocky light to her own gorgeous eyes, and he enjoyed that immensely.

"It had nothing to do with you," she said. "With this. It was for—"

"Medical reasons?" He slid a finger beneath the elastic band.

She managed a tight nod, then her eyes shut on a long moan of satisfaction, as he slid his finger deep inside her.

"Damn convenient timing," he said, enjoying himself far too much.

"You can say that again." She gasped as he pushed more deeply inside her. "Again."

Jake gladly complied. She was so damn responsive. He loved how she moved at his touch. It was incredibly heady, having this power over her.

Then it hit him. No condoms meant one more barrier removed. In this case, one made of latex. He'd truly feel her, rubbing all wet and tight directly against the full length of him. His body tightened so violently, he felt the rush surge right to the very tip.

Slow down, savor this. But it was almost impossible to do. He wanted inside her now. Hard, fast, with that powerfully crushing climax he knew would happen an instant later. Yet, as badly as he wanted that, he wanted to make it last. For both of them.

So he turned his focus to her and recalled what had started this whole thing—this time.

He rolled off her, gently removing her seeking hands and pinning them by her side. He straddled her and pushed their joined hands up until they were on either side of her head. "Keep them there," he told her as he slid his fingers free.

She said nothing, merely held his gaze in a way that told him she was up for this game, but that she was more than willing to turn the tables at any second. The fact that she might, and that she'd likely succeed, only jacked up the sexual tension.

He opened her blouse fully, then pushed the silk cups of her front-clasp bra completely to either side, fully exposing her to him. He'd done this before, had her submit to him looking at her. As he recalled, they'd both enjoyed that more than a little. Now he wanted to take that to the next level.

"Look how your nipples peak when I look at you." He lightly brushed his fingertips over first one, then the other, eliciting a soft moan and the sweet pressure of her hips lifting into him. He swallowed hard and pushed on. "You like being looked at, don't you, Natalie."

She slowly turned her head.

"Yes, you do. Your body doesn't lie."

"This is different."

She knew where he was going. And she was right.

"Because I'm pushing you. And we're totally alone."

She nodded, her eyes never leaving his.

"So the idea that any one of those businessmen in that restaurant this morning might enjoy looking at you, picturing what your sweet breasts look like beneath that designer silk blouse, with crushed strawberries dripping red, sticky juice all over them..." He let his gaze linger as he slowly looked from one rosy peak to the other, then back to her eyes. "That does nothing to you?"

Her hips were squirming under his, even as she shook her head no. His grin was slow and knowing. "Don't lie to me, Natalie. Here, in this room, or whatever room we're in...we're honest with each other. And more importantly, we're going to be honest with ourselves." He let his fingers barely whisper over the tips of her breasts, eliciting a strangled moan from her. "We can do anything, say anything...admit anything. And it stays here." He leaned down and circled one tight, still sticky bud with his tongue, then traced after it with his finger. "Between us."

She was grinding beneath him now, her eyes sliding closed.

"Look at me, Nat."

She did. The need and passion all but glazing her brown-sugar eyes close to undid him the rest of the way. But they were going to see this all the way through.

"Imagine yourself back at the restaurant."

A tentative nod.

"Imagine those men, watching me feed you."

"Imagine their appreciation of you, how your lips close over my fingers as you suck the fruit from them. Imagine them growing hard as they watch you lick the sugar off me."

Her hips continued to rock.

"What if you knew you were making them hard?"

She said nothing. But she didn't have to.

"Would that turn you on, Natalie? Would you maybe lick my finger a little longer, pull it deeper into your mouth?" He pressed his finger into her mouth. "Would you purposely go to the ladies' room, making sure you walked past every one of them? Maybe even lick the tip of your finger as you went by?"

She pulled his finger deep into her mouth, sucking on him, her hips pistoning now.

"Would you like it if I followed a moment later? I'd come into the ladies' room, lock the door and take you right on one of the sinks. They'd know exactly what we were doing in there, Natalie. And you would know they were thinking about it with every thrust I made." He pulled his finger out of her mouth, then pushed it back in. "Would you try not to scream as you came, Natalie?" He leaned down then, close to her mouth, and slowly slid his finger back out. "Or would you want them to hear you come?" He leaned in and slid his tongue deeply into her mouth, taking his wet finger and rubbing it over her nipple.

Her scream filled the back of her throat as she roared over the edge into an almost convulsive orgasm. He kept at it, pushing her over again. Then again, until she trembled limply against him.

He was panting hard, fighting his own climax with everything he had left. He was going to be deep inside her when he came. As deep as she could take him.

She was ripping at him now, clutching at him to fill her. He shoved her skirt the rest of the way to her waist and tore off her panties, then, without waiting, thrust hard into her. She screamed, and he felt her clench around him as she climaxed again. He came instantly. It was a hard, fast rush, and he gave himself over to it totally. As if he had a choice.

They lay side by side, their bodies sweaty and limp. He had no words to tell her what the gift of her trust meant to him. He was almost afraid to look at her, afraid he'd see embarrassment now at where he'd taken her, what he'd made her understand about herself.

As it turned out, he didn't have to worry about that.

She turned her head to where he'd buried his against her neck and whispered in his ear, "Next time, I sit on top. And I tell the tale."

He turned his face so it pressed against the fine line of her jaw, already grinning. "Gee," he said hoarsely, "twist my arm."

She chuckled, and it was a supremely self-satisfied sound. He decided he rather liked it.

"If you think I'm going to torture you with visions of women watching you, you're wrong. You're a guy. Of course you'd like that."

He lifted his head now, surprised. "A tad sexist, don't you think?"

"You're saying the idea of knowing you're turning a woman, or women, on in a public place is something you'd have to force yourself to imagine you'd enjoy?" She just looked at him. "I was there this morning. I don't think you're going to sell that one."

"You know, I've never once done anything like that. In fact, I wasn't even thinking about it being a public place, until you blushed."

She promptly blushed again. Which he enjoyed the hell out of, considering what they'd just done and discovered together.

"So you want that scenario?" She paused, pondering. "Nope. Too easy a sell. Not far enough outside your comfort zone. You took to the game far too easily today."

It was on the tip of his tongue to tell her this wasn't a game, not to him. But the fact he'd even thought it, and so quickly, so naturally, stopped him. This *was* just for fun, he reminded himself. He could handle this and not get attached. It was the thrill of discovery he was attracted to here, not her. Not in that way, anyhow. Because he couldn't. That would ruin everything. So he just wouldn't allow himself to go there.

Even as he shoved the whole thing out of his mind, the first teensy thread of worry began to form.

"So what will it be?" he asked, getting his head firmly back into the game. Such as it was.

Now her smile was downright wicked. "Oh, I don't know. It will take some time to figure out."

His heart leapt inside his chest. *Because of the sex,* he told himself. What else would it be? "So you'll see me again?"

"If we can work it out."

He wanted to leap up and do a dance on the bed. Instead he lifted his head enough to run his tongue along the shell of her ear. "When do you have to leave today?"

She craned her neck, looking for a clock. "Four. I've got to turn my rental in before I board."

Jake felt around behind him until he found the linen napkin he'd filched the fruit in. He plucked a blueberry from the folds, amazed they hadn't smashed all the fruit. He rolled it between his fingers in front of her face. "What say we give breakfast in bed a try?"

Her eyes widened a bit as she watched him roll the berry back and forth. "I thought you had a meeting."

"I'll reschedule. Now, breakfast in bed?" He put the berry between her breasts and began slowly rolling it down the center of her body. "I'm still hungry. And I'm thinking this would taste really good dipped in you."

Her head dropped back and her hips actually undulated. "I give up," she groaned in pleasure. "You're way better at this than me. Who knew cowboys were so imaginative?"

He continued rolling the berry over her belly, nudging it into, then back out of her navel. "Who knew lawyers could be so...responsive." She gasped when he let the berry tickle through the first few curly wisps. "Why don't you let me lead today. That will give you until next time to think up a few things. Research a few...briefs."

He nudged it over the edge, and she arched hard as it hit her clitoris. "Yes," she gasped. "God, yes."

"To hell with the bed," he growled, already growing hard again. *How did she do that?* He nudged the berry along her wet lips, then rolled his tongue in right behind it.

She groaned, long and low, as her climax took her slowly but body-shakingly hard. She was still twitching as she all but yanked him inside her.

He gladly complied. This time, however, he didn't come for a long, long time.

Chapter Eight

"DATING SUCKS." Liza swirled the cherry in her drink, then bit it off the stem in one vicious snap.

Natalie almost choked on her drink. "What? You're the one always telling me how fabulous the men in L.A. are and how I should race out here and enjoy the endless 'beef buffet,' as I believe you termed it."

"Yeah, well, I'm switching to chicken and fish."

Natalie laughed, glad her flight had been delayed, after all. Liza had been happy to meet her at a restaurant near the airport for dinner. Now she knew why. Girl talk. She didn't mind. It would help take her mind off what she'd been doing only hours earlier. She still couldn't quite believe it herself.

"Please. Just because Conrad decided to have an affair with his soap co-star fling-of-the-week doesn't mean the whole dating world has gone to hell."

Liza set her drink down. "I'm not saying the whole world has gone to hell. Just the men in it. What is up with them, anyway?"

"Aren't *you* usually the one who gets irritated when a man starts to get all clingy with you?" Natalie had lost count how many times she'd sat just like this, either in person or on the phone, and talked Liza through yet another breakup. Only it was usually Liza doing the breaking up. Since the shoe was on the other foot this time, it wasn't surprising that her friend wasn't taking it well. "I know it's a blow to the ego, but come on, you only have…what? Ten, twelve, twenty others dying to take Conrad's place?"

Natalie had expected an annoyed look followed by a rueful laugh, and then it would be over and they could finally go eat dinner. Instead Liza's expression sobered, then she looked away and started twirling her cherry stem.

When several moments passed and she still hadn't responded, Natalie leaned down to catch her eye. "Liza?"

"Okay. So maybe he wasn't the fling I'd hoped he'd be."

"Then, why are you so upset?"

Liza looked up, and Natalie was stunned to find her eyes swimming. "I didn't mean he wasn't a good fling. He was. Too good. So good, in fact, I'd sort of forgotten about the fling part and started to get serious." Then she shocked Natalie further by starting to cry.

Liza had never cried once since Natalie had known her.

"And then the jerk goes and sleeps with another woman. How could he do it to me, Nat? He was actually shocked when I told him I wouldn't see him again. Like I shouldn't mind sharing!" She sniffed. "Well, I minded."

Natalie quickly abandoned her stool and hugged her friend. "Oh, sweetie, I'm so sorry. I had no idea. I wouldn't have teased you like that if I'd known. It's just that you never get—"

"Serious?" she said, hiccuping through another sob. Her mascara was a mess and her cheeks were splotchy. "Well, I guess we all fall sometime."

Natalie instantly thought of Jake, and then shut the picture out. It had just been a reflex reaction, to think of the last man she'd been intimate with. The fact that he was also the next man she planned to be intimate with made no difference. Jake was not a forever man.

Liza hiccuped again. "I don't want...to date anymore." She sniffed, then blew her nose on a cocktail napkin. "It's not...worth it. I don't want...to ever...feel like this again." She wiped her face, still sniffling, and gently pushed Natalie back to her stool.

"I know what you mean, but honestly, Liza, it was bound to happen at some point. It's surprising it hadn't happened sooner. Last time I looked, it was a fairly normal reaction between a woman and a man she finds attractive and fun."

"Don't forget good in bed," she added with a watery chuckle.

Natalie rolled her eyes, trying to ignore the heat in her cheeks as she recalled just how good in bed Liza had thought Conrad was. After all, she'd heard firsthand.

"But just because you got stung once doesn't mean you should give up altogether."

"I know." Liza sighed and used another napkin to blot her face. "You're right." She downed the rest of her drink, choking a bit as it stung her throat. "Still sucks."

Natalie sighed along with her. "I know."

Liza turned a considering look to her. "Since when?"

"Oh, no, we're not going there. You know very well that I've led the opposite kind of social life from you, so it's not at all surprising that it hasn't happened to me."

"You sure sounded like the voice of experience."

Natalie backpedaled faster. "I was just sympathizing. I mean, look who I date."

"Lawyers, investment bankers and rich idiots your dad and sisters shove at you. I know. Still, who would have thought, with all the hot, amazing men I've dated, I'd lose it for a dumb soap stud?"

Natalie couldn't help it; she lowered her voice and said, "Well, I can think of one or, well, multiple reasons why you might have."

Liza sighed again, but in abject appreciation this time. "Yeah, well, there was that. A lot of that." She laughed. "Maybe that's why I'm crying."

Natalie snickered, then they both lost it and laughed.

But Liza wasn't one to be dissuaded from a mission. The considering look returned as soon as the laughter died.

Natalie held up her hand. "Please, we'll do my love life next time."

"So." She folded her arms and leaned forward. "There is a love life. I've been wondering. You're holding something back on me. I could hear it in your voice." She leaned even closer and peered into Natalie's face. "It's in your eyes, too." She grinned, obviously more than happy to shift the conversational target to her friend. "Spill it."

Natalie had debated telling her friend. God knows, they shared everything else. Liza was the one person in her life she could tell anything to, including the fact that she'd heard her and Conrad at the end of that party. So what if she'd sort of omitted the fact that when she'd slipped out for coffee, it had been with Conrad's childhood buddy, and they'd ended up in bed together?

It was so unlike anything she'd ever done. And now she'd done it twice. And it was still so amazing, so stunning to her...well, she simply couldn't give that up for conversational fodder. Not yet, anyway.

"Well, the only exciting thing on the dating spectrum for me is another one of Sabrina's charity balls," Natalie said. At least it was the truth. "To make it worse, Melissa has managed to dredge up the one remaining eligible bachelor under the age of fifty that she hasn't already shoved at me. At least, I assume he's under fifty. I don't think she's gotten that desperate."

Liza smirked. "Yet."

"God help me when that time comes."

"'When' is right. There is no 'if' with your sisters. When they set their minds to something, nothing so trifling as a twenty-year age gap would stop them."

Natalie merely nodded, taking no offense, especially as Liza was absolutely correct in her assessment. In fact, Natalie was ever grateful for Liza's take on her whole family situation. It made her feel less like an ungrateful spoiled brat and more like the intelligent woman she hoped she was—one who'd naturally run screaming from a family as controlling as hers.

"So, who's the victim *du jour?*"

Natalie made a face. "Preston Albert Markwell III. Sounds about as dreamy as a tax audit, doesn't he?"

"Only if he actually calls himself Preston Albert."

Natalie grinned. "Probably does."

Liza pretended a swoon. "Oh, Preston Albert, do it to me again!"

Natalie swatted her, but laughed all the same.

Thankfully the maitre d' came over and told Liza their table was ready, saving her. Natalie was able to turn the conversation to the menu, which then launched Liza into tales of the latest weird diet fads of some of her celebrity clients. All of which they discussed and analyzed as they wolfed down their filet mignon and cherries jubilee. Natalie would have to drag herself off to the gym as penance in the morning, but that was hours away. In the meantime, she dug in and enjoyed the time with her friend.

And tried like hell not to think of what Jake could do with those damn cherries.

"YEAH, DAD. I've worked through the probabilities schematic and I think I've got the shipping problem figured out. It's not going to be cheap, but they stand to do pretty well if they can move the beef overseas more easily." Jake flipped past the notes he'd been consulting and picked up the engraved manila envelope he'd tucked underneath. "I'm meeting with Ray and John this afternoon." He turned it over, looking at his name in neat, black ink on the back. "Yes, they'll go for it if they want to deal with us." He chuckled. "Yes, Dad, I'm playing hardball just like you taught me. I expect to be out of here by six. I've already contacted the pilot, and he's filed our flight plans."

Company jets were an absolute luxury, but they were the one perk he'd guiltlessly accepted after too many years of cramming his six-foot-two body onto crowded commercial flights heading to points all over the globe. "Give Mom my love and tell her I'll see her this weekend." He hung up, still fingering the envelope, then finally gave in and pulled out the single folded piece of stationery that was inside.

He read the note for what was probably the twentieth time since it had arrived at his hotel the night before, then folded it and slid it back into the gold-edged envelope. Good thing he was alone. He had a permanent grin...and what he feared was a permanent hard-on. And probably would be until he laid eyes...and hands on the sender of that note.

"An art museum," he murmured, shaking his head. A very public one, too, as it was the Art Institute in Chicago, where they'd both be doing business ten days from now.

Doing business. He supposed that was one way to put it. Best damn business meeting he'd ever had the fortune to look forward to. She'd taken two weeks to come up with something for their next rendezvous. But an art museum? *What in the hell does she have in mind?*

He laughed as all sorts of ideas popped into his way-too-fertile-of-late mind, but he doubted they were what she'd come up with. He sorted through a pile of folders on his makeshift hotel-room desk, trying hard not to think about what they'd come up with the last time they'd been together.

One thing was for sure: he had a whole new respect for fruit as a major food group.

Still grinning, he tried like hell to get his mind back on the meeting he was to run in less than fifteen minutes. It really wasn't like him to let a woman distract him this way. But he'd never met a woman like Natalie Holcomb.

His gaze drifted briefly to his laptop. He knew they weren't supposed to talk about work or family or anything other than what they wanted to do with each other when they were together. But they hadn't ever actually said they couldn't explore a little when they weren't together. So, one night shortly after their last encounter, he'd given up on trying to sleep with a raging erection, taken a cold shower...and booted up his laptop. If he couldn't satisfy himself physically with her, he'd thought maybe learning more about her personally would assuage the need she'd so effortlessly roused in him.

He knew she came from a wealthy family with her talk of boarding school and family chefs. So he'd done a little digging into her family history and come across Holcomb Industries, which had started with Natalie's great-grandfather as an investment firm. The young banker had cagily branched out just before the stock market crash. Now they were into a host of other things, all profitable and overseen by her father and brother. Many charitable works bore the Holcomb name, and the names of her two sisters popped up on a regular basis in all manner of social and charitable works attributed to the company. Their husbands, along with Natalie's older brother, Chuck, also popped up regularly in the newspaper business news sections for one major deal or another.

None of those things struck him as unusual, as his own family's background was similar, even if the industry itself was wholly different. The glaring difference was that he, along with his two brothers and one sister, were all involved happily in the family business with his father, mother, several aunts and uncles. Even his aging, retired grandfather still kept a hand in at board meetings.

Jake enjoyed his work, and loved working with his family, although his schedule kept him from seeing them every day. He smiled. Maybe distance was the key to family harmony in the workplace. He shook his head. Whatever the case, they each gave the business their all and took immense personal pride from its continued success. None of the Lannisters had ever felt like the world owed them anything, nor did they expect to get anything without working to achieve it.

Granted, it was a lot easier to work toward a goal when you had the bankroll to finance the education and whatnot to help get you there, but he'd never taken it for granted. His family was also heavily involved in philanthropic endeavors, one part of which he'd personally developed—grants and college scholarships. His siblings and parents devoted their time to their pet charities in addition to their other work.

Which led him back to the glaring omission from Natalie's family history. Sure, he'd found out where she worked as an up-and-coming attorney with Maxwell & Graham, a law firm in Manhattan that handled everything from corporate to family to entertainment law. She was involved in the corporate side, although she'd been doing work for one of the new partners, who was their new entertainment specialist.

It had taken a little digging to uncover all this information through his buddy's access to the legal network. It would have been a lot easier if she worked for her family, considering they were in the news all the time. Her name was occasionally mentioned in the social columns when she attended this wedding or that ball, usually as an afterthought in a list of "other attendees."

He didn't find her associated with any of the other high-profile charities her family was so abundantly proud of being involved in, nor did he find her involved in any way with the family company. Ever. He'd discovered she'd gone to Georgetown on an academic scholarship and finished law school in the upper quarter of her graduating class. He assumed she'd passed the bar on her first try judging by the time frame between graduation and her first job…where she was still employed to this day.

All in a night's work. A long night, but he'd been unable to stop digging once he'd started. And rather than suppress his appetite for her, it had only whetted it further. Why the division between family and work? Why had she gone rogue and left the family fold? She was the black sheep, and yet she came off as an overachieving corporate climber, dedicated and serious about making her mark in the world. To all appearances, this would have made her golden to her family business.

Unfortunately, there were no answers for those questions on the Internet or anywhere else. Pumping Liza was out of the question, although he'd considered it at about four in the morning, when anything seemed possible.

Unless he came out and asked, he wasn't going to learn any more about her. But he couldn't do that. And was, therefore, dying to find out. At least, that was what he told himself. He was the family troubleshooter and he was exceptionally good at his job. He didn't sleep until he'd figured out how to solve a puzzle. So it was only natural that he was avidly curious about her.

He wasted a minute wondering if she was curious about him, as well. Maybe they could bend the rules, have one long question-and-answer session, then shut the topic down. Even as he thought it, he knew that wouldn't fly. He could hardly be her secret thrill if she knew everything about him. And maybe knowing would remove too much of the mystique, cloud the time they had with too much reality. And, after all, wasn't reality what they were trying to escape from with one another?

He slapped the folders shut and shoved them in his brief-case, then slid his laptop and software in after them.

Maybe it would ruin things for her. But he knew a great deal about her now...and it only made him want more.

"Dangerous game you're in, buddy," he muttered to himself. If he was smart, he'd play it safe and keep it simple. He shook his head and gave a rueful grin as he let himself out of his room. Since when had he ever played it safe?

Chapter Nine

NATALIE STARED at the abstract painting in front of her. She'd known before coming to Chicago for her meeting with Johanssen and Associates that Jake would be in town at the same time. She'd thought of little else in the weeks since their last…meeting. Now she was wishing she'd never sent the note to Jake's hotel. She felt foolish standing in the cool, quiet hall of the Art Institute, looking for all the world like a patron of the arts in her simple black suit, sensible designer pumps and fitted suede jacket.

When what she really was, was a woman on the verge of hormonal overload, waiting for a man she was planning to have hot, steamy sex with. Her body gave a little shudder of excitement at the thought, which was why she was still standing there. She only hoped "I'm having a wild fling" wasn't written all over her.

Maybe he couldn't come—he hadn't responded to her note. But then, he'd have no way of doing so. Their relationship had sort of become a "come if you can" type of situation. *And boy, am I willing to come.*

She covered her mouth and pretended to cough as she choked on a laugh. What had gotten into her?

Actually, it was who. *Jake.*

And she wanted him into her again. And again.

She thought about him all the time. And who wouldn't, considering the pleasure he'd given her both times they'd been together? But that wasn't what bothered her. What worried her was that when she thought about him, it wasn't always in conjunction with sex. Which was bad. Because that was all they could be for each other. That was the deal. If he had any idea she harbored even the remotest fantasy that this unusual liaison they'd formed would lead to anything more permanent, he'd disappear in a blink and she'd never hear from him again.

So she resolutely did not think about what he might be doing at any given point during the day. She certainly didn't wonder who he might be doing it with, because that would mean she had some sort of imagined claim on him, which she certainly did not. She sighed and pretended to look at the next painting. Liza might be cut out for this type of thing, but Natalie was fast learning she was not.

Of course, knowing that hadn't stopped her from sending the note. In fact, she was fairly certain nothing could have stopped her. Could a person get addicted to sex? Well, really great sex, anyway?

"Hi."

She jumped a foot and only barely managed not to let out a squeal.

Jake laughed and held her arm to steady her as she turned around. "I'm sorry. I guess you were really absorbed in that painting. I didn't mean to startle you."

It was on the tip of her tongue to tell him she was only absorbed with one thing: him. But he was standing right there in front of her, looking every bit as spectacular as she'd been certain her mind had deluded her into thinking he was. Her body actually ached for him to touch her. The spot on her arm where his fingers brushed her had already come alive. God, she was addicted to him.

Or what he could give her, she corrected herself. Certainly, like any good craving, when she'd had her fill, she'd move on to some other…hobby.

He leaned down so his eyes were level with hers. "Are you okay?"

I am now. "Fine."

He held her gaze a moment longer, looking skeptical, but simply smiled and held out his arm. "So, we're off to see a specific exhibit? Or just wander aimlessly?"

"Specific exhibit." She took his arm, wishing she could get her raging libido in check. This was her day, her plan, and she'd be damned if she wouldn't handle it with the same easy aplomb he'd handled their last outing. An outing that hadn't even lasted long enough for them to finish breakfast, she recalled, feeling a little better.

Of course, last time there had been no expectation on either of their parts that the meal would lead to what it had. This time was different. And it was up to her to prove she could handle this like the well-educated, mature, world-traveled woman that she was.

He slid his hand down her arm and linked fingers with hers, gently rubbing his thumb along her wrist. Her knees weakened considerably.

She was in deep trouble.

She moved on, hoping he didn't notice how unsteady she was.

"This exhibit must really be something special," he said.

"What?" She heard the thread of amusement in his tone, then realized she was all but racing them down the hallway. So much for sophistication. "Okay, so I'm a bit nervous."

He squeezed her hand. "Yeah, me too."

"Right."

He looked surprised. "No, really."

"You *are* the same man that fed me strawberries in front of an eager dining audience at Aunt Sue's, are you not?"

"That was different."

"How?"

"I didn't plan that. It just sort of happened."

He actually did look a tiny bit uncomfortable. His big rangy body was clothed quite handsomely in casual trousers and a pullover sweater beneath a worn leather and suede jacket. He looked rugged and sexy, but polished too, every bit the casual kind of art admirer that might frequent the Institute. And for all she knew, he'd been here hundreds of times. Except when she looked in his eyes. There was a certain deer-caught-in-headlights look to them when he took his eyes off her and looked around. As if she might expect him to make some kind of educated analysis about each piece.

And that fish-out-of-water feeling was what she'd banked her entire plan on. She'd been spoonfed an appreciation of the arts since birth. She'd never particularly enjoyed having it shoved down her throat, but in this case, she hoped to gain an edge, so to speak, by being in a location where she might feel more at home than he did. She sent a silent thank-you to her Aunt Mildred for giving her a *Fine Art* subscription every year for Christmas. She rarely read the thing, but when she'd seen this exhibit featured on the latest cover, her plan had begun to take shape. She smiled to herself. Oh, if Mildred only knew the sort of learning experience her niece was actually deriving from her not-so-veiled attempt at continuing her art education.

"So, you haven't been here before?" she asked.

"No, I don't get much sight-seeing in when I travel. I suppose I should."

He didn't look too upset about it. She understood exactly how he felt. When she traveled, it was to work. Her various aunts and uncles had dragged Natalie and her siblings all over the world growing up and she had burned out on cathe-drals, monuments, statues and museums before the age of twelve. She still couldn't get all that excited about another piece of ancient pottery or Impressionist oil painting.

She'd definitely never been remotely excited about the idea of exploring more of it as an adult. Until now. Exploring anything with Jake could be exciting. Who knew, she might even learn to love ancient pottery.

"Do you like art?" she asked.

"I can appreciate it as much as the average person, I guess. But I'm not educated about it, if that's what you mean." He smiled. "I'm always open to new things, however."

"Good. Now, I know we're supposed to be expanding our sexual boundaries." She lowered her voice when a passing patron looked their way with a raised eyebrow. She blushed, anyway, when she caught the teasing light in Jake's eyes, but forged ahead. "But, well, I thought you might enjoy this and…" She stopped trying to explain, suddenly nervous about her choice. Would he think it too personal? "It's this way." She tugged him out of the wing they were in and steered him toward the exhibit, before she lost her nerve.

"You seem to know your way around here. I take it you have been here before."

"Several times."

"A real fan of the arts, then."

She laughed. "No." She turned the corner and paused. "In fact, I loathe them on principal. Haven't been here since I was fourteen and never planned to come back."

He looked understandably confused. "What changed your mind?"

"Like you said, I'm open to trying new things. I want to see art through your eyes. Might give me a new outlook on the medium." She grinned. "Sort of like the new apprecia-tion you gave me for oatmeal."

Jake laughed, then shrugged. "I try."

"You succeeded. Now it's my turn."

He gestured in front of them. "Lead on."

Natalie had been uncertain about how patient he'd be with this idea. They had limited time together, as usual, and by issuing an invitation at all, she'd basically tacitly agreed to go to bed with him again. Some men wouldn't want to take any detours on their way to the good stuff. She'd been hoping Jake would indulge her. She was more than pleased to find him up for the adventure.

She barely got through the door, when he was tugging her over to a small bronze in the corner.

"I'm sorry, but I had to see this up close."

Natalie just smiled and let him go. Yes, this was going to be another fun adventure, after all.

"Would you look at this," he said in a hushed tone, stopping in front of a small sculpture of a Native American man on horseback. "You can almost feel the power of the horse, the muscles bunching beneath the rider."

Natalie felt muscles bunching, too. Hers.

"You can actually see him clenching his thighs against the side of the horse as he leans over his neck. Amazing."

Natalie's throat went dry. "Yes," she managed to say. So, okay, maybe she could appreciate art. She started to say something, anything, but he was already dragging her over to see another sculpture. She couldn't help but smile at his honest enthusiasm. Never let it be said the man didn't tackle new things with gusto. She barely held back a sigh. Boy, what gusto.

"The same artist," he said, reading the small plaque mounted to the front of the pedestal.

This one was another bronze. It was a Native American woman kneeling, her hands cupped to her mouth as if sipping water just scooped from a stream. He said nothing as he studied it, but Natalie found herself studying him instead of the piece.

He was totally focused, taking in every detail. As he had before, when he found something that fascinated him, he blocked everything else out. She'd learned that with the blueberry.

"You can almost see her throat working as she swallows." His voice was hushed, his respect for the artist obvious.

Natalie could only swallow hard herself. Was it her, or was it getting warm? She'd hoped he'd enjoy the sculpture, but she hadn't had any idea just how sensual a study it would be. She looked at Jake—the smooth, hard lines of his face, the determined look in his eyes as he studied the piece. He seemed so rugged, too rugged to be such a sensualist. But she looked again at what he was wearing and realized the fine fabric of his trousers and lush warmth of his pullover were probably chosen for how they'd feel against his skin. Comfortable and plain enough. And yet undeniably sensual, when you thought about it. She had to curl her fingers inward against the urge to run her hands over the leather jacket he wore, the suede sleeves, the soft weave of the sweater stretched across his chest.

"Makes you wish you could touch her, doesn't it?" he said, totally unaware of the direction her thoughts had taken her. "Feel the power of what the artist created under your fingertips."

"Yes," she said, and the word was heartfelt. Only, she wasn't looking at the sculpture.

Her body vibrated at the idea of his long fingers exploring her with the same intensity he had focused on the bronze. If there was any way to make him leave right now and take her directly to bed, she would do it.

She caught herself and almost laughed. Now who was rushing ahead, impatient for the good stuff?

She took his hand, enjoying the rough warmth of his palm against hers. Had she known she could get so turned on in an art museum, she'd have come here daily. "Come over here," she said, determined to get her mind back on track. "There is a piece I want to show you." It was the piece from the cover of the magazine, the one that had given her this idea.

He glanced around him as she led him to the adjacent room. "This is all early Western art, isn't it? Or inspired by the early West."

"Different artists, but yes, the theme is the Old West. You come from the West, said your family had been there a long time, so I thought you might enjoy it." She hoped that wasn't treading too close to taboo territory, but he smiled.

"My ancestors were on one of the wagon trains well over a hundred years ago." He paused by a painting just inside the door. It was a watercolor of the sun setting over the Rockies. "But I never thought of that history in terms of art." He was silent for a moment, then looked down at her. "Thank you for this."

It stunned her a little, how good it made her feel to please him. "You're welcome." When he looked at her the way he was right now, it made her want to do whatever it took to continue to please him. She cleared her throat. "The sculpture I want to show you is this way."

He squeezed her hand and wove his fingers more tightly between hers. "How long is this exhibit here?"

"A few months, I think. It just opened."

"Good. I'd like the chance to see more of it."

She stopped. "I'm sorry. I'm rushing you again."

"No, no, I want to see this through your eyes, too." He pulled her a bit closer. "I can come back later. Right now, I want to see what you want."

What she wanted. Dear God, if he only knew how badly she wanted.

"You're sure?"

"Absolutely. Show me the way."

"It's over here." She slowed. "Of course, now I've made this big deal out of it and it's not really. I just...well, I saw it on the cover of a magazine and it made me think of—" She broke off, realizing she was probably revealing more than she should about how much of her thoughts he'd occupied of late.

"Think of what?" When she balked, he turned slightly and pulled her against him. There was no one near them, but Natalie still stiffened and tried to pull away. He simply put his arm around her and tucked her right back against him. Grinning now, he said, "Think of what?"

"Let me go, and I'll tell you."

"Tell me, and I'll let you go."

She gave him a look, but he gave it right back.

"I'll start taking penalty kisses right here the longer you make me wait," he said.

That should have ticked her off. Instead it made her wet for him. "I shouldn't tolerate this kind of treatment."

"Yeah, it's pure torture, I know."

It *was* pure torture, and he knew it. Making her ache like crazy while fighting against her natural desire to not be so public about that ache. But she didn't force him to end it, either, which she knew he would have if she asked.

He leaned in and took a quick but devastating taste of her mouth. "Clock is ticking."

She trembled but said nothing.

The second kiss was slower, bordering on being too passionate and personal for a public place. It also bordered on making her not care too much about all that.

"Show me first," he said, his voice a bit rougher. "Maybe I'll figure it out on my own."

He was giving her an out. She should take it. She didn't.

"You. It made me think of you." *I think about you too much. All the time*. She only hoped that wasn't written all over her face.

"Thank you," he said softly. He kissed her gently on the corner of her mouth, then released her. Which conversely made her want him even more. "Show me."

This was not how she'd planned this. She should have known that anytime the two of them got together, this would be the result. *And the problem with that was?* she asked herself. The problem was, she was coming too close to revealing her growing feelings for him. Feelings she had to get under control if she was going to continue this. And Lord, she wanted to continue this.

"It's over here."

He stopped short several feet away from it, pulling her to a stop, as well. The sculpture had been carved from a tree stump that had been stripped of its bark and polished to a rich golden sheen. Erupting from the base of the trunk was a stampede of long horns. Above that, looking like he was bursting from the top of the cut stump, but actually carved from the tree itself, was a cowboy on horseback. His body was bent close to the horse's neck, his hand raised over his head with a looped rope poised to be thrown over the small steer that had broken away from the herd.

"It's…" He didn't finish.

She looked from him to the sculpture, unable to name how she felt in the face of his obvious awe. She'd felt that same tug when she'd seen it. She knew his family bred and sold cattle, but he was hardly a cowboy. And yet something about this piece, even on glossy magazine paper, had pulled her right in and demanded her full attention.

"I know," she whispered.

She couldn't say how long they stood there. Jake finally pulled her forward so he could look at the artistry more closely, from all sides, never once releasing the tight grip he had on her hand.

She couldn't deny how good it made her feel to know she'd moved him like this. But she also couldn't deny how nervous it made her. This feeling she had right now had nothing to do with pushing sexual boundaries and everything to do with pushing personal ones.

She wasn't sure how it would feel to make love to him now. How could it not start to be more than just two people exploring pleasure?

You're being silly, she told herself. She was reading way more into this than there was. Likely he was very glad to have been introduced to art that was so personal to his past, but it wasn't going to alter anything else.

For him, anyway.

Still, maybe they should just go back and look at the entire exhibit, she thought, skip the rest of this go-around.

Then he turned to her, and the look on his face told her there was going to be no skipping what came next. She should be strong enough to read the danger signals screaming inside her, but she wasn't Superwoman. No matter what he was or wasn't feeling, what she was feeling was too overwhelming to be denied.

"You ready to leave?" he murmured.

She could only nod.

He traced one finger along her cheek. "I'll be back to see the rest, but right now I want to spend some time alone with you." He leaned down and kissed her softly. "Thank you for this, Natalie," he whispered next to her ear. "I want to take you. Right now. Do you know that?"

She shuddered with pleasure.

"Wonder what we'd look like in bronze."

"Dear God."

"On horseback."

She moaned softly.

He grinned and headed toward the exit.

Chapter Ten

THERE WAS NOTHING GENTLE about the way they made love this time. And Natalie didn't mind in the least. It was probably better this way. No mushy sentimentality to cloud the real reason they were together.

Jake had her up against the wall of the elevator as soon as the door closed. Thank God her room was on the tenth floor, or she might have been unclothed by the time she got to her room. And not have cared.

"Key card," he said in a heated groan against the side of her neck.

She fumbled it out of her coat pocket. It took both of them several tries before the green light flicked on.

They stumbled into the room, coats dropping, shoes flying before he tumbled her to the bed. "I want inside you right now," he demanded.

"Please."

She pulled his sweater off, he unbuttoned her blouse. He did stop to admire the lacy cream bra and panty set she wore. For about two seconds, before all but tearing it off of her. She heard a hook *ping*.

"I'll replace it," he said, his mouth already on the heated skin just between her breasts. "You taste too damn good, Natalie."

She slid his belt free, almost frantic to feel his bare skin against hers. She had no idea what had launched them into this sensual frenzy. But ever since the museum, when he whispered he wanted to be inside her, the two of them had done everything possible to achieve that single goal. The cab ride to her hotel had been torture. The walk through the lobby even worse.

For once Jake didn't push it, make it harder or the ache more exquisite by making her wait. He was in as much a rush as she was, and they had all but run through the lobby. And the ache couldn't have been more exquisite.

She tried to focus on his chest, the way the skin stretched over his muscles, the slight scattering of hair that swirled ever-so-perfectly across his pectorals. But she kept seeing his eyes, the way they looked at her, into her, when he'd thanked her for showing him the sculptures. And it was that look that had her hotter and wetter than ever before.

She couldn't block it out, so she stopped trying. So there was mushy sentimentality, anyway, no matter the ferocity of their need at the moment. It would likely be weeks before she saw him again. Plenty of time to come back to her senses.

"Slide your legs up over my hips, Natalie," he instructed, his hands already lifting her as he climbed over her. "God, you smell good."

He paused and dipped his head toward her belly, already pushing her back, but her body was primed for him, and she wanted to feel every inch of him pushed well inside her. Her muscles were aching to clamp down on him, hold him tightly inside for as long as she could.

"Uh uh. I want you now." She tugged his head up, her nails sinking into his shoulders.

He grinned up at her. "Demanding. I like that." He delayed just long enough to grasp her nipple between his lips. "But I will be back."

"Yes, yes. Just move up inside— Yes! God, yes."

"Here?" He pushed deeper inside her and stopped. "Is this where you want me, Natalie?"

"Yes." Her hips were already pumping, and she could feel the effort it took him not to move. His arms were like steel beneath her clutching fingers—quivering steel.

"Tilt up," he instructed hoarsely.

She did, and he reached and grabbed a pillow, shoving it under her hips. She groaned long and loud as the position enabled him to sink even more deeply inside her.

"Please," she murmured, not even sure what she was asking for anymore. Just more of this. Hours of this. Days. Weeks. Eternity.

He held her pinned to the bed, letting her hips barely move up toward him. "Push," she commanded, almost wild with needing him.

"Say please."

She opened her eyes in surprise, but although he was grinning at her, the sweat on his brow and the vein ticking in his forehead told her how much this was costing him.

"Maybe," she managed to say breathlessly. "Maybe not."

He blew out a long breath of his own as his hips bucked slightly. "You don't play fair."

"Guess who I learned that from?" She locked her legs more tightly around his hips and pushed against him as hard as she could, her back arching her off the pillow.

His immediate loss of control came in a long, sweet groan as his body took over and gave her what she wanted. He pumped into her hard. She shrieked with the pleasure that plunged through her as she met him thrust for thrust.

He lost control first, his climax an intense release that made him shout. She followed immediately, the sound of him driving her over the top.

Dizzy with the force of their mutual release, she expected

him to fall heavily and limply upon her, which he did, but only for a moment. He pushed her hair from her face and found her mouth with his, kissing her long and hard, with more energy than she'd thought he'd have at this point.

Then he left her mouth and began the slow, sinuous trek down her damp, heated body.

"Jake."

"No way."

She smiled and let him do what he wanted. After what they'd just accomplished, she feared she might be too sore...then discovered to her grateful surprise just how restorative a gentle tongue could be.

Her head lolled back, her body relaxed...and then he slowly drove her up that sweet peak. Once, then twice...and then one more time—just because he could.

Finally, when she was nothing more than a languid pool of pleasure without an ounce of energy left in her, he climbed up along her body and silently rolled her against him. He pulled her leg over his thigh and tucked her against his chest, stroking her hair until she drifted off to sleep. Her last thought was that her dreams couldn't possibly top reality.

JAKE STARED UNSEEINGLY across the hotel room, as Natalie's breath evened out beneath his stroking fingers.

Boy, he was in big trouble.

He didn't even have to look down at her to know just how much trouble he was in. He'd never wanted anyone so desperately as he'd wanted Natalie today. It should scare him how badly he'd needed to make love to her. And it did. Just not enough to make him get up, get dressed and get the hell out of there before he did anything even more stupid. Like tell her he was beginning to get serious about her.

You've only seen her three times, he argued with himself.

Of course you think you're falling for her. The sex is great. What's not to like?

But that wasn't it, and he knew it. Yes, he was incredibly physically gratified at the moment. But, as much as he'd like to believe that was all there was to this sudden tender spot in his heart, it didn't explain the way he'd felt earlier when she showed him that cowboy sculpture. It should seem sort of silly now, to get all dopey over some old carving. But he didn't feel remotely dopey or silly.

She settled heavily against him as she fell more deeply asleep. He felt that queer dip in his stomach as he gave in to the need to look down at her. Yeah, she was something else in bed, no doubt about that. He pushed a few damp strands of hair from her cheek. But he wasn't thinking about that at the moment. He kept seeing her, cheeks blooming, when she thought she was being overheard talking to him about sex in the museum. Not that she had any problem talking directly, and quite boldly for that matter. But it tugged at him that for all that she was bold and smart and not afraid to show it...when it came to some things, she was very private and a little shy. And though he liked to push her, he honestly didn't want to change that.

As long as she wasn't shy with him.

And then there was the way she'd gone about choosing what they'd do today. She didn't know him, not really. And yet, she did. She saw things in him others didn't. Certainly none of his associates or friends ever would have looked at him and thought, "Hey, bet ol' Jake would like to hit the local art museum." But she had.

Perhaps it was because she didn't know him in a professional or family capacity, leaving her free to get to know the real him, with no other knowledge coloring her perceptions.

Whatever the case, she'd deliberately chosen the exhibit today because she thought it would move him...and because she'd enjoy giving him that. And she had enjoyed it. Even when he'd been bowled over by the exquisite detail of the artwork, he'd felt her eyes on him. Him. As if he were as fascinating to her as the piece was to him.

He felt almost...awed by the pleasure she took in giving *him* pleasure. What was really startling was that, rather than feel tied down or fenced in, he wanted to do the same for her. It made him feel incredible to give her pleasure, in ways that had nothing to do with sexual gratification. Maybe too incredible. Maybe that was why he pushed her, teased her, when they were in bed together. To keep it a game, something they were doing for kicks.

Rather than something he was doing because he was falling in love with her.

You don't know her, he argued. But he did. And not because he'd dug up stuff about her family. He knew *her.* Maybe not her favorite color or favorite food. But he knew she was sharp and funny and endearingly shy. He knew she could give as good as she got, that she was competitive with herself but not necessarily with others. She expected the best from herself and was frustrated when she couldn't live up to her own expectations. Which might explain why she'd pursued her own path in life, rather than take the predetermined family path.

He wanted to ask her about that. To find out what made her happy, what made her sad. He wanted to know what her favorite color was and if she left the cap off the toothpaste and every other little thing.

Yeah, he was in big trouble.

He must have drifted, because when he looked at the clock again, an hour had disappeared. Natalie was still snuggled next to him. He hated to wake her. It made him wonder what it would be like to wake her up every day.

Apparently his little nap hadn't restored common sense. When she turned her head to nuzzle his chest, he leaned down and kissed her forehead, then her temple. For such a small action, the pleasure that rippled over him was intense. He really had to get out of this bed. Maybe fresh air would clear this fog from his brain.

And his heart.

He jiggled her arm. "Natalie. Time to get up."

She only snuggled more deeply.

He sighed. Mostly because he liked it. And he probably shouldn't. Not that much, anyway.

"Time to get up. Plane to catch," he said softly.

She mumbled something, then tucked her hand beneath her face, her lips parting on a sigh.

If he could have, he'd have made a call and changed her flight to a later one so she could sleep. Tomorrow maybe. Or never. But he had work to do, as well. Dammit.

Well, he knew one sure way to wake her up.

He started by tracing his fingertips down the gentle slope of her back. She arched into him, and he stirred against her. He shifted forward, rolling her to her back. She moaned and arched again as he closed his mouth over the tip of her breast. So damn responsive.

"Jake," she whispered roughly.

"Mmm."

She gripped his head when he would have lifted it. He gladly complied with her wishes. He slid his hand down over her stomach and found her wet and waiting for him.

If this is how she woke up every morning, maybe making a commitment wasn't such a scary thing. For the first time, he questioned his all-work lifestyle. But that thought, along with every other one he might have had, vanished when she pushed him on his back and climbed on top of him.

NATALIE ALMOST MISSED her plane. She strapped herself in and leaned her head back. She should feel harried and frustrated. She hated rushing, hated not having every detail taken care of so things ran smoothly. Which didn't explain the smile she couldn't seem to wipe from her face.

Jake had surprised her by asking to accompany her to the airport. He'd claimed that it had been his fault for initiating their last little activity and that getting her safely on her way was the least he could do.

But Natalie hadn't been so sure. She couldn't put her finger on it, but something seemed to have changed between them.

Just because you want it to doesn't mean it did, she told herself. Jake might be an exuberant lover in bed, but he was also a gentlemen. He always held doors for her and put her first. Even with orgasms, she thought, suppressing a very un-Natalie-like giggle. There was something to be said for good manners, she decided.

Not that she wasn't perfectly capable of opening her own doors, and she certainly had no problem with seeing to his pleasure—in bed or out—before seeing to her own, but she definitely wasn't going to complain if he wanted to take turns at it.

Thinking about pleasure brought her thoughts back to their museum trip earlier today. He'd said his ancestors had settled in the West over a hundred years ago. Her ancestors had come over on the Mayflower. Only, he was more involved in his current family than she was. She knew he worked for the family cattle business, but nothing more. It was odd that she felt as if she knew him so well when, technically, she really didn't know much about him at all.

But it went beyond facts and figures. Even after such a short time together, she could read his moods, sense when he was teasing and know almost before he did when he was going to turn serious. But that didn't mean he was the kind of man she could live with or even want to spend a significant amount of time with. Sure, he was charming and wonderful when they were together. Wasn't that the whole point? That they share the best of themselves and leave all the reality dreck outside the hotel door?

Hotels. That was another thing. She was already counting the hours until they saw each other again. New Orleans. A shiver of delight raced through her. One of the most decadent cities in the country. And it was his turn to plan.

But she didn't want another hotel room. She couldn't explain it. It wasn't that it made her feel tawdry or anything. It was hard to feel tawdry in a five-star hotel. But she wanted something more… personal.

Dangerous wish there, Nat.

She wondered what his home looked like, wondered if he'd like her loft in the city. She imagined what it would be like to see him sprawled on her sheets, sleep on the pillow he'd slept on, smell his scent on her towels.

God, she was becoming obsessed.

Which was exactly why she'd turned down Jake's offer to take her to the airport. She needed to get her head back on straight about just what the two of them were doing together. Lingering kisses at the gate were only going to further cloud her already cloudy mind. She was already reading things into his every look that probably meant nothing more than that he was having a good time. And why wouldn't he be? But it didn't mean anything else. Did it?

Nothing else had changed. He was still a workaholic dedicated to his career, as was she. Even if they both wanted to take this relationship to a more serious level, how would that work?

She knew the answer to that. It wouldn't work. If she wanted to see him at all, she'd have to suffer with the rules they'd set up. But could she? Could she handle her growing feelings? And when it inevitably came to an end, would she wish she'd ended it sooner, before her heart got any more involved?

Because it was definitely involved.

She sighed and looked out the window as the plane took off from O'Hare. She had three weeks until New Orleans. The work she'd done in Chicago wasn't her best, even though she'd gotten the job done. If she was going to stay on the upwardly mobile track at work, she'd damn well better find a way to keep her mind focused on work, and off Jake.

He'd be in New Orleans. They'd have fun. Nothing more than that, and no reason to look forward to it any more than she would a party with Liza, or a work-free weekend. No reason to let thoughts of him interfere with her career. After all, that was exactly why they'd made up the stupid rules in the first place.

She relaxed as the plane reached cruising altitude, and started drifting to sleep. Only, she didn't dream about making partner before she hit thirty-five. She didn't dream of the corner office with the view or finally proving to her family that she was perfectly capable of making her own dreams come true.

No, she dreamed of a cowboy riding bareback, roping a rogue calf, taming it to submission...

When she woke as the plane landed, she actually found herself rubbing her wrists, checking for rope burns.

She stayed in her seat as others disembarked.

"You're in big trouble, Natalie Holcomb," she muttered beneath her breath. There was only one way to get herself out of it. Cancel New Orleans.

Chapter Eleven

AS IT TURNED OUT, Natalie would have to cancel New Orleans whether she wanted to or not. Her father suffered another heart attack three days after she returned to New York. She'd flown home and spent thirty hours straight at the hospital, only going back to New York when it was clear her father would make it.

But it hadn't ended there. In fact, that had been only the beginning. She'd been having running arguments with one family member or another since she left Connecticut.

"You have to come home, Nat. You're the only one he listens to."

Natalie massaged the now-constant ache in her temples as she fought once again with one of her sisters. "How many times can I explain that I can't just up and walk away from my career, from my life, to take care of Dad? He's a grown man. A grown man who can well afford round-the-clock care."

Sabrina made an impatient noise. "Don't you think this rebellion thing has lasted long enough? Daddy needs you now, and all you can think about is yourself."

"What Daddy needs is to realize that he is not immortal, and he needs to listen to his doctors. I've been on the phone with him every day. You know that. I'm not neglecting him, but I can't force him to get better."

Then the waterworks started. "I can't believe you're being so cold and unfeeling about your own father." She sniffled.

Natalie swallowed an impatient sigh. Sabrina was an Oscar-caliber crier who used her tears very effectively on just about everyone else. Usually Natalie was impervious, but right now, despite her tough talk, she was feeling very shaky and vulnerable. Enough so that, even though she knew she was being manipulated, she couldn't stop the guilt from assaulting her.

For a short time her father had actually been clinically dead. In fact, the doctors brought him back not once, but twice, on the operating table. It had shaken her badly to realize just how fragile a bond she had with her only remaining parent. And if he didn't follow his doctor's instructions to the letter this time, there would be no next time. His cardiologist had explained the grim reality to her personally, and had also beseeched her to do what she could to help her father, as if he somehow knew she was the only one in the family who could. It didn't comfort her in the least that his intuition was on the money.

Even in the best of circumstances, Chuck and Natalie's two sisters simply didn't have the patience to deal with their father, nor he them. They all worked for the same common cause: to make the Holcomb name synonymous with everything elite and powerful. But they went about it in very different ways. Normally her father was content to let them go about their own business in their own way, as long as the bottom line was maintained. Which was just as well, since trying to tell her siblings how something was going to be done was only marginally more havoc-wreaking than them trying to tell their father what to do.

Right now, they were telling her what to do. They saw no

reason why she couldn't end this "foolish escapade in New York" and come home where she belonged, to take care of the man who had always taken care of her.

She could have argued that she'd taken care of herself since graduating from prep school, but there was no point. She also knew that her return was not going to be the miracle cure her siblings thought it would be. Living with her father would be one huge, ongoing battle of wills. The very idea made her head pound.

But his life was on the line. How could she just walk away?

"Natalie? Are you listening to me?"

No. I'm listening to myself. She had to squeeze her eyes shut to keep the tears at bay. "It will take me a little time to put things in order here." She took no measure of comfort from the relieved sigh on the other end of the line. *What have I just agreed to?*

She hung up the phone, tempted to lay her head down on her desk and cry. But that would solve nothing. She turned her thoughts to the tasks ahead. This wasn't going to be easy.

She had to ask her boss for a sabbatical. She would probably get the leave, but she knew she was dooming what success she'd busted her backside to achieve. Others would pass her by, and when she returned she'd have to work doubly hard just to earn her way back in. She'd seen it happen time and again with other women who'd taken even a brief maternity leave. No matter how many laws they passed to protect women's rights in the workplace, the old boys' network managed to find some way around them. And nowhere was that more clear than in her testosterone-dominated law firm.

Which was why she'd long ago decided to claw her way up as high as she could, to junior partner at the least, before even considering trying for a serious relationship, much less a family. Women had children in their forties all the time, she'd reminded herself every time her biological clock threatened to start ticking.

Jake instantly flashed through her mind. She managed a hollow laugh. Biological clocks and Jake. Had she really been trying to persuade herself that she could still carry on with him and not get more serious? She'd lost sleep trying to convince herself she could handle a whole weekend in New Orleans without falling more deeply in love with him.

So much for that worry. No job meant no travel. No travel meant no Jake. But she knew she'd have had to end it, anyway.

Her heart literally ached, and she stared unseeing at the piles of folders on her desk. Temper flared through the pain, and she had to fight the urge to clear her desk with one sweep and give in to a well-deserved tantrum over the sudden destruction of everything she'd worked for.

But that was counterproductive. She knew the only way she'd feel better was to take action, put the plan in motion. Then she'd at least feel she was in control. So she picked up the phone and dialed her boss. There would be no pouting. Her father needed her.

FOUR HOURS, one airline reservation and several packed suitcases later, however, she still hadn't managed to leave that note for Jake.

"It wasn't supposed to last forever," she reminded herself. But saying it out loud—again—did not make her feel any better.

He was going to be in Dallas in three days. All she had to do was send a note to his hotel for him to pick up on arrival. It was the only way to contact him. She knew he'd understand. He had a close family.

She knew this because she'd just happened to stumble on some information about a cattle ranch in Wyoming while

doing some research for a merger deal for one of her partners and— Okay, okay, so it hadn't been specifically Jake's
cattle ranch. But since she was poking around, she'd gone
and looked up other cattle-related industry in Wyoming and,
lo and behold, she'd stumbled across Jake's family business.
Empire was more like it.

Only, it had seemed to her a rather happier empire than
the one that had brought her into the world. Both parents,
several aunts and uncles, children from various families including all four children in Jake's family, as well as their
spouses worked for the company. Literally one big happy
family.

She hadn't found much in the society pages beyond the
weddings of Jake's three siblings and three or four cousins.
Nothing had popped up on the political front, but when
she'd dived into charitable contributions she'd hit the mother
lode. The Lannisters loved giving money away almost as
much as they enjoyed making it, or so it seemed.

It was odd, though. Finding out he came from a large family with substantial holdings should have made her feel closer
to him, considering her own background. Instead it had
made her feel a bit lonelier. Maybe a bit needier. Which was
more than a bit disconcerting, as she'd long ago come to grips
with her family's various dysfunctions.

Their families didn't really have much in common beyond
their corporate bottom line. Sure, her family was into charities, but they made certain their contributions were duly
noted in the news so as to enhance the company's image.
They dominated the society and political pages for the same
reason.

From what she could tell, Jake's family kept their charitable work relatively quiet and seemed to be content to stick
to business when discussing anything with the media, keeping the family part in the family.

She'd sighed, wondering how things might have been different in her own family if they'd put family first.

She tossed the pencil down on her desk. Honestly, she had to stop this. So what if his family was happy? It still didn't mean she knew him any better. When she got right down to it, beyond his ability to bring her to multiple screaming orgasms, she really didn't know him at all.

She snorted as she imagined Liza's probable response to that bit of information. "What else does a girl need to know?"

But seriously, did he leave the toilet seat up? Was he picky about what he ate or how things were done? What was his favorite music? Did he like to stay home and read, or was he a party animal, needing to be around others all the time? What was his favorite vegetable? Did he always lose his keys? Did he remember important dates, or was he completely hopeless when it came to birthdays and anniversaries?

No, her little foray into his family and business background hadn't answered those questions. Questions she almost desperately wanted answers for…questions destined to remain forever unanswered, as soon as she placed that call to Dallas.

She reached for the phone, then paused. So what if she didn't know his favorite vegetable? She already knew all the really important stuff. He had a good heart. He was a gentlemen to the core, but willing to push her when he thought she needed it. He was honest. He refused to take the easy way if a more difficult path might prove more beneficial in the long run. So what if she'd learned these things in bed? Surely they applied to the man himself in any situation. Her heart knew.

She yanked up the phone and called Liza. "Thank God," she said, when her friend answered her phone at work.

"What happened?" Liza asked instantly.

Liza was great about skipping the small talk. It was one of the many things Natalie cherished about their friendship.

She'd already told Liza about her father's heart attack. She'd called from the hospital. Now she told her the rest, from her sister's call onward. She told her about everything except the one thing she really wanted to talk about. Jake.

"Oh, honey, I'm so sorry!" Liza said when she was finished. "Can't they hire a nurse or something?" She didn't even wait for a reply; she knew Natalie's family very well. "I know, I know. Wishful thinking. It's just that it's not fair that you have to give up everything and run home to Papa."

Natalie already felt better. She might not throw tantrums over things, but it never hurt to have someone else do it on her behalf. "I don't have a choice. Not this time. But thanks for sticking up for me."

Liza snorted. "Yeah, yeah. Like you need hand-holding. I'm sure you've already made all the plans and taken care of everything. God forbid you mope and whine. Lord knows, I would. But then, the last person my folks would turn to for help is me." Liza's parents had divorced when she was a teenager, leaving her mostly to her own devices as they spent most of their time wrapped up in themselves.

That pattern hadn't changed in the years since. She rarely heard from them, and when they did call it was usually to announce some new engagement or marriage. Liza had stopped attending these events somewhere around wedding number four for each of them. She loved them both, but pretty much left them alone, as they did her, and everyone was the happier for it.

Natalie sighed. "Yeah, well, I'd trade you at the moment."

"Be careful what you wish for."

Wishes. She knew what she'd wish for. An endless weekend in New Orleans with Jake. Her stomach knotted and her heart hurt as the reality that she was never going to see him again truly began to sink in. "Liza, I have to tell you something."

"There's more?"

"I'm making up for lost time."

"Hey, are you implying that I've taken the lion's share of whining lately?"

Natalie smiled. She might be putting a career on hold and losing her secret thrill, but Liza would always be there for her. "You? Whine?"

"Okay, smart-ass. I'll let that go, basically because I can't defend myself against it and we both know it. So. I'm totally ready to wallow in your misery. Bring it on." Then she gasped. "Oh, no. You're not giving up the loft, are you? Is that what you wanted to tell me? Because I know you love that place. If money is the problem, then let me help you. You can pay me back whenever. Personally, I think you should make an exception about that trust fund of yours and finally dip into it. After all, it's your family that is forcing this sacrifice on you—the least they should do is foot the bill for this. You shouldn't have to lose everything just because you're the only one who takes no guff from that hardhead of a father of yours." She paused for a breath, then dove back in. "And what will he say about this? He might argue with you about your career choice, but you know damn well he's proud of your independence."

"Only because he truly believes I'll eventually see the light and give it all up to come to work for the good of the family. He can be a very patient man when it comes to proving a point. Of course, he'll gloat for life if that ever comes to pass, so in his mind it's a worthwhile gamble."

Liza didn't laugh this time. "Maybe, but he's going to throw a fit when he finds out he finally won, but only because he's weak and needs taking care of. Talk about pissing the old guy off. You might kill him just showing up."

"Liza," she quietly admonished. Liza was her one sounding board in the occasional rail and rant against her family, and it was a fairly typical statement for Liza to make. But the memory of standing in that sterile little room, waiting for the surgeon to come out and tell her if she was indeed an orphan or not, was simply too fresh.

"I'm sorry," Liza said sincerely, even if Natalie knew she held little affection for her father. But her compassion for her friend was boundless, and Natalie embraced that. She was strong, but everyone needed compassion once in a while.

"I just hate this for you," Liza added quietly.

"I know. I do, too. But it's what I have to do, you know?"

"Yeah. But I don't have to like it."

Natalie found a smile despite the burning sensation behind her eyes. "But as for the loft, don't worry. I've got some stock options I can cash in to keep up on rent for at least the next couple of months. After that, we'll see." She managed a laugh. "Besides, I'll need a place to escape to for the weekend when the slings and arrows get too heavy at home."

"You can always fly out and see me."

"Not on my currently nonexistent personal expense account, I can't. No more company flights, remember?"

"Promise me you'll let me fly you out if you need a break. Even if it's only for a weekend. And whenever I'm in New York, you'll come in and we'll do something wild and frivolous. On me. Deal?"

"Deal," she said, knowing Liza wouldn't accept anything else. "You're the best, you know that?"

"I certainly am. And don't you forget it!"

"Not a chance." It wasn't until Natalie hung up that she realized she'd never told Liza about Jake.

It was just as well, she decided. It was too fresh right now. Maybe in the distant future when they were sitting around discussing their love lives, or lack thereof, she'd dredge up this one perfect little affair and share it.

It wasn't like she was going to forget even the tiniest detail of it, no matter how much time passed.

She glanced at the clock and realized her cab would be here momentarily. She looked at the name of the Dallas hotel, written out in Jake's own hand from the itinerary he'd left her that first time they'd been together almost three months ago. All she had to do was call information, get the number, leave a message, and all would be taken care of. Neat and tidy, just the way she liked it.

But then there was a honk from below. Her cab was here. She looked at Jake's handwritten list and told herself the sensation rushing through her was not relief. She was merely putting off the inevitable. But though she knew the list by heart, she grabbed it and stuffed it in her purse. She'd call from Connecticut after she settled back in at home.

Home. Maybe it wouldn't be as bad as she remembered.

She knew it would be worse. She hadn't lived at home in ten years, not since she was eighteen.

Liza was right. Her father would be none too pleased to discover his baby had only abandoned her stubbornly held dreams to come take care of him. No, he wouldn't like that at all.

"Well, that makes two of us, Daddy." But like it or not, she was going to help him get well. Even if it killed them both.

Chapter Twelve

JAKE TOSSED the pile of notes on his hotel bed, dumped his garment bag and laptop case on the other one and headed straight for the shower. Damn, but he wished he was in New Orleans and not Dallas. He wished Natalie was waiting for him. It had been the week from hell, and if he never saw the inside of another hotel room he'd be more than happy. Unless that hotel room contained the woman he couldn't get off his mind.

He stepped under the hot spray and groaned in appreciation. He soaped up and tried like hell to convince himself what a bad idea it would be to give in to the urge to call her at work. He knew the number by heart now, having picked up the phone and dialed it several times since she'd left him in Chicago.

Getting back to work hadn't remotely helped him put their relationship back in perspective. He wanted more than this physical romp they'd agreed to share. He wanted to be able to hear her voice whenever he wanted to. So what if they lived across the country from one another? With their travel schedules, surely they could sustain some kind of committed relationship if they could call and talk between actual face-to-face visits.

He wanted to talk about her work, her day; tell her about his. Share the good news, family news, bad news, and just shoot the breeze. He found himself constantly wondering what she'd think of this or that, and was getting increasingly frustrated by the boundaries they had set up.

Would she be open to stretching them a little? He knew she was as harried in her business life as he was, and just as committed to succeeding. If he demanded more from her than their occasional meetings, would she run?

He shut off the water and climbed out. Could he risk losing what they did have? He dried off and wrapped a fresh towel around his waist before heading back into the bedroom. As a matter of habit, he scooped up the messages again, but tossed them back down a moment later after skimming the first two or three. More problems, more meetings. It was endless.

He truly enjoyed the work, but lately it seemed that he solved one problem only to have three more crop up. His dad kept telling him to train a few other people so he could dole out the workload a bit more and not travel as much. But he'd never had a reason to really contemplate it. His life was his job, and he hadn't minded it taking all his time and attention. Until he'd met Natalie.

He sat down on the side of the bed, for the first time thinking that delegating might not be such a bad idea. He wasn't a control freak by any stretch, but he'd always been the one to handle the serious glitches and it was hard for him to admit he couldn't keep up with the demand. Harder still to step aside and trust someone else to handle them as thoroughly and with as much dedication as he would.

He glanced at his laptop, thinking about the e-mail his dad had sent with a list of names he might consider. He knew he wasn't giving up control or responsibility. What really bothered him was that he wasn't cut out to be a manager. It wasn't a role he looked forward to playing. That was his sister Julie's forte.

He liked being his own boss, his only responsibility to get the job done for the company. If he had to start worrying about how everyone else was handling the job... His head throbbed at the mere thought of it.

Which left him precisely where? He found his thoughts drifting back to the home ranch. His great-great-grandfather, Lamont Lannister, had been the one to start the family cattle business after he'd settled in the West. Jake wondered if he'd ever in his wildest dreams thought it would lead to an internationally respected holding.

He'd been raised on that land, in the original house, or at least the part of it that remained. But no matter where he traveled, his heart was back on that ranch. He'd always had a love for the basics of ranching, the intricacies of breeding. It was a fascination he shared with his father. Of course he loved his job, but more and more lately Jake found himself thinking of the Double L. His parents still called that home, although they spent less and less time there.

It was too cold, his dad complained. His mom had surprised him by agreeing, and three years ago they'd bought some land in Arizona, close to their corporate offices there. Both parents were still integrally involved in the company, but his dad now indulged in breeding some newer types of longhorns, mostly for fun rather than profit, and his mom had become involved in several organizations in Tempe and was more relaxed than he'd seen her in some time.

The Double L, by rights, would go to his older brother, Tom. But Tom lived in Casper and wasn't much for the ranching life. Julie and his younger brother, Steve, were both married and enjoyed the city corporate life, as well. He supposed he did, too, as his condo was downtown, but he was rarely there. When he thought of home, he automatically thought of the ranch. *Where are you going with this?*

Quite honestly, he didn't know. Of course, his parents would jump on this with both feet if they knew. They'd say he was ready to settle down. He was the only unmarried child left in the immediate family. Fortunately Steve's wife had just given the family a third grandchild, so the focus was off him for the moment. He wondered what they'd think of Natalie.

He shook his head. From babies and settling down, right to Natalie. He needed a break from the near-constant travel, that was all. Natalie had simply come to represent the rest and relaxation he'd somehow lost along the way. He was making way more out of his preoccupation with her and the ranch than was warranted. He'd already been in two other cities since Chicago, and there were three more unscheduled trips now penciled in for the next ten days, one overseas. Maybe after that he'd take a weekend off and head out to the Double L.

Then there was New Orleans. Two days with Natalie with only a few hours needed for work. What would it be like to have the whole night with her? To wake her up in the morning and not have to rush off to the airport?

He wondered what Natalie would think of the ranch.

"Okay, enough." He set about unpacking. Besides, she was a city dweller, like his siblings. She'd probably hate it. One more reason not to call her at work and push what was, in every other way, the perfect relationship.

He dug out a pair of jeans and a sweatshirt, trying to ignore how little comfort he'd drawn from that conclusion. He had some work to do before his dinner meeting. The first of which was going to be to look at that list and start the ball rolling on training some help.

He'd get over the management duties part of it. It was bound to happen at some point. Although Tom would likely be the one to take over the helm of the company when his parents finally decided to fully retire, Jake knew the time would come when more would be expected of him than the rogue troubleshooting role he played now. He just wished he was more excited about it.

Of course, if he delegated more now, it would mean less travel, less chance of total burnout. Also less chance of scheduling time with Natalie. Unless he went ahead and pursued her openly, and to hell with the boundaries.

That made him pause. "Well, hell, Lannister, if you're going to make some changes, might as well start with the one you want most." And just like that, before he could change his mind, he scooped up the phone and dialed her office number.

Two minutes later and several tries to cradle the receiver later, he was still attempting to deal with the blow he'd just taken.

"I'm sorry, Ms. Holcomb has taken a sabbatical. May I direct your call to her temporary replacement?"

He'd sat there, dumbfounded, long enough for the person on the other end to repeat the message. Just in case he wasn't sufficiently blown away the first time. He'd managed to mumble something and end the call.

He stared at the stack of notes on the bed and snatched them up. He tore through them, knowing this was the only place she'd try to contact him. He went through the stack twice. No note.

"What the hell is going on?" He threw the notes on the bed. Was she still going to meet him in New Orleans? Damn! He hated feeling so bewildered, so helpless. Where was she? Did she need him? Why in the hell had she left her firm, even temporarily? He realized just how little he really knew about her. Where would she go? Was she home? Was it her pal, Liza? Her family?

He stood and paced the room. Should he call her place in New York? He had that number, too. He sat heavily on the side of the bed. If she needed him, she knew she could contact him here in Dallas. What was really upsetting him was that something had happened to her...and she hadn't turned to him for help.

He braced his head in his hands. *Wasn't this precisely what you wanted?* his inner voice taunted. *No snags, no real life problems, no annoying problems left for you to solve?* He shoveled his fingers through his damp hair. So, okay, yes, that's what he'd thought he wanted. He swore long and loud and flopped back on the bed. And it had stopped being what he wanted the moment he'd first made love to her.

"So where in the hell does that leave me?" he asked the ceiling. He glanced over at the phone and knew he wasn't going to call her. What he was going to do was start making some changes in his life. Then hope like hell she showed up in New Orleans. After that, all bets were off.

"YOU'RE ACTING like a child." Natalie waited outside her father's bedroom door. His *locked* bedroom door. "Okay, fine. I'll send Nurse Ratchet up instead." She counted to ten, then smiled wearily when she heard the lock click off.

She entered the room to find her father standing at the window, looking out on the rear formal garden. "I don't understand why I can't simply be left alone. I am, after all, a grown man."

If Natalie wasn't so tired of this discussion, she'd have pointed out the petulance in his tone. But that would get her nowhere. Neither would whining or kowtowing. No, what worked with her father, or at least had the best chance of working, was directness.

"Yes, you are a grown man. But even after this, you think you are indestructible."

He swung around, ready to defend himself, but she cut him off. Quietly, but effectively.

"I happen to love you. Very much. That's why I'm here." She found a small smile in the face of her father's sudden discomfort. It shouldn't be endearing, but it was. It was perhaps his greatest weakness, but one she forgave him for. His guidance and advice might be misdirected, but she knew he loved her. "I came home because I was very afraid that, left to your own hardheaded ways, you'd end up in the hospital again." Her breath caught and surprising tears rose to her eyes. "I don't want that to happen. I don't want to lose you."

Had he been another kind of man, he might have opened his arms and welcomed her into them. But she didn't expect what he wasn't able to give. That way she wasn't disappointed. He did have to clear his throat before he spoke, and she took her measure of comfort in that small, but telling, action.

"I'm not used to being dictated to, Natalie. I can certainly appreciate the scare I gave you and the others. I wasn't too keen on the experience myself." He looked to the window again. "For that I apologize."

"Dad—"

He lifted his hand to stall her, but remained facing the window. Apologies came hard enough to him, so she didn't push. "But I won't stand for your mollycoddling, Natalie."

She sighed. He was such a stubborn fool.

He turned, and she was taken aback again by just how much this latest episode had aged him. Or at least revealed the fragility of his health. He'd always been robust of frame and of voice and temperament. Larger than life, even though he was barely taller than her. Now he looked...well, like a senior citizen. "I hardly think making sure you've taken your medication is mollycoddling."

"There is a nurse here for that."

"And this is already nurse number—what, three? Four? It's only been ten days."

"I can't help it if they can't handle their responsibilities." He waved away the discussion, a common tactic when he was fighting a battle he might not win. "I didn't ask you in here to discuss the sorry state of medical professionals." He folded his hands in front of his thick robe. "You know I'm glad to have you back home where you belong."

Natalie knew where this was heading, just as she knew it was pointless to argue. "Shouldn't you be sitting? You're not supposed to be up for long periods."

"Nonsense. I spend far too much time in that bed as it is. Now, don't redirect the topic here."

She smiled then. "Sorry. I learned from the best."

That brought a grudging smile from him. "Yes, well, don't you forget it. But also remember you can't outfox a fox."

"Boy, don't I know it," she murmured beneath her breath.

He narrowed his eyes, but went on determinedly. "I'm proud of you, Natalie. Of how hard you worked for your degree, for the bar. I could use you. The family always needs a sharp lawyer. In fact, I have some files I'd like you to read over. I could use your advice."

Natalie wisely said nothing. He would pull her in with the promise of a legal position, but she'd be shifted into management in the blink of an eye. He'd want her in a position of as much power and control as possible, as he did her brother and both sons-in-law. Her sisters wielded their power in the boardroom with their stock holdings, and in the ballroom. The latter, at times, being more a center of power than the former.

She was the lone wolf, the one that had to be brought back to the fold and put in her proper position. Which was on a pedestal. A distinctly uncomfortable place, and one she'd sworn never to inhabit.

"You need to rest, Dad. We'll discuss this later." She went to his bedstand. "And you didn't take your two o'clocks."

For once, he let the discussion go. He was a fox and he well knew when to push and when to sit and wait. *Well, he was in for one hell of a long wait.*

She handed him his pills and poured some water out of the carafe. "Here."

He took them without argument—likely to put her off her guard. Well, she had been born and raised a Holcomb. She knew the game almost as well as he did. She moved quickly toward the door before he could resume negotiations.

She paused in the doorway. "I'll be back in a couple hours, after you've rested." For his four o'clock round of pills, she thought, but wisely didn't say so out loud. "There is one other thing—"

He'd taken a seat by the warmth of the immense fireplace and had picked up a sheaf of papers. He paused in the act of putting on his spectacles, and looked at her. Likely he was expecting her to admonish him for working, but she knew what battles to pick. It was enough that he was in his room, sitting and not badgering the house staff to bring his golf cart around for a little trek about the grounds. An activity she'd only barely managed to thwart this morning.

"I will need to be out of town next weekend. Just overnight. I'll be leaving early Friday and will be back here no later than Saturday afternoon." She'd calculated the time frame to reduce the risk to him as much as possible. Plus, she'd already scheduled a family dinner for Friday, which guaranteed he'd go to bed early just to escape the end-less nattering.

"Where are you headed?"

"New Orleans." She crossed her fingers behind her back that he didn't interrogate her further. She could stand up to her father with no problem, but she couldn't lie to him.

"Business?"

"Of sorts."

He merely nodded and went back to his papers, probably as relieved as she that this little interaction was over.

She closed the door and leaned back against it with a deep sigh. She'd realized soon after coming home that there was no way she could simply send a note to Jake explaining everything. She'd gotten in way over her head with him, had broken the rules they'd so carefully set. And now, with the situation with her father...well, there was simply no other choice but to end it with him. But this was something that had to be done in person. As much for herself, as for Jake.

At least, that was her reasoning and she was sticking to it. So what if at night, when she finally fell into bed, exhausted from tangling with her father all day in addition to taking the constant checkup calls from her various siblings, she dreamed of seeing him in New Orleans for entirely different reasons than saying goodbye?

Which was why she'd purposely set up her trip so that she'd have limited time with him. Her plan was to send a note and meet him Friday evening, end it, then cry herself to sleep, or maybe call Liza and pour her heart out, then get the hell out of there as early as possible on Saturday.

She pushed away from the door and headed toward the kitchen. Right now, she had other things to worry about. She had to give the cook an alternative menu to the one she knew her father had ordered. Steak and potatoes with sour cream. The man was a walking death wish. And she'd thought working for Maxwell & Graham was exhausting. She should be thankful, though. Her mind constantly occupied with keeping her father out of trouble, she only thought of Jake every other minute instead of every single minute.

She was going to New Orleans. She shouldn't be looking forward to it—it was going to be painful in the extreme. But her heart didn't want to hear that. Her heart was all a-flutter about the fact that she'd get to see him again.

Even if it was for the last time.

Chapter Thirteen

JAKE COULDN'T REMEMBER ever being so nervous. He paced the foyer of the French Quarter guest house where he'd reserved a room. He'd wanted something different, and this beautifully restored house at the residential end of Bourbon Street was perfect. Quiet and yet very close to all the excitement the Quarter had to offer. He could sit on his balcony and smell the spicy foods and hear the music that seemed to spill from every corner, literally feeling the vibrancy that seemed to rise like steam from the street below. All he needed to make it perfect was for Natalie to come walking through that door.

She'd never contacted him to say she wasn't coming. Had he not called her office, he'd never have known things had changed for her. So he'd left a note at the hotel where he would have been staying, telling her to meet him here as soon as she got into town. And now he waited. And hoped. And it was pure hell.

If she didn't show, he'd simply have to accept it was over and walk away. Yet deep down he didn't think she was the kind of person to simply disappear without a word.

Which left him with another dilemma. What if she did show up, but made no mention of what had caused her to leave her job? There was no reason to think she would, as it was part of their agreement not to talk about things like that. But could he pretend he didn't know? No. If she didn't say something, he would. That was the other decision he'd made. If she walked through that door, he was going to lay it all on the line and tell her he wanted more.

Which was why his palms were sweating and he felt like he might lose his breakfast at any second.

And then she was there, standing nervously just inside the huge plank door. "Hi."

He immediately noticed the difference in her. She wasn't in her usual business attire. She wore black flats, pleated black slacks and a short-sleeved peach sweater. Polished but not "lawyerly." Her hair was the same, but her eyes weren't. They were…sad.

He went to her immediately, but stopped just short of taking her into his arms, when she took a tiny but telling step back.

"What's wrong?" he asked, trying not to let his own anxiety show.

She looked beyond him, her gaze skirting the sitting room situated just behind him. "Is there someplace we can go?"

"We can talk in here," he said, nodding toward the sitting room. "Or I have a balcony off my room, if you'd prefer more privacy."

He could see that she actually had to think about it, which made his heart sink even further. Something was terribly wrong.

"Your balcony would be fine," she said finally. "I—we need to talk."

"I can see that." His tone was sharper than he'd intended, but she seemed too distracted to really notice. He motioned to the wide staircase opposite the foyer. "All the way up, second door to the left."

He followed behind her, his heart hammering in his throat. He'd finally found a woman he could get serious about, and she was going to walk. He wasn't an idiot, he knew damn well what she was going to tell him. It probably had to do with her taking leave from her job, although why that should change things, he had no idea. Whatever had caused her to make this big change, whether it was her family or because she'd had a sudden change of heart about her career or something had happened at the office or—

He froze on the steps. Or she'd met somebody else and had stopped working because she was going to relocate somewhere else. With *him*. He tried to tell himself it was an absurd conclusion to leap to, and yet that was the one stipulation they'd made. If either of them met someone else, it would be over, no questions asked.

Dammit! Why hadn't he ever thought about that?

He knew why. He'd been so wrapped up in her, it had never occurred to him that she might not feel the same. He hadn't dated anyone since he met her, not even casually. From the moment he'd met her, other women had simply ceased to exist for him.

She paused and looked over her shoulder questioningly. Realizing he was just standing there, he motioned her to keep going and continued climbing the wide, carpeted stairs behind her. Well, he only had himself to blame for the pain she was about to inflict on his heart, he told himself.

Apparently he was an idiot, after all.

He stepped in front of her and opened the door, then moved aside so she could go in first.

Damn, but she smelled good. His body leapt to attention as she brushed by him. His heart leapt right along with it. It was all he could do not to reach out and pull her into his arms.

"This is gorgeous."

He didn't even look at the room. He knew she was right; he'd chosen it specifically with her in mind. All the furnishings in the room were period pieces, each dated, many with a detailed history that was available from the hosts upon request. The fireplace worked; the marble mantel was topped by a huge framed mirror that reflected the bed on the opposite side of the room.

The bed was the real masterpiece, though. A hand-carved four-poster, according to their hosts, with a carved headboard and footboard, as well. It sat so high off the ground, there were footstools provided to climb into it. It was topped with a thick, down duvet and ringed with a canopy of white muslin to keep the heat of the afternoon out if they wanted to open the balcony doors. He'd thought it would appeal to her. Looking at her now, he knew it did.

Temper rose along with the pain. How could she leave him for someone else? It was stupid to feel so possessive over her, and yet he did. He wasn't the sort. Or he hadn't been before. But maybe that was only because he'd never met the woman who was supposed to be his. She belonged to him, dammit. And what was more, he belonged to her.

She turned back to him. "This is really lovely." He didn't miss the fact that she'd carefully avoided looking at the bed. "Is the balcony through here?"

"Yes." It came out as more rasp than word, as his throat had closed over. It was on the tip of his tongue to just go to her and beg her to give him a chance. But he wouldn't do that to her. They'd had an agreement, and even if it killed him—which it damn well felt like it would—he'd not make it any harder on her.

He cleared the lump from this throat. "Right through here—" He pulled back the heavy draperies and opened the doors, which, like all the other doors, rose the full height of the fifteen-foot ceilings. The balcony was a lacy pattern of wrought iron, covered from end to end with pots spilling over with bougainvillea and impatiens. But he noticed none of the lush decadence that had captivated him before. "Can I get you some coffee?"

She shook her head.

"Oatmeal?" It just popped out, but once he'd said it, he was glad he had.

It caught her off guard. And made her smile. "No. Thank you," she said, some of the familiar dryness back in her voice.

He'd missed that, their easy banter. Dammit, he *knew* her. There was no reason to dance about this. He sat down across from her. "What's wrong, Natalie? I can see bad news written all over your face." Better just to get this over with, he decided. It would be easier for them both. "You've met someone else, haven't you."

She looked so honestly shocked, it shocked him, as well. And then his heart took off and there was no quashing the hope that filled him.

"I—no. What made you think that?"

"You haven't let me touch you since you walked in. You said we 'needed to talk.' Never a good sign. We had one rule and that was if we met someone else, it was over, no questions asked." He shrugged. It was that or get up and dance around the balcony and shout down to the street below. "So I assumed since you looked all serious and sad that…"

She touched him then, covering his hand with hers. He immediately flipped his over and wove his fingers through hers.

"It's not someone else. But it's still—" She looked down at their joined hands, then out over the mass of blooms crowding the balcony's edge. "I still have to end this."

He tugged her hand until she turned back to him. "I think I need to tell you something first. Then you can decide what's best."

She looked almost afraid, as if her will to get through this was shaky already and this was pushing her to the limits. He shouldn't have rejoiced at that, but it meant her heart wasn't really in this goodbye. Well, if he had his way, no one's heart was going to ache today.

"I called your office," he blurted.

Her eyebrows shot up. "You did? Why?"

There were a hundred ways he could have answered that question, but he chose the simplest, and perhaps the most direct. "I missed you."

She blinked, opened her mouth, then closed it again.

He rubbed his fingers over the pulse in her wrist. "Things were happening...in my life. I had some changes to make. I...wanted to talk about them with you."

She simply stared at him. "Why?"

This wasn't so easy to explain. If she honestly didn't have the same growing feelings for him as he did for her, then this might push her away. But what in the hell did he have to lose?

"I have a confession. I know we made rules, but, well, I don't want to play by them anymore. In fact, I haven't been playing by them for some time now."

She frowned. "What do you mean?"

He looked right into those eyes that had haunted him every night since the last time they parted. "I know this is supposed to be a secret thing, where real life doesn't intrude. But you have been intruding in my real life. For weeks."

Her mouth dropped open and, surprisingly, a faint pink stain bloomed high on her cheeks. "But that's not true. I didn't even know anything about you until just last—" She broke off when his own eyebrows lifted.

So. He grinned and began to relax. He wasn't the only one who'd been drawing outside the lines. "What did you find out just last week?"

She swallowed. "I—well..."

He simply sat and waited.

"I was doing some research for one of the partners, and

it happened to involve a business in Wyoming. A ranching business."

"The Double L?" He was really surprised now.

"No. But...well, I knew your family was in ranching, too, so I kind of, sort of—"

She broke off and swallowed, then sat up straighter, and he knew she was about to put it all out there. It was one of the many things he enjoyed about her. When push came to shove, she didn't dodge. She handled things directly.

"I did some research on you. Your family, anyway. Just business stuff. I was...curious. I wanted to know more about you."

"And what did you learn?"

She frowned. "Not a hell of a lot." When he grinned, she gave him a look. It only made his grin widen. "Okay. You want to know what I learned? I learned your family is pretty much on par with mine wealth-wise, and they've been in this country almost since the dawn of time—but from there on, we're about as opposite as night and day. You have two brothers—one older, one younger—and one sister, all of whom work for the company, which is still run by your mom and dad. Your mom's brother and two of your dad's brothers and some of their children also work for them. Even the spouses have joined the happy harmony of Lannister Cattle Company.

"As a rule, the Lannisters steer clear of politics and any other spotlight-inducing endeavor, preferring to make their mark inside the industry, out of the public eye. Weddings and birth announcements are about the only things that make the papers outside the business section. You are one of the most philanthropic families I've ever come across, and possibly the only ones who work as hard to keep their charitable contributions out of the public eye as most companies do to keep theirs *in* the public eye.

"You went to college close to home—I'm guessing so you could continue working for your parents—and graduated in the top ten of your class with a double degree, one in business administration, the other in agricultural something-or-other." She leaned back and blew out a breath. "There's more, but you get the gist."

"Pretty formidable."

She shrugged. "I'm a corporate lawyer underling with an eye on a partnership. Research is my life."

He leaned forward. "So, why did you walk away from it?"

"Not because I wanted to." She took a moment, then finally met his eyes again. "It's a family matter."

It stung that she didn't tell him. But then, what did he expect? It was just an example of how little they really new each other. But they could change that fact.

"It's your family, isn't it," he said quietly.

She instantly became wary. "What do you know about my family?"

He looked directly at her. "Your family has been around since dirt and probably invented it. You have two older sisters and one older brother. He and your two brothers-in-law work for Holcomb Industries, your sisters work equally hard to keep the family name in the society columns to the best of their abilities, which are as formidable as yours are in research. Your mom passed away when you were a kid, your dad never remarried. You got an academic scholarship and put yourself through college and law school even though your family probably could have put most of your graduating class through college.

"You graduated early and in the top twenty in your class. Then, unlike your siblings, you moved away from the family manse to the big city, otherwise known as New York. You passed the bar on the first try and landed a job with Maxwell & Graham. You're the family black sheep because you don't work for Daddy, but his health has been in question of late, although your family has done an equally formidable job of keeping that information out of the press. I'm guessing none of them can function without you and probably drive you crazy." He leaned back and sighed. "And you're right. Our families are as different as night and day."

She looked stunned. "And you say *I'm* formidable?"

"I told you I wasn't playing by the rules. I'm a troubleshooter for an international company and not without some research abilities of my own. Unfortunately, none of this answered any of the real questions I had."

"What the hell else did you want to know? My bra size?"

He grinned. "That I knew." He tightened his grip on her hand, when she went to yank it away. "I'd say we both did some digging and came up short of our real goal. Which was to get to know each other better." He leaned forward now and tugged her forward, too. "I want to get to know you better, Natalie. I don't want to play by these stupid rules. I want us to see each other beyond just the occasional meeting in a hotel. I want to be part of your whole life and I want you in mine."

Tears sprang to her eyes, but they were not the tears of joy he'd hoped for. "Jake." She pulled his hand to her mouth and kissed his fingers, then gently disentangled hers. "If this were another time in my life, I might try to make this work. But right now, I don't see how we can. Your life and mine, especially now, are so different. I think it would just be too frustrating and too difficult, and we'd both end up suffering for the attempt."

"Natalie   "

"No, listen to me. I've thought about this a lot. Nonstop it seems. I was going to just send a note here, but I couldn't do that to you. No matter what you felt for me, you'd become too important to me for me to just walk away without a word. You deserved—we both deserved—a personal goodbye. You've meant more to me, shown me more about myself, than anyone ever has."

"Then, don't do this. Whatever the situation is, we can find a way."

She shook her head. "I don't think so. And even if you could, I don't think I can. Not right now. My life is completely upside down. For how long, I have no idea."

Jake wanted to argue with her. But words would be wasted. She was as stubborn about things as he was. So he'd go about it another way. Just as he'd shown her sides of herself, he'd show her how it could be for them if she'd only try.

"How long are you in town?"

His question seemed to catch her off guard. "My flight goes out tomorrow at noon."

"Then, we have almost twenty-four hours."

"Jake—"

"We started this relationship as a means to escape from reality. Your reality doesn't sound too wonderful at the moment. If you're not willing to give me more, at least let me give you twenty-four hours away from it. Let me give you—us—this."

"I don't know." But it was clear from the leap of excitement in her eyes that while her mind might not be sure, her heart definitely was.

He stood and pulled her into his arms, thanking God and every other deity he could think of, when she didn't push him away this time. "Please, Natalie," he said, brushing her lips with his. "Give yourself this. We can say goodbye tomorrow."

Unless, between now and then, he could convince her otherwise.

He kissed her then, taking her mouth and reveling in her instant response. "Say yes." She was breathless, and he could feel her heart pound against his chest. He nipped at her mouth, trailed his lips along her chin, then kissed that tender spot just beneath her ear. "Say yes." He didn't care if he seduced it out of her. He was a desperate man. He ran his hands up along her back, then down her sides, brushing his fingers alongside her breasts, then cupping her to him. She gasped as he pushed against her, and he had to swallow the deep groan of satisfaction in his throat.

"Say yes, Natalie. Stay with me one last night."

And every other night I can convince you to give me.

"Say yes." He turned and leaned against the railing, pulling her between his legs. "Say it."

"Yes," she said, trembling hard against him. "Yes. Now, can we please go inside?"

He grinned and wrapped her up in his arms. "Oh, yes."

Chapter Fourteen

NATALIE'S BODY was on a rampage. She wanted all of him, right now. Her mind was so clouded with need, she couldn't think straight and didn't bother to try. She had until tomorrow to regain her sanity and her strength to walk away from his man.

But for now, his mouth was on her and nothing had ever felt so damn good.

He tossed her so she landed in a fluffy heap of duvet and pillows atop the high double bed that dominated one end of the room. The muslin draping fluttered shut behind him as he climbed up on the bed after her. She distantly realized he'd left the balcony doors sitting open, but she didn't care. The sultry air filled the room, making her clothes stick to her skin. As Jake moved toward her, she didn't think that was going to be a concern for very long. And she was right.

He moved his hands to her sweater top, but something made her stop him. "No, let me."

She crawled to her knees and pushed him against the headboard. "There," she directed.

If this was truly to be their last time together, then there was more exploring she wanted to do. She'd intended to take the upper hand in Chicago, when it had been her turn, but it hadn't ended that way. They'd both been too hungry for one another. Well, her appetite hadn't abated, not a bit, but she was nothing if not determined to have her way this time.

Jake smiled at her, pushed some of the multitude of pillows up against the headboard and leaned back against them, propping his head on his hands.

"And keep them there," she said, nodding to his hands.

"Anything you say."

She couldn't help but notice the formidable bulge pressing against the front of his jeans. The same sweet bulge she'd felt against her out on the balcony. She almost lost her nerve right then, the ache between her legs intensifying.

She looked to his face instead, and there she found what she needed. He wanted her, badly, but he was also willing to let her do what she wanted. It was this trust between them that would be the hardest to walk away from.

She didn't think about that now; she reached for the hem of her sweater and slowly pulled it over her head. She had to smile as she realized what she had on. Plain bra and panties, no lace, no frills. "Not exactly the siren apparel I'd have worn if I'd known we'd end up like this."

"You're just fine," he said, his voice hoarse. "Fine."

Right then, she'd never felt finer.

She straightened on her knees and slowly unbuckled and unzipped her trousers, sliding them down her hips. Then she turned and laid on her back across the bed, lifting her hips and undulating as she pushed them down her legs, along with her hose and shoes, until they fell off the bed to the floor. She rolled toward him then, wearing nothing more than her panties and bra. She had no idea where her boldness came from. Actually, she did. As long as she looked him in the eyes, she had the power to do anything.

She rolled to her back and lifted her chest so she could unhook her bra from the back, then she slowly peeled the soft white cups over her breasts. She sighed as she covered them with her own hands, letting the straps trail down over her arms. A sudden groan from Jake made her jerk her eyes open. She hadn't even been aware of closing them.

"You're breaking the rules," she said on a stunned whisper. He was stroking himself through his pants.

"Sue me," he choked out. "Just don't stop."

Natalie had never done this before, had always thought it would feel somehow demeaning to… perform like this, for a man. Only now did she realize it was the exact opposite. The power was heady, in fact. And seeing him like this…she wanted to see him stroke himself for real. He'd done it once, one stroke, but she wanted more. Just picturing it made her entire body blush and heat at the same time.

"Take off your pants," she instructed.

His eyes widened a bit at the harsh command. But she was so needy now, she didn't care. As long as he complied.

And he did.

Not as slowly as she had, but no less provocatively. He all but ripped them off—jeans, briefs, socks shoes, everything.

"Shirt, too."

Gone.

She was shuddering with need. He was rock-hard for her. "Don't—" She had to gulp air. "Don't stop what you were doing."

He grinned now, and there was something almost primal about it. "I won't if you won't."

Could a person faint from pleasure overload when she wasn't even being touched? She wasn't sure, but she might find out.

He touched himself, watching her as he did so. She swallowed hard as he wrapped his fingers around the pulsing length and slowly moved his hand up, then down.

She raised her hands to her breasts. His deep groan as she

fingered her own firm nipples was one of the most gratifying sounds she'd ever heard.

She somehow managed to climb to her knees again, the trembling in her limbs so strong, she felt almost clumsy with it. His smile was bold, encouraging, the desire in his eyes so wondrous a thing that she almost climbed on him right then. But this wasn't over yet.

She turned her back to him and slowly slid her panties down over her hips. She bent forward just slightly and heard him gasp. It made her bolder, so she slid them down to her knees, then kicked them away, affording him a complete view of her most intimate self. It wasn't anything he hadn't seen up close and personal before, but somehow, displaying herself for him this way made it seem far more intimate...far more erotic.

His stroking increased and his hips were moving, as she peeked over her shoulder at him. And somehow her hand ended up between her own legs. She wanted to push him further, harder, higher. She let him watch her stroke her fingers along herself.

"Dear...God...Natalie." His groan was more a growl this time, his jaw clenched so hard, his throat so tight, she thought he was about to burst. And perhaps he was.

She crawled to him, moving between his legs.

"Oh," he grunted as she replaced his hand with hers. "My," he managed to say as she lowered her head. "God," he finished on a long, satisfied groan, as she took him deep into her mouth.

His hips rocked hard against her, but she didn't care. She'd never felt so strong, so sure, so...sexual.

Then his hands were on her shoulders, pulling her up. "Now, Natalie, for the love of Christ, now." He all but plunged her on top of him.

She shrieked as he filled her, thinking she'd never felt such a rocketing sense of pleasure in her whole life.

"Hold on."

She gripped his forearms, and he gripped hers as he moved beneath her. She wasn't even sure who rode who, and she didn't care. Moans filled the air—hers, his, she lost track. She was panting, screaming, writhing. Her climax was right there, just beyond her reach. He'd move her back, then pull her up tight, knowing just where to rub and just what to do to prolong it.

Until she couldn't take it anymore. She grabbed his hand and shoved it between them, pushing his fingers where she wanted them. Her climax was so powerful, she swore she saw stars.

She fell against his chest, mind and body swimming. But he wasn't done yet. He rolled her to her back so she was beneath him.

"Roll over," he said, his voice barely more than a rasp.

Her body was still clenching from the aftereffects, and he was still deep inside her, setting off sparks with every breath. She didn't understand what he wanted—hell, she couldn't have told him her own name at that moment.

So he did it for her. She whimpered when he pulled out. "But—"

Then she was on her stomach, and his hands were on her hips. "You liked being on your knees before."

She almost came again, just hearing him say that.

Then he pulled her back onto him, and she shuddered so hard she thought she might come. He pushed into her, again and again. God, he was so deep. Then his hands were sliding up her waist as he bent over her. She braced their weight on her hands, then cried out as his fingers rubbed her nipples. "Oh God, oh God." She'd thought herself wrung out, but Jake always seemed to realize there was one more waiting.

One hand stayed on her breasts, his thick fingers moving from one nipple to the other until she was begging him to finish her. From this position there wasn't the right friction, wasn't the right—

And then his other hand slid down over her belly. His hips were like pistons now, the entire bed was rocking. Her body seized up, every muscle tightening, as she silently begged his hand to get *there*. Now.

"That's it," he said, panting himself. "Hold on."

"Now," she begged. "Now, dammit."

And damn him if he didn't laugh. Breathlessly and with a little groan of his own. "God, you are so tight, so wet, so mine."

Yes, she thought. *God help me, I am.* "Jake." She was pleading.

"I want...to be...together...this time."

"Just...touch...me." They were both panting in the rhythm of his thrusts.

"Come for me...Natalie," he said in a rush. "Now!" And he slid his fingers over her just as he pushed as deeply into her as he could. He shouted as his climax finally thundered through him. Her shout was muffled by the bed as they fell forward, burying him more deeply into her, his fingers pushing into her pulsing wetness, both of them shaking and shuddering, until finally he rolled off her.

Natalie couldn't move. Wasn't sure if she ever would. Their heavy breathing filled the room, as did the sultry smell of their bodies. The air was heavy with it. She saw the muslin flutter and remembered the open balcony doors, but was so satiated she didn't care.

"That is possibly the most satisfied smile I've ever seen," Jake said, his voice gravelly and wonderful.

She turned her head to find him propped up on one elbow, looking at her. "Yours is pretty damn satisfied, as well."

"Appropriately so," he said, then sighed and rolled to his back.

"I'm surprised we didn't get a cheer from the street."

He laughed. "Are you sure we didn't? It was so loud in here, we might not have heard it." He moved. "I could go check."

Her hand came out to stop him. "Jake."

He laughed even harder, making her finally move enough to prop herself up on her elbows. She'd been with this man now in every way she could imagine, but not until now had she felt so perfectly comfortable in her own skin around him. What she'd done today, taking control the way she had, at least in the beginning, had changed her. Them. Again. As they seemed to change and grow every time they were together.

Sadness threatened to overwhelm her, as the reality of the fact that this was their last time— No, she wouldn't do that to herself. Not now. Nothing had changed. Just because everything felt like it had didn't mean it had.

"What's so funny?" she asked, forcing her mind back to the moment.

"You."

"Me?"

He rolled to her and kissed the tip of her nose, then tugged her closer and kissed her mouth. It was a lingering kiss filled with such tenderness that it made her eyes water.

"What about me is funny?" she asked, rolling to her back and pushing her hair from her face, giving herself a moment to clear her eyes.

"You are this unbelievable siren one moment, then so proper the next."

"What, because I didn't want you parading onto the balcony in your birthday suit, I'm a prude?"

"Trust me, this street has seen far more provocative displays."

"I don't even want to imagine."

"See?" He laughed again.

But she truly didn't mind his teasing. In fact, she liked it. Too much. She laid her head down and let her eyes slowly shut. Maybe if she just drifted off to sleep, when she woke up she'd have her sanity back, along with the strength she'd need to walk away from him. Because right at this moment, she simply couldn't imagine it.

JAKE HELD HER HAND as they walked through the French Market. He was surprised they were both walking and not limping. *Explosive* didn't begin to describe what had taken place a few hours ago.

Then Jake had seen the clouds shadow her eyes and decided it might be best to get them up and out. Besides, his plan wasn't to make love to her until she couldn't walk away from him. Although, he wouldn't have minded her using that tactic on him. Except, she didn't have to. He wasn't going anywhere. He certainly wasn't walking away from her and what they might have together.

But he wanted them to spend time together outside the bedroom, the way they had that morning in the museum. He ignored the fact that their trip to the museum had led them directly back to bed. They were combustible. He wouldn't be surprised if they were still dragging each other off to bed fifty years from now. If he were that lucky.

He tucked her hand more deeply in his and let her set the pace. She enjoyed the vendors, sampling the food in some, examining the artistry of the wares in others. He simply enjoyed her. He'd heard it said that falling in love opened your eyes to a whole new world, but he'd never believed it. Until now.

He'd always thought himself very aware, but it was as if everything was amplified now. He smiled. Life in Dolby stereo. But that was how he felt, and he was beginning to understand where the feeling came from. Now when he saw something, felt something, even smelled something, he thought of her, wanting to share the moment with her. So yes, everything was in fact amplified. By two.

His stomach chose that moment to growl.

She looked sideways at him, blushing a little because they were standing at a booth where she'd been trying on bracelets, and clearly the artisan had heard the rumbling sound, too. Jake just shrugged and grinned. "I'm a growing boy."

They were at the end of the market, and the lady pointed up the block. "You might want to try Otto's on Decatur." She beamed. "My nephew's place. He makes the best muffelattas."

"Thanks," Jake said. "I've never tried one, but I'm into trying new things lately." He squeezed Natalie's hand, making her blush again. She'd likely make him pay for that comment later. He couldn't wait.

"You two enjoy."

"I'm sure we will," Natalie said, and Jake saw she was trying not to laugh.

He scooped up the bracelet she'd been admiring and said, "How much?"

"Jake, no, really."

He ignored her. The vendor's eyes narrowed as she sized him up. In the end he didn't haggle and paid her named price. She merely shook her head and said, "Love. Makes men's heads go thick."

"Yeah," he said with a grin, "but it's good for business, no?"

She laughed and started to carefully wrap the trinket, but Jake shook his head. "Not necessary. She'll wear it."

"Oh, she will?" Natalie asked, but there was a teasing light in her eyes.

"Yes," he said, looking directly into them. "She will."

He enjoyed watching her pupils dilate. She fumbled with the bracelet. "So she will," she murmured, as he pushed her hand aside and clasped it together himself.

He shot a wink at the vendor as they turned to go.

"You keep that one," the lady called out as they left. "He is good for you."

Jake wanted to agree with her, but he restrained himself. "So, you up for trying a muffelatta? If I'm not mistaken, they're huge. We can share one."

She looked up at him from beneath her lashes and said, "Why, I'm sure I can handle a huge one all by myself."

Jake almost choked. Natalie laughed outright.

It was right on the tip of his tongue that very moment to tell her he loved her. That he loved how she kept him guessing, kept him wanting more.

He actually had to force the words back. But he *would* tell her, when the time was right. They walked up the block, the sun bouncing off the bracelet, almost, but not quite, as bright as her smile. He was thankful the clouds were gone from her eyes. For now.

And if he had his way, forever.

Chapter Fifteen

EVENING FOUND THEM boarding the *Natchez* steamboat for a dinner cruise down the Mississippi. They ate amongst the general chaos of the other couples and families aboard, then wandered out back to listen to a zydeco band. There was a small dance floor, and Jake headed right for it.

"Jake, wait."

He paused. "Come on, it'll be fun. All you have to do is shuffle and wiggle a little."

"That's just it. I'm not a good wiggler."

He looked at her. "I say different."

"Not that way," she retorted.

"Hey, wiggling is wiggling."

She pulled him close. "If I wiggle with you out there the way I do in private, we'll be thrown off the boat."

Jake pretended to think over the idea, then laughed when she swatted him again. "Yeah, okay, there are children on board, after all." Then he kept on toward the dance floor.

"Jake."

He loved it when her voice got low and warning like that. It usually just meant she was nervous. He could help her with that. He swung her around in front of him and took both her hands as they hit the dance floor. "Just follow me.

If you're not having fun by the time this tune ends, we'll quit. Deal?"

He was having to shout to be heard over the raucous singing and fiddle playing. She nodded. But only after sticking her tongue out at him.

He swung her around so her back was to his chest. "Be careful with that. We are in public." Before she could take aim at his shins, he swung her out again.

Three songs later, he was the one pulling her off the floor.

"Can we come back later?" she begged, still swinging her hips.

"Water" was all he managed to say.

She laughed and tugged him toward the gift shop. "Come on, I want to browse."

So they browsed, and he swigged a soda, and then she was tugging him back for more dancing.

"You're a quick study," he said, as she swung around him. He grinned. "I like that in a woman."

Her smile faltered, but just slightly. Enough for him to notice, even in the waning light. He'd been joking, but somehow it had reminded her of the tenuous nature of their relationship. He drew her close and shuffled her to the edge of the dance floor. He leaned his lips down to her damp neck and kissed a trail to her ear. "I like that in *my* woman," he amended.

He felt her pulse trip beneath his lips and felt the soft gasp against his skin. But she said nothing. He guided her off the floor altogether. "Come on, I want to show you something."

She laughed. "I thought we'd discussed doing that on board."

"Very funny." She rebounded quickly, another thing he loved about her. But she also used that sharp wit to mask whatever else she might be thinking. He'd have given a great deal to know what she was thinking right now. He tucked her hand in his and led her to the side railing. "Look—"

"Oh, wow. It's stunning." The sun was setting, painting a golden crescent above the city. They passed the RiverWalk with the white lights outlining the waterside shops, and he pulled her back against his chest and simply enjoyed feeling her against him as they watched the sun set.

"This is nice," she said quietly, after some time had passed.

It can always be like this, he wanted to say. It was getting more and more difficult to not press his case more directly. Time was drifting past as quickly as the river beneath them, and he wasn't at all sure she was even thinking about changing her mind.

"Tell me about your family," he asked, holding her more tightly when she stiffened against him. But dammit, he just couldn't stand there, holding her, smelling her, feeling her heart beat against him, and do nothing.

A moment passed, then she said, "You already know most of it. I have two sisters, one brother and a very stubborn father who I'm trying to keep from killing himself."

"Why don't you work for the company?"

Another long pause, then a short sigh. "I suppose I chafe under being told what to do."

He grinned, and leaned down and kissed her hair. "I don't know. I think you take direction really well."

She tilted her head back so she could look up at him, but she was smiling. "Don't be smug."

I love you. It was right there, burning the tip of his tongue. "So, you're the black sheep," he said, forcing it out over the sudden lump in his throat.

She settled back against him and watched the passing riverside. "I suppose. My sisters never minded having Dad direct them, but that was because they want the life he picked out for them. I guess that just rubbed me the wrong way. Probably because I'm too much like him instead of like my mom."

"I can't imagine losing a parent," he said quietly.

"It definitely sucks." She squeezed his hands at her waist. "She was sick for a long time. Cancer. I don't really remember a time when we weren't taking care of her, rather than the other way around. Of course, we had nannies and the like, anyway. I think my mom was always pretty fragile. Probably having four kids didn't help any, no matter how much help she had after we were born." She sighed a little. "Which is probably what my dad saw in her. His own parents were pretty tough on him, and here was this lovely, fragile Southern flower who wanted only to be taken care of. I think he enjoyed being her sun and moon. He did love her tremendously."

"Is that why he never remarried?"

She nodded, then he heard the smile in her voice. "That and there wasn't anyone else who could tolerate him. He's very set in his ways. She didn't push him as long as he took care of her, and he did a very good job of that."

"You said you've been trying to keep him from killing himself. Is that why you left your job? To take care of him full time?"

She stiffened again, but only for a second. Then she nodded. "He actually died this time—they had to revive him." She shuddered, and he pulled her around so she faced him, then tucked her against his chest.

"I'm so sorry, Natalie."

"I am, too."

"I take it he's not being a good patient?"

"Hardly. And my sisters mean well, but putting them in the same room with him... Well, let's just say they aren't cut out to be nurses. As for my brother... Well, this kind of thing is really uncomfortable for Chuck. He never handled Mom's illness real well, either. His idea of helping is to keep things running as smoothly as possible at work for Dad. And to stay as far away from a sickbed as possible."

There wasn't any rancor in her tone, but there was resignation. "So you got elected. I'm guessing you're the only one who can get through to him."

"You guess right."

"I'm also guessing he wasn't thrilled with your decision."

"Give the man a Kewpie doll." Now there was a touch of bitterness in her tone, but she quickly swallowed that. "I may have chosen to do things on my own and go my own way, but my dad has worked hard to provide us with everything we could ever want. Sometimes too much, although I'm the only one who saw it that way. And yet, he was there every day by my mom's side." She looked up at him. "Someone has to be there beside his."

He leaned down and kissed her. It was a long, lingering kiss filled with more emotion than he could ever remember feeling. "I know he appreciates it, Natalie, even if he resents having to accept the fact that he needs it in the first place."

"He wants me to work for him. He always has. In fact, he has been waiting for me to get tired of slaving my way up the ladder in New York and come home where I'll be appreciated. He doesn't understand that I want to stand on the merits of my work, not my name. Regardless, this isn't how he planned to get me home, that's for sure."

For the first time he heard the fatigue, the weariness in her tone, and pulled her more tightly against him, wishing he could infuse her with his strength. The very least he could do was provide a place for her to seek a bit of solace. He wanted to do so much more.

They stood that way for a long time, her face turned out to the river, his bent down looking at her.

"What about your family?"

It was quietly asked, but nonetheless it set his heart pounding. A tentative step, but a step. And she'd made it on her own.

He didn't know where to begin. He felt uncomfortable telling her about his big, happy family, when hers was anything but. "Well, you already know how many brothers and sisters I have. And you're right, we do all work for the family." He paused, not sure where to go from there.

She glanced up at him, a dry smile on her face. "You don't have to feel guilty because your family is happily functional, you know." She nudged him. "Come on, I want to hear how it's supposed to work."

He shrugged. "I'm not sure why we all get along so well. My parents' attitude, I guess, and we just all really enjoy what we do."

"But?"

He looked surprised. "But what?"

She moved back a bit and looked more closely at him. "But something. I can hear it in your voice. I know you like what you do, but...?"

It was disconcerting to truly realize how well she'd come to read him. He wasn't used to anyone questioning him about how he felt about anything. Outside his family, anyway. He liked it.

"I, well, as I started to tell you earlier, I've made some changes recently."

"What changes?" She shot him a look. "Don't tell me you're going renegade like me and leaving the family fold."

He shook his head, wanting to laugh with her but realizing that even more, he wanted to talk with her about what was really going on inside him. "I'm not leaving. I guess I've just come to a crossroads. I hired some people to help me out with what I do. I can't maintain the workload any longer."

"It's tough delegating, trusting other people to do things the way you would, as thoroughly as you would."

He'd thought the same thing, but it made him feel much

better hearing her say it. "Exactly. But I've met with them, started their training, and actually, I think it will go okay. Better than I thought."

"So that's it, then? You're feeling unnecessary?"

Now he did laugh. "No. That's not it."

She leaned back against the railing, no longer paying attention to their leisurely cruise. "So what is it?"

If he wasn't so caught up in trying to figure that out, he'd have enjoyed her absolute focus on him and his problem. But he didn't really have a problem. Or did he?

He finally shrugged. "I don't know, Natalie. I guess I wasn't too keen on moving into a more managerial role. I'll still be traveling, doing the work I was doing before, only now I'll be directly overseeing the rest of the troubleshooting team." He paused as if that fact were just now sinking in, and maybe it was. He laughed, but with little humor. "Troubleshooting team. Who would have thought it?"

"You're very successful, like the rest of your family. Why does it surprise you? Isn't it a mark of how well developed your business has become that you need more people to handle things like this? I mean, business will never run smoothly, so you'll always need this kind of support. I'd think this would be a good thing for all."

"It is, it is." When she put it like that, there was really no other way to look at it. So why did he feel so…unsettled? "I guess it's still all new and under development. Probably when we get it off the ground and running, I'll feel better about it."

She looked at him several moments longer, her expression a shade skeptical, but she finally smiled and said, "Well, I think you'll make a wonderful upper-management type. You're very good at giving orders." She wiggled her eyebrows, and he felt his entire body heat up. Just like that, he was primed and ready for her. He couldn't be sure, but he'd be willing to bet one look was all it would ever take.

Now, how in the hell could he convince her of that?

"Well, coming from someone who wants to climb to upper management and beyond, of course you'd be prejudiced."

Her smile froze. Only for a moment, but he was already kicking himself. He reached for her. "Go ahead and yell at me. I'm sorry, I wasn't thinking."

She shook her head, but went into his arms willingly. "It's okay. I'll eventually go back." She tried for a bold smile. "I'm young and still hungry. I'll get it back."

Now it was his turn to look at her more closely. "But?"

She gave him a look. "No buts."

"There's a but. I see it. Are you really afraid you won't be able to climb back to where you were? I know you, Natalie. You're a very determined woman. When you want something, I don't see anything stopping you from getting it." *I just wish what you wanted was me.*

"Thank you. I wish I had your confidence. It's pretty brutal out there."

He stroked her hair, and she shifted so she was once again leaning back against him. They were coming back to dock. Jake wished he could do something, anything, to keep them out on the river longer. Until he figured out how to make things work between them.

"What made you decide to head to New York? Has that always been your dream? Being partner in a prestigious firm?"

He'd expected an easy answer and was surprised when she was silent for a while. As open as they were being, he didn't think he'd been insensitive this time, but when the silence stretched out, he finally said, "I didn't mean to—"

"No, no. It's okay. I guess it's just that no one has ever asked me. In quite that way, anyway. I don't even remember why I decided to become a lawyer. Isn't that funny?"

It might have been, but she wasn't laughing. Neither was he. "Do you enjoy it?"

She laughed now. "You know, I've always been so busy trying to chart my corporate climb, I never really stopped to ask myself that. I mean, it's not supposed to be fun on the way up, right?" She shook her head, then swore and fell silent again.

Jake didn't know what to say. He hadn't meant to open a can of worms. Just as he was sure she hadn't meant to, with her earlier probing.

So they both were each lost in their own thoughts, as the boat docked and people began disembarking.

There were photos displayed for purchase that had been taken during the cruise. He spied one of him and Natalie dancing. She was whirling and smiling brightly. He was looking at her, and there was no mistaking the expression on his face. She didn't stop to look, still lost in her thoughts. He escorted her out to the lot, then said, "Wait here. I'll be right back."

"Jake?"

He just waved at her and jogged back up the line. He wanted that photo. He wanted that moment in time, a permanent recording of how he'd felt then. Because he had a sinking sensation that whatever had just taken place on board, in the end it hadn't helped his case at all.

Chapter Sixteen

NATALIE'S MIND was a complete jumble. She couldn't get her thoughts to stay in order; they kept careening from the evening she'd just spent with Jake—the dancing, being held by him as they watched the sunset, how incredibly at peace she'd felt standing there like that—to an eruption of feelings about the life she'd dedicated herself to. *Was she happy?* And that was all complicated further by the reality of her current situation with her father, which made even thinking about the other two things almost impossible.

Jake had remained silent on the long stroll back through the Quarter. He'd held her hand as they walked, as lost in his thoughts as she was in hers. He'd seemed surprised by her questions earlier, about his work. If her head hadn't been pounding, she'd have laughed at the two of them. Here they were in one of the most decadent cities in the world and all they could think about were their respective careers.

How pathetic was that?

Her smile faded. *Yeah, Natalie, just how pathetic was that?* Had she given too much of her energy and dedication to this big career she'd dreamed of? She'd always had some vague image that it would all be worth it in the long run. Dedication and sacrifice now, for the big payoff later. But what if the payoff was just more of what she was doing now? *Do you enjoy it?*

She glanced up at Jake. What if the payoff wasn't what she thought it would be? Was she walking away from what would make her truly happy?

And what the hell difference did it make? She couldn't pick either one. Right now, her priority was her dad's health and general well-being. No matter what might be in store for her down the road, at the moment she didn't have a choice.

A sudden blast of music had her looking around in sudden awareness of where they were. At the other end of Bourbon. Their guest house was several blocks ahead. And between here and there, it looked like one huge party.

The street had been blocked off and it was swarming with people. Clubs and shops lined the street, and music literally thumped in the humid evening air. People were dancing, laughing and drinking on the sidewalks, in the streets, even up on the balconies above. Strands of shimmering Mardi Gras beads were sold in every store and looped around everyone's neck. More of them were being flung by young men and women on the balconies in hopes of seeing a bit of skin flashed below.

Natalie's eyes widened at the bewildering number of men and women who were more than willing to comply.

"Did she really just pull up her shirt?"

Jake grinned. Apparently the sight of bare flesh had pulled him from his thoughts, too. "She sure did."

Natalie elbowed him, but she was laughing in disbelief.

"You want some beads?" he asked her.

"Don't even think about it."

"Hey, I wasn't thinking about you." His hands went to his belt, and there was an immediate roar of approval from the women—and some men—on the balcony directly above them.

"Sorry, ladies," Natalie called out, placing her hand firmly over Jake's. "And gentlemen. The only show he's giving tonight is for me."

There were general groans, but the throng quickly moved on to encourage their next hopeful. One of the girls did fling a few strands of beads, which Jake deftly caught in one hand.

"For your private show," the young woman yelled down.

Jake just laughed and pulled Natalie onward through the throng. "So, it's a private show you're wanting, is it?" He wiggled his eyebrows.

She didn't know what had come over her back there—only that if he was going to take his pants off for anyone, it was going to be for her. At least, this one last night.

Her heart squeezed painfully at the thought, and she ruthlessly shoved it away, along with the rest of her angst. She wasn't going to waste the last night they had beating herself up over things she couldn't control.

JAKE LED THE WAY up the stairs of the guest house and barely managed to get the door closed behind them before pulling her into his arms. He felt her pulling away from him, and he didn't know what else to do. But this was what had started it all between them, and if this was how they were going to finish, he intended to go out with a bang.

He pushed her toward the bed, lifting her up so her hips made it to the mattress. She went to pull him down on top of her, but he stepped back. "I believe someone said something about a private show?"

Her brows lifted in surprise, but that was quickly followed by a grin. "Why, yes, I do believe someone might have mentioned something about that, as I now recall." She scooted up to the headboard and relaxed back on the pile of pillows. "Do we require music for this particular show?"

Jake had only been teasing her, but her playful mood was infectious. *What the hell?* He strode to the balcony doors and pushed them open. A cacophony floated through the door, jazz mixed with zydeco mixed with the blues and plain old rock and roll. He turned back to Natalie and actually had a momentary attack of modesty.

It was one thing to tease, it was another to willfully put on a display. Visions of the display Natalie had put on for him earlier today sprang vividly to mind. He supposed he owed her. And she'd seemed to actually enjoy it, once she got started. Maybe he'd feel the same.

She was laughing now.

"What?"

"Cat got your fly?"

"I'm...getting there." He was not blushing. Not after all they'd done together.

She crawled to the side of the bed and motioned him over to her. "Do you need some help with that heavy buckle?"

"Ha-ha, very funny."

She just grinned and gave him a provocative once-over. "I see. So you're all tease and no fulfillment, is that it?"

"I think you know better than that."

"Well, then, show us the goods." She slid off the beads he'd put around her neck and dangled them from one finger. "If you're good enough, I'll throw beads."

"You're really enjoying this, aren't you."

"You have no idea."

He couldn't help it—he laughed then, and whatever inhibitions had come over him fled. Here, with her, was truly the one place he could bare all. And not just his flesh. Insecurities, doubts, worries, fears. All of them were safe with her. How in the hell was he supposed to let her walk out that door?

He resolutely shut that mental track down. A bang, he'd promised himself for them. And a bang he would deliver.

He lowered his head, then looked up at her from beneath

his lashes, a slow grin spreading across his face. His hands went to his belt buckle and slowly slid the leather flap from the loop. His head came up as he ripped the belt through the loops, and he took immense gratification when her smile faltered and her throat worked.

Well, well. Maybe he could get used to this, after all.

He moved his hips, just a little. Then, when he noticed her eyes were riveted to that motion, he moved them some more. Slowly, sinuously. He unbuttoned his pants and slowly tugged the zipper down, making sure his fingers brushed over him as he did. The beads slowly slid from her fingers, and he felt a surge of power that wasn't quite like anything he'd ever felt before.

He tugged his shirt from his pants and rotated his hips and body in full circle as he slid it up over his back and head, then turned to face her as he pulled it down and off his arms. He tossed it to her, and smiled when she snatched it out of the air. He swore he could feel her pulse pounding. Or maybe it was his. God knows, he was turned on.

He pushed off his shoes as his hands went back to the waistband of his pants. He ground his hips more deeply, moving closer to her as he did, then slid his pants over his hips and down his legs and stepped out of them, pushing off his socks at the same time, until he was left standing in front of her in only his briefs. Briefs whose limits were being sorely strained.

He moved closer to her, enjoying her visible swallow and the way she wet her lips. He pushed at the elastic band of his briefs as he moved right up in front of where she knelt at the side of the bed. She shifted, sitting with her legs dangling over the side. The height of the bed allowed him to move directly between her legs.

She groaned when he moved his hips so that he brushed against her. He slid his hands up and over his chest, reveling in the obvious pleasure she was taking from this.

"Take your clothes off for me, Natalie. I want you to feel me against you."

Her pupils shot wide, and he did see the pulse leap in her throat as she scrambled back and undressed for him.

"Now, come sit on the side of the bed again. And bring those beads."

She shuddered with pleasure, and he felt it ripple over him, as well. He only hoped he lasted long enough to do what he wanted to do. He moved between her legs again, rubbing against her until her hips began to move.

"Help me take these off."

She lifted trembling hands to his hips and with torturous slowness, peeled his briefs from his body until he could kick them away. The feel of the humid air caressing him made him twitch with pleasure.

"I think I deserve some beads, don't you?"

She nodded, still squirming as he moved up tight between her legs again, brushing her but not entering her. It was all he could do not to push her back and crawl up and into her. His own pulse was thundering now.

He reached out and toyed with one of the two strands she'd put back around her neck, twirling the emerald-green beads between his fingers. He pushed harder against her as he rolled the strand first over one nipple, then the next.

She gasped, the moan deep in her throat, and he couldn't help it, he entered her, hard and swift. She screamed with it, immediately pushing her hips against him and tucking her legs around him to keep him from withdrawing. "No, don't. Dear God."

He pushed back into her, hard, and groaned himself. "Hold me, then," he said roughly, and his knees buckled when she squeezed tightly around him. "Dear God is right," he managed to say.

Her head dropped back as she leaned back on her elbows

and arched against him. Her position pushed her breasts up toward him, and he took full advantage, rolling the beads again and again across her nipples until she was writhing and groaning, her eyes shut against the waves of pleasure he could feel rumbling through her.

He tugged on the beads then, until she sat up.

"Wrap your legs tighter around me."

She did, and with one arm around her back, he hoisted them both onto the bed, at the same time moving deeper inside her. They both trembled, and he couldn't stop himself from pushing her back into the mattress and letting his body take what it so badly wanted. She met him thrust for thrust, and he could feel himself losing the battle of control. But he wasn't done yet, dammit.

It took all he had to move out of her and slide down her body. He pushed her back when she sat up in protest. "Grab the headboard."

She looked down to where he'd slid between her legs.

"Trust me," he said.

She smiled then, and his heart turned completely over. Where would he ever find such a true match for him? Would he ever trust anyone as he did her, or be trusted as fully as he was with her? Again he shoved that aside as she laid back down and tucked her hands beneath the base of the headboard.

He climbed up her body and slipped the strand of violet beads over her head, then slid them the length of her body. He slithered them around her breasts, dragging them over her nipples, then let their coolness pool on her belly before slowly, so slowly dragging them downward. Brushing one bead after another between her legs.

"Keep your hips still."

"I can't," she moaned.

"Try."

She ground her teeth on a long, low growl. But that was

quickly followed by an even deeper growl of satisfaction when he lightly brushed the beads over her wet, waiting cleft. She screamed in her throat and she fought to keep her hips from thrashing, when he lowered his mouth over the beads and manipulated them directly on her swollen clitoris—until finally she lost the battle and screamed as she climaxed.

He let the beads slide to the bed as he climbed up her body, his tongue following the opposite path the beads had traveled moments before, until he was at her neck.

"Let go of the headboard and grab my hips, Natalie," he murmured into her ear.

She all but clawed him to her, which was good because he felt every bit as primal.

When he entered her this time, there was no gentleness in either of them. She commanded every bit as much force as he could give. He was surprised the bed didn't splinter beneath the fury of their lovemaking. She climaxed again before he finally went screaming over the edge himself.

I love you, Natalie.

The words had been so loud, so clearly spoken in his mind, that, for a moment, he thought he'd said them out loud. In fact, he wasn't sure how he could have kept them locked in a moment longer. But he managed, somehow. If he ever said the words to her, it would not be in the heat of lovemaking, even lovemaking as powerful as what he discovered every time they were together.

No, he wanted her to hear the words clearly, to understand how deeply he felt them and would always feel them, even if she did walk away from him. He understood her dilemma and honestly had no idea, given his current life and career, and her situation with family, how they'd make it work. Maybe she was right, and it would only lead to heartache and frustration. Maybe it was best to walk away when it was still perfect and beautiful. Maybe there would come a point in the future when they could meet again and make it work.

And maybe he would have to realize that he couldn't have everything he wanted, no matter how badly he wanted it.

He pulled her to him and kissed her as he stroked her hair. She nestled against him, against his still-pounding heart. He felt her relax, felt her fall asleep with the drumming of his heart beneath her ear. His eyes burned, and his heart squeezed. There had to be a way, dammit. He just had to find it.

When sleep finally claimed him, the solution was still beyond his grasp.

Chapter Seventeen

MORNING CAME far too soon. Natalie kept her eyes closed, hoping she could stay afloat in her dreamworld. A world that had her and Jake staying together for eternity.

But that wasn't going to happen. She opened her eyes. The room was still dark, even though a quick glance at the bedside clock told her it was well after daybreak. A deep rumbling sound shook the balcony doors, and she realized what had woken her up.

"Wonderful," she muttered. A thunderstorm.

Well, she supposed it was only fitting that the weather match her mood. She rolled gently to her side and looked at Jake, willing her heart not to ache. *How am I supposed to say goodbye to you?*

She'd woken up at some point in the middle of the night to use the bathroom. She'd been wrapped tightly in Jake's arms and found herself wondering how she'd ever slept alone. That thought, and the realization that sleeping alone was going to be that much harder now, had propelled her up. She'd closed the balcony doors; then, rather than sliding right back into bed, she had leaned against them and watched him sleep in the waning moonlight.

He was the proverbial right man at the wrong time. She'd

spent the next hour watching him and trying to figure out how to make things work between them. But she had no idea how long she'd be staying with her father. She'd even briefly thought about giving in the rest of the way and going to work for the family. Perhaps it wouldn't be too bad, maybe she would find her niche there.

But she knew that wouldn't be the case. Even if her father allowed her to work her way up, earn her place in the legal echelons of Holcomb Industries, her brother was not going to be an easy man to work with, and she shuddered to think of having to get involved in all the company politics. There were politics enough where she worked now, but at least they weren't tangled with family responsibilities and expectations.

No. Working for her father was not what she wanted. But what if Maxwell & Graham wasn't what she really wanted, either? What if clawing only led to more clawing? Is that what she wanted? She loved law, she knew that much, but why had she decided on the big firm partnership? Because it was prestigious and because she would be respected for working there. Respected by whom?

And that was when things had all fallen into place.

She'd crawled back into bed and laid staring at the ceiling. She'd chosen Maxwell & Graham to impress her father. To prove to him that she could make it on her own in a big city with a big firm. He'd have to respect that, right? And for what? So he'd finally be forced to admit she didn't need him?

She'd laid next to Jake, his heat and vibrancy filling the room even when he was asleep, and cried silent tears. *How stupid had she been?* And why had it taken her so long to figure it out? She shifted closer to Jake, feeling the solid strength of him next to her. Maybe because she'd never had a reason to question her choices. Until now.

So now what? She'd already come to the conclusion that

moving home for good wasn't the answer. She would have to get over needing her father's approval. It wasn't going to happen, and she wasn't going to continue living her life for him. It amazed her to realize that even in leaving supposedly to live her own life, her choices had been dictated by him, or by her relationship with him. If she hadn't been so stunned by the revelation, she'd have been furious with herself for not seeing it sooner.

Liza had been right: he *was* proud of her, of her success and her determination. She did have that, even if he wasn't happy with how she'd achieved it. And that would have to be enough. Because she was finished choosing her goals to prove something to others. It was time for her to figure out what *she* wanted. For herself.

And it shocked her to realize that she had no idea.

Now, in the gray light of dawn, she simply felt lost.

Jake was there beside her, his muscular body so tempting. But she knew she was going to have to figure out on her own what was next for her. And even that would have to wait until her father was well on the road to recovery. She'd stand by him, but she was also going to have a talk with him, explain herself, and let him and her family know that while she loved them and appreciated that they thought they knew what was best for her, she was going to have to find out on her own what made her happy. She only hoped they loved her enough to let her do just that, without censure or inducement of guilt.

She smiled for the first time in hours, even though her eyes burned. *Yeah, that was going to happen.* She knew her family too well and doubted they'd change, no matter how gently she explained herself to them. But she'd just have to live with that, too. She hadn't come this far in life because she caved when the going got rough. She just wished she had a clue where in the hell she was going.

Jake's hand searched her out, pulling her close as the thunder shook the dawn skies again. He was still asleep, and it made her weepy again to realize that he'd reached for her so naturally. She went willingly into his arms, and when his body grew more aroused at the contact and he finally woke, she closed her mind to everything and reveled in the slow, sweet lovemaking they shared while the lightning and thunder shook the windowpanes.

And afterward, when he was asleep again, she dressed and wrote him a note. She knew she should have been a bigger person and said her goodbyes directly to him. But in the end she simply wasn't strong enough.

Dear Jake, I can't even begin to describe what you've come to mean to me. If I were at another time and place in my life, I'd pursue this...thing we share with all my heart and determination. But we're both heading in such different directions—it simply wouldn't be fair to either of us to take this on as well. I will never forget you. You'll always be my secret thrill. Yours, Natalie.

At the door she paused to look back at him, tears falling. "I love you," she whispered, then closed the door behind her before she lost what little nerve she had left.

JAKE SWORE and barely resisted crumpling the note in his hands. The storm was over outside but it had only begun inside. He couldn't believe she'd left him sleeping! He'd never asked her if she had reservations anywhere or what airline she'd taken, so he had no way of finding her. But he knew her final destination: Connecticut.

The phone rang and he pounced on it. "Natalie, thank God."

"Uh, no, this is your father. Who's Natalie?"

Jake almost heard his father's grin, but wasn't in the mood. "Sorry. What did you want?"

There was a pause. Jake knew his father didn't appreciate the abruptness, but it was the best he could do at the moment.

"Well. I've been waiting a long time for this moment," he said quietly, the gentle humor still evident in his voice.

Surprised, Jake was at a loss how to respond. "What are you talking about?" He blew out a long breath. "Listen, I'm sorry for the way I answered the phone. It's…personal. But I know I've got meetings this afternoon and evening, and I'm on top of things."

His father actually chuckled. "Not from what I'm hearing in your voice. And I'm not talking about business," he added. "That's one area I've never had to worry about."

Jake actually felt his cheeks heat up. He and his dad had had many a frank conversation in their lives, but he couldn't recall women ever being the subject. "Dad, you don't have anything to worry about now, either. Trust me. I'll…handle it." He couldn't even sound convincing to his own ears.

"You know, just because I'm an old married man doesn't mean I can't appreciate how difficult relationships can be. In fact, *because* I am an old married man, I probably have more experience in that area than most."

"You and Mom are perfect together."

"And if you think it's been easy staying that way for over forty years, think again. Nothing worth having comes easy. And nothing has been more worth having than the life I've spent with your mother."

Jake paused and let the wisdom of his father's words sink in. "Even if it makes you question everything else about your life?" The words were out before he realized it.

There was a pause on the other end, and Jake wanted to

kick himself. He wasn't ready for this conversation. Hell, he'd just discovered the only woman he'd ever loved had walked, without giving him a chance to—*What? What else could he have done?*

"So, that serious, huh? But then, I think I got that from the way you answered the phone."

"Dad, listen—"

"When you're ready to talk, I'm here. Okay? The reason I called you is that I need some help."

Jake sighed in relief. "Sure, what can I do for you?"

"Jim called this week. He's going to retire."

Jim Mulligan was their majordomo at the Double L and had been for as long as Jake could remember. It shouldn't have come as such a shock; Jim was certainly well past the age of retirement. But it was impossible to think of the Double L without him.

"He's certainly earned it," Jake said, at a loss to sum up his feelings.

"I know, son. I know. But that leaves us with the task of replacing him. I'd like you to come out and help me interview new managers and foremen. With your mom and me spending as much time in Arizona as we are now, we're not going to be at the ranch much. So, I'm thinking of splitting up the job, making it a bit easier to manage."

"I'd be glad to, but shouldn't Tom be the one to help with this?"

"Jim will be there, as will I. But you know as well as I do that Tom has no real interest in the Double L. Neither do Steve or Julie. They're sentimental about the place, they were born and raised there, but it's your opinion and advice I'm asking for now."

Jake didn't know what to say. He'd never made a secret of his attachment to the ranch, but this still came as a surprise. And an honor. "I've got a number of meetings scheduled this week and that St. Louis deal to contend with, but I should be able to clear up a day next—"

"No can do. I need you out here by Tuesday."

That was only three days away. "I'm not sure I can reschedule—"

"So don't. Delegate, boy. That's the beauty of having people work for you."

"But they're still in training."

His father merely snorted. "Every one of those men and women was already primed for this job. All they need is the documentation and your position on the situation, and you can cut them loose. Best way to deal with things is to get in and get your fingernails dirty."

"But—"

"If something goes wrong, they'll know where to reach you." He chuckled. "You're so like your mother. It's taken me forty years to finally get her to relax and let go a little. I don't know why I think I could make it happen any faster with you." Then his tone sobered. "One thing I've tried to instill in all of you is the secret of true success. If you don't enjoy the process, then the reward is worthless. Because it's the process of the achievement that is its own goal."

"I think we've all lived by that. We all enjoy working for the company and take a great deal of pride in its success."

"Don't confuse success with fulfillment."

Jake shook his head. "I don't think I have."

"Perhaps. But goals can change, fulfillment can be found doing many things. Don't be afraid of acknowledging that. Pride should be about fulfillment. Lord knows, I've always been proud of you— Now, I've got to run. Your mother wants me to go to some civic luncheon thing she's set up. All a bunch of women—I have no idea why I need to be there. Anyway, we'll talk more when you get to the Double L. I'll be flying in on Monday." He paused, then added, "And bring this Natalie if you'd like. I don't know the situation between you two, but if some time alone would help, she's more than welcome."

Jake was still trying to understand what his father was trying to tell him. Natalie's name popping up only added to his confusion. "Uh, thanks, Dad. But I don't think she'll be coming with me. I appreciate it, though. Give my love to Mom. And behave yourself at the luncheon. I'm sure being in a room full of women won't be too much of a hardship on you."

"You haven't met this crew," his dad replied, laughing, then said his goodbyes and hung up.

Jake cradled the phone, but didn't move beyond that. Had his dad understood more than Jake had given him credit for? Maybe more than Jake himself had understood? Because he didn't need Jake's input to hire a majordomo—not when he had Jim there to help him out. But it seemed important to him. Important and specific.

Jake's gaze fell to the empty side of the bed, and his heart tightened. It was that or let it shatter. It would be a good time to head back to the Double L. He had a lot of thinking to do, and there was no better place on earth to clear his head…and his heart, than the ranch.

He took a shower, then got on the phone and took the first step to sorting things out. He delegated. It wasn't nearly as hard as he'd thought it would be.

If only the rest of his problems could be resolved so smoothly, he thought as he packed. He'd already made reservations at a hotel downtown for the remainder of his stay. He couldn't stay here. He glanced at the picture from the dinner cruise, but it hurt too much. He slid it in his briefcase, took one last look at the tumbled bed covers, the Mardi Gras beads in a tangle on the nightstand. The sun was peeking out from the remains of the storm clouds and shone through the balcony doors. Everything was bathed in a golden glow, the air washed fresh and clean, like a new beginning.

He closed the door behind him, wishing it were that simple.

Chapter Eighteen

"I LEFT SOME PAPERS in your room for you to look over."

Natalie sighed inwardly, but kept her voice even. "Dad, I've already told you that as much as I appreciate your faith in me, I won't be working for Holcomb."

She'd come home from New Orleans a week ago, and had had a serious talk with him about her desire to rethink her goals. She'd tried to explain why working for Holcomb wouldn't fulfill her any more than Maxwell & Graham had. For all the good it had done. Her father had listened up to the part about her uncertainty regarding her career choices and had skipped past the rest. She should have known better. But she'd felt it important at least to try.

"Just read the papers over." Her father was sitting by the fire in his bedroom.

The evenings were getting chillier now that autumn was giving way to winter, and she thought about having a fire in her own room. The sheaf of papers her father had been leaving for her would be the first thing she added for fuel. He slid his glasses on and turned his attention back to the documents he was looking over, assuming as he always did that she would be the dutiful daughter and do as she was told, no questions asked. Though she had no earthly clue why, since she never had before. He was nothing if not dogged, however.

Well, if he'd paid any attention, he'd know she was just as dogged. "Good night, Father. Don't forget to take your pills. Dr. Cunningham is coming by tomorrow."

He just gave a distracted nod and waved her off.

She shook her head and left quietly, going straight to her room. Her brother and both brothers-in-law were downstairs, but she wasn't going anywhere near them. They'd been twice as bad as her father, who'd naturally told the whole family about her "finally coming to her senses," as he'd put it. They'd done nothing but badger her about when she was moving back, which real estate agent she should use, what part of town was "in," and where she should buy her clothes. New York fashion was apparently far too edgy for the conservative Connecticut crowd. Her brother was faxing her daily with details of various projects they wanted her to work on. None of them had appealed to her, and even if they had, she'd have said no, since acceptance of any project came with the lovely bonus of having him as her immediate boss.

She loved her family dearly—someone had to—no matter how misguided they were and despite often wondering if she'd been adopted or simply left on the doorstep. They did mean well, and she could hardly fault them for being stubborn and determined; those were two of the very few traits they did share. But if she couldn't live with them, she certainly wasn't going to attempt to work for them.

She closed herself in her bedroom and, seeing the fire had already been started, immediately felt better. Maybe she'd just curl up and read something. Anything other than legal documents or contract plans. She flipped through some magazines she'd bought to keep her mind off Jake on the flight back from New Orleans, but they did their job no better now than they had then.

She sat on her bed. It was Friday, which meant he was in Tulsa. She looked at the phone, as she'd done at least a thousand times since she'd gotten back. She still felt horrible for walking out the way she had—but what had really changed? Her father's health was steadily improving, but she was no closer to making a decision on her future plans now than she was a week ago. Maybe she would just go back to New York. Maybe this whole thing with Jake and her dad had just shaken her confidence in her goals, and when she got back she'd feel that surge of competitiveness that had driven her this far.

She flopped back on her bed. "Or not," she muttered. She sat up again and grabbed the phone. It was early in L.A., but Liza could be out on the town by now. Well, Natalie needed to confide in someone, and it was way past time to tell her best friend what was really bothering her.

Liza picked up on the fourth ring. "This is Liza. Aren't you lucky?"

Natalie laughed, already glad she'd made the call. "Yes, I am. But I should give you fair warning that I'm about to sob all over your shoulder. So you might want to come up with a good excuse to get off the phone quickly."

"Not even if Brad Pitt was waiting for me."

Natalie laughed. It was that or give in to the tears that she'd been on the verge of shedding. "You do know how much I love you, right?"

"Of course I do. Now spill."

"And so sentimental, too."

Liza laughed. "Okay, okay. I'm in no rush here, so take your time and omit nothing. This sounds potentially juicy."

"You have no idea."

"Oh God. Hold on. I need to get some chocolate. I swear I wish I could just beam myself across the continent so I could see your face."

"Why?"

"You're going to tell me that what's-his-name, Preston Albert whatever, turned out to be a hunk and has proposed and you've accepted, thereby winning over your entire family and turning into a Stepford Holcomb all in one fell swoop."

Natalie choked on a laugh. "You know, you should be writing screenplays instead of doing public relations. Your imagination is frightening. You'd fit right in."

"You jest, but I have a secret or two of my own," she said coyly. And there was a trace of...something else in her voice.

Natalie scooted back on her bed and rested against the headboard. "Don't tell me, you're having some wild fling with a director—no, a producer, you'd go for the money—and he's convinced you to write something for him."

Instead of the sassy laugh she'd expected, there was a long pause.

"Liza?"

There was a deep breath, then she said, "I know this is your dime and you have something earth-shattering to share, so I should let you go first. But I can't."

Natalie didn't mind in the least. In fact, this was the first time in a week she could honestly say something was taking her mind off Jake and the rest of her problems. "No, please. Share, share."

"Okay, but we're going to get back to you. I am armed with chocolate now."

"Just spill it."

"I'm not dating a producer. In fact, I'm not dating anyone." She didn't let Natalie comment, but hurried on to explain. "After Conrad, I had a personal epiphany of sorts. I'm almost thirty and I'm just tired of fooling around with anyone who catches my fancy. I don't have the energy for it anymore. Or maybe I don't have the heart. I'm not sure. What I am sure of is that I don't want to play anymore. I'm only going to go out with someone who really catches my attention and who I think is worth my time and effort."

"Whoa."

Now there was a smile in Liza's voice. "Yeah, I know."

"Good for you, Liza."

"Well, of course, I knew you'd approve, but there's more to it than that. I've also realized that most of my friendships, except with you, are superficial. And that's because they are all business related. It's all one big game out here, and while I love it and can't honestly imagine not being in the thick of it...I don't know. You're going to think I'm crazy, but I decided that rather than be the one who gets other people the deals, maybe I'd get myself one." She laughed, but there was a definite vulnerability to it that Natalie had never heard before. "So you really weren't that far off, but I'm doing this for me. Not to impress a guy, and not because it will get me something. All I want is the satisfaction of knowing I'm doing this for me. Something that fulfills my needs instead of someone else's."

Natalie was nodding the whole time. "Maybe this is why we're so close. We even have our major life crossroads at the same time."

That got Liza's attention. "We are? Do tell."

"Well, first I have to tell you how proud I am of you. Not only for realizing you needed to make a change in your life, but for having the guts to do something about it once you realized it. I've realized I need to make a change, too, but I have no idea what I want to do about it."

"You're not going back to Maxwell & Graham? You know, I can't say I'm surprised. I never saw you as the type to always slave for others. Even partners there have hierarchy. It's not you."

That made Natalie pause. Liza just might have hit the nail on the head. "Well, that explains why I can't work for my family, either. I love them, but you're right, I need to be on my own. I've explained that to them—"

"Oh, and I'm sure they're hearing everything you have to say. How many proposals have they sent your way? Are your sisters shopping for your house? Do you have a list of acceptable designers to wear, and when is the big coming-out party?"

"You know them too well," Natalie said, laughing.

"Which is why I'm glad I'm not with you at the moment. I now wish I could beam you here, instead." Her tone shifted, grew gentler. "You sound like you could use the break. Think things out, figure out what you do want."

"I wish I could," she said with a deep sigh.

"Well, then, why don't you? You know, I have some contacts out here in entertainment law. Maybe—"

"Thank you, Liza, but that's not for me, either. You're right, maybe I do need to work for myself." It was such an obvious choice, she wasn't sure why she'd never thought of it before. But what kind of practice did she want? And where? Her mind spun with the possibilities.

"God, I'm doing the same thing your family is. I'm sorry. I just want to help." Liza paused, then said, "Wait a minute. You said there was juicy stuff. If it's not Preston Albert, then who?"

"What makes you so sure there is a 'who'?"

"I might have turned over a new leaf, but I have a whole tree's worth of old leaves, most of them with men's names scratched on the back. I know when a man is involved. It's a gift. Or a curse. So go on, tell Liza all about him."

"Okay, okay, so you're right. It's about a man. His name is Jake." Natalie felt a little of the weight lift already, just saying his name. "I should have told you about him earlier."

"There's been an earlier? Just how long has this Jake been in the picture?"

"Since the night of Conrad's big bash at The Maxi."

Liza was nothing if not sharp; she put it together in a blink. "Oh my God. Jake Lannister. You went out for more than coffee, didn't you." She hooted. "Oh, this is great! Here I am feeling pangs of guilt for all my bad-girl ways, and all along you're out there— Exactly what were you out there doing?"

Natalie groaned. "God, what *didn't* we do?"

There was a *thunk,* followed by some hollow-sounding noises as Liza picked the phone back up. She started to talk, then had to stop to clear her throat. "You go, girl. I take it this has been going on for more than that one night?"

"Oh, yeah."

"If I wasn't so blown away, I'd be hurt."

"I know, and I'm sorry I didn't tell you. It was so…I don't know, so different from anything I've ever done."

"What, you were ashamed? I'm the last person—"

"No, no, I wasn't ashamed. It was just, well, it wasn't exactly a normal relationship. We were sort of just together for…"

"The sex?" Liza hooted even louder now. "I *love* this!" She actually gave a cheer.

Natalie let her have her moment; she certainly owed her that much.

"All I can say is, it's about damn time," Liza went on. "I think this is great. So what happened?" She didn't even let Natalie respond. "Oh, no! The same thing as Conrad. You fell for him and he dumped you."

"No, no, that's not it. I think we both sort of fell. But I was the one who left."

"You *what?* Wait a minute, here. Let me get this straight. The sex is so great that even you were willing to compromise your oh-so-strict moral code to see this guy. And you know I want details so bad it's killing me even though you probably haven't relaxed those codes enough to tell me.

Dammit. Anyway, the sex is great, the guy is sweet, you fall, he falls—and *you* walk away? What's wrong with you?"

Only Liza could make her laugh at a time like this. "Gee, Liza, I'm so glad I turned to you in my moment of pain and heartache."

Liza had no remorse—not that Natalie had expected any. "You're going to have to explain this to me. Connect the dots, here."

Natalie sighed now, no longer feeling like laughing. "He comes from a big family, too."

"Yeah, yeah, they're into cows or something, right?"

"Cattle. And his bottom line is right in the same ballpark as mine, wealth-wise."

"Match made in heaven. You both have money, you both come from a family business. What, you don't want to spend your life with cows?"

"Cattle. And I never even thought about that, because I can't see how our lives could even get to that point. He's a troubleshooter for the company, he travels all over the world."

"Then, how did you make it work this far?"

"We...well, I traveled a lot, too. When our paths crossed, we—"

"Had wild, uncontrollably lustful sex," Liza happily supplied.

Natalie refused to blush or feel guilty. And with Liza, she didn't. "In fact, yes. But it got to be more than that."

"How many times did you see him?"

"Three. I know, I know, that doesn't sound like much, Liza, but I can't explain to you what it was like. He's—" She couldn't finish, but she didn't have to.

"I understand," Liza said. "Quantity isn't what it's about. It's quality. When it's the right person, your heart just knows." She laughed, but there was little humor in it. "My heart's just a little slow on the uptake is all. I mean, what was I thinking with Conrad, anyway?"

Natalie smiled sadly. "I guess maybe that's the answer for me, too."

"Is Jake a jerk, too?"

"No, not at all."

"Then, you're the jerk."

Natalie laughed. "Gee, tell me how you really feel."

"So, he travels a lot and you don't know what you want to do with life. It sounds like you know one thing you want, anyway. You want him. Was he willing to try?"

Natalie opened her mouth to argue, but there was no argument to make. "I am a jerk," she said finally.

"Exactly. Can you call him?"

"I have his itinerary, at least for another couple of weeks, anyway."

"When is the next date?"

"Now. He's in Tulsa."

"And you're talking to me when you could be calling him. This call is so over."

Natalie laughed, but there were tears in her eyes, as well. "I didn't tell you all of it. I, well, I saw him a week ago and I sort of left without really saying goodbye. He might not be happy to hear from me."

"Think back to the last time you spoke to him, looked in his eyes, listened to his voice. And then ask yourself if he'll want to talk to you."

Liza's words triggered a montage of images: the two of them together, both in bed and out. It made her body achy with need...and her heart simply ache.

"I honestly don't know, Liza."

"Well, there's only one way to find out."

"Yeah. I know."

"Call me back if you need to, okay? I'm in for the night."

"I will. And Liza? Thanks."

"Yeah, yeah," she said softly. "Thank me later, after you talk to him."

Natalie hung up, but it took her a full twenty minutes to work up the courage to pick up the phone again. She called the hotel, but no one by that name was registered. She wasn't sure what to think. Had his itinerary changed? It was certainly possible.

She dialed Liza back, not wanting to keep her in suspense. "He's not there," she said, when Liza picked up.

"When is the next date on the itinerary?"

"Wednesday. St. Louis." Natalie already felt better; Liza's matter-of-fact tone quelled her panic.

"So, you call him there. Or you track him down at work."

"No. I'm not going to interrupt him with something like this at work. We sort of agreed to never do that." Although, he'd called her once. Still, this was not the sort of call to make while someone was at work. It would be better if he were alone in his hotel room. That way they could talk frankly.

"What do I say to him, Liza?"

"That you changed your mind. That you can't live without him and want to find a way to make it work. He'll have to pick up the ball from there. You'll figure it out."

"I hope so." She hung up, but it was a long time before she went to sleep that night.

It was an even longer four days till Wednesday.

She didn't let herself hope for too much, but when she called the hotel in St. Louis and he wasn't registered there, either, she realized she'd hoped a great deal more than she'd thought.

She was devastated. He'd never changed his itinerary before. One change wasn't unusual. But two? In a row? And immediately after New Orleans? No, he was making sure it was over.

Liza urged her to call him at work, so Natalie finally broke down and did it. Only to find he wasn't there, either. When she asked where she could contact him, the secretary suggested she leave a message, instead. And what in the hell was she supposed to say? She left her name. But there had been no return call.

She'd hurt him and she'd also given him her final answer. He'd taken her at her word.

Now she'd have to live with that.

Chapter Nineteen

NATALIE WINCED as Sabrina's brittle "kissing up" laugh filled the air. She saw her sister fawning over Ned Tarlington, CEO of TarlComm Corp., who was at least a hundred years old. He was grinning and so was Rina, so that laugh had probably just added a few zeroes to his donation check. Natalie just shuddered.

It had been three weeks since her unsuccessful attempt to contact Jake, and she was no closer to healing her broken heart or figuring out what she was going to do next. But one thing she wouldn't be doing was hosting charity luncheons like this one. Not if it meant flirting with old guys and laughing like Barbie on speed. Honestly, you'd never know her sister had a degree. Natalie wasn't even sure Sabrina remembered.

She sipped her tea and wished like hell she was anywhere but here. Jake's face swam into her mind. As it was wont to do about, oh, every other minute. Another reason for her foul mood. No Jake, ever again, *and* she had to pretend she cared about— Hell, she wasn't even sure which cause they were supporting this week. Whichever one got them the opening spot on the five o'clock news and first mention in the society column.

She pushed her grilled pineapple and zucchini pasta curls

around on her plate, absently wondering who in their right mind had thought those two things should ever be cooked together, and managed a smile for one of her dad's many vice-presidents and his wife as they passed by. She speared a noodle, but let her fork drop back to her plate when it made a weird squishing noise.

She'd expertly avoided her brother and both of her sisters through the entire event. They'd threatened to announce her arrival at Holcomb Industries today, and she'd threatened to kill each and every one of them if they did. Okay, so she'd done that in her head. Out loud she'd merely voiced her concern that this was to be her father's day, and any announcements about her future plans, which she pointlessly reminded them were not concrete, should be held for another time.

Of course, it would have been better if she could have given them those concrete plans, but since she didn't have any, there wasn't anything she could do about it.

And it didn't help that she couldn't stop thinking about Jake. Everything reminded her of him. Liza was upset with her because she refused to call him at work again, but her heart had taken enough of a beating. She'd heard the silent message he'd sent loud and clear. If he'd wanted to hear from her, he would have called her back.

Which left her here. At a luncheon with a bunch of people she didn't know and didn't want to know. Maybe this was her clue. If she couldn't figure out what would make her happy, maybe she should do what would make everyone else happy. Maybe she could even learn to like pineapple-zucchini pasta.

If Jake fed it to her, maybe.

She tossed her fork down and stood up. Enough. She was making herself sick with all her moping and whining. It didn't help that one stray thought of him had set her body off. Again. As often as thinking about him pained her heart, her stupid body went on full alert every time. And Liza hadn't helped any by not-so-casually mentioning that Jake had probably ruined her sexually for any other man. Natalie would have hated her for that, if it weren't quite probably true.

God, she had to stop this. She stood and searched the crowd for her father. This was his coming-out party, of sorts. Not that he was happy about it. He'd envisioned a black-tie dinner party or an A-list soiree, something of that nature. Tea parties weren't generally his thing. But she'd argued that he needed to take small steps. His doctor had given him the go-ahead to move slowly back into the business, on a greatly reduced schedule. Her brother had been running things fairly efficiently in her father's absence, and she knew they all hoped he'd ease gracefully into a sort of semiretirement.

This benefit was a start in that direction. It was being held at their country club, with her sisters as hostesses, so he was among both business associates and family friends. Not too taxing, yet public and important enough to assuage his ego.

She spied him talking to Mrs. Fentweather, head of the ladies' auxiliary at the club. Natalie felt a momentary pang of guilt as she watched her father force himself to ignore the ungodly peacock feather hat she wore, the fronds of which were bobbing and weaving around his head and into his drink, all the while feigning interest in Lord only knows what cause she was spouting on about. She smiled and silently applauded him as he deftly foisted the old biddy off on an unsuspecting board member. *Smooth as always, Dad*.

She was forced to admit that he looked good. His color was back and his weight up. Only she would notice the tiny lines of fatigue that pulled at the corners of his mouth. Thankfully, the event was nearing conclusion. She'd have to call the house and make sure his room had been made up so he could rest a few hours before dinner.

Her gaze narrowed when he sipped at something clear and fizzy. No alcohol, he'd agreed. But then she spied the twist of lemon, realized it was probably sparkling water, and relaxed. For all his general bullheadedness, he'd essentially followed his doctor's wishes. Well, with her there forcing him to. But regardless of how he'd gotten there, she was finally beginning to believe that he was really going to be okay. And that he might even stay that way for a while.

Which meant she'd better come up with some plans soon or the next luncheon would be honoring her coming home to work at Holcomb.

Maybe she would take Liza up on her offer of a retreat. The never-ending L.A. sunshine might be just the thing to help her clear her head. And her heart.

Just then, Melissa came up behind her and tugged her elbow, almost making her spill her drink. "Natalie," she hissed, "there is someone here looking for you."

Natalie managed to save her dress from being splashed and turned to face her sister. If the tone Melissa had used hadn't made it clear, her sister's expression did. Whoever had arrived was *not* on the approved guest list. Which didn't make sense to Natalie. She hadn't invited anyone because she didn't know anyone, and even if she had, she wouldn't have subjected a friend— Oh! She craned her neck, suddenly feeling tons better and even a bit guilty for all her mean thoughts. "Is it Liza?"

It had to be. Liza could hobnob with the best of them, and had—but this wasn't L.A. and her family had limited acceptance for anything that didn't drip blue blood. Or tasteful diamonds and pearls. Natalie wouldn't put it past Liza to show up wearing thigh-high leopard-print boots and a spike wig. But rather than panic, she grinned. This was exactly what she needed: something to shake her out of her heartbroken stupor.

Her sister's frown was as deep as Natalie's grin was wide. She smoothed a finger over Melissa's cheek. "You'll get wrinkles scowling like that, you know." Her sister's expression smoothed with almost comical swiftness, but Natalie was too excited and relieved to enjoy it. "Where is she?"

"Oh, for heaven's sake, it's not Liza. It's some—"

She never got to finish. The crowd had gone suddenly silent except for a few gasps and one or two *Oh my*'s.

Confused, Natalie turned toward the door...and froze when Jake came striding through the crowd.

She blinked. Twice. But it still looked just like him. The outfit had thrown her off. He was wearing faded jeans, well-worn cowboy boots, his beat-up leather jacket...and what had to be a Stetson. It all looked incredibly good on him. But more than that, he looked at home in them.

He stopped right in front of her, and Natalie was fully aware that every eye in the room was on them, her family's most of all.

"Hi." She was totally flummoxed by his sudden appearance. Her heart was pounding so hard, it was like a drum in her ears, and her insides were all but quivering with unstoppable joy. Her mind was simply mush.

"How is your father?"

"What?" Of all the possible opening sentences she could have imagined—and she'd lost a ton of sleep imagining every possible scenario, or so she'd thought—this never would have made the list.

"My father is doing really well."

"Good, I'm really glad to hear that."

Melissa shouldered her way between them. "I'm very sorry, but this is a private function and—"

That snapped her out of it. "Oh, for heaven's sake, Lissy, get a grip." She turned to the rest of the crowd, and for the first time in her life couldn't have cared less what any of them thought of her or the situation. "I'm sorry for the interruption, everyone." Then she took Jake by the elbow and said, "We'd better step outside if we're going to have any hope of a conversation."

Jake merely shot the crowd that grin of his, tipped his hat and followed her. Natalie swore she saw several women fanning their faces as he strode past. It shouldn't have made her smile, but it did. She had no idea why he was here or what he planned to tell her, so she had no business letting herself get remotely excited about—

They'd barely made it through the doors into the lobby area when he took hold of her arm and spun her back to him. "I know this is possibly the worst time and place to do this, but I couldn't wait any longer. I called at your house and they gave me directions here."

"That's—that's okay. Worst time to do what?"

"I haven't been able to stop thinking about you. I know you think we don't have a chance, but—"

Now she interrupted him. "That's not true. That's why I called you."

He stopped, seemed stunned. "It isn't? You did?"

Hope began to unfurl inside her heart. "I tried to contact you in Tulsa and again in St. Louis, but the hotel didn't have you registered. I took that as a sign that you didn't want to hear from me again, but Liza talked me into calling you at work. You weren't there, and I didn't know what to say, so I just left my name."

"You're kidding. I never got the message. I'm…I'm not working for Lannister Cattle. At least, not directly." He looked honestly confused, but that was nothing compared to her confusion.

"You're not working for your family?"

He was still shaking his head. "I didn't know. God, I can't

believe—" He shook it off and turned back to her. "I'm running the Double L."

"So why did you come here?"

He shrugged, and that vulnerable look he sometimes got, the one that melted her heart, flickered over his face. "Because I love you. I never told you. And with all the other decisions I've made, that's one thing I'd decided to do. I should have told you the first hundred times I wanted to." He fingered the brim of his hat. "Maybe you wouldn't have left me in New Orleans."

"Maybe I wouldn't have." *He loved her!* She could hardly think straight, but it was important that she did because she had to explain. "But maybe I would have. I...a lot of things happened to me that night in New Orleans. I came to some conclusions about why I wasn't going back to Maxwell & Graham, but no idea where I did want to go. And I still had my dad to worry about and help. I didn't think it was fair to drag you into my life when I had no idea which end was up at any given moment."

"I'm willing to be part of your life no matter where it's headed. Just tell me one thing. Will you give me—us—a chance?"

"Yes. I do love you, Jake."

He whooped and swept her up in his arms. As he spun her around, she vaguely noticed that everyone was packed at the doorway, watching the entire exchange. She didn't care. She threw her arms around his neck and held on tight. He was kissing her before her feet touched the ground, not that she could feel the ground, anyway.

He tasted better than she remembered, and she wanted all of him right that very second. She fought for control, the clearing of a throat behind her helping her along, and managed to disengage herself from Jake. But she grabbed his hand as she turned to face the owner of the cleared throat.

"Dad, this is Jake Lannister."

Jake offered his hand. "How do you do, sir. I'm very pleased to meet you. I've heard a great deal about you."

If her father was surprised by the polished way Jake spoke, so at odds with his cowboy-fresh-off-the-range appearance, he didn't show it. *Smooth as always, Dad,* she thought again with a tender smile, even as her heart continued to pound.

"Yes, well, I would like to say the same, but my daughter hasn't spoken of you. I take it the two of you are more than casual acquaintances?"

Now Natalie blushed. "Dad."

He looked squarely at her. "I'm only commenting on how things look. If I'm misunderstanding, please enlighten me."

"No, you aren't misunderstanding. I met Jake several months ago in New York."

Jake stepped forward. "I understand she's been staying with you, and I'm sure her help has been immeasurable, but I'm hoping you can spare her for at least a short while. I'd like to take her to Wyoming."

"Wyoming?" Both Natalie and her father spoke simultaneously. She might have heard echoes from her sisters still in the doorway as well.

"And why are you asking my father? I'm a grown woman, I—"

"Hush, Natalie, let the man speak," her father said. "It's obvious the boy was raised to respect his elders. And I respect *that.*"

Natalie only rolled her eyes, but then Jake tugged her around to face him. "I want to show you the ranch, Natalie."

"Your family is in ranching, you say?" her father asked.

"Yes," he said, turning back to her father. "Lannister Cattle Company."

"I don't think I've heard of them, but then, I don't have any dealings in that area."

He grinned. "We've been around almost as long as Holcomb Industries has."

Her dad chuckled at that. "Well, that's saying something right there." He turned to Natalie. "We won't need to have you involved in any meetings here for a while, so if you'd like to take a short vacation, I don't see why—"

Natalie surprised her father and everyone else by moving away from Jake and hugging him tightly. She kissed his cheek, then said, "Dad, I'm not going to work for you. I love you dearly. And I want to keep on loving you dearly. But I'm not cut out for corporate life and I'd rather keep family as family and not as co-workers." She looked at Jake, then glanced at her sisters pressed in the doorway behind them. "I want to open my own practice. I don't know where or even what yet. But I think I'm better off being my own boss."

Her father actually blushed at the public display and had to clear his throat several times. His voice lowered so only Natalie and Jake could hear his reply. "Yes, well. You always were more like your mother."

Natalie was honestly surprised at that. "Mother was sick almost all her life. How am I like her?"

He smiled, and Natalie saw the love he had for her shining in his eyes. "She was an adventurer. Oh, her body might have been too fragile to allow her spirit to soar for real, but that never stopped her from wanting to. Had she been healthy, I think she'd have been a lot like you. Independent, single-minded, and ornery about it." His eyes clouded then. "I suppose she wouldn't have needed me, then. I've always felt a bit guilty for that. Not that I wouldn't have wished her well, even if it meant losing her." He shrugged, looking suddenly uncomfortable, as if he'd just realized what he'd revealed. "Maybe that's why I wanted to keep you close. You're the best part of her."

"Oh, Dad." She hugged him again and felt tears run down her cheeks. "I never knew. I do love you."

"Go to Wyoming, Natalie." He set her back, already well outside his comfort zone, and so publicly, too. So she gave him his space and let him reclaim his control. He straightened his tie and cleared his throat, his voice now back to normal. "I hope you find what you're looking for." He smiled then, and the father she knew and loved, the fox, surfaced once more. "Naturally, if it doesn't work out, I always have a position available for you here."

Natalie laughed and sniffled at the same time.

Jake stepped forward and shook her father's hand. "Thank you, sir. I promise I'll take good care of her."

Her father gave him a look. "Oh, I'm not worried about that. You might want to get some help, though. You'll have your hands full just keeping up with her."

"I'll take the advice under consideration."

Natalie pinched his arm, but Jake just laughed and tucked her hand in his. The crowd had pushed into the lobby now, her sisters leading the pack.

"Come on," he said, "before the mob descends on us. I want you all to myself."

She couldn't argue with that. "Well, what are you waiting for? Isn't this the part where you sweep me off my feet?"

He grinned. "As a matter of fact…"

Rule number one: Never taunt him, Natalie thought, squealing as he swung her up in his arms. *Oh, what the hell,* she amended. Taunting was fun. And if there was one thing she'd learned, it was that life should be more fun.

With that in mind, she waved at the crowd assembled behind them, noting with great pleasure that many people were applauding. Her sisters' faces were blank masks of confusion.

Well, it was a pity they didn't understand, but if she'd learned anything, it was that she wasn't responsible for their happiness or for their understanding hers.

Well, she did have a certain proprietary feel for the happiness of the man who held her in his arms.

"Please tell me there isn't a horse waiting in the parking lot," she said, wrapping her arms more tightly around his neck. "I never did finish riding school."

He kissed her soundly. "No horse. But there are one or two back at home I was hoping to introduce you to. I'd like to show you our land, but horseback is the only way to really see it properly. It takes a couple of days. We'd have to camp out. There's a cabin, too, but I haven't been that far to check out the condition of it. We don't use it anymore—"

"Camping, huh?" She was open to new things, right? She had the feeling this was only the beginning, and that was fine by her. She reached up and licked the spot beneath his ear. "Would we be alone on the trail, hoss?"

He stopped at the curb and let her slide down his body. "Why, yes, little lady, we would be," he said with that teasing grin of his.

"God, I've missed you," she said softly.

He pulled her close, and she reveled in the hard strength of him. Her body was clamoring for him already, but she was more than willing to wait. She had all the time in the world. Or she would, if she had anything to do with it. And she would. Single-minded and determined. Yep, that was her.

"I missed you, too." He tilted her chin up. "Natalie, you have to promise me one thing."

"What?"

"If you hate the ranch, if it's not for you, you have to tell me. We can find a compromise. We can have more than one home. Casper is close by, and if that's not big-city enough, then—"

She pressed her fingers to his lips, trying not to moan at the contact. God, she'd never been like this with anyone else. And she wanted to be like this forever. "I just want to be with you." It was the one thing she knew above all else. "We'll figure the rest out. As long as you're willing to let me find my own way, then I'm sure we'll make this work. At least, I want to do everything I can to try."

"Me, too." He kissed her, running his hands down her sides, brushing over her already hard nipples with his fingers.

She did moan this time. "Did I mention I *really* missed you?"

"I believe you did," he said, sounding a bit hoarse himself. But rather than tease her the way she'd expected, he tipped her chin up again, looking more serious than she'd ever seen him. "I do love you, Natalie."

"I don't think I'll ever get tired of hearing you say that. I love you, too, Jake." Tears stung her eyes, and she thought his eyes were a little glassy, too. "Come on, cowboy. Show me this ranch of yours."

He motioned with his hand, and a stretch limo pulled around the circle and stopped. A uniformed driver stepped out and held the door for them. "Mr. Lannister, Ms. Holcomb."

"Some steed you have here, cowboy," she said, climbing into the depths of the shiny black car.

He climbed in after her. "Well, I might be a rancher, but I'm still a Lannister."

"I see that." The driver got in and the car pulled away from the curb with a *purr*. "I also noticed the glass between the front and back is tinted."

"I noticed that, too," he said, sliding along the seat until he was right beside her.

"Did I mention how much I missed you?" she asked, tugging his coat open.

"Several times."

"Well, you've never been slow on the uptake."

"No, that's one thing you can't accuse me of."

She smiled. "Then, what are you waiting for?"

He yanked off his jacket, then reached over to open the small refrigerator. He pulled out a bottle of champagne.

"Very nice. But the taste of you will be just fine," she said.

He lifted his eyebrows and popped the cork. "Pretty bold talk."

"I'm feeling pretty bold at the moment."

"I can see that. Take your blouse off."

She tried to keep an even expression, but the suddenness of the command, coupled with the heat in his eyes, caught her off guard. She slowly unbuttoned her top, enjoying watching his grip on the bottle tighten.

"Now the skirt."

She eyed him, but did as he said.

Then he leaned forward and trickled the champagne on her stomach, following it with his tongue. "I'll never be able to drink it any other way now, you know."

Natalie was still gasping, from both the chill of the sparkling wine and the heat of his tongue. "I'd like to share in that addiction." She managed to sit up enough to take the bottle away from him. She smiled at him, then slid her hand down the neck of the bottle. "Now it's your turn."

Jake grinned and unbuckled his pants.

She crawled over to him as he slid his jeans and boots off. "Keep the hat on, cowboy."

"Sure thing, ma'am."

She poured champagne over him and licked up every drop. His hips were jumping…along with the rest of him, as she got done her very thorough taste test. "I see what you mean. Highly addictive."

"I'm thinking it's time for your first riding lesson," he teased her.

She climbed on top of him, and he put the hat on her head. "Can we drive all the way to Wyoming?" She slid down over him, making them both groan. "I'm sick of airplanes."

"Give us a chance...to get to know...each other...better." He ground the words out. "Dear God, Natalie."

"I know," she managed to say. "I love you, Jake. Take me home." And he did.

Epilogue

"I FOUND the perfect place!" Natalie was bouncing on the balls of her feet, so excited she could barely hold on to the phone.

"Not possible," Jake responded automatically.

"Hey, just because I've been a little picky about location…"

"A little?"

"Even your mother thinks I should make sure it's just right before jumping in. Starting my own practice is going to be scary enough." And she couldn't wait to start.

Jake laughed. "I know, sweetheart. The only reason I said you couldn't possibly have found the perfect place is because I was in the perfect place, oh, about two hours ago."

"Two hours ago we were in bed mak— Oh, ha-ha. And thank you." She fell in love with him more every day. He made her laugh, he made her think, and he made her heart pound just by looking at her. "Now, can you come into town today? I don't want to sign on this until you've seen it."

"Have you talked to Mom?"

"Well…"

"She's there with you, isn't she."

Natalie grinned. She'd bonded quickly with Helen. She only wished Jake's mom was planning to spend more time in Wyoming. "She just left. She thinks it's perfect, too."

Jake just laughed. "So what do you need me for?"

Natalie lowered her voice. "If you have to ask that, then we need to do what we did this morning all over again."

"Thank God my mom's not standing there."

"I love it when you get all modest on me." She leaned against her car and shifted her cell phone to the other ear. "Can you meet me?"

"I've got to make a few calls and meet a client about a bull he wants to buy, but if you can give me about two hours, I'll be there."

"Great. And Jake?"

"Yeah, I know. I love you, too. Pretty damn wonderful, isn't it?" He hung up before she could respond.

She just smiled and kissed her phone. She'd been in Wyoming for three months, but it had taken less than three minutes to fall in love with the Double L, Casper and the incredible sight of the Big Horn Mountains.

It was spring, but there was still snow on the ground, so she climbed in the ranch Rover to stay warm and picked up the packet that had just arrived at the post office for her. Her sisters had sent an arsenal of bridal information, complete with typed lists of all the things Natalie had to do.

She was touched by their enthusiasm, and hadn't the heart to tell them she wasn't using a wedding consultant or a personal designer. They were still reeling from the news that she was getting married on the Double L and not the family chapel in Connecticut. Liza, of course, had been thrilled and had readily agreed to being maid of honor. She was flying out in several weeks, and they'd do most of the planning then. Natalie couldn't wait. But most important was the fact that her father was healthy enough to fly out and had already agreed to walk her down the aisle. She got teary just thinking about their last phone call, when he'd given her his blessing.

Jake pulled up just then, honking the horn of his pickup and making her jump. She leaped out of the Rover and raced into his arms. "You're early."

"I postponed my meetings. It's good to be the boss."

She grabbed his hand, and turned and gestured to the small storefront in downtown Lamont, the small town named after Jake's ancestor who'd originally settled here. She'd decided on a small local practice instead of something in Casper. She wanted to stay small, and stay close to the ranch and Jake—and the family she one day hoped to have.

"What do you think? I know it's not on the main street and it's a bit run-down, but I can work on that. The brick is in good shape, the siding needs to be washed and probably painted. The electricity and water are up to code, though, which is good. It will need some new drywall and repainting, and the carpet definitely has to go, but—"

Whatever else she had to say was cut off by Jake's kiss. Someone drove by, honked a horn and gave a holler. Natalie didn't even try to squirm loose.

"I love you, Natalie," Jake said when he finally lifted his head.

"And the whole town knows it. Or they will in about ten minutes when that guy heads into Darlene's Place."

"I can see this bothers you greatly."

Natalie couldn't seem to stop smiling these days. "Well, I think it's only right that the town's new family lawyer is part of a family herself. Don't you agree?"

"I agree that it's damn cold out here. Come on, show me around your new offices, counselor."

"Right this way, sir." Natalie loved the fact that Jake was as interested in her work and pursuits as she was. And in turn, she'd been taking riding lessons and reading up on the care and feeding of cattle and general farm management. She was thinking about getting some Nubian goats after reading an interesting article about them. But she'd talk to him about that later.

"Now, don't get discouraged. I told you about the paint and the—"

He opened the door, pulled her inside and had her up against the wall.

"Jake! There are no blinds on the windows." She laughed when he hiked her legs around his waist and moved them out of view. "I don't mind the locals knowing I'm part of a family, but—"

"I was thinking we ought to christen the place. It's good luck."

Natalie giggled when he started licking the side of her neck. "As in, get some champagne and have a little party?"

"We don't need champagne." He shifted her legs around his hips and pressed into her. "And you're all the party I'll ever need."

"There are several rooms," she managed to say, as he pushed at her clothes. "We should...christen them all, don't you think?"

"Absolutely."

"So, I guess...this means...I can sign...the lease?" She was panting now, tearing at his clothes.

He tossed the rest of their clothes away and pushed inside her, making them both groan. "Definitely." Then he was moving and she was holding on and they both growled into each other's mouths as they came.

Natalie laughed even as she tried to get her breath back. "I can't believe I'm going to have clients in here. Every time I look at this wall..."

"It will be our secret thrill."

Natalie beamed up at the man she'd given her heart to. "You'll always be my secret thrill."

"Bet on it." He kissed her deeply and slowly, and the

sweet tension began to build again. "I believe you mentioned something about other rooms?" He traced a finger over one bare nipple, then slid it down her body.

"Why, yes," she gasped, nipping at his ear. "I believe I did."

"I think maybe it's your turn to thrill me," he said in that taunting tone of his.

She grinned at him and slid her hand down his body. "Bet on it."

GOOD TIME GIRL
Candace Schuler

To all the good girls of the world who are yearning
to take a walk on the wild side—go for it!

Prologue

ROXANNE ARCHER designed her strategy like a four-star general—or a stalker.

The first part of the plan involved laying the groundwork. She studied her subject carefully. She plotted her itinerary. She listed her needs and requirements, defining and refining them as necessary. She carved out the time she would need. She saved the necessary funds. She acquired the necessary skills.

That had taken nearly six months to accomplish.

The second part of the plan involved general reconnaissance and one-on-one surveillance. She trailed several possible subjects, observing them in their natural habitat for several days before narrowing the field down to one. And then she trailed that one, learning his preferences, his habits, his predilections and inclinations.

That had taken nearly two weeks.

The third part was more hands-on. Bravely, she turned herself over to the experts and let them arm her for the coming campaign. She was plucked and waxed, trimmed and highlighted, buffed and filed and polished within an inch of her life. Then she selected and donned her camouflage so she would blend in with her surroundings.

That took nearly two days.

She was now as ready as she would ever be.

It was time to go get herself a good-looking, dangerous cowboy.

Chapter One

"WELL, I'M HERE to tell you, sugar, rodeo cowboys are a whole hell of a lot of fun but they're the most irresponsible sons o' bitches in the world when it comes to women. You can't trust 'em any farther than you can throw 'em, and you sure as hell can't believe a word they say. Especially the good-lookin' ones. They're the most dangerous kind, you know, 'cause they've been gettin' by on looks and charm their whole lives and they got it down to a science. I'm tellin' you the pure honest-to-God truth here, sugar. You got to keep an extra sharp eye on the good-lookin' ones or you'll get your poor little heart broke for sure."

Roxanne Archer heard those cautionary words of advice echo through her mind as she pulled into one of the few remaining parking spaces in front of Ed Earl's Polynesian Dance Palace, and resolutely reaffirmed her decision not to let the dire warnings of one crusty old ex-barrel racer from San Antonio put a damper on her quest.

She was going to get herself a cowboy.

A good-looking one.

The most dangerous kind.

If she got her heart broken in the process, well, so be it. It was no more than she expected, in any case. And a bro-

ken heart had to be better than one that had shriveled up
from disuse. Not to mention a few other body parts that were
in imminent danger of dehydration from prolonged neglect.

She turned off the ignition of her rented candy-apple-red
Mustang convertible and sat there for a moment, her fingers
still clasping the key, her foot on the parking brake, staring
blindly at the flock of pulsating pink-neon flamingos atop
the roof of Ed Earl's, and contemplated the series of events—
the series of *non*-events, actually—that had brought her to
a cowboy honky-tonk on the outskirts of Lubbock, Texas,
in the middle of her summer vacation. It was simple, really.

Roxanne Archer had been a good girl—a very good girl—
for the entire twenty-nine, uneventful years of her life. She
wanted to take a crack at being a good-time girl before it was
too late. If it wasn't already too late. She'd been mired in
good-girlness an awfully long time, and it was an awfully
deep rut to climb out of—even with the help of a dangerous,
good-looking cowboy.

Provided, of course, that she actually managed to get herself one.

"I just won't go home *until* I get him," she muttered stubbornly, and reached up to flip open the lighted makeup mirror in the visor so she could check her lipstick—glossy
candy-apple red like the car—and make sure her hair hadn't
blown all to pieces on her drive over from the Broken Spoke
Motel. It had. But as promised by the young woman who'd
cut it for her in Dallas just two days ago, being blown all to
pieces had only improved the style. Roxanne smiled at herself, delighted by the chunky, layered cut that tangled with
her eyelashes and caressed the back of her neck with such
reckless abandon.

It was amazing what a new hairdo could do for a woman.
Not to mention a new shade of lipstick. And new clothes.
Especially when each and every item of those new clothes—

right down to the leopard-print bikini panties and matching push-up demi bra—were so radically different from what said woman usually wore.

Feeling wild and wicked and blessedly unlike her usual boring self, Roxanne pushed the car door open, swung her feet out onto the graveled parking lot, straightened up to her full five feet nine inches...and teetered precariously as the high, stacked heels of her brand-new, lipstick-red Sweetheart of the Rodeo cowboy boots sank into the rocky, uneven surface. She made a hasty grab for the top of the car door to steady herself, wondering if maybe the high-heeled boots had been a mistake. She always wore flats at home, or sensible pumps with little one-inch heels so she didn't tower over people—men—any more than necessary.

But, then, no, she told herself firmly, good-time girls didn't wear sensible shoes, whether they towered over people or not.

And, besides, she'd always wanted a pair of red cowboy boots, ever since she was a little girl growing up in Greenwich, Connecticut, secretly dreaming about riding the range as a dangerous outlaw queen like Belle Starr or Cat Ballou. Although it didn't actually say so in any of the books she'd read, she'd been absolutely positive an outlaw queen would wear red cowboy boots. She'd gathered up her courage and asked her mother for a pair.

Charlotte Hayworth Archer had lectured her nine-year-old daughter about her poor choice of role models and footwear, then bought her proper brown leather riding boots and a proper English saddle and signed her up for proper riding lessons, no doubt believing all that wholesome, healthful propriety would rechannel Roxanne's interests and ambitions in a more socially acceptable direction.

Which it had.

Sort of.

Roxanne learned to keep her admiration for unconventional women to herself, and she never mentioned her desire for red boots again.

After a while, she *almost* forgot she'd ever wanted them. Dressage riders didn't wear fancy red boots, nor did honor students or members of the debate team or the Latin club, and certainly no class valedictorian had ever pranced across the stage to the podium in red boots. A cheerleader might, of course, or a member of the drama club, but Roxanne was too tall and too inhibited and…well, just too plain geeky to belong to either of those cliques. A girl like Roxanne had been during her high school years—tall, gangly, scholarly, shy—would never wear or do or say anything to attract attention to herself. It got to be a habit, and Roxanne passed out of her awkward teens and into her marginally less awkward twenties without attracting any undue notice from anyone.

Shortly after her twenty-fourth birthday she became one half of a mature adult relationship with another teacher at the exclusive private school were she taught English Lit and beginning Latin to fifth graders, but she never really attracted his attention, either. Not completely. In the three years they spent together as a couple, he never once remembered how she liked her coffee—a *half* a spoonful of sugar, damn it!—or noticed that she faked her orgasms.

Which, in a roundabout way, was the reason she was standing in front of a cowboy honky-tonk outside of Lubbock, Texas, in the middle of her summer vacation, wearing red cowboy boots and the shortest, tightest skirt she'd ever worn in her life.

Roxanne Archer was finally ready to call some attention to herself, to cut loose, to kick over the traces, to take a walk on the wild side and find out what all the shouting was about. In the immortal words of Auntie Mame—another admirably unconventional woman with a flamboyant fashion sense—Roxanne was ready to "live, live, live!"

For the duration of her vacation, anyway.

She let go of the car door, then reached down with both hands—freshly manicured with glossy fire-engine-red polish instead of her usual tasteful French manicure—and carefully smoothed her sweaty palms over the curve of her hips to make sure her tiny denim skirt was still covering everything it was supposed to cover.

Someone whistled appreciatively

Roxanne started at the unexpected sound, her body stiffening instinctively, as if to ward off a threat or an insult. And then, deliberately, remembering her mission, she forced herself relax. She'd dressed to attract attention, hadn't she? Well, she'd attracted attention. Now she just had to figure out what to do with it.

She turned her head slightly, glancing over her shoulder, and flashed what she hoped was a saucy smile at her admirer.

The response was immediate. And immensely gratifying.

He puffed up like a rooster and swaggered toward her with the loose-limbed, bow-legged gait of a man who'd spent a lot of time on a horse. "Well, hey, there, baby doll," he crooned appreciatively as he honed in on her.

He was six foot four, at least, with shoulders like a bull, a trophy buckle the size of a pancake decorating his belt, and a smile as wide and open as a Texas prairie beaming out at her from under the rim of a cream-colored Stetson. An honest-to-goodness cowboy. Good-looking, too, in an open, aw-shucks, country boy sort of way that, unfortunately, wasn't the least bit dangerous.

Roxanne had her heart firmly set on dangerous.

Still, a cowboy was a cowboy, even if he had freckles and a snub nose. And she could certainly use the practice. She fluttered her eyelashes experimentally.

"Hey, yourself, sugar," she drawled. Her accent was a near perfect imitation of the San Antonio barrel racer who had warned her against trusting cowboys. The flirtatious tilt of her head was the result of two weeks' worth of close observation and diligent practice in front of a mirror. Amazingly, it worked.

The cowboy swaggered a bit closer and leaned in, putting one big, beefy hand on the open car door. The mingled scents of horses, saddle soap and a musky men's cologne, liberally applied, engulfed her. "You here alone, baby doll?"

Roxanne stifled the urge to take a quick step backward, out of range of that too strong cologne and the unfamiliar burden of his undivided attention. It was what she would have done. Before. Now, she shut the car door with a sassy little thrust of her hip, dislodging his hand, and gave him what she hoped was a provocative look from under the fringe of her chunky blond bangs. "I'm meeting someone inside."

"Girlfriend?" he said, looking so much like an eager, oversize puppy that Roxanne couldn't help but smile at him again.

"Boyfriend." She touched the manicured tip of her index finger to the center of his massive chest and pushed lightly, backing him up. "And he's real jealous, sugar, so I'd be careful if I were you."

The cowboy's grin widened. "I'm willing to take a chance if you are, baby doll. We could run away together before he even knows you're here. My truck's right over there."

Roxanne laughed and shook her head, causing her tousled flyaway cut to shimmer in the pink neon glow of the flock of flamingos gracing the roof of Ed Earl's. "I wouldn't want your death on my conscience, sugar. But thanks for the invitation." She sighed regretfully. "It was a real sweet offer and if I wasn't otherwise engaged, I'd be tempted." She batted her eyelashes again for good measure. "I really would."

She patted his chest and turned away, tucking the car key into the pocket of her stretch denim skirt as she sauntered across the parking lot—slowly, because of the unaccustomed height of her boot heels and the graveled surface beneath her feet. The careful pace made her hips sway seductively, in a way they never did in her usual flats.

"Man, oh, man," she heard him say reverently, and she slowed down even more, exaggerating the fluid movement of her hips, enjoying the moment, reveling in her unexpected success.

Oh, it had been so easy! Who would have ever believed it would be so easy?

With a triumphant, self-satisfied smile tugging at the corners of her glossy red lips, Roxanne pulled open the front door of Ed Earl's Polynesian Dance Palace and sashayed in like she owned the place.

It was as if she had stepped into another world and—like Dorothy torn from her black-and-white life and thrust over the rainbow into a brilliantly colored Oz—she could only stand there and blink in stupefied amazement. It was loud, smoky, and tacky. Unapologetically, unrepentantly, *gloriously* tacky.

Chinese paper lanterns were strung from life-size wooden cutouts shaped like palm trees. Brightly colored plastic fish dangled from the ceiling. Bedraggled fisherman's netting, studded with glass floats, striped beach balls and pink plastic flamingos of various sizes, was draped across the walls. Gyrating hula dolls—the kind found on the dashboards of cars of people with questionable taste—decorated each table. The wait staff wore gaudy Hawaiian Aloha shirts and paper flower leis with their Wranglers and boots. The four members of the twanging cowboy band stood on a small, raised stage constructed to look like a log raft. The crowded dance floor was huge, kidney-shaped and painted a vivid blue.

Roxanne's cocky smile faltered a bit as she watched the dancers' whirling, skipping, kicking progress around the scuffed blue floor.

Dancing had never been her strong suit. Not that she didn't love to dance. She did. But girls who were five feet nine inches tall by the time they were thirteen, especially girls who were brainy and wore glasses, too, didn't get much opportunity to learn all the latest dance moves. Her mother had insisted she learn all the standard ballroom dances, of course—and what a wretched embarrassment those lessons had been, being waltzed around the room by an unwilling partner whose head barely reached her chin!—but she'd never danced any of the popular dances all the kids her age were doing back in high school. Not in public, anyway.

Determined not to be left out this time around, she'd secretly taken a six-week series of dance lessons in preparation for her Wild West adventure, but none of the half a dozen country-western dances she'd so painstakingly learned bore more than a passing resemblance to the bewildering series of steps currently being performed on the floor of Ed Earl's Polynesian Dance Palace. Obviously, her instructors—a fresh-faced young preppie couple in matching pastel plaid shirts—had never been in a Texas honky-tonk. Or six weeks of lessons hadn't been nearly enough. Either way, she couldn't possibly—

"Dance, ma'am?"

Roxanne shifted her gaze from the dance floor to find another cowboy smiling at her from beneath the rim of a broad-brimmed, black cowboy hat. This one was lean and rangy, with dark, soulful eyes and an uncanny resemblance to a young John Travolta. Unfortunately, he was also no more than twenty, at most. Still, it was heartening to be hit on as soon as she came in the door, as it were. Another sign, if she needed one, that her transformation from party pooper to party girl had been successful. If she hadn't been ninety-nine percent sure she'd fall flat on her face, she might have taken him up on his offer, just out of pure gratitude that he'd asked.

"Thank you, no." She smiled at him to cushion the blow. "I'm meeting someone." She gestured across the sea of dancers toward the bar and pool tables on the other side of the blue lagoon. "Over there."

"How 'bout I dance you over that way, then? Little bitty slip of a thing like you might get stomped on, you try to make it through this rowdy crowd on your own."

Even without the warning from the San Antonio barrel racer about a rodeo cowboy's proclivity for stretching the truth, Roxanne knew a line when she heard one—and his was long enough to hang clothes on. No one had ever, in all her twenty-nine years, referred to her as a "little bitty slip of a thing." She'd been called skinny. Scrawny. Bean Pole. String Bean. Arrow Archer. But *never* a little bitty slip of a thing. And by someone who was smiling at her as if he really, truly meant it. At the moment, anyway. It was irresistible.

"All right, sugar," she drawled, suddenly feeling powerfully, erotically female. *Little bitty slip of a thing.* If she could call forth that kind of shameless flattery from a young, good-looking cowboy by just standing there, she could do anything. Even dance in public without disgracing herself. "For that, you get one dance. The man I'm meeting can wait."

He whooped as if he'd just won the lottery and snagged an arm around her waist, whirling her onto the floor before she had a chance to change her mind.

"One dance," she reiterated as they joined the enthusiastic throng.

They danced two dances.

After all, the first dance hardly counted, as the song was more than half over when they joined in. And the second dance was the Cotton-Eyed Joe. It would be an affront to Texans everywhere to leave the dance floor when the Cotton-Eyed Joe was playing. Roxanne acquiesced to that argument, spurious though it was, but managed to stand firm when he tried to cajole her into a third go-round. Cute as he was—and he was darn cute!—she had other plans for the evening. And it was about time she quit stalling and put them into action.

"I'm meeting someone," she stated firmly, resisting when her dance partner tried to twirl her into the two-step that was just beginning. "And you said you'd dance me over there—" she gestured with her free hand "—after *one* dance, now didn't you, sugar?"

The cowboy gave an exaggerated shrug, pantomiming both compliance and disappointment, and obligingly two-stepped her backward through the crowd. As they approached the edge of the dance floor, he spun her in a series of quick, showy turns that ended with her pressed up against his lean, rock-hard young body, their joined hands clasped against the small of her back. Breathless, laughing, Roxanne clutched at his shoulder with her free hand for balance and found herself looking into his face from only inches away. The expression in his soulful brown eyes had her reconsidering her definition of dangerous.

"Oh, my." She slid her hand from his shoulder to his chest in an effort to give herself a little more breathing room. Unlike the cowboy who'd accosted her in the parking lot, he didn't budge. "Well...um, that was certainly invigorating," she said brightly, forgetting to drawl. "Thank you."

"Thank *you*," he purred, and dipped his head with unmistakable intent.

Roxanne drew back sharply, as far as the arm encircling her waist would permit.

"Is that a no?" he murmured.

"No. I mean, yes. That's a no," she stammered, fighting a curious combination of schoolgirl panic and equally schoolgirlish triumph.

He wanted to kiss her!

It was out of the question, of course. He was just a kid. Younger than her youngest brother, Edward, who was a junior at Brown. But still...this young John Travolta lookalike wanted to kiss *her!* It was a heady thought and if he were a few years older or she were a few years younger, she might be tempted to let him. Maybe.

"Sure I can't change your mind? I know lots of other—" his arm tightened fractionally, pressing her closer to his over-heated body; his voice dropped an octave, becoming intimate and suggestive "—invigoratin' things we can do together."

"Yes, I'm quite sure you do," she said primly, wondering how she'd gotten herself into this. And how she was going to get out of it. "But I'm meet—" She sucked in her breath, startled into silence when he reached up and brushed her cheek with the back of one finger.

"You sure have soft skin," he murmured, his finger wandering down her cheek to the side of her neck. His dark eyes sizzled with potent male heat. "You this soft all over?"

Roxanne reached up and grabbed his hand, stopping its unerring descent toward the scooped neckline of her lace-edged camisole blouse. "No," she said firmly, with no equivocation in her voice this time, and no indecision in her expression that might lead him to think she could be convinced to change her mind.

The young cowboy sighed and let her go. "I enjoyed the dance. Dances," he said with a smile, as earnest and polite as if he hadn't just tried to cop a feel. "And if you change your mind about anything—" his voice took on a playful, suggestive timbre "—you just give a holler and I'll come runnin'."

His easy, good-natured capitulation to her rejection boosted Roxanne's confidence another notch. Obviously, she was better at this man/woman thing than she'd thought. Or, rather, her sexy alter ego was better at it.

"And just who should I holler for, sugar?" She tilted her head, looking up at him from beneath her lashes. "If I do happen to change my mind, that is."

"The name's Clay." He offered his hand. "Clay Madison."

Roxanne put hers into it. "Roxy Archer," she said, giving him the version of her name she'd decided went with her new persona.

"Well, Roxy, it's been a real pleasure." He lifted the hand he held to his lips and brushed a careless kiss across her knuckles before letting it go. "You remember what I said now, hear? Holler if you change your mind."

"I'll do that," she promised mendaciously, knowing it wouldn't happen.

Clay Madison knew it, too. He touched two fingers to the brim of his hat in a brief cowboy salute, then turned and left her standing at the edge of the dance floor while he zeroed in on a big-haired, big-bosomed young lovely in skintight jeans and a skinny little tank top that exposed a great deal more cleavage than Roxanne could ever hope to possess, even with the help of a push-up bra.

"Oh, well," she said to herself, watching without rancor as he twirled the delighted girl onto the crowded dance floor with the same smooth moves he'd used on her. "Easy come, easy go."

She had no doubt at all that if she'd been willing, it could have been her out on the dance floor, plastered up against young Clay Madison with his hand inching inexorably toward her butt. It was a comforting thought. Before Clay and the cowboy in the parking lot, her belief in her ability to inspire that kind of lustful feeling in a man had been based on little more than research and hope. Now, it was established fact. She could do it. She *had* done it. She could do it again. All it took, apparently, was a short, tight skirt, a provocative smile, and the ability to flutter her eyelashes.

She was utterly amazed it had taken her nearly twenty-nine years to figure out something so simple, but now that she had, she was going to put her new knowledge to good use. With a confident toss of her head, Roxanne turned and headed for the bar with a sultry, hip-swinging stride that drew more than one admiring male glance.

"Lone Star," she purred when the bartender smiled and asked her pleasure.

She waved away the mug he brought with the beer, wrapped her hand around the frosty long-necked bottle and swiveled around on her bar stool so she was facing the pool table tucked into the far corner of the honky-tonk. She raised the beer to her lips and took a long, slow swallow, surveying the men playing pool over the upturned end of the bottle.

There he was.

Her cowboy.

The good-looking, dangerous one.

She lowered the beer, resting the cool frosty bottom on her bare knee, and watched him as he circled the pool table with the cue in his hand. He wasn't movie-star handsome like young Clay Madison, but Roxanne didn't want movie-star handsome. She wanted craggy and rugged. She wanted virile and manly. A real cowboy, not the rhinestone version.

The cowboy playing pool was as real as it got.

He was long and lean, an even six feet according to his stats, although his boots and hat made him seem taller. Broad at the shoulders and narrow at the hips with the strong, hard thighs of a horseman, he moved around the pool table with the ambling, easy, loose-kneed gait of a man who knew

the value of patience. He was older than most of the other
rodeo cowboys—an important consideration to a woman
staring her thirtieth birthday in the face—with tiny lines of
experience etched into the tanned skin around his eyes, and
laugh lines creasing his lean cheeks. His dark hair was conservatively cut, neither short nor long, with the appealing ten-
dency to curl from underneath the edges of his hat. His
snap-front, Western-cut shirt was a plain, pale blue; his jeans
were snug but not tight; the silver trophy buckle on his belt
was moderately sized. His whole manner bespoke quiet,
rock-solid confidence with no need to advertise either his
physique or his prowess.

Roxanne had been surreptitiously watching him for the
past two weeks, sizing him up from the safety of the stands
and around the rodeo grounds. Now, her decision made, her
quarry in sight, she leveled her gaze at him from across the
room and stared openly, her interest obvious to anyone who
cared to look.

The object of her interest stood, hip cocked, head down,
the brim of his hat shadowing his face, his upper body bent
over the pool table as he lined up his shot, seemingly oblivious to the woman watching him.

Roxanne kept staring, willing him to look up. According
to all the books she'd read and the research she'd done in
preparation for her Wild West adventure, the easiest and
most direct way for a woman to signal her interest in a man
was with eye contact. Prolonged, direct eye contact. The
trick, she realized now, was to get him to look at her in the
first place. The books and magazine articles had made it all
sound so simple. Catch his eye, lick your lips, trail your fin
gertips suggestively over your cleavage or the rim of your
glass, all the while holding that all important eye contact, and
he'd come running. That was the theory, anyway. Unfortunately, nothing she'd read had mentioned what to do if he

was so intent on his next pool shot that he didn't even notice you were staring at him.

She was just about to switch tactics, steeling herself to slide off the bar stool and saunter over to the pool table for a more direct approach when, suddenly, his shoulders twitched under the pale blue fabric of his shirt. His hands stilled on the pool cue. He raised his head, slowly, his upper body still positioned over the felt-covered table in preparation for his shot.

She saw the chiseled angle of his jaw first as it emerged from beneath the shadow of his hat...the full, sculpted curve of his lips...his blade of a nose...the strong, angled cheekbones under skin the warm golden color of old doubloons...and then, finally, the startling blue of his eyes as he looked straight at her from under the brim of his hat.

Their gazes locked.

Held.

Roxanne felt the jolt all the way down to her toes. *Steady,* she told herself, fighting the urge to lower her gaze. *Steady.* Now wasn't the time to get all girlie and flustered. She'd caught his attention. Now she had to engage his interest enough to make him approach her. Deliberately, with a gesture she'd practiced a hundred times in front of the mirror in preparation for this moment, she lifted her free hand and touched her crimson-tipped fingers to the lace-trimmed edge of her scoop-necked blouse, brushing them lightly, languidly, back and forth over the cleavage produced by the push-up bra.

The cowboy's eyes widened and his gaze flickered downward, following the sultry movement of her fingers on her skin. The expression in his blue eyes when they came back to hers was hot, focused and intent, rife with speculation and frank sexual curiosity.

Roxanne felt equal parts fear, excitement and sheer female

power sizzling through her at the success of her ploy. She'd done it. She'd hooked him. Now all she had to do was reel him in.

Come to mama, she thought, and smiled in blatant, unmistakable invitation.

Chapter Two

IT TOOK TOM STEELE a good ten seconds to convince himself the hot little blonde at the bar was actually aiming her come-hither stare at him. Not that he hadn't been the focus of a come-hither stare before. He did all right with the ladies. Always had. But the trophy-hunting buckle bunnies who hung out in places like Ed Earl's usually went after bigger trophies—and younger, flashier studs. There was nothing flashy about Tom Steele.

His last birthday had put him on the far side of thirty, for one thing, making him a good five to ten years older than most of the peach-fuzz cowboys in the honky-tonk. And even in his younger days he'd never been one of those Fancy Dans who went in for wildly colored custom-made shirts, glittery bat-wing chaps or oversize silver belt buckles. He was a circuit cowboy, and proud of it. A weekend competitor who fit his rodeoing in around a job and a ranch and an eighty-hour workweek.

Or rather, he *had* been a circuit cowboy.

This year—his last year before he quit for good—he'd decided to go hog wild and really live it up, competing in as many rodeos as possible, traveling from one go-round to the next, living, eating and breathing the foot loose and fancy free life of the professional rodeo cowboy for one full season. So far, that meant he spent a good deal of his time behind the wheel of his pickup, chasing the rodeo from one dusty Podunk town to another, living on fast food and bad coffee, and getting tossed around by snortin' mad broncs on a daily basis instead of just on the weekends.

It was a good life, as far as it went. The days were mostly hot and dirty, comprised of long periods of boredom and inactivity interspersed with eight-second intervals of heart-pounding, teeth-rattling, bone-jarring excitement. The nights were mostly spent on the road or in honky-tonks like Ed Earl's. He had no responsibilities to speak of beyond making sure he was paid up and on time for each of his events. And no worries beyond wondering which bronc he was going to draw in the next go-round. About the only thing missing from his last fling was, well...a last fling.

It appeared things might be looking up in that department.

"Well, hell, Tom. You gonna stand there, starin' at that little gal like some big dumb critter what ain't got no sense, or you gonna take your shot?"

Without shifting his gaze away from the woman at the bar, Tom straightened and handed his pool cue to the cowboy who'd asked the question. "I'm going to take my shot," he said.

"Hey, you got a twenty ridin' on this game," the cowboy reminded him.

Tom didn't even glance at the crumpled bills under the shot glass on the edge of the pool table. "Consider it forfeit," he said. "I think I've just found a more interesting game to play." Then, paying no attention to the hoots and hollers that followed his comment, he rounded the end of the felt-covered table and headed toward the blonde at the bar.

He moved slowly, purposefully, the way he did when he was approaching the chute to climb aboard his next ride. His gait was measured and even, his boot heels clicking against the floor with every deliberate step, neither his gaze nor his pace wavering as he unerringly honed in on her through the noise and smoke of the jam-packed honky-tonk. She didn't fidget, didn't look away, didn't blush or giggle or toss her hair. She simply sat there, perched on the bar stool as regal as a princess—her back ramrod-straight, her long slim legs crossed at the knee, her hand playing idly at her breast—and watched him come to her.

She was a tall, cool glass of water, for sure, a far cry from the usual oversprayed, overdone, overeager groupies who congregated around rodeo cowboys. Long and lean with a glossy, high-tone polish, she had a pampered, well-bred look to her underneath the fancy packaging, like a Thoroughbred racehorse all decked out in a show pony rig. And, hot damn, what a rig!

Her short blond hair was kind of rumpled and tousled-looking, as if she'd just rolled out of bed and wouldn't mind rolling back in. Her lips were red and shiny, as if she'd just licked them. The tiny little skirt she was wearing showed off miles of slender, well-toned leg and clung like denim-colored Saran wrap to the sweetest curve of hip it had ever been his privilege to see. The neckline of her white blouse dipped just low enough to offer a tantalizing glimpse of cleavage. And those long, red nails...

Damn, she knew just what she was doing, brushing those glossy red fingernails back and forth above the scooped neckline of her blouse, all nonchalant and casual-like, as if she had no idea she was doing it or what the sight did to a man, with that mysterious, knowing little smile curving those matching red lips, offering compliance and challenge without a word being spoken. And all the while staring at him as if she meant to gobble him up when he got close enough.

It riveted a man's attention, for sure, and got the blood

pumping through his veins harder than it did when he was in the chute, sitting on top of twelve-hundred pounds of quivering horseflesh and waiting for the gate to swing open.

Tom did what he always did in that situation. He narrowed his focus to the task at hand, settled in, and prepared to take hold, determined to assert his dominance from the get-go. Women or horses, he'd always figured the game plan was pretty much the same. A man had to show 'em who was boss, right off, or he'd end up getting stomped on. Especially with the high-spirited ones. And he could tell at a glance the long-legged blonde with the cool, glossy polish and the hot come-hither look in her eyes was definitely one of the high-spirited ones. If a man let a woman like that get the upper hand, he'd never get it back.

He came to a stop directly in front of her.

And then he just stood there, his jeans-clad knees inches from her bare dimpled ones, his wide shoulders blocking her view of everything except him, and silently offered up a hot-eyed challenge of his own.

Her sassy little smile faltered a bit and the tip of her tongue came out, licking nervously at her bottom lip, but her gaze never wavered. "Buy you a drink, cowboy?" she purred.

Her voice was low and husky with a hint of something foreign and exotic under the drawl, as if she were from someplace other than Texas. Tom liked exotic, especially when it was sleek and blond and brazen. He pushed the brim of his hat up a fraction of an inch with the tip of his thumb, then, still silent, leaned in and put his hand on the bar beside her.

She shrank back, just slightly, and her gaze dropped for a split second. Then her spine stiffened and her chin came up, and she met his eyes. Five long seconds passed in silence as they stared at each other, deep blue eyes gazing into pale golden brown, male to female, yin to yang, speculation, curiosity and pure undisguised sexual energy crackling back and forth between them like static electricity as they silently jockeyed for position in the age-old battle of the sexes.

Then one of her eyebrows rose, all hoity-toity and imperious. "Well?" she said, and there was a snap under the cornpone and molasses in her voice. "Do you want a drink or not, sugar?"

Tom bit back a grin—damn, he liked a woman with sass!—and put his other hand on the bar, caging her between his outstretched arms. "How 'bout we skip the preliminaries, Slim," he said, his voice low and husky and suggestive, "and just get right to it."

Her eyes flared wide for a second, and he would have sworn he saw her gulp, but the angle of her chin stayed the same. "Skip the preliminaries?"

He leaned in just a bit closer, all but surrounding her with his size and strength in a deliberate attempt to overwhelm her with the none-too-subtle body language of the dominant male animal. The grin he couldn't quite control curved his lips, quirking up one corner of his mouth when she refused to give ground by shrinking back a second time.

"No sense wasting time when we both know what we want, now is there?" he said silkily, close enough now so that his knees were bumping hers and the brim of his hat shadowed her upturned face.

Roxanne lifted her free hand in automatic reflex, putting it against his chest in an instinctive effort to preserve what little space she had left, and opened her mouth to inform him in no uncertain terms that she wasn't that kind of girl. Fortunately, she remembered in time that she was, for the duration of her vacation, anyway, *exactly* that kind of girl. The problem was, she had no idea what that kind of girl would do now, with six gorgeous, well-muscled feet of cowboy all but pressing her up against the bar.

"Well...um...." She stared up at him, her head tilted back,

her hand resting lightly against his broad chest, her mind working frantically.

He was so close she could feel the warmth of his breath on her cheek, so close she could feel the brush of his shirt-sleeves against her bare arms. The look in his deep blue eyes was confident and cocksure, as tempting as sin on a hot Saturday night. The heat of his body was an almost tangible thing, reaching out to curl around her like the loop of an expertly thrown lasso.

Her heartbeat quickened in response, sending an answering heat surging through her, making her nerve endings sizzle with a heady combination of panic and excitement as she tried to decide what her next move should be.

None of her carefully orchestrated plans for her fall from grace had included the possibility of falling quite so fast—and without any of the preliminaries he seemed so eager to dispense with. She'd expected at least a few minutes of getting-to-know-you pleasantries over that drink she'd intended to buy him. Maybe a dance or two to warm things up and put them both at ease. A little sweet talk and romantic nonsense to disguise what was really going on. Apparently, her good-looking, dangerous cowboy didn't believe in wasting time with subterfuge or romantic nonsense.

So, how would a real good-time girl handle the situation?

Hold him off?

Or urge him on?

Tom stood stock-still, waiting, his hands on the bar on either side of her, the little half smile still turning up one corner of his mouth, an unholy gleam of masculine devilry and undisguised anticipation lighting his face, and watched the whirl of emotions parade through her big whiskey-colored eyes as she debated the issue with herself.

He knew he'd disconcerted her with his directness—that had been his intent, after all—and he had read, quite clearly,

the first flash of instinctive, feminine outrage at his masculine arrogance and presumption. He also saw the flicker of
uncertainty that replaced it, the swift calculation and consideration, the bubbling excitement beneath it all that got his
own juices flowing fast and hot...and, then, suddenly, surprisingly, the unmistakable glint of steely-eyed resolve.

Tom bit back a curse and prepared to be slapped down—
verbally, at least—for daring to presume too much, too soon.
Any man with good sense knew the high-spirited ones, be
they equine or human, didn't take kindly to being rushed.
And no woman, high-spirited or not, reacted favorably to the
assumption that she could be too easily had. Even when she
could be.

"You're absolutely right," she said briskly, surprising
him again just as he was about to pull back and regroup by
asking her to dance—and pretending that's what he'd meant
all along.

"Ma'am?" he murmured vaguely, stalling for time while
he tried to figure out what he'd been right about.

"No sense wasting time when we both know what we
want." She turned slightly and set the bottle of beer on the
bar behind her with a decisive little click. "Let's get to it,"
she said, and slid off the bar stool into his wide-open arms.

Tom reacted automatically, shifting his weight backward,
lowering his hands from the edge of the bar to catch her as
she all but fell into his embrace. He bracketed her hips in his
wide palms, holding her upright, meaning only to steady her
until she found her balance before he let her go again. But
she was a warm, fragrant armful of woman, sleek and sexy
and soft.

Incredibly soft.

Everywhere.

Her hair was soft against his jaw.

Her breath was soft against his neck.

Her breasts were soft against his chest.

And he was suddenly, incredibly, excruciatingly hard.

Everywhere.

The unexpectedness of it caught him completely off guard. The intensity of it short-circuited his brain, urging him to bypass the teasing, testing first steps of the mating dance they'd been doing in favor of the pure, primal male instinct to dominate and possess a willing female. Between one breath and the next, he forgot he'd been going to ask her to dance, forgot they'd only just met, forgot he didn't even know her name. Instinctively, without conscious thought or premeditation, he tightened his hands on the curve of her hips, pulling her solidly against his suddenly aching erection.

Roxanne gasped and her eyes widened, the pupils dilating until they all but obscured the golden brown of her irises. But she didn't stiffen. She didn't pull back. She didn't move by so much as a fraction of an inch. And she didn't look away.

Couldn't look away.

They stood there in the noisy honky-tonk in front of the long, busy bar, chest to breast, belly to belly, groin to groin, and stared at each other as if they were the only two people in the place. The heat sizzling between them built exponentially, second by second, growing higher and hotter and more intense, until it was zigzagging back and forth like lightning on a stormy summer night. No words were spoken. None were needed.

He wanted her.

She wanted him.

It was as simple, as basic, as elemental as that.

Obeying rampant male instinct and the hot female invitation in her eyes, he bent his head and kissed her. One hard, ravening, devouring kiss, unmistakable in its carnality and erotic intent, as intimate and intemperate as if they were alone in a quiet bedroom. She kissed him back the same way, deeply, avidly, instinctively, her mouth open, her tongue tangling wildly with his for a long, hot, mindless moment out of time. And then they drew apart a fraction of an inch, both of them flushed, both of them breathing too fast, and stared at each other for another long moment. His hands were hot and hard on her hips, holding her securely against him. Hers were curled around his biceps, her shiny red nails pressing into the unyielding muscle beneath his pale blue shirt. Questions were asked and answered, decisions made as they stood there, silently staring into each other's eyes.

"Are you sure?" he growled, low, just to make certain he was reading her right.

"Yes," she murmured breathlessly, and then, more firmly, "Yes, I'm sure," she said, and nodded her head for added emphasis.

Incredible as it seemed, she'd never been more sure of anything in her entire life. There wasn't a shred of doubt in her mind. Not a smidgen of hesitation. Not a second thought to be had. The earlier niggling fragment of panic had receded into absolute nothingness, wholly replaced by reckless excitement and wild anticipation for what was to come. She'd been waiting for this moment, fantasizing about it, her whole life. She wasn't about to chicken out now that the fantasy was within her grasp.

"*Yes.*" The word was an affirmation—and a vow.

"You'll leave with me now?" he said, giving her another chance to come to her senses. "Just walk out of this bar with me right now? This minute?" His gaze was still inexorably locked with hers. His erection was unmistakable, pressed firmly against her pubic mound. His fingers bit into her hips. "Even knowing we're going to end up naked and sweaty ten minutes after you do?"

She nodded again. "Yes," she said, her tone unequivocal

and rock-steady, despite the erratic fluttering of her heart and the rush of heat that flooded her body at his words and the feel of him against her.

"Then let's get the hell out of— Damn!" The word was a hot expulsion of air against her lips. "I don't have a room. I was planning on hitting the road later tonight so I didn't book a room."

And all the nearby hotels and motels would already be chock-full of the cowboys who *weren't* hitting the road until the next morning.

"Damn," he said again, his brows drawing together as he struggled to think through the thick cloud of lust in his brain and come up with an alternate plan.

There was always the front seat of his truck, but that didn't seem quite gentlemanly. And, besides, the way he was feeling, he was going to need a lot more than the front seat of a pickup to maneuver in, even if it was the biggest damn model Chevy made. Maybe he could work a trade with one of his buddies, or offer a little monetary incentive to someone to give up their room or... Hell, if there were absolutely no other accommodations to be had—and he was pretty sure there weren't—he was hot enough to forget his gentlemanly scruples in favor of the front seat or the sleeping bag stashed in the bed of his pickup or an empty stall at the—

"I do," she said, interrupting his train of thought.

"Do what?"

"Have a room."

Lust instantly fogged his brain again, shorting any and all remaining thought processes. He could only think of one thing. *She had a room.* "Where?" he growled, barely managing to croak the word out.

"Ah..." The way he was looking at her—as if he wanted to devour her where she stood—had her struggling to remember. "About five miles down the road. West of here. The Broken Spoke Motel."

Without another word, he peeled one of her hands from the sleeve of his shirt, grasped it firmly in his and headed for the glowing red Exit sign on the far side of the dance floor. He plowed through the loud, surging crowd with the single-minded determination of a man hell-bent on getting laid before the night was very much older.

"Hey! Hey, Tom!" A short, bandy-legged cowboy with an energetic dance style stopped mid-twirl, blocking their path. "You comin' back?"

Tom threw him a narrow-eyed look that made the other cowboy grin.

"That mean I need to find myself another ride to Santa Fe?"

"Oh, hell. I forgot." Tom stuffed the first two fingers of his free hand into the front pocket of his jeans and extracted a couple of keys on a ring. He started to toss them to the cowboy, then hesitated and shot a glance at Roxanne. "You got transportation, Slim?"

"A rental car," Roxanne said. "Out front."

Tom nodded and tossed the keys to his grinning buddy. "I'll catch up with you tomorrow in Santa Fe. Don't put any dents in my truck," he ordered as he swept on by the man, towing Roxanne in his wake.

She tripped along behind him, nearly floating, her heart pounding, her knees shaking, her breath sloughing in and out of her lungs, one single, triumphant, giddy thought uppermost in her mind.

I did it! Oh, my God, I really did it! I got myself a dangerous, good-looking cowboy!

And she knew *exactly* what she wanted to do with him.

Chapter Three

TOM HAD EVERY INTENTION of keeping a tight rein on himself until they got to the Broken Spoke Motel—he sincerely believed some things rightly belonged behind closed doors, despite that kiss in the bar—but she stumbled on the loose gravel of the parking lot as he dragged her through the warm night air toward the flashy little car she'd pointed out to him. Her small soft breasts pressed against his arm, her rounded hip bumped his, and all his good intentions disappeared in a firestorm of mind-numbing heat. He swung around, braced his hips against the low-slung red sports car and hauled her into his arms. "Com'ere, Slim," he growled, and crushed his mouth down on hers.

Roxanne gave one soft, startled yelp, then melted against his chest like hot wax, reaching up to clutch his shoulders as he pulled her tight against him. His body was like iron against hers. His hands were hard and hot on her back. And his mouth was…oh, his mouth was delicious. Indescribably delicious.

She hadn't really had time to appreciate that first kiss in the bar. It had happened so fast and been over so soon, and she'd been so…well, overwhelmed was the only word that came to mind. But now that he was taking his time she could fully appreciate his skill. Oh, yes, she could *definitely* appreciate his skill.

Her dangerous, good-looking cowboy was a wonderful kisser.

A glorious kisser.

Indisputably the best kisser who'd ever puckered up.

His lips were soft and firm at the same time, both greedy and generous as they plucked and nibbled and sucked at hers. Not too wet. Not too dry. Just moist and hot and absolutely perfect, all passion and impatience and wild intemperate lust, with no thought for rules or propriety or her good-girl reputation. She was being ruthlessly, ravenously, thoroughly kissed by a man who knew exactly how it should be done.

It was one of her most cherished fantasies come to life.

With a little sigh of pure unadulterated pleasure, Roxanne wound her arms around his neck to pull herself closer, and parted her lips to suck his clever, marauding tongue deeper into her mouth, determined to give as good as she got.

No way was *this* man going to be able to accuse her of being a cold fish. No way was he going to have to ask if she'd come. No way was she going to lie and tell him she had when she hadn't. And no way was she going to censor even the tiniest, most insignificant element of her response to keep from shocking him. She was going to give him her all. Every sigh. Every moan. Every shudder. She was going to match him kiss for kiss, caress for caress, demand for demand. And before it was over, she was going to have *all* her fantasies fulfilled.

Every hot, lascivious scenario she'd ever imagined.

Every wistful romantic daydream.

Every passing erotic thought.

"Everything," she murmured fervidly, the words hot against his lips. "I want everything. Now."

Tom gave a low, ragged groan, like a man mortally wounded, and slid his hands down her back, cupping her tight little buttocks in his palms. "Lord, Slim, you're killing me here," he growled as he lifted her into the V of his splayed thighs.

Roxanne whimpered in helpless delight and squirmed against him with the wild abandon of a buckle bunny out to get herself another notch on her belt. With no more thought than any healthy female animal in heat, she raised her knee, brushing it up along the outside of his denim-clad thigh, and rubbed herself against his leg in a paroxysm of mindless desire.

Tom slid his hand from the rounded curve of her buttock to the back of her bare thigh, lifting and turning her in one smooth movement so that she was sitting on the front fender of the Mustang. The glossy surface was cool against the backs of her thighs; his lean horseman's hips were hot and hard between them. His fingers dug into her flesh, one hand high on her leg, the other still cupped around the curve of her butt. He pulled her forward—one harsh, quick, convulsive movement—so that the crotch of her leopard-print panties was pressed up against the straining fly of his jeans.

All of Roxanne's fantasies suddenly paled into insignificance against the reality of what was happening. No fantasy, no matter how vivid, could have prepared her for his elemental, unrestrained sexuality—or her own recklessly hedonistic response to it. Awash in sensory overload, swamped by the strength and immediacy of her arousal, she forgot all her carefully laid plans for seduction and simply let herself react to the moment. And she had only one thought in mind at that precise moment. One goal. One overwhelming, pulsating, driving need. Shuddering, sighing, her slender arms locked tight around his neck, Roxanne pulled him down with her as she fell back onto the hood of the car beneath his encroaching weight.

They were chest to breast now, their breathing rasping and heavy, their hearts racing, just as they had been in the bar, but now he was between her thighs, his narrow hips moving in a slow, maddening grind that pressed the hard, heavy bulge beneath the fly of his jeans against the rapidly dampening crotch of her panties. His hands were flexing and kneading her buttocks through the denim of her skirt, lifting them to meet each deliberate downward thrust. His mouth was melded to hers, his tongue probing and exploring, devouring, rapacious and utterly devastating.

Roxanne strained against him, one booted ankle locked behind his thigh to hold him to her, her tongue dueling with his, her hands frantic, skimming over the long, hard muscles of his back, over the swelling mounds of his shoulders, searching for a way beneath the soft cotton fabric of his shirt to the flesh beneath. She found bare skin above his shirt collar—warm, satiny, slightly damp—and pressed her glossy red nails into it, making him moan and arch away, lifting his mouth from hers as he drove his hips forward and down.

She slid frantic fingers up over the back of his head to keep him where he was, found his hat in the way and yanked it off, tossing it blindly away so that it flew over the windshield and landed on the floorboard in the front of the car.

He moved one hand up her side, gliding swiftly over a rounded hip and the gentle dip of her waist, skimming the side of one soft breast, over her smooth, bare shoulder, to fist in the soft, tousled hair at her nape. He drew her head back, forcing her body to bow beneath his, instinctively reasserting his control over her, and dragged his open mouth down the long, elegant line of her throat to the tantalizing swell of cleavage revealed by the scooped neck of her blouse.

Roxanne's response was unhesitating, unapologetic, and wildly uninhibited. She clutched his head in both hands and arched under him, pressing her breasts forward, urging him to take more. To take all. To take everything.

He obliged with flattering speed, his mouth open and

sucking at the soft flesh of her breast above her blouse. One hand moved down to her bare thigh, then began inching upward again, sliding under the bunched-up hem of her tiny denim skirt. She felt his fingers skimming along the leg opening of her panties, and then they were edging under it, tracing the sensitive crevice at the top of her thigh, touching the soft crinkly hair that covered her mound, moving inexorably toward the throbbing, heated core of her.

She tensed. Breathless. Waiting. Wanting. Her nerves screaming with anticipation. Her body screaming for release.

"How do you like to be touched, Slim?" he murmured, his voice low and heated, just on the edge of ragged. "Slow and easy?" He skimmed her clitoris with his fingertip, gently, like a man lazily strumming a single string on a guitar.

Roxanne gasped as heat forked through her, and rolled her head against the hood of the Mustang, lifting her hips upward, pressing closer, straining.

"Or fast and furious?" He flicked the swelled nubbin of flesh, quickly, as if he were doing hot licks on a banjo string.

Roxanne bucked wildly beneath him and her hips began to piston in silent demand. She was as taut as an expertly coiled rope, the tension in her arched body a palpable thing that held her, quivering and breathless, on the edge of release, needing only the right touch to send her flying.

"Talk to me, Slim," he growled, his head lifted now so he could watch her face as he held her there, trembling on the brink. His eyes were like blue lasers, hot, intense, and focused. "Tell me how you want to be touched."

Roxanne moaned, incoherent with need and excitement, and reached down to grab his hand, intending to direct his fingers to where she most wanted them to be, to show him what she wanted with every fiber of her being.

"No." He resisted the silent demand. "Tell me."

"I...I... Oh. I don't. I can't. I... Oh, please. *Please.* Just touch me. Touch—"

"Well, hot damn, would you look at that." The voice rang out across the parking lot, boisterous and male. "Yahoo! Ride 'em, cowboy!"

The two people sprawled on the hood of the Mustang stiffened, stilled in a frozen tableau of passion rudely interrupted. Tom's hand was under her skirt, inside her leopard-print panties, a millimeter from where she needed it to be. Roxanne's fingers were clamped around his wrist, the nails biting into his flesh in a futile effort to guide him to the right spot.

"Come on, Hank, honey." It was a woman's voice, high-pitched and giggly. "It ain't polite to stare."

"Well, hell, darlin', it ain't polite to do the wild thing in public, either, but—"

"Come *on*, Hank. Let's just go inside. I want to dance."

They could hear Hank grumbling but he went, his boot heels crunching in the gravel as he followed "darlin'" into the honky-tonk. The door to Ed Earl's creaked open, spilling music and light out into the parking lot, then closed again, surrendering the night to the garish pink glow of the flamingos on the roof.

Roxanne bit back a strangled whimper of frustration and loosened her grip on Tom's wrist, hating the loudmouthed cowboy and his giggling girlfriend with her whole heart. She'd been so close. So tantalizing close! All she'd needed was one more second. Just one more measly little second and she knew her good-looking, dangerous cowboy would have taken her all the way to paradise.

Tom swore ripely and withdrew his hand from Roxanne's panties, silently thanking God or whoever was in charge of looking out for damn fools that Hank and his darlin' hadn't come by two minutes later. He'd been that close—*that* close—to unbuttoning the fly of his Wrangler and giving it to her right there on top the car. Two minutes more—hell, less than two minutes!—he'd have been bare-assed, his jeans around his knees, thrusting into her with no more thought for time and place than a stallion covering a mare.

And no cowboy yahooing in the parking lot would have stopped him until he'd gotten them where they both wanted to go.

Even now, it was a near thing. His control—such as it was—wouldn't survive another close encounter. The next time he put his hands on her, he wouldn't stop until both of them were naked, sweaty, and too exhausted to do more than moan in satisfaction. And, damn it, they needed a bed and some privacy for that!

"Come on, Slim." He stepped back and took hold of both her hands, pulling her upright. "Let's get the hell out of here before we get ourselves arrested."

Bemused, befuddled, her body humming with unfulfilled desires, her brain fogged by unsatisfied lust, Roxanne slid obligingly, even eagerly, off the fender of the car—and then just stood there, staring up at him with a soft, besotted expression on her face. Lord, he was good-looking. And sexy. And she wanted him so much. So very much. More than she'd ever wanted anything or anyone in her entire life. She swayed toward him, her face raised, her lips parted, her eyes drifting closed.

He took a quick step back and dropped her hands. "No."

Her eyes snapped open, widened at his abrupt, almost-biting tone.

"We lock lips again and, I swear, I'll hoist you right back up on the hood of this car and finish it," he warned, his voice low and soft and strained. "Every last cowboy in the bar could come tromping out to watch and I wouldn't stop. Not until we were both too tired to move. And maybe not even then."

Roxanne smiled beatifically, thrilled to the core by his ragged admission. "I wouldn't want you to stop," she said, her voice as ragged, as strained, as his. "I didn't want you to stop before."

Tom gulped audibly and his hands fisted at his sides.

The jolt of pure female sexual power that surged through her at that small, telling gesture was utterly intoxicating, adding another layer to her simmering sexual excitement. No man had ever threatened her with ravishment before. No man had ever had to fight to restrain himself from carrying out that threat, either. It made her feel irresistible. Invincible. Intensely, totally female. At that precise moment, good girl Roxanne Archer disappeared completely. In her place was good-time girl Roxy.

And Roxy was hot.

Roxy was itchy.

Roxy wanted a man—*this* man—and didn't care who knew it.

She tilted her head, looking up at him from under provocatively lowered lashes, and gave him the same slow, seductive come-to-mama smile that had drawn him to her in the bar. But this time there was no calculation in it, no planning or plotting. She was acting on pure feminine instinct. "I guess we'd better do as you suggested, then, shouldn't we?" she said, and licked her lips. Slowly.

Tom made a low growling noise and took a careful step back, away from her and the temptation she so blatantly offered.

Roxanne's smile turned positively feline. Her eyes glowed. Without shifting her gaze from his, she reached down with exaggerated slowness and slid the first two fingers of her right hand into the pocket of her skirt.

"The key," she said, and held the plastic Hertz key ring up in front of his face with the key dangling. "To the car," she added, when he just stood there, staring at it as if he'd never seen a key before. "So we can get the hell out of here before we get arrested," she prompted.

When he still made no move to take it, she reached out, hooked the tip of one long red fingernail on the edge of his shirt pocket, pulled it away from his chest and dropped the key inside. "You drive," she said, and then turned and sauntered around the hood of the car to the passenger side, hips swaying seductively, glossy red nails trailing over the glossy red car. She made a show of getting into the car, affording him a leisurely, heart-stopping view of her cleavage as she bent over to pluck his Stetson off the floor mat, snuggling her butt into the soft leather of the seat, adjusting the hem of her minuscule skirt over her bare legs with a languid, caressing gesture, as if she enjoyed the feel of her own fingers on her skin.

Tom stood stock-still, watching her, unable to move, unable to respond, unable to speak, as dumbstruck as a wet-behind-the-ears, peach-fuzz cowboy who'd just been tossed on his head by a bronc and still hadn't got his breath back yet.

She set his Stetson on her head, adjusting it so that it set, low and sexy, over her forehead, then tilted her head and looked up at him from under the brim. The invitation in her eyes was blatant, unashamed, unwavering, with nothing held back, nothing hidden. She smiled seductively, slowly, and licked her lips again.

Damn, she was...she was... Hell, he didn't know *what* she was!

Except gorgeous.

And hot.

And so damned sexy it made his insides ache and his palms sweat.

One look, that's all it had taken. One long, slow, hot-eyed look from a tall, cool glass of water, and he'd wanted to grab and take and possess. He *had* grabbed and taken and—very nearly, anyway—possessed. And that surprised him. Shocked him, actually. He wasn't normally a man with a short fuse. Ask anybody who knew him and they'd tell you Tom Steele was one careful hombre. He took his time. He considered his options. He weighed all the pros and cons. Steady, that was Tom Steele. Not a man to rush off half-cocked, or to get all hot and bothered and lose his head over a pretty little piece of tail.

Except that he had.

He stood there in the parking lot of Ed Earl's, in the pink-neon glow of those ridiculous flamingos, his heart thudding against the wall of his chest, his cock full to bursting against the fly of his jeans, and his hands... Good Lord, his hands were actually trembling.

He unclenched his fists, flexing his fingers like a gun-fighter about to take that long walk down the middle of a dusty street, and took a couple of deep, deliberate breaths in a effort to bring down his heart rate. It didn't work.

"Ah, the hell with it," he muttered, and reached for the door handle of the car. The only thing that was going to slow his heart rate was the exhaustion that came after a fast, furious bout of hot, sweaty sex. Maybe.

She turned toward him as he slid behind the wheel, reaching out to run her hand down his arm.

He didn't even look at her. "Keep your hands to yourself, Slim," he ordered, tight-lipped, as he fished around in his shirt pocket for the key. "And don't say a word." He jammed the key into the ignition and gunned the engine to life. "Not a word until we get to the motel."

Roxanne gave a soft gurgle of laughter, a low, throaty sound of feminine triumph and challenge, and settled back into her seat, her hands folded demurely in her lap. It was only five miles to the motel and judging by the rooster tail of dust and gravel he'd left in Ed Earl's parking lot, they'd be there in less than five minutes. She could wait that long. Barely.

Chapter Four

THE FACADE of the Broken Spoke Motel was cheap Hollywood Western, with an unpainted barn-board exterior, a split-log hitching rail running along the front, and horseshoes bracketing the room numbers on each of the doors. A red-neon wagon wheel, one spoke seeming to swing back and forth as it flashed on and off, sat perched atop a pole in front of the motel office, right above the unblinking No Vacancy sign. A bank of vending machines stood on the cracked concrete apron just outside the office door, in clear sight of whoever was manning the registration desk. At the moment it was empty, with a hand-lettered sign advising would-be guests to ring for assistance.

Tom pulled into the first open parking space in the lot, jammed on the parking brake, and was out of the car almost before the engine stopped idling. His boot heels sent up little puffs of dust as he rounded the hood, purpose in every deliberate step, burning lust in his eyes, one thing on his mind. Roxanne sat in the passenger seat in stupefied delight and watched him come to her, come *after* her, thrilled beyond belief to be the object of such single-minded desire. With a sense of delighted amazement, she realized she could actually feel her nipples, rigid against the satiny fabric of her leopard-print bra, could feel the wetness soaking the matching fabric between her legs, could feel the blood pounding through her veins. She had never been so aware of her body, never felt so sensitized, so aroused, as if every nerve ending was on red alert. She was tingling all over...her lips...her fingertips...her thighs...every part of her quivering with anticipation and wanton, intemperate need, making her wonder how she was going to manage to stand up and walk to the room without collapsing into a quivering heap at his feet.

She didn't have to try.

He yanked open the door and bent down, scooping her up into his arms. "Which room?" he growled as he shoved the door closed with his foot.

It was another cherished fantasy fulfilled. Being swept off her feet. Carried off to be ravaged by a dangerous cowboy. The old Roxanne would have likely fainted from excitement; the new Roxy looped her arms around her cowboy's neck and tickled his ear with her tongue, as if being swept off her feet were an every day occurrence.

Tom's whole body tensed at her teasing caress, and his hands tightened on her thighs and back as a spasm of sheer sexual pleasure shot through him. If he didn't get inside her in the next sixty seconds he was going to come in his jeans. And that hadn't happened since he was fourteen. "Which room, Slim?"

"Seven." She sighed the word into his ear, her breath hot and moist. "Lucky seven." She slid her tongue down the side of his neck, and then up again, as if he were her favorite flavor of ice cream and she was intent on savoring every last delicious drop. "Second door past the office."

Tom turned on his heel and headed toward the promise of paradise with long ground-eating strides, while the woman in his arms did her best to drive him to his knees before they got there. He stumbled slightly when she stuck her tongue in his ear, but managed to regain his balance with a quick, light-footed move that brought him to a halt directly in front of the trio of vending machines in front of the motel office. One offered the usual soft drinks, another candy bars and chips, the third had toiletries for sale...miniature tubes of toothpaste, tins of aspirin, palm-size packets of tissue, condoms. A mental picture of his battered canvas carryall, still stowed behind the front seat of his pickup, flashed through his mind.

Roxanne left off nibbling on his earlobe to raise her head. "What?" she murmured, her eyes wide and hazy with arousal, her voice softly slurred.

Tom indicated the offerings in the vending machine with a jerk of his chin. "Am I going to need those?"

Her arms still locked securely around his neck, Roxanne glanced over her shoulder to see what he was talking about. "I've got one inside my bra."

His eyes blazed. "Only one?"

"And a whole box in my room," she assured him. "There are a dozen in it. Well—" she loosened her hold on him with one hand and touched the little foil packet of protection tucked inside her push-up bra, inadvertently drawing his eyes to the creamy mounds of flesh above the neckline of her blouse "—eleven, anyway," she managed, watching his eyes heat and burn.

"A dozen just might do it. Maybe." He bent his head and nuzzled the scented valley between her plumped-up breasts, breathing her in with a long hungry gulp of air. "Or maybe not," he said softly, the breath rushing out of him in a tremulous sigh.

And, just like that, Roxanne fell a little bit in love. Not the happily-ever-after, till-death-do-us-part kind of love. She wasn't that much of a fool. But it was love, nonetheless, a light-headed, lighthearted, giddy kind of love, as insubstantial as moonbeams and neon, as temporary as the victory after a championship bronc ride. But it made what was about to happen just that much more wonderful and exciting. More thrilling. More everything. If she hadn't already been dewy with need, that one sweet, tender gesture would have done it.

"Hurry," she whispered, and nipped his earlobe for emphasis. *"Hurry."*

Tom hurried.

"The key?" he said, letting her slide down his body as he set her on her feet in front of the door to room number seven.

"That's in my bra, too."

"Get it."

She leaned against the door, her hands behind her back, her breasts thrust out, and looked up at him from beneath the brim of his hat. "Why don't you get—"

"No." It was the same abrupt tone he'd used in the parking lot when he'd backed off from kissing her. But this time he didn't back off. He simply stood there, looking down at her with hot dangerous lights dancing in his blue eyes. "I'm on the thin edge of control here, Slim, and if I put my hand down your blouse now, I'm going to end up fucking you where you stand, right here against this door, in front of God and everybody. Is that what you want?"

She almost said yes. The word hovered on the tip of her tongue for a dangerous moment, enticing them both with the possibility of flagrant debauchery. And then Tom put his hands on her shoulders, jerked her away from the door, and turned her around. "Get the key, Slim, and open the damned door."

Roxanne fumbled for the key, fumbled as she fit it into the lock, fumbled as she turned the doorknob and stepped over the threshold. She should be aghast, she knew. Ashamed of her lack of control. Appalled at her willingness to make a public spectacle of herself. Yesterday, she would have been.

Maybe tomorrow, she would be again. But right now, she wasn't. Couldn't be. Right now, she was on fire, burning up from the inside out, trembling with desire. The only thing on her mind, the single driving thought in her head, was the overwhelming need to assuage the heat, to quench the aching desire, to find sweet release with her good-looking, dangerous cowboy.

And then the door crashed closed behind her, and his arm encircled her waist, and he spun her around, crushing his mouth to hers, and she ceased to think at all.

He propelled her backward toward the bed, his mouth fastened to hers, feasting, his hands moving over her body, frantically molding her breasts and back and the sweet, subtle curve of her bottom through her clothes. Her kisses were as greedy, as wildly intemperate as his, her hands as frantic, touching him everywhere she could reach. The backs of her knees hit the edge of the bed and she tumbled onto it, pulling him down on top of her. They bounced once, sending the cowboy hat she still wore somersaulting over the edge of the mattress to the floor. Entwined like tangled kudzu vines, they rolled across the bed and crashed into the headboard. It banged against the wall and they rolled away, mouths still hotly fused, hands still moving frantically, bodies pressed together, legs entangled, hips grinding together. Tom's foot hit the rickety bedside table, causing the equally rickety bedside lamp to wobble on its base, sending shadows flickering precariously across the walls and ceiling, counterpoint to the intermittent flash of red neon from the motel sign pulsing through the slanted blinds on the window.

Neither one of them paid it any heed. Neither of them would have noticed if the lamp had gone crashing to the floor. The only thing that registered was the searing wildfire need that ricocheted back and forth between them, the only thing that mattered was satisfying that need.

Immediately.

Now.

Tom shoved both hands under her tiny denim skirt, pushing it up to her waist, and curled his fingers under the low-slung waistband of her leopard-print panties. And then he paused, still on the thin edge of control, and stared down into her wide, whiskey-colored eyes. She stared back at him, her gaze avid, unwavering, and unabashedly eager, without coyness or equivocation, primed and ready for whatever came next.

"This first time is going to be a fast, hard ride," he said, his voice low and guttural. "If that's not what you want, say so now."

She bent her knees, planting her boot heels on the edge of the mattress, and lifted her hips. "It's what I want."

He yanked her panties off, tugging them past her raised hips, dragging them down her legs, wrestling them over her boots, and tossed them on the floor. His hands went to his fly, his fingers working frantically at the metal buttons to free his erection as he slid his body back up between her legs. He grasped her bare thighs, his strong callused fingers digging into her flesh as he spread them wider, meaning to drive himself into her, hard and fast the way they both wanted, to take her with elemental, unthinking fury.

But something about the way she lay there, her minuscule skirt pushed up around her waist, her bent knees splayed, her soft, hot, woman's body open and vulnerable to his every desire, had him suddenly gentling his approach. She was so pretty and fragile there between her legs, all plump and pink and glistening, with the feeble light from the bedside lamp glinting on the smooth pale skin of her thighs, and the red neon pulsing like a heartbeat, giving her an all-over rosy glow. The soft blond hair between her legs had been waxed or shaved or whatever it was that women did, into a narrow little rectangle that barely covered her mound. It was rawly sexy, and inexplicably, elegantly refined. Just as she was.

He softened his grip and slid his palms down the inside of her thighs, slowly, caressingly, until his thumbs just touched her vulva. Her body jerked beneath him, a tiny involuntary movement that could have signaled rejection or acceptance of his intimate invasion. He raised his gaze to her face again. She stared back through the frame of her splayed knees, her lips moist and parted, her cheeks flushed, the expression in her eyes as soft, as hot, as open and vulnerable as her body.

Slowly, still holding her gaze with his, he slid his thumbs down and then up, then down again—once, twice, three times—gently skimming her most sensitive flesh. Her body undulated, like a field of ripe wheat rippling in the wind, and she uttered a breathy little sound, half moan, half sigh, that shuddered out between her lips.

"You're wet." His voice was low and caressing, his gaze voracious and admiring. "Hot and wet and slippery."

"Yes." She didn't blush. Didn't look away. "I am."

"I want you wetter. I want you—" he moved his thumbs inward a fraction of an inch, pressing down, closing in, capturing her distended clitoris between them in a sensuous little squeeze play "—dripping."

Her body tightened, straining, and the sound she made was definitely a moan. A deep, throaty, on-the-edge moan.

He eased his thumbs back a teasing fraction of an inch from her slick swollen center and watched her eyes flare wide in mindless entreaty, watched her bite her lip against protest and plea. Her desire was palpable, her anticipation a living, breathing thing between them.

He knew exactly what she wanted.

Needed.

Had to have.

In another mood, he might have made her say the words,

might have teased her—and himself—by making her ask for what she wanted. Instead, he slid his hands under her hips, slid his body down off the bed until his knees were on the floor and his shoulders were wedged between her thighs.

"We'll save the hard riding for later," he said, and buried his face between her legs.

Roxanne nearly levitated off the bed at the first heated, silken stroke of his tongue against her throbbing clitoris. Her back arched like a bow. Her hands clutched at the worn chenille bedspread, gathering it into her clenched fists. Her booted heels pressed down into the edge of the mattress. She moaned. Loudly. And then more loudly still as he brought his fingers into play again, opening her more fully to his lasciviously talented tongue.

It felt as if every nerve ending in her body began and ended in that one tiny nubbin of sensitized flesh between her legs. She throbbed. She ached. She vibrated with need. And, then, in a blinding, incandescent blaze of sheer primal lust, she came. It was gut-wrenching. Breath-stealing. Mind-blowing. *Sublime*.

"More," she demanded, when her breath finally shuddered back into her lungs and she could breathe again. She released her death grip on the bedspread and reached down, fisting her hands in his dark, silky hair, pressing him closer, straining for another peak. "More."

He acquiesced with satisfying gallantry and greed, with no hint of hesitation or resistance, as if continuing to pleasure her with his mouth had been his intention all along. And, maybe, it had been. She was sweet and tender, so incredibly hot and responsive that it was pure, unadulterated pleasure to give her what she wanted. Because it was what he wanted, too.

Making her scream with ecstasy had been high on his list of priorities since the first moment he'd seen her in the bar.

He'd thought to do it by pounding her into the mattress. He still meant to do it that way. Later. Right now, he was determined to tease those screams of ecstasy out of her with his tongue. She'd uttered that one, long, shuddering, gasping breath when she came the first time; he wanted a full-throated scream the next time she went over. He slipped his hands back under her bare squirming bottom to hold her more securely, and set about getting what he wanted with the same single-minded focus he applied to everything.

In minutes, he had her writhing between his hands. Her hips undulated against his mouth in mindless entreaty. Her head thrashed against the bed. Her breath came in throaty little whimpers and panting moans, interspersed with disjointed pleas and fragmented demands.

"Oh, God... I... Yes. Oh, yes. There. Oh, please. Yes. Right there. Yes. Yes. *Yes!*"

The last yes came out as a strangled shout, a muffled scream that barely echoed off the thin walls of the motel room.

Satisfied with that, Tom lifted his head and pressed a soft kiss to the soft crinkly hair that covered her mound.

"Inside," she demanded raggedly, nearly delirious with need. She yanked on his hair, trying to pull him up her body. "I need you inside me. Now. Right *now.*"

Tom didn't have to be asked twice. He levered himself on top of her with a supple shift of his body, sliding up between her splayed thighs. His engorged penis nudged her slick folds, seeking the entrance to her soft, hot woman's body. It took every ounce of his considerable willpower to keep from plunging into her. Instead, calling upon his last reserves of control, he pushed himself up onto his knees and reached for the top button on her blouse.

"The condom." The words were gritted out between clenched teeth. His hands were trembling. "Where's the damned condom?"

Roxanne pushed his groping hands away to retrieve it herself. "I'll do it," she said, curling the foil-wrapped packet into her fist when he would have taken it from her. "I want to do it."

"Then do it," he ordered. "*Quick.*"

With hands that were surprisingly steady given the raging storm going on inside of her, she peeled the two halves of the foil wrapping back, tossed it aside, and reached down with both hands to sheath him. His penis was incredibly hot to the touch. Incredibly hard. She curled her fingers around his steely, latex-shielded length and guided him into her.

"Ride me, cowboy." The words were a demand. A plea. A prayer. "Ride me hard."

He drove himself into her with all the finesse of a sex-crazed adolescent mounting his first woman. His body was tense and quivering, muscles straining, hips pistoning wildly, madly, almost violently. Pounding into her, taking her, possessing her, riding her. Hard. Roxanne cried out, a feral sound of surrender and triumph both, and drove her hips upward, meeting him thrust for thrust. It was hot and wild. Untamed. Uncivilized. Out of control. Damp flesh slamming into damp flesh…breathing hot and labored…long callused fingers digging into soft giving flesh…long red nails pressing into hard straining muscles…lips parted, gasping for air…eyes closed tight to better savor the battering maelstrom of sensation… relentlessly driving each other to completion.

The mattress creaked beneath them, counterpoint to each powerful thrust. The headboard banged against the wall. The lamp wobbled on its stand. And still they hammered at each other, striving, straining, battling toward the ultimate peak of physical sensation.

And then all of Roxanne's small inner muscles began to spasm. Hard. Fast. Unstoppable. Inevitable. The movement spread outward, tightening the muscles in her belly and back and thighs, drawing her nipples into stiff aching buds, arching her body up off of the bed until she was as taut as a quivering bow. Tom thrust into her twice more—deeply, powerfully, heavily—deliberately pushing her over the edge. She fell with a high keening cry, trilling her satisfaction and pleasure with the same lack of restraint she'd shown in going after it in the first place.

With a hard convulsive shudder, he let go and went over himself. The feeling began between his legs, pulling everything tight and hard, nearly painful in its intensity, radiating outward in pulsating waves that curled his toes inside his battered Tony Lamas and nearly caused his eyes to roll back in his head.

They collapsed onto each other, *into* each other in a boneless heap, trembling and damp, wrung out, replete, utterly satisfied. Several minutes passed in silence as they lay there, panting, still entwined, still intimately joined, and waited for the world to right itself around them.

Roxanne surfaced by slow degrees, the sensual haze clouding her mind dissipating bit by bit as she came back to herself. She could feel the hard round shape of his belt buckle pressing into the soft flesh of her inner thigh, feel the pearl snaps on his shirt pressing into her breasts and belly through the thin cotton fabric of her eyelet blouse. His breath was hot against her neck. His hands still cupped her bare bottom. His penis was still snug inside of her. He was a dead weight on top of her, a hundred and eighty pounds of exhausted, hard-muscled male, but she lay there quietly beneath him for several long contented minutes, her body deliciously relaxed and sated, and deliberately took stock of the situation.

Common sense would dictate that she should be feeling ashamed, or guilty, or at least foolish about what she had just done. Instead, she was absurdly pleased with herself. Good-girl Roxanne Archer had picked up a good-looking, dangerous cowboy in a tacky honky-tonk, taken him back to her tacky motel room, and had wild, raunchy sex with him. Nobody back in Connecticut would believe it. She could hardly believe it herself. And, yet, there she was, spread-eagled and flat on her back beneath said cowboy, still wallowing in the afterglow of a monumental, toe-curling, mind-bending orgasm—and thinking about doing it again as soon as humanly possible. Or as soon as they both got their breaths back.

She smoothed her hand down the long damp curve of his spine, under the pale blue shirt he still wore, to the hard swell of his bare buttock. "I don't mean to complain, sugar." She patted his fanny lightly, appreciatively. "But you're smashing me flat."

He grunted, a purely male sound that delighted her feminine soul, and levered himself up onto his elbows to relieve her of most of his weight. His head hung down between his shoulders, as if it were too heavy to lift just yet, his face still buried in the curve of her neck. She could feel his eyelashes, soft as butterfly wings, flutter against her skin as he opened his eyes, and then he raised his head and gave her a slow, sexy, self-satisfied smile.

"You get the license number of the truck that hit us?"

Roxanne smiled back, pleased and gratified by the implication that she wasn't the only one who been broadsided by the big O. "What truck was that, sugar?" she said playfully, and fluttered her eyelashes at him.

"Big ol' eighteen-wheeler roarin' down the highway at ninety miles an hour, at least. Knocked the stuffing right out of me."

"Oh, I don't know. You still feel pretty—" she made a little thrusting motion with her hips "—stuffed to me."

Tom's smile widened into a teasing, lopsided grin. "You've got your anatomy wrong, Slim. You're the one who's—" he countered the teasing movement of her hips with a quick thrusting movement of his own "—stuffed."

Roxanne's appreciative chuckle turned into a low throaty moan. Her hands tightened on the cheeks of his butt. Her back arched.

And, just like that, he was rock-hard again, as hot and horny and hungry as if he hadn't just exhausted himself between her thighs. His teasing grin faded. The lazy glow in his eyes sharpened and focused. He pushed himself up onto his hands, pressing her hips more deeply into the mattress, and stared down at her, incredulous and amazed. He was thirty-one years old, for God's sake! He wasn't supposed to be ready for Round Two so soon.

"This is crazy," he murmured, fighting the urge to begin thrusting like a wild man again. "*We're* crazy. You know that, don't you? Completely crazy."

"Yes." She tightened her hands on his backside, trying to press him closer, deeper. "I know. Crazy."

"We're both of us still half dressed." He gave in to temptation, and the silent demand of her hands on his butt, and rotated his hips, grinding his pubis against hers. "Still got our boots on."

"Yes," she agreed. "Boots. We should take our boots off and— Oh! Oh, yes." The word was a long drawn-out hosanna of inarticulate appreciation. "Do that again."

"I don't even know your name." He made another small, deliberate grinding motion. "You don't know mine."

"I know your name." The words fluttered out in little panting breaths. "Your name is Tom Steele. And mine is Roxan—Roxy," she corrected, catching herself. "Roxy Arch— Oh, yes! Again. Please." She wrapped her legs around his waist, locking her booted ankles at the small of his back to keep him inside her when he started to withdraw. "*Again!*" she demanded.

He did it again.

And then again.

Very slowly.

Very deliberately.

Very gently.

Roxanne bucked beneath him, her hips pistoning as she tried to increase the pace, and the pressure. "Faster," she panted. "Harder. Oh, please. *Harder*."

He gave in to one demand and resisted the other, pressing down harder, while at the same time restricting the movement of her hips with his until they were barely moving at all.

"Take it easy, Slim." The words were low and soft, gritted out through clenched teeth as he struggled to resist her passionate demands and the inclinations of his own body. He wanted it to last a good long while this time, and that wasn't going to happen if he let go and started thrusting like a madman. "Real slow and easy," he murmured, suiting words to action as he ground his pelvis against hers. "Let's make it last this time."

Roxanne uttered an inarticulate protest and strained against him, her legs clamped around him like a vise, her thighs and belly taut and quivering, her back arched, her teeth clamped over her lower lip as she fought to take what he held just out of her reach.

"Easy," he said, and ducked his head, brushing his mouth over hers, skimming his tongue over her abused lip. "Take it easy. Just let go and take it easy. We'll get there."

He continued to rotate his pelvis against hers, his engorged penis rock-hard and motionless inside her, his pubic bone pressing against her clitoris in a tiny, focused, unrelentingly gentle motion that seemed to go on forever, winding her tighter and tighter, like barbed wire being slowly, carefully tightened with a winch, stretching every muscle and nerve ending to the very edge of release, holding her there until she gave in and went limp beneath him, letting him take her where he would.

He rose, then, catching her legs in the crook of his elbows as they slid bonelessly from around his waist. He leaned forward, pulling her legs high and wide, opening her fully, and placed his hands on the bed beside her shoulders. And, finally, he began to thrust. Deep and slow at first, long, deliberate strokes that gradually—oh, so very gradually!—became faster and harder as she began to writhe beneath him.

Faster.

Harder.

Faster.

Harder.

Until, suddenly, it was too much and too hard and too fast, and everything broke loose in a wild, uncontrollable whirlwind of nearly unbearable sensation, like a hundred strands of bared wire that had snapped under intolerable pressure.

She screamed this time. It was a full-throated, unselfconscious scream of triumphant release that had the occupants of the neighboring room pounding on the wall and demanding quiet. Ignoring their demands, Tom uttered his own exultant shout of satisfaction and followed her into the spinning vortex.

"Next time," he promised, just before he collapsed on top of her, "we'll get our boots off first."

ROXANNE WAS DEFINITELY sans boots when she woke up the next morning. She was also sans everything else, including blankets of any kind. She lay on her side on the rumpled bed, her knees drawn up, her naked flesh pebbling under the arctic blast of the air-conditioning unit in the window. Bright Texas sunlight glittered through the slatted blinds, creating a ladder-like pattern on the worn carpet, over the scattered articles of clothing and bed linens that littered the floor, and across the broad golden back of the naked man lying in bed beside her.

Her good-looking dangerous cowboy hadn't disappeared with the morning's light as she'd half feared he might, but lay facedown, taking up a full three-quarters of the motel bed, snoring ever so softly into his pillow.

Roxanne couldn't help the idiotic grin that spread across her face at the sight of him. She also couldn't stop herself from reaching out to run her hand over all that glorious masculine pulchritude. She would have thought she'd have gotten enough of him sometime during the long, sweaty, tempestuous night that had gone before, but she hadn't. If anything, last night had only made her want more. More touching. More kissing. More of him. More of herself the way she was with him.

She'd never been so uninhibited. Never been so voracious and greedy. Never been so effortlessly responsive. It was a side of herself she hadn't previously known existed and she wanted to explore it.

At length.

In depth.

Right now.

She tiptoed her fingers back up his spine and tickled the nape of his neck.

He stirred beneath her touch, the long lean muscles of his back flexing, the smooth rounded muscles of his shoulders bunching ever so slightly under his golden skin as he turned his head toward her. He blinked owlishly, not quite all there. "I wasn't sure you'd be here this morning," he said.

Her fingers stilled. "Are you disappointed that I am?"

"Lord, no!" He rolled to his side, levering himself up onto his elbow, catching her hand before she could draw it away. "I thought maybe I'd dreamed you, is all."

"Then I must have been dreaming, too."

He grinned. "Hell of a dream," he said, and lifted her captured hand to his lips for a quick kiss. "I hate to see it end."

"Who says it has to?" she said, and felt her heart flutter at the audacity of what she was about to suggest.

"Don't you have someplace you have to be?" He cocked an eyebrow at her. "A home? A job? Something?" He hesitated. "Someone?" he suggested.

"Nope. I'm free as a bird for the rest of the summer. There's nowhere I have to be until September. No one I'm accountable to." She looked up at him from under the veil of her lashes. "You interested?"

"In?" he said carefully, not quite sure she was suggesting what he thought he was suggesting. No man could be *that* lucky.

"You. Me." She tugged her hand out of his, slid it down his torso, curled it around his penis. It hardened instantly, filling her hand to overflowing. "This." She squeezed him lightly. "All. Summer. Long."

Tom nearly swallowed his tongue. He had to consciously tell himself to take a breath before he could speak. "And when the summer's over?"

"When the summer's over, we go our separate ways. No fuss. No muss. No strings. And no looking back."

Good God Almighty, Tom thought, as what she said sank in. He'd just been offered a last fling that was going to take him nearly to the end of the rodeo season. And then she'd disappear from his life. A man *could* be that lucky!

"So, how about it, sugar?" She squeezed him more firmly, adding a leisurely up-and-down stroke for good measure. "You want to take me on for the rest of the summer?"

Chapter Five

THE DRIVE from the Broken Spoke Motel in Lubbock, Texas, to the rodeo grounds in Santa Fe, New Mexico, was nearly eight hours long, which gave Roxanne more than enough time to think about what she'd done the night before—and what she'd agreed to do for the remaining two and a half months of her summer vacation.

The first was an event she had planned for as carefully and completely as she did her class curriculum each year. Like the thorough, conscientious, obsessively good girl she was, she'd considered her options, made her decision, then spent a good six months laying the groundwork for getting laid. She'd taken country-western dance lessons, researched the rodeo, read every sex manual, erotic novel and women's magazine article on attracting and seducing the male of the species that she could get her hands on. From there, it had taken nearly a week of attending rodeos to decide on the cowboy she wanted. And then another week of careful study to transform herself into the kind of woman he might conceivably want in return.

The second event, however, was a decision her sexy alter ego had made on the spur of the moment, in the heat of passion, so to speak. And Roxanne wasn't entirely sure if she was comfortable with that decision. Could she *be* Roxy for two and a half months? Could conservative, stick-in-the-mud, good girl Roxanne Archer sustain the transformation to good-time girl Roxy without reverting to type and blowing her cover? Did she have the stamina and the cunning to stay in character for that long? More importantly, did she have the wardrobe?

She'd only planned on a weekend of sexual excess—a week, if she got really lucky—and had purchased accordingly. A pair of cowboy boots, one denim miniskirt, a pair of jeans, a couple of skimpy tops and some sexy new underwear weren't going to last her an entire summer. If she was going to do this—and, she realized, she *was* going to do it, was *already* doing it, despite the misgivings still niggling at the back of her mind—she needed to supplement her new wardrobe. Otherwise, she'd be reduced to wearing the khaki slacks and linen camp shirts that were her usual summer uniform. And that wouldn't suit Roxy, at all.

"Having second thoughts?"

Roxanne hooked a strand of flying hair behind her ear with one long red nail and looked over at her good-looking, dangerous cowboy. He sat in the driver's seat of her rented convertible, his left elbow on the car door, his right wrist draped over the steering wheel, his hat pulled down low over his eyes, piloting the car down the long, lonely ribbon of highway at speeds that just begged a cop to stop them. If there had been any cops, that is. She hadn't seen anything besides the occasional eighteen-wheeler for miles.

"I beg your pardon?" she said politely, and then belatedly remembered her San Antonio drawl. She fluttered her eyelashes to cover the lapse. "You say something, sugar?"

"You've been sitting over there, lost in thought for the past thirty minutes. I was wondering if you were having second thoughts."

"Second thoughts about what?"

"About us." He flicked the hand he had draped over the steering wheel, the gesture eloquent in spite of its brevity. "This."

"I never have second thoughts," Roxanne said airily, lying through her teeth.

Roxanne *always* had second thoughts. And third and fourth ones, too. But she was sure Roxy didn't. Roxy was a decisive, daring, devil-may-care, fly-by-the-seat-of-her-pants kind of girl; the kind of girl careful, conservative Roxanne had always secretly envied.

"Once I make a decision—bam—" she snapped her fingers in the air between them "—it's made. Second thoughts are a waste of time. Unless..." She felt her stomach clench as one of those second thoughts she denied having popped into her mind. "Are *you* having second thoughts, sugar?" She shot him a sliding sideways glance, rife with deliberate insouciance in case he was. "Because, if you are, we can dissolve this—" she ran her fingernail along the top of his thigh "—partnership—" she said, encouraged when his quads tensed "—at the next truck stop. You just say the word and I'll be gone. No muss, no fuss, remember?"

She patted his thigh and lifted her hand, only to find it captured beneath his. He drew it to his crotch, pressing it down over the rapidly hardening bulge beneath his fly. "Does that feel like I'm having second thoughts?"

Roxanne's cherry-red lips turned up in a wicked smile of pure feminine satisfaction—and relief. "It sure feels like you're having some kind of thoughts." She squeezed him lightly. "You want to stop somewhere and act on those thoughts, sugar?"

His smile was as wicked as hers. "I wasn't thinking about stopping at all," he said, and moved her hand in a suggestive up-and-down motion before releasing it.

Roxanne felt an illicit thrill zing through her. Here was

another fantasy, hers for the taking, if she dared. She'd never done what he was suggesting, not in a moving vehicle. Not in a vehicle at all, actually. Not anywhere. The world of lovers' lanes and teenage sex in the back seat of Daddy's car hadn't been one she'd ever been invited to enter. There had been no heavy petting in somebody's rec room or fogging up the windows in a parked car. She'd been nearly twenty-four, a responsible adult with a job and her own apartment when she surrendered her virginity. By then, there had been no need for furtive sex or forbidden thrills. She'd always wondered what she'd missed. What it would be like to indulge in frenzied sex acts that stopped short of intercourse.

Now was her chance to find out.

She couldn't resist.

Didn't *want* to resist.

Feeling decadent and daring, she squeezed him slowly, leisurely, measuring the length and hardness of his erection beneath her palm. He was satisfyingly hard, deliciously long, gloriously thick. She made a purring sound in her throat and tiptoed her fingers up the straining bulge to the metal button at the top of his fly.

His stomach muscles contracted.

She flicked the button open.

He drew in a quick, hard breath.

She grasped the waistband of his jeans between her thumb and forefinger and gave a sharp little tug. The remaining buttons of his fly popped open, one after the other, slowly—pop, pop, pop—each one a tiny explosion of sound that was more felt than heard. Without giving herself a chance to chicken out, she flattened her palm against his washboard stomach, slid her fingertips under the elastic edge of his briefs, and burrowed down between his legs.

His breath hissed out between clenched teeth and he

shifted in his seat, spreading his knees to accommodate her and give her room to explore.

She caressed his balls, cupping them gently in her palm for a delicious moment, and then curled her fingers around his hot, rigid flesh, and began a slow squeezing stroking meant to drive him mad.

He seemed to swell in her hand, becoming harder and longer and thicker with each stroke. He had both hands on the wheel, now, his knuckles white with the ferocity of his grip. His breathing was fast and shallow. His upper lip was beaded with sweat. His foot was a lead weight on the accelerator.

Roxanne was surprised to find her excitement matching his. Her breathing was fast and shallow. Her pulse was racing. Her body was tingling. She hadn't realized it would be like that, hadn't imagined that being the seducer would be as thrilling as being seduced. She felt incredibly powerful, incredibly sexual, incredibly female.

She wanted—desperately—to make him come with just her hands alone.

She released her seat belt and shifted in her seat, twisting her body sideways so she could reach over the console with her right hand and cup his balls through his jeans. With her left, she continued the long squeezing strokes, using her thumb to spread the pearl of moisture that appeared at the tip of his penis and increase the friction, moving her fist faster and faster as she felt his tension build.

Tom stiffened and made a low, guttural sound deep in his throat. The car swerved, the back end fishtailing wildly, spewing up gravel as he steered it onto the shoulder of the road and stomped on the brakes. Roxanne's body was propelled forward, and then back against the seat, but her rhythm never faltered. She was intent on one thing, and one thing only, and wasn't stopping until she got it.

And then it happened.

With his hands tight on the steering wheel, his arms rigid, his boot heels pressed against the floor, his head pressed back into the headrest, Tom uttered a harsh, rasping cry, and erupted in a spectacular orgasm. Roxanne watched it happen, entranced and enthralled.

She had done that.

She had made him lose control.

She had made him come.

She felt triumphant. Exultant. Victorious. Smug.

"Your turn," he said, and grabbed her by the shoulders, dragging her across the console to sprawl awkwardly in his lap. She lay on her side, her upper body wedged between his chest and the steering wheel, her hip balanced on the console between the seats, her booted feet against the passenger door. His mouth came down on hers, hot and hard and ravaging. His hand went between her legs, rubbing her through the heavy seam of her jeans. That was all it took. She was already wet, already aroused, drunk on passion and power and the excitement of the new and forbidden. She came hard, her body arching, her nails digging into the hard curve of his shoulders, her thighs clamped tight over his hand. It didn't stop his fingers from moving, though. He drove her up again, and then yet again, until she was quivering in his arms, until she was shivering and panting and making gasping little whimpering sounds, begging him to please, please fuck her. He brought both hands up to her head, then, cradling it between his wide callused palms, and gentled his kiss, going from ravager to protector in an instant.

His lips plucked at hers, softly, moist and tender, raining kisses to soothe them both, easy, gentle caresses that fell on her lips and cheeks and eyelids, meant to cool their roiling passions and take them to a place where they could draw an even breath. She sighed tremulously, her breath catching like a child who's cried too hard and too long, and melted into his arms, tucking her hot face into the damp curve of his neck while he stroked her temple with his thumb and drew soothing little circles on the back of her head with his fingertips.

They stayed that way for several long minutes, just holding each other, quietly, coming down off the edge together, until an eighteen-wheeler rolled by, buffeting the little convertible with its passing, blowing a long, loud salute on its air horn. Roxanne put her hands against his shoulders and pushed, squirming backward into her own seat. Tom levered his hips up slightly, reaching into his back pocket for the bandana he always carried. He cleaned himself with it, then folded it and passed it to Roxanne to wipe her hands while he rearranged and rebuttoned.

"It's nearly lunchtime," he said, after they had set themselves to rights. "You hungry?"

"I could eat, I guess," she said, without quite meeting his eyes.

She was a little embarrassed, now that it was over. It was, after all, one thing to have wild raucous sex in the relative privacy of an anonymous motel room. It was quite another to jerk a man off in an open convertible at high noon on the side of the highway. She couldn't help but wonder if she had crossed the line from good-time girl to, well…slut.

"There's a truck stop a few miles up the road, just the other side of Tucumari. Pete's Eats. They've got great burritos. That sound okay to you?"

Roxanne nodded. "Sounds fine," she said, and leaned down, snagging her purse off the floor. She began rooting around in it, ignoring him.

Tom knew by the way she was acting that he had fallen short somewhere. That he hadn't done or said whatever the right thing was to do or say in a situation like this. But, damn, he'd never had a woman do that to him, not in an open car, speeding down the highway. Not while he wasn't busy returning the favor. He hadn't expected her to do it, either. His gesture had just been a tease. A dare. He'd expected her to give him a little squeeze through his jeans, a little pat, maybe make some risqué comment about holding his horses until a more appropriate time.

But then she'd unbuttoned his fly and taken him in her hot little hand, and all his expectations were shot to hell in an explosion of panting lust and excitement that was fueled as much by *how* she did what she did, as *what* she did. She'd been avid and intent, her excitement as hot and palpable as his. He'd never had a woman give that way, completely unselfishly, focused on his pleasure alone and asking nothing in return until he'd dragged her into his lap and made her beg.

Tom didn't know what the hell to say to that, how to act. He felt gauche and grateful, and totally inadequate, like the callow inexperienced boy he hadn't been for many years. Knowing he had to do something, say something to let her know what her actions meant to him, he reached over and captured her chin, interrupting her careful application of a fresh coat of lipstick as he turned her to face him.

"You're something else, Slim," he said softly, his tone admiring and appreciative and awed. "Damn, you are just something fucking else."

Roxanne smiled beatifically, her confidence restored, and pursed her lips in a ripe, red air kiss.

THEY HAD A QUICK LUNCH of beans and burritos at Pete's Eats and took their coffee in to-go cups to save time and get back on the road more quickly. Roxanne added a precise half teaspoon of sugar to hers, stirring it thoroughly to make sure it dissolved.

"Why bother?" Tom said, watching her as she daintily tapped her spoon on the edge of the cup and set it, bowl down, on the corner of a paper napkin.

"Because that's the way I like it," she said, and snapped the plastic lid on with a firm click. She picked her purse up, slung it over her shoulder and held her hand out, palm up. "Key, please," she said, and wriggled her fingers imperiously.

Tom covered his shirt pocket with the flat of his hand. "You got some objection to my driving?"

"Nope." She reached over and slid her fingers into his pocket, snagging the key ring with the tip of her fingernail. "It's my turn to drive, is all."

"This is Texas, Slim," he said as he followed her out to the car. "Real men don't let women drive 'em around in Texas. It ain't manly."

"In case you didn't notice, cowboy, we crossed the border into New Mexico more than fifty miles back. I think your manhood's safe." She tossed her purse onto floor behind the driver's seat and opened the door before he could come around the car to do it for her. "Why don't you close your eyes and take a nap," she suggested breezily as she adjusted the seat and the rearview mirrors to her shorter stature. "You're going to need your rest for tonight's ride."

He slanted her a wry, wicked look out of the corner of his eye as he folded himself into the passenger seat. "Is that a proposition? So soon?"

"For the *bronc* ride, cowboy." She reached out and tapped the brim of his hat, tipping it down over his face. "Sleep," she ordered sternly, and then spoiled the effect by shooting him a teasing sidelong grin. "The proposition comes later." Her grin widened. "If you're lucky."

"Oh, I've always been lucky." He pulled his hat completely down over his face, crossed his arms over his chest, and leaned back, angling his body into the corner formed by the seat and the car door. "Especially lately," he said from beneath the hat.

Five minutes later, he was sound asleep. He didn't wake

up until she slowed down to take the exit ramp to the rodeo arena. As he had that morning, he woke slowly, a muscle at a time. His shoulders rolled under the pale-blue fabric of his shirt. His arms unfolded. His legs shifted. He lifted the hat from his face, ran his other hand through his hair, and re-settled the hat.

"We make it on time?" he asked, yawning hugely as he extended his arms straight out in front of him, fingers laced, palms turned outward in a bone-popping stretch.

"You tell me," she said, as she turned the Mustang into the parking lot and began circling, looking for an empty spot among the Volvos, BMWs, and bright shiny sports utility vehicles that dominated. Unlike most rodeos, which drew fans from surrounding ranches and small towns, the Rodeo de Santa Fe was an uptown, upscale affair. The fans were mostly big-city tourists and the artsy locals who'd made Santa Fe a style as well as a place. Beat-up pickups and dusty "ranch" cars were few and far between. Her glossy red rental car fit right in. "The lot's pretty full," she said anxiously. "And I can hear someone singing the national anthem. Does that mean you're too late to compete?"

"Not if I hustle."

"Well, hustle, then. Don't worry about me," she said, when he hesitated. "You go on and do what you have to do. I'll find a parking place, get a ticket and a soft drink, and be in the stands in time to watch you ride. Go on." She waved him away. "Go."

"YO! TOM! Over here." Tom's bandy-legged traveling part-ner hailed him as he came out of the rodeo secretary's office with his draw and his competition number in hand. "I didn't think you were gonna make it in time." The man grinned las-civiously. "That little blonde you were with last night looked all lathered up and hot to trot. I'll bet she gave you one hel-luva ride."

Tom ignored the comment. "Pin this on for me, would you?" he said, and turned around so the other cowboy could pin his number to the back of his shirt.

"Well, come on, pard. Give. Was she as good as she looked?"

His number fastened on, Tom turned around to face his friend. The other cowboy appeared to be made mostly of barbed wire and bone; he stood a mere five-six with his boots on and weighed a scant hundred and thirty pounds, flak jacket and all. He was a championship-caliber bull rider, currently number eight in the rankings, which put him squarely in contention for the finals in Vegas come December. He and Tom had been friends since they were just a couple of snot-nosed troublemakers on the Second Chance Ranch in Bowie, Texas. For that alone, Tom was willing to cut him some slack.

"You didn't dent my truck, did you, Rooster?"

"'Course not. It's parked over yonder, all safe and sound." He jerked his chin, indicating the direction. "On t'other side of the hay barn where there ain't too many other cars 'cause it's so danged out of the way. So—" He waggled his eyebrows. "How was she? Hotter than a firecracker, I bet." His eyes sparkled with vicarious pleasure. "The kind that rides a cowboy real hard and puts him away wet, I'm thinkin'."

"Keys?"

"Got 'em right here." The wiry little cowboy dug into the front pocket of his jeans. "You're not gonna share any of the juicy details, are you?" he complained as he dropped the keys into Tom's open palm.

"Nope."

"Well, hell," he groused. "I don't know why you're bein' so mean-spirited and close-mouthed about some buckle bunny you picked up at Ed Earl's. It ain't like she's anything special or—" The look in Tom's eyes had him reconsidering. "Or is she?"

ROXANNE FOUND A PARKING place between a gleaming BMW convertible and an equally gleaming Cadillac Escalade SUV. After retrieving her purse from the back seat, she made her way across the tarmac to the ticket booth. The air was brutally hot and dry, despite the lateness of the day. The sky was a bleached-out blue, as if it had faded in the unrelenting glare of the sun. The hillsides surrounding the rodeo grounds were barren and brown, except for the expensive new homes—most of them Spanish-style adobes—nestled among their folds.

The ripe smell of livestock permeated everything, mingling with the scents of popcorn, beer and cotton candy from the concession stands, enlivened by drifting hints of sagebrush and hay, overlaid by the somehow fertile smell of the sun-baked land. It was nothing at all like the cool green smell of Connecticut, or the chalkboard-and-glue smells of her regular daily life in the classroom at St. Catherine's. She took a deep breath, savoring the differences, finding them exciting and exotic even after two weeks of constant exposure.

The singer had long since finished her rendition of "The Star-Spangled Banner" by the time Roxanne had paid her entrance fee and entered the rodeo grounds. As she strolled toward the arena, she could hear the announcer extolling the virtues of cowboys in the upcoming steer-wrestling event. Knowing she had plenty of time before the bronc riders would be competing, she stopped to buy a cowboy hat to protect herself from the sun and help her blend in with the crowd, and then she lingered a little longer, selecting just the right hatband to go with it. The one she chose was bright red, like her boots and tank top, a narrow, braided lariat of leather. The ends dangled down over the edge of her hat brim and were finished with flashing silver beads and fluffy little red feathers that nearly brushed her shoulder. She felt like a sure 'nuff cowgirl with it decorating the crown of her straw cowboy hat as she wandered toward the arena through the labyrinth of concession stands that surrounded it.

Besides the usual food and souvenir stands that could be found at nearly any rodeo, there were miniature clothing boutiques and art galleries meant to appeal to the uptown, upscale patrons that frequented the Santa Fe rodeo. In quick succession, Roxanne found herself plunking down her credit card for a snug little denim vest decorated with silver conchas and leather fringe that fit her like a glove, a pair of soft butterscotch leather chamois pants cut like a pair of jeans, a turquoise and silver lariat necklace, a Western-cut shirt with pearl snaps, and a completely impractical white-eyelet skirt with a ruffled hem that she didn't even try to resist. Her purchases just about busted her vacation budget, but what else was a vacation for, if not overindulgence and mindless extravagance? And, besides, she—or, rather, Roxy—needed the clothes.

The barrel racers were doing their thing by the time she finally made her way to the stands, guiding their quick little cow ponies in figure-eight patterns around barrels set up in the arena, the fringe on their Western-cut shirts and their long hair—most of them had long hair—flying as they raced the clock. Roxanne stood at the base of the bleachers, her purse and a bulging plastic shopping bag looped over her shoulder, a large Dr Pepper clutched in one hand, a glossy rodeo program in the other, shading her eyes as she searched for a seat in the jam-packed arena. Spying one about halfway up and off to the far side, she made her way up the metal steps, sidling past a pseudo cowboy in electric-blue, lizard-skin boots with a cell phone pressed to her ear, past the trio of stylish pseudo cowgirls in beaded buckskin blouses, past an artsy couple in gauzy pastel linens and elaborate turquoise jewelry, to a seat next to the metal rail that separated the stands from the bucking chutes and the staging area just beyond them.

The area was bustling with activity. There were wranglers—people who handled the animals and made sure they were where they needed to be—rodeo bullfighters in their outrageous clown outfits, contestants readying themselves for their individual events. Roxanne had been following the rodeo long enough to know that most cowboys had their own special rituals before an event, just like any other athlete. Some wouldn't ride without a picture of their wife or sweetheart tucked in the breast pocket of their shirt; some always wore the same hat or the same pair of socks; some checked and rechecked their gear; others paced, or sat quietly, staring into space, or praying, or just repeating a special mantra over and over.

Roxanne craned her neck, searching the area for a glimpse of her good-looking dangerous cowboy. The saddle-bronc riding event wasn't for a while yet, but she knew Tom's routine from having surreptitiously watched him for the past two weeks.

First, he would sit down, right in the dirt beside one of the pens if there was nothing else to sit on—and, often, there wasn't—lay his saddle in his lap, and go over it meticulously, inch-by inch, checking the cinches and webbing for wear or weakness, brushing off dust, picking off bits of straw, polishing the smooth leather seat with his bandana until it gleamed. A bronc rider's saddle was his most precious possession; he carried it from rodeo to rodeo, the only constant on every go-round. The horses were different each time, the venue constantly changed, but the saddle was always the same. A smart cowboy took good care of it.

She finally spied him, sitting on a wooden bench near one
of the pens. He'd changed his shirt—that's why she hadn't
seen him at first glance. It was beige now, instead of the blue
she'd expected. The Western yoke and pocket flaps were
outlined in dark brown, making his shoulders look impossibly wide, his hips impossibly narrow in contrast. His head
was bent over the saddle, his face shielded from her sight by
the brim of his hat, but she could see his hands, moving
slowly, almost caressingly over the saddle, giving it the same
undivided, single-minded attention he'd given her when she
was under those hard, competent hands. She gulped audibly,
her throat suddenly dry, her pulse suddenly pounding, her
face flushed from more than the heat of the sun. She took a
long noisy sip of her soft drink in a useless effort to cool off,
and wondered how soon they could steal away and find a
motel room.

Chapter Six

SATISFIED WITH the saddle's condition, Tom rose from the wooden bench, slung the saddle over the blanket on the top rail of one of the unoccupied pens, and ambled on over to view the action in the arena. The barrel racers had given way to the calf ropers, who would soon give way to the bare bronc riders. And then it would be his turn.

Saddle-bronc riding wasn't the glamour event of the rodeo anymore, not the way it had been back in the early days— bull riding held that spot now, thanks to ESPN—but it was *the* classic rodeo event, the one everybody thought of when they thought of rodeo. Style mattered just as much as staying on, and it took years of practice to do it well, which gave the older, more experienced cowboys the edge. Tom wasn't the top-ranked cowboy in the event, but his score in yesterday's rodeo in Lubbock had pushed him to number eighteen in the rankings, close enough to the magic fifteen to make a place in the finals in Las Vegas a distinct possibility.

He glanced up toward the stands, wondering if *she* would still be with him then. They'd agreed they'd only be together until the end of summer, and the finals were in December, so it wasn't likely. Not that he wanted her to be there, anyway. That would make his life way too complicated because he'd already halfway decided that if he made the finals, he was going to ask Dan Jensen's daughter Jo Beth to come to Las Vegas and watch him compete. Dan was a neighboring rancher, with a nice little spread that ran right alongside the Second Chance, back home in Bowie, Texas. Jo Beth was Dan's only child. She was a nice-looking little gal, sweet-natured and hardworking, knew her way around a barn the way most women knew their way around a dance floor. And she'd had a crush on him since she was sweet sixteen. Not that he'd ever looked her way back then; at twenty-four he hadn't been the least bit interested in sweet little girls. But she was a woman now, "full-growed and haired over" as the saying went, and she was back on her daddy's ranch after four years at Texas A&M with a degree in animal science, and marriage on her mind. Her folks had thrown a big shindig to welcome her home and halfway through his first two-step with her, he'd begun wondering if maybe it wasn't time to start thinking about getting married himself. A man could do a lot worse than to marry a woman like Jo Beth Jensen. Especially when the man in question was a rancher who was retiring from the rodeo circuit and settling down to raise cattle and kids. He had a good start on the cattle, but for the kids he needed a wife. And Jo Beth had been tailor-made for the role.

He hadn't asked her, though. He hadn't even hinted that he was thinking about it. And now he was damned glad he hadn't. It wouldn't have set right with his conscience to be engaged to one woman while he was rolling around on motel beds, tearing up the sheets with a different one. Once the summer was over, that would be the time to get things settled with Jo Beth. In the meantime…

He glanced up at the stands again, looking for a tall blond glass of water in a red tank top but couldn't pick her out of the crowd—until she suddenly stood, a big smile on her face, and waved frantically. He started to lift his arm to wave back when he realized she wasn't looking at him. He turned his head, following her line of sight to the young cowboy who sat perched on the top rail of the arena fence with his boot heels hooked on the rung below. The cowboy touched two fingers to the brim of his hat, returning her wave with a jaunty salute and a gallant dip of his head.

A sharp sliver of something very like jealousy pricked Tom as he recognized the other cowboy.

Clay Madison was an up-and-comer, a good-looking young bull rider who was already making a name on the circuit while still in his first year of professional competition, and giving Rooster a run for his money into the bargain. Despite the hot-pink and black-striped shirt and the elaborately fringed and inlaid chaps, which might suggest otherwise to the uninitiated, he was as tough as nails. He was also pretty enough to have more than his share of buckle bunnies panting after him when the rodeo was over. A few of the bolder ones pursued him shamelessly, to the point of hanging around outside the cowboys' locker room like a bunch of cats in heat, waiting for him to come out so they could pounce.

Tom didn't like to think that Slim might be one of them. He didn't like it at all. He was thinking seriously of marching up into the grandstand to tell her so, in no uncertain terms, when the announcer broadcast the news that the saddle bronc event was next up.

ROXANNE FORGOT ABOUT Clay Madison between one breath and the next, turning her attention toward the bucking chutes as she sank back down in her seat. The announcer was reeling off the lineup, extolling the virtues of each horse and man, waxing poetic about the contests to come. Roxanne was only interested in finding out which horse Tom had drawn. The horse counted for half of a contestant's score. A lackluster performance on the part of the horse could bring the score down no matter how well the cowboy rode. A good bucker, on the other hand, could push the score up into the winning numbers, provided, of course, that the cowboy managed to stay on for the full eight seconds.

Tom had drawn Hot Sauce. The two had been paired up several times before, and Tom was a little bit ahead in the win column. He'd managed to ride her to the horn more times than she'd managed to toss him on his butt in the dirt. She was a good bucker, a worthy opponent, a horse who would do her part to put points on the board.

Roxanne watched, her hands curled around the rolled-up program, as Tom climbed up onto the platform behind the bucking chutes and leaned over the rail to gently place his saddle on the mare's back. Most injuries occurred in the chutes where the narrow confines left little room for maneuvering if a horse panicked and started bucking prematurely. But Hot Sauce stood calmly, as much a pro as the man who was saddling her.

She was already wearing the flank strap, a sheepskin-lined, beltlike apparatus that fit loosely now, but would be pulled tight when the chute opened, providing added encouragement to buck. The added weight of the saddle didn't seem to concern her in the least. Tom made a small, careful adjustment to the way it sat on her back, then used a long, hooked pole to fish for the cinch hanging down the other side of her barrel. He pulled it under her belly, drawing it up her side until he could reach down with his free hand to bring it up the rest of the way. Handing the pole to a waiting wrangler, he leaned into the chute to feed the end of the cinch through the O-ring and tighten it down to secure the saddle. The mare tried to swing her head around to see what was going on as the cinch tightened, but she was restricted by the narrow confines of the chute. She kicked out with her back feet to show her displeasure with the situation, and rattled the lower rail. The sound startled her. She whinnied in fear and temper, kicking again, and then tried to rear and lost her balance.

Tom's arm was pinned against the rails as thirteen hundred pounds of horseflesh slammed into the side of the chute. Roxanne's fingers tightened around the rolled-up program, but she managed to stifle the frightened scream that rose to her throat.

"EASY, GIRL," Tom murmured. "Easy." He put his free hand against the mare's neck and pushed gently. "Move over, now. That's a good girl," he crooned as she shifted her weight and freed his arm. He flexed it, checking for broken bones or torn ligaments. It throbbed like a son of a bitch, but was otherwise intact. Fortunately, it was his left arm, so he could still ride. Not that he would have considered doing otherwise, even if it had been his right. He'd have just figured some other way to hang on to the reins. Like with his teeth, maybe.

"You okay?" Rooster said from the other side of the chute. "She get you bad?"

"Nothing an ice pack and a cold Lone Star won't take care of." Tom finished securing the saddle with one good hard yank, patted the mare one last time to let her know he was still there, then slowly eased himself over the top rail and lowered his butt to the saddle, careful not to graze her with his spurs and set her off again.

Hot Sauce, apparently over her little tantrum, didn't so much as flick an ear in his direction.

Tom sat equally still, the reins clutched tightly in his right hand, his left resting lightly on the top rail, his attention now entirely focused on the coming eight seconds that would constitute the entire duration of a successful ride. He ran down a mental checklist—reminding himself to keep his legs stretched high, toes turned out, eyes straight ahead—while he sat there, stock-still, waiting for the moment when everything felt just right. Hot Sauce snorted and shifted beneath him, impatient to begin.

"Ready?" someone said.

Tom lifted his left hand from the railing, letting it curve up over his head, and gave one quick, decisive nod.

The gate swung open.

The flank strap pulled up tight.

Hot Sauce screamed in fury and bolted out of the chute, then jerked to an abrupt halt, head down between her legs, front hooves slamming into the ground with enough force to rattle his teeth as she kicked out with her back feet and tried to toss him off over her head. Tom swung his boots down along the mare's sides with the first buck, letting them snap up to her shoulders as her rear hooves slammed back to earth, then bringing them back down as she bucked again. His butt stayed glued to the saddle, his free hand waved in the air, his body swooped and swayed with the wildly gyrating horse as if they were dancing an intricate pas de deux, rather than fighting for supremacy. When the horn sounded, signaling the end of the ride, he let his left leg swing up and over the mare's neck, and jumped lightly to the ground.

"Man, that was one pretty ride," the announcer enthused. "Probably the prettiest ride I've ever seen."

The judges agreed, awarding him a score of ninety-two out of a possible one hundred.

Tom raised his hat to the crowd as they roared their approval.

ROXANNE WAS ON HER FEET and screaming with the rest of them. She wasn't quite sure whether she was cheering because of his phenomenal score, or because he'd escaped unhurt when Hot Sauce slammed him up against the side of the chute. She suspected it was some giddy combination of both, combined with a healthy dose of lustful feelings for the conquering hero. It might be politically incorrect and unliberated of her, not to mention horribly shallow, but seeing him compete—and win!—had her creaming her jeans. She couldn't wait to get her hands on him and show her admiration and approval in a more direct and satisfying way.

Unable to think of a good reason why she *should* wait, she stuffed her crumpled program into her purse, slung it over her shoulder with her shopping bag, and headed down the steps of the grandstand. There was a guard at the entrance to the livestock area, presumably checking passes, which she didn't have. The old Roxanne would have politely waited outside the fenced-off area until Tom finally appeared. The new Roxy waited until the guard was occupied with someone else, then slipped through the rails and went to find Tom herself.

"Hi, there, sugar," she said, batting her eyes at the first cowboy she saw. "Can you tell me where I might find Tom Steele?"

"He was headed for the locker room, last I saw him." The cowboy motioned toward one of the outbuildings near the main barn. "I'm right here, though. Sure I can't help you, instead?"

"You already have, sugar. Thanks ever so," she said, mixing a little Marilyn in with the San Antonio barrel racer before she turned and headed toward the cowboys's locker room.

"Hey, Roxy. Roxy! Wait up!"

Roxanne looked around at the sound of her name to see Clay Madison bearing down on her. "Well, hey, good-lookin'," she said by way of greeting, and then narrowed her eyes in mock suspicion. "You followin' me?"

"I thought *you* were following *me*. I decided I might as well make it easy on both of us—" he flashed her a good-natured, good-ol'-boy grin designed to make him look as harmless as a puppy "—and let you catch me."

Roxanne wasn't fooled. She'd seen that John Travolta grin before, up close and personal, and knew the lethal charms it disguised. "Well, sugar, I do appreciate the offer, but I'm afraid I'm going to have to decline. I'm meeting someone."

"Again?"

Roxanne laughed at his hangdog expression. "Tell you what, sugar. You can escort me over there. Just like you did last night." She tucked her hand into the crook of his elbow. "I'm headed for the cowboys' locker room."

"You mind tellin' me who's beatin' my time?" he asked as he fell into step beside her. "Maybe it's someone I can put out of commission."

Roxanne had her doubts about that. "Tom Steele." She slanted a glance up at him out of the corner of her eye. "Think you can take him?"

Clay had his doubts about it, too, but, "Hell, yes!" he said because that's what she expected. "Would you be mine if I did?"

"Hell, yes," she said, and they both laughed, knowing it was all in fun, knowing they had gotten past whatever attraction might have been between them last night and emerged on the other side of it with nothing more than the potential to be friends.

Tom didn't know it, though.

He exited the cowboys' locker room, hat in hand, just in time to see Roxanne lean in and plant a kiss on Clay Madison's peach-fuzz cheek. That little sliver of something that might have been jealousy grew into a throbbing green monster. He slammed the screen door to the locker room just a little harder than necessary to close it. Both Roxanne and Clay turned their heads toward the sound.

And then, before anyone could say a word, Roxanne whooped like a cowboy at a Fourth of July parade, dropped her purse and packages, and launched herself bodily at Tom.

He dropped his hat and caught her, automatically, easily, his hands cupping the curve of her jeans-clad bottom as she wrapped her legs around his waist and wound her arms around his neck. And then her mouth smashed into his, her lips opened hungrily, her tongue came seeking, and the big green monster that had taken hold of him turned a deep, pulsating red. He flexed his fingers against the tight curve of her butt, pressing her more firmly against the rock-hard bulge in his jeans, and kissed her back. He was just about ready to fall to his knees and take her down with him, when she pulled away and smiled into his face.

"God! You were fabulous!" She planted another one on him. Quick and hard and sweet. "You *are* fabulous!" Another smacking kiss. "That was the prettiest ride I've ever seen. Well—" she grinned, her hot whiskey-colored eyes smiling into his "—the second prettiest. Last night was the prettiest." She hitched herself a little higher against him and put her lips against his ear. "I'm so hot for you right now, I'm practically melting," she whispered.

He practically melted, too, right then and there. Would have, too, if he hadn't suddenly spied Clay Madison over Slim's shoulder, standing there grinning like a skunk eating cabbage. Her very public display of affection—talk about cats in heat, he thought!— had gone a long way toward soothing the green-eyed monster, but the sight of the young bull rider standing there as if he were waiting his turn, brought it roaring right back to the forefront again. He let go of her butt and slid his hands up her sides to her arms, curling his fingers around her biceps to loosen her hold on him.

She let go immediately, unlocking her legs from around his

waist and her arms from around his neck. "What?" she said, instantly sensing the change in him. "What is it, sugar?"

"While you're with me, *sugar*, you're a one-man woman." His fingers bit into her biceps. "Or you aren't with me."

She stared at him for a full five seconds, her eyes wide and uncomprehending, her mouth half open, as if she meant to say something but couldn't think what it might be. And, then suddenly, understanding dawned. Her eyes narrowed. Her teeth snapped together. "Just what are you accusing me of?"

Without a word, Tom dropped his hands from her arms and stepped back, jerking his chin toward someone behind her.

Roxanne glanced back over her shoulder. Clay. She'd completely forgotten he was there. "Go away," she said, and turned back to Tom without waiting to see if she'd been obeyed.

The old Roxanne would have waited to make sure he was gone, loathe to make a scene in front of witnesses. Then she would have soothed and explained, wanting only to smooth things over before the situation escalated and feelings got hurt, before anyone yelled. The new, improved Roxy let 'er rip.

"How dare you!" she said, and there was nothing soothing in her tone. There was also nothing of the San Antonio barrel racer in it, either. It was all clipped New England indignation. "How dare you stand there and accuse me of being a promiscuous tramp."

"I never said you were a tramp."

"As good as. *While you're with me...you're a one-man woman. Or you aren't with me.*" She spat his words back at him. "Just who else was I supposed to have been with between now and this afternoon?"

Tom lifted an eyebrow and shifted his gaze to the man standing behind her.

Roxanne didn't even turn around. "And just when was I have supposed to have fucked him?" she demanded, using the most shocking, the most graphic term she could think of. "Hmm? Out in the parking lot, maybe? Under the bleachers of the grandstand during the steer wrestling event? When?"

"I didn't say you fucked him! And keep your voice down, goddammit. Do you want everyone to hear you?"

"I don't care who hears me." She was right in his face now, toe to toe and nose to nose, blood pumping with righteous indignation. "I want to know what—*exactly*—you're accusing me of."

"You kissed him," Tom said, and knew, as he said it, just how ridiculous it sounded.

"I *what?*"

"Kissed him," he mumbled.

"I kissed him? Is that what this is about? I *kissed* him?" She turned to Clay, a look of mock confusion on her face. "Did I kiss you, Clay?"

"Yes, ma'am." Eyes sparkling, he touched his finger to his cheek. "Right here. It was quite a little smacker. Very nice, if I do say so as shouldn't."

"That wasn't a kiss." She reached out and grabbed him by the ears. "*This* is a kiss," she said and pressed her mouth to his.

She gave it all she had—lips, tongue, teeth, and a good deal of squirmy body language. It was a wet, seductive, blockbuster of a kiss. When it was over, she thrust him away from her and whirled back to face Tom.

"Now you have something to be pissed about," she said, and socked him in the stomach as hard as she could. It was a good solid jab, with her body behind it, and it took the wind out of him.

He made a surprised-sounding "Woof," and hunched over.

She smiled evilly, satisfied she'd made her point. "See you around, *sugar,*" she said, and then turned away, deliberately, and bent over from the waist, her bottom pointed at him like a dare—or an insult—and scooped her belongings off of the ground.

Without a backward glance, she straightened, regal as an affronted queen, and stalked off with her head held high.

If she had a flag, she thought, she'd be waving it. She felt that high, that triumphant, that strong. She'd raised her voice. She'd created a scene and used vulgar language, and—ohmygod!—she'd actually *hit* another person. She'd said exactly what she wanted to say, exactly when she wanted to say it, and she felt *wonderful*. Almost as good as she had last night in the midst of her fifth—or was it sixth?—glorious orgasm. Or this afternoon on the side of the road, when he'd come apart in her hands.

All in all, she decided, there was a lot to be said for unbridled emotional excess. She should have tried it a *lot* sooner.

Behind her, Tom straightened slowly, one hand still clasped protectively over his stomach, and watched her walk away. Maybe it was best this way. He had Jo Beth to think of, after all. A man shouldn't spend the summer tomcatting around when he was seriously thinking about getting engaged come fall. And there was the season to think about, too. He couldn't keep riding like he had today if he was doing a different kind of riding all night. A body could only take so much.

"Man, that little gal sure packs a hell of a wallop," Clay said, grinning when Tom shifted his gaze to glare at him. "In more ways than one," he added, and tugged at his lower lip. "Be a shame to let her get away."

"Hotter than a firecracker," someone else said, and Tom shifted his gaze farther to find that Rooster had apparently been standing behind the screen door of the cowboys' locker room the whole time and had seen the whole sorry incident. Which meant everyone else was going to hear about it before the day was over because Rooster didn't have a discreet bone in his whole wiry body. "It's going to take a whole heap of grovelin' to get back on her good side," Rooster said.

Disgusted with the both of them, Tom shifted his gaze back to the woman who appeared to be walking out of his life. Her back was ramrod-straight, her hips were swinging, the ridiculous red feathers dangling from her hatband were dancing in the breeze. She didn't hesitate, didn't pause, didn't look back over her shoulder. Tom told himself again it was better this way. He told himself he had no intention of trying to get back on her good side. But he didn't believe it for a minute.

She was a tall cool glass of water with a scalding hot spring inside, and he was one sorry-ass son of a bitch who had a whole heap of groveling to do if he wanted to get back in her bed.

Which he did.

In the worst goddamned way.

"Shit," he said.

Chapter Seven

ROXANNE'S HIGH LASTED through the time it took her to walk across the rodeo grounds and the parking lot to her car. It lasted through the time it took her to drive to the nearest motel and get checked in. It lasted through her leisurely bath and a careful application of fresh makeup and the ritual of getting dressed for the evening—*Take that, Tom Steele,* she thought as she buttoned the snug little denim vest she'd bought over nothing but soft, perfumed skin. It lasted on the drive to the Bare Back Saloon, where all the cowboys hung out after the Rodeo de Santa Fe in the hopes of finding some horizontal action.

It faltered a bit when she stepped inside the smoke-filled honky-tonk and saw Tom leaning up against the bar, talking to a certified, card-carrying buckle bunny, the kind who collected belt buckles as trophies and had perfected the art of gnawing the little red tag off the back pocket of a cowboy's Wrangler while he was still wearing them.

She felt a sharp little jab in what she hoped was only her pride, although it felt uncomfortably close to her heart. Was she really so easily replaceable? Could he share what he'd shared with her last night and this afternoon, did the things he'd done, say the things he'd said, and then blithely go out and find someone else to do them with tonight? And if he could switch partners that easily, damn it, then why was he so incensed when he thought *she* had? What difference could it possibly make to him if it was so easy for him to do the same?

Were men and women really *that* different when it came to sex?

She was about to conclude that, yes, indeed, men were pigs and the San Antonio barrel racer had been right—rodeo cowboys *were* irresponsible sons o' bitches and you *couldn't* trust them—when he looked up suddenly and captured her gaze from across the room. Roxanne abruptly decided that maybe she wouldn't pack up her poor little broken heart and head for home, after all.

He still wanted her.

Badly.

It was all there in his eyes. The burning lust that was twin to her own. The injured male pride. The determination not to be the first to give in. Roxanne felt all her confidence return at that one nakedly yearning, stubbornly male look and decided, then and there, that if Tom Steele wanted her, and she knew now that he did, he could have her. But he was going to have to make the first move. And he was going to have to grovel. And she knew just how to make him do both. Hiding a smug little smile of satisfaction, she lifted her chin and turned away, the ruffled hem of her brand-new, white-eyelet skirt swishing around the tops of her red Sweetheart of the Rodeo cowboy boots, and tapped the closest broad shoulder.

"Dance, cowboy?"

TOM FELT the old green monster rear up again as she melted into the arms of her partner, and deliberately tamped it down. She wasn't really interested in that grinning idiot she was dancing with. She was only doing it tick him off and make him come to heel.

"And I'll be damned if I'll dance to her tune," he muttered, and slugged back a long swallow of the single Lone Star he was allowing himself for medicinal purposes.

The rodeo doctor had given him a cortisone shot and a couple of pain pills to take later if his arm started aching. It hadn't—the cortisone had worked just fine—but he didn't want to complicate matters by adding too much alcohol to the mix, just in case.

"What was that, darlin'?" The physically gifted buckle bunny who'd been trying to engage his interest since he walked in the place pressed her gifts up against his arm and giggled in his ear. "I didn't quite hear what you said, sweetie. The music's kind of loud."

He raised his arm to dislodge her and took another pull on his beer. "I said, nice tune," he said.

"Yes, it is." She giggled again. "Would you like to dance?"

"No."

"Oh. Well." She didn't seem to know what to say to that.

Tom took pity on her—and took the opportunity to get rid of her—by tapping a passing cowboy on the shoulder. "Hey, Rooster, I'd like you to meet— What was your name again, honey?"

"Becky."

"Well, Becky, meet Jim Wills. You can call him Rooster, though. Everybody does. He's a champion bull rider—took first place today in the bull riding event, didn't you, Rooster?—and he's one fine dancer, too."

"First place?" she said, her eyes lighting up as she turned her limpid gaze from Tom to Rooster. "Was that you?"

Rooster stuck his scrawny chest out. "Sure as shootin' was."

"He's got a great big silver buckle to prove it, too," Tom

said. "He'll probably let you look at it later if you ask him real nice."

Becky giggled and let Rooster sweep her onto the dance floor. The disparity in their heights put her overgenerous breasts nearly at nose level on Rooster, but neither one of them seemed to mind. Rooster liked women in all their myriad sizes and shapes, and Becky appeared more than satisfied to be dancing with a prize-winning bull rider.

Grinning, Tom lifted his beer bottle to his lips for another sip just as Roxanne two-stepped through his field of vision, smiling up into the face of a grinning young stud who was holding her much too close. Tom barely restrained himself from biting the top off of his beer bottle.

"WHY, that's just *so* interestin', sugar," Roxanne heard herself say, and thought she sounded just like Scarlett O'Hara on the porch of Tara with the Tarleton twins. "I had no idea ridin' bulls was such a complicated process. I mean—" she batted her eyelashes to distract him from the utter inanity of her conversation "—I knew it was *dangerous* an' all, but I had no idea it was *scientific*. You're so brave. And brilliant, too. A regular scientist. My goodness." She lifted her hand from his shoulder and touched her fingertips to her temple. "It's enough to turn a poor girl's head, sure 'nuff."

Oh, my God, she thought, *now I'm* channeling *Scarlett.* If Tom didn't step in pretty soon and rescue her, she was going to make him eat dirt when he finally did show up.

"You're just a double-edged sword, aren't you, sugar?" she said to the cowboy, who seemed to have no idea that she sounded like a character from one the world's best-known novels. "And you've been ridin' bulls for—how long did you say it was?"

"I started riding calves when I was two," he said, and launched into a long explanation about how his daddy had followed the training apparently laid down by rodeo's all-time greatest bull rider, Ty Murray. It included a regimen of fence walking, unicycle riding and sessions on the bucking machine that lasted into the wee hours.

Thankfully, Roxanne didn't have to say much after that. She just smiled until her jaw ached and silently cursed Tom for the no-good, low-down, good-looking, dangerous cowboy he was.

"WHY DON'T YOU just go get her?"

Tom stopped glaring at Roxanne and her dance partner long enough to turn his head and glare at Clay Madison. The young cowboy was decked out all in black—black hat, black shirt, black denim jeans—in an effort, Tom suspected, to capitalize on his resemblance to the Travolta of the *Urban Cowboy* era. "Mind your own damn business," he snarled.

"You know you want to," Clay said.

"What I *want* is to rearrange your pretty face for you."

"You're welcome to try." Clay seemed unperturbed by the implied threat. "Any place. Any time. We can take it outside right now."

Tom seriously considered it. Smashing anything right now would probably make him feel better. Smashing the face of the man who'd swapped spit with Slim while he stood there and watched would make him feel a whole *lot* better. But it would only be a temporary fix. Besides, Clay wasn't the one who'd been doing the kissing. Regretfully, Tom shook his head. "It wasn't your fault," he said.

"No," Clay agreed. "It wasn't." He took a sip of his beer. "It was yours."

Tom wanted to argue with that. He really did. But the kid was right. It *was* his fault. Slim had only done what she'd done—what she *was* doing—because of what he'd said to her. Tom sighed, and went back to watching her whirl around the dance floor.

She had switched partners and was doing the Schottische with one of the rodeo bullfighters, who was still in his clown get-up. Rumor had it that some of the buckle bunnies had a thing for the bullfighters, but had trouble telling who they were without the makeup and baggy pants. Apparently, this guy wanted to make sure he didn't miss out on any chance for some action. Slim was batting her eyes at him, making him think there was a possibility he might actually get it.

"She isn't even remotely interested in him," Clay said helpfully.

"I know that," Tom snapped. Why the hell wouldn't this guy go away and leave him to stew in peace?

"It's all an act. She's doing it to make you suffer."

"I know that, too."

There was a beat of silence as they both watched her partner spin her in a series of quick, showy twirls. Her ruffled white skirt flared high and wide, exposing the tops of a pair of lacy, white, thigh-high stockings and sleek bare thighs before it fluttered back into place. Both men sighed appreciatively.

"Man, she *really* wants to see you crawl," Clay said.

Tom jerked his gaze away from Roxanne long enough to shoot the young cowboy a half irritated, half admiring glare. "How the hell do you know so much about women? A kid like you?"

Clay shrugged. "I've made a lot of 'em mad." He up-ended his beer, pouring the last of the brew down his throat, and then set the empty bottle on the bar. "The thing is," he said, as he signaled the bartender for another one, "you know you're going to do it sooner or later—a guy's *always* going to do it sooner or later, if he has feelings for a woman—and the sooner you cowboy up and get it done, the sooner you'll be the one she's dancin' with instead of that clown. You leave it too late, though, and you run the risk of leavin' here alone tonight." He picked up his fresh beer and took a long swallow. "Or else you'll end up watching her walk out of here with someone who ain't so pigheaded and prideful."

Tom knew the awful truth when he heard it. "Shit," he said.

AFTER THE THIRD skipping turn around the dance floor with the painted cowboy, Roxanne decided she'd waited just about as long as she was going to. If Tom wasn't going to come crawling after her on his own, she was going to have to do something to give him a little added incentive. And that incentive was dressed in black and standing next to him at the bar.

"All this dancin' is making me feel a little light-headed," she said to the bullfighter, fanning herself for effect. "Would you mind awfully if I sat the rest of this one out?"

"Would you like something to drink? A beer? A glass of water?"

"Oh, no, thank you, sugar. I think I'll just go to the ladies' room and run some cold water over my wrists for a few minutes. That should perk me up some. Don't feel like you have to wait for me." She patted his arm. "You just go right on ahead and find yourself another partner. I'll probably be a while."

On her way to the ladies' room, she just happened to sashay down the length of the bar. She walked on past Tom as if she hadn't seen him, then stopped and turned a brilliant smile on the man standing next to him. "Hey, there, good-lookin'," she purred, as if he were the only man in the room.

"Hey, yourself," he said, and grinned at her. "Having fun?"

"Sure am." She put her hand on his chest and leaned in a bit, smiling at him from underneath her lashes. "I'd be having more fun if you'd dance with me," she invited in a breathy little voice.

"Well, now, that's the best offer I've had all night." He

reached behind him to set his beer on the bar. "I'd consider it an honor to dance with you."

"No," Tom said.

Roxanne stiffened and turned her head toward him, slowly, as if he were some strange species of bug that had suddenly spoken. "I beg your pardon," she said in her frostiest tones. "Were you speaking to me?"

"You know damned well I'm speaking to you." He reached out and curled his fingers around her forearm, pulling her hand away from Clay's chest. "If you want to dance, dance with me."

"What if I don't want to dance with you?"

"Damn it, Slim, don't push me."

"I wasn't aware that I was even talking to you." She looked down at the hand on her arm, and then back up at him. The look in her eyes was pure temptation. Pure fire. Pure female cussedness at its most contrary. "And if you don't remove your hand from my arm, I'm going to have to ask Clay to remove it for you."

Tom decided he damn well didn't want to wait a minute longer to have her in his arms again. Damn, he liked a woman with sass! "I'm sorry, Slim."

Yes! she thought, mentally doing a little victory dance. "Really?" she said, as if she couldn't care less. "What for?"

"For acting like a jealous fool."

"And?"

"And for yelling at you like I did."

"And?"

"And what?" he said, exasperated. "What else did I do?"

"Well, let's see, now. What else *did* you do? Oh, yes, I remember. You called me a tramp."

"Damn it, don't start that again. I didn't call you a tramp."

"You may not have said the actual word, but that's what you meant."

"I did not call you a tramp," he insisted.

"I'm not going to argue semantics with you. You all but came right out and accused me of having sex with Clay right after I'd had sex with you. In my book, that's calling me a tramp." She looked over at Clay. "What do you think, sugar? Did he call me a tramp?"

"Close to," Clay said diplomatically.

"I did not call you a—" Tom clenched his teeth on the word, clamping down on his temper at the same time. Because she was right. And he knew it. He hadn't actually called her a tramp, but that's what he'd implied. Without any proof, without even a hint of tramplike behavior on her part, he'd let suspicion and ego override good sense. Knowing there was no way out of it, Tom suppressed a sigh and did what he had to do. He groveled.

"I'm sorry," he said. "I'm sorry for yelling at you. I'm sorry for implying that you were a tramp. I'm sorry for acting like a goddamned jealous jackass. I was wrong. And stupid. And—" He groped, searching for another word, any word, that would satisfy her and get him back in her good graces. "I was just flat-out wrong, is all. And I'm sorry."

Roxanne smiled beatifically. "I forgive you."

Tom eyed her suspiciously. "That's it? That's all I had to say? You're not going to make me eat shit?"

"Dirt," she said. "I was thinking of making you eat dirt. And no, I'm not."

He couldn't quite believe that's all there was to it. "Why not?"

"Because when I walked in here tonight and saw you talking to that silicone-enhanced little chippy, I wanted to tear her bleached-blond hair out by the roots."

Tom smiled. "You were jealous." He all but crowed the words.

"When you're with me, sugar, you're a one-woman man. Or you're not with me."

Tom's smile widened into a grin. He slipped an arm around her waist and pulled her close. She melted against him, her hands flat on his chest, her face tilted up like a flower to the sun, her luscious ruby-red lips a kiss away from his.

"So," he said, and his voice wasn't quite steady. "You wanna dance?"

She shook her head, brushing her lips back and forth across his in an almost kiss. "No."

"Drink?"

Another brushing butterfly kiss. "Uh-uh."

"What, then?"

She leaned in that tiny, necessary fraction of an inch and pressed her lips to his. When she finally drew back, a long delicious minute later, she had his lower lip between her teeth. She nipped it lightly before letting go. "I've got us a room down at the Round Up. How 'bout we skip the preliminaries and get right to it?"

THEY DIDN'T MAKE IT to the Round Up Motel. They didn't even make it as far as the car. They were hardly a dozen steps past the front door when Tom pulled her into the dark, concealing shadows at the far side of the building and pressed her up against the unpainted plank wall.

His mouth crashed down on hers, lips open, tongue seeking, teeth nipping and nibbling, his hands on either side of her head to hold her still for his invasion. He didn't come up for air until their lips were red and wet and swollen. Just like certain other parts of their collective anatomy.

"I missed you," he said, and skimmed his mouth down the side of her neck with tender, avaricious hunger. "I know it's only been a couple of hours, but I missed you something fierce."

She tilted her head to give him better access, then sighed when he took it. "I missed you, too."

He smoothed his hands downward, palms open, fingers curved, letting them glide over the curves of her shoulders and arms and breasts. "I've been miserable ever since you walked away from me."

"Me, too." She moaned and arched into his caress, lifting her hands to the backs of his to press them more firmly to her breasts. "Oh, me, too."

"I couldn't do anything but think about you." He flicked open the first button on her denim vest. "About this." He flicked open another button, and then another, and another. "These," he said as he brushed back the sides of the vest and exposed her breasts to the warm night air.

The two ends of the silver lariat necklace she'd purchased that afternoon hung between her breasts, the vivid blue stones dangling on a level with her erect nipples, making her look more naked, more sensual than she would have without the added adornment.

Tom sucked in his breath. "You have the sweetest little breasts," he murmured raggedly, and cupped his hands over them, enveloping them completely, squeezing them together so they plumped up in delicious little mounds of flesh that overflowed his hands and caused the turquoise stones on her necklace to disappear into her cleavage. "Sweet little cupcakes." Slowly he drew his hands away, bringing his fingers together in a pinching motion at the tips of her breasts. "With sweet little cherries on top," he said as he rolled her nipples back and forth between his fingertips.

Roxanne felt everything inside her turn warm and liquid and wanting. She arched her body even more, thrusting her breasts outward, pressing her head back against the rough-hewn wall. "Please," she said.

Tom smiled into the night. "Please what?"

"Touch me."

"I am touching you."

"With your mouth."

"Where?"

"On my breasts. Put your mouth on my breasts."

He bent his head, flicked a nipple with his tongue. "Like that?" he said, knowing he was teasing her, knowing she wanted more.

"Yes. Like that. More."

"More how?" He flicked her nipple again. "Like that? Or like this?" He circled his tongue around the hard, distended little bud, slowly, making it thoroughly wet, then drew back and blew on it.

She shuddered.

"Tell me," he murmured. "Tell me what you want and you'll get it."

She put her hands on either side of his head and tried to draw him closer. "More," she said, her voice low and petulant and rasping, a mere breath of sound.

Gently, he took her wrists in his hands and pushed them down to her sides. "Keep them there," he said, and pressed her palms flat against the wall. "And tell me what you want." He leaned in close for a minute, swaying against her, letting the fabric of his shirt rasp against her sensitive nipples. "You can have anything you want," he crooned. His lips hovered a tantalizing inch above hers. "Anything at all. But you have to ask for it."

"Kiss me," she said.

He did. Thoroughly. Completely.

"Now what?"

"Kiss my breasts."

He scattered a wealth of baby-soft kisses over the upper slopes of both breasts.

"My nipples. Kiss my nipples."

He placed a soft sucking kiss on the tip of each breast.

Roxanne's fingers pressed into the wood beneath her palms.

"Tell me," he murmured again, his voice rough and ragged. She'd lost her cornpone-and-molasses twang again and it drove him nearly crazy to hear her talk dirty in that starched New England accent. He circled his tongue around her nipple, slowly, stopping just short of giving her what he knew she wanted. "Tell me what you want, Slim. Tell me and you'll get it."

"Suck them," she said, and moaned when his mouth closed around the tingling tip of one breast.

He drew it deep, taking as much of her breast as he could into his mouth.

She bit back a whimper as he began to suck, and then let loose a low, aching moan when he cupped his hand around the other breast and began rolling the nipple between his finger and thumb.

"Ohmygodohmygod*ohmygod!*"

Tom lifted his head. "You came, didn't you?"

"Yes."

"Do you want to come again?"

"Yes."

"How? No," he said as she reached for his hand, "put your hands back on the wall and tell me. That's the only way you're going to get what you want."

Quivering, aching, feeling thwarted and rebellious and all the more aroused because of it, she did as he ordered and pressed her palms flat against the wall.

"Good girl." He kissed her approvingly. "Now. Tell me what you want."

"Put your hand between my legs. No. No, under my skirt. Inside my panties. Rub me. Yes, like that. Please. Oh, yes. Yes. Just like that. Right there. Oh. Oh. Oh, please. Oh, Tom. Please, Tom."

"Hands against the wall," he ordered, stopping the tantalizing manipulations of his fingers when she clutched his arms. "And keep your hips still."

Shooting him a fulminating glare, she slapped her palms against the wall and went rigid, biting down her bottom lip in an effort to stay that way.

He rewarded her with the soft, slow strumming of his thumb against her clitoris, just the way he knew she liked it, drawing it out, waiting…waiting… waiting until she was on the screaming edge before he slipped two long fingers inside of her and stroked her G-spot. Her body convulsed as a torrent of feeling burst inside her, her whole body clamping down in an orgy of wild, intemperate, unstoppable sensation.

"Again?" he said, when she'd caught her breath.

"Yes." The word was nearly a sob. "Yes. But I want your cock in me this time," she said, telling him before he could ask. "And I want to touch you."

"Be my guest," he invited, angling his hips so she could get at the fly of his jeans.

She flicked open the metal button on the waistband, then grabbed the two sides and pulled, popping the rest of the buttons in a single motion. His erection bulged through the opening, covered now only by the white knit fabric of his briefs. She grabbed the elastic waistband with both hands and pulled it down. His erection sprang free, iron-hard and pointing straight up at his navel. She trailed her fingertips up its length and then down again, slowly, watching it jerk in response.

Roxanne all but licked her lips in anticipation. "I want this inside me."

"Lift up your skirt," he ordered.

Her gaze on his face, she gathered the eyelet fabric in her fists and pulled it up, slowly, revealing the tops of her red boots and the lacy white stockings. The stocking tops stopped midway between her knees and crotch, held up with lacy elastic bands that gently hugged her thighs. Above them her legs were smooth and bare all the way to the high-cut legs of her white lace panties.

His eyes glazed over, his gaze riveted on the tiny triangle of white lace between her thighs. "Take them off," he said, indicating the panties with a jerk of his chin.

Transferring the froth of fabric to one hand, she attempted to remove the panties one-handed.

Evidently, she was taking too long. "Let me help." He curled his fingers over the waistband, and yanked.

Hard.

The fragile lace split without a protest.

Roxanne nearly came again, right then and there.

Tom grabbed her hips in his hands, curling his fingers under her bare bottom, pulling her forward and lifting her all in one smooth motion.

She started to come again as soon as he entered her.

"Not yet. Not yet," he murmured desperately, pressing her hips hard against the wall to keep them both from coming.

It was too late for Roxanne. She went up and over, her face buried in the curve of his neck to muffle the sounds of ecstasy.

Tom managed to hang on, holding back until her spasms subsided, and they could begin again, together. And then he began moving. Slowly. Powerfully. Pumping in and out of her in unconscious time to the heavy beat of the music pulsating against the wall at her back. The band was playing "Wild Thing," the unlikely hard-rock anthem of the rodeo cowboy. The crowd was really into it, stamping and screaming, rattling the walls of the old barnlike building from the inside, while they shook it from the outside to the same wildly sensual beat.

Wild thing, I think I love you!

Oh, no, Roxanne thought, as she tumbled over the edge again into the mindless abyss of blinding physical sensation.

Did she?

Chapter Eight

ROXANNE TURNED IN her Mustang at the Santa Fe airport on the theory that there was no reason to waste money on a rental when they'd be driving to the same places all the time.

"If you get sick of us, you can always rent yourself another car and be on your way," Rooster said as they all settled into the cab of Tom's pickup for the one-hour drive from Santa Fe to Albuquerque.

It was one of the extended crew cab models, big and black and macho, so there was plenty of room for the three of them as well as the occasional fourth passenger—or even a fifth, if nobody minded getting cozy and they ran across a cowboy in need of a lift to the next rodeo. The truck bed was fitted with a low, windowless camper top that could be locked to secure their gear. It was equipped with an inflatable mat and a double sleeping bag, so it was even possible to sleep in shifts, if not actual comfort, during the frequent overnight hauls between venues. Given that it was the virtual home-away-from-home for two men, Roxanne found the interior of the truck was surprisingly neat and tidy. There was a big cooler behind the driver's seat for soft drinks and cold cuts, and a plastic bag for the inevitable trash one accumulated on a long road trip. There was a thick stack of well-worn maps stuck under an elastic band on the visor, a jumble of mostly country-western CDs mixed in with several books-on-tape in a shoebox on the floor, a radar detector mounted under the dashboard, and nearly a dozen paperbacks and as many magazines strewn over the top of it.

Someone, Roxanne noted, was quite fond of the more sensational tabloid magazines, which, together with the books, made for a very eclectic mix of literature. There was a copy of the most recent *Prorodeo Sports News,* of course, three or four of the requisite Louis L'Amour and Zane Grey westerns, a couple of Robert Parker and Sue Grafton detective stories, a Tony Hillerman, a meaty Wilbur Smith novel, a recent Oprah pick, and—

"Harry Potter?" she said, picking up the young magician's latest adventure.

"That's Tom's," Rooster pointed out quickly, in case anyone thought he might be reading a kid's book.

"I like to keep up with what my students are reading," Tom said. "Turns out, it's a real good book. Have you read it?"

Roxanne goggled, just a bit. "'Students?'"

"Tom's a teacher," Rooster said helpfully. "When he's not rodeoin' he spends most of his time trying to pound some learnin' into the young hooligans at the Second Chance Ranch."

Roxanne really did goggle then. She couldn't help it. Her good-looking, dangerous cowboy was a *teacher?*

"Surprise," he said softly.

IT WAS NEARLY an eight-hour drive from Albuquerque to Phoenix, if you kept to the speed limit. It was considerably less if you pushed it. After only two days in their company, Roxanne had already learned that cowboys *always* pushed it. Even cowboys who taught school. It was simply the nature of the beast, and the way the rodeo game was played if you wanted to win.

A cowboy had to compete at a lot of rodeos to make a living. And a lot of rodeos meant a lot of traveling.

"Say you win first place at one of the big venues and pull down fifteen hundred, maybe two thousand dollars for a single event," Tom said quietly, talking mostly to keep himself awake on the long overnight haul. "That's considered big money because, more often, you're looking at a couple of hundred dollars, max. But say you win that two thousand. You've got to pay your entry fees out of that, and those can be four or five hundred dollars at a top venue. You've got to pay all your own traveling expenses. If you're a family man, with a wife and kids waiting for you at home, you've likely got expenses there, too. A cowboy can be a top rodeo star and still make less than a hundred thousand a year, gross. Usually way less."

She wanted to ask what he'd "pulled down" for the third place he'd taken in the saddle bronc event that afternoon, but didn't. It wasn't any of her business what he made or didn't make. "Then why do you do it? Why does anybody do it?"

"Why did Joe Namath play football with braces on both knees? Or Steve Young keep playing after his sixth concussion? Sure as hell, neither one of them needed the money."

"So you're telling me it's the love of the game? That you actually *like* being tossed on your head at regular intervals?"

"Hey, now, no need to be insulting," he chided. "I don't get tossed my head on a regular basis. Just often enough to keep it interesting for the paying customers."

"But to risk life and limb for that piddley amount of money! That's just crazy, is what it is."

"No, darlin'," he drawled, "that's rodeo."

"HERE, ROXY, take a sip of my Co'-Cola," Rooster said, thrusting the familiar red-and-white can at her when she paused to clear her throat. "Wet your whistle. We can't have you gettin' dry, now, can we?"

Roxanne took the can from him and took a small sip. It was the full-octane version of the soft drink, chock-full of caffeine and sugar, too sweet for her taste and warm, to boot, from being clenched between Rooster's hands. But she'd been reading out loud for the past two hours and needed, as he'd said, something to wet her whistle. Having done so, she handed it back to him with a smile, silently vowing to make sure they added diet cola and a six-pack of spring water to the contents of the cooler in the back seat at the next refueling stop.

"For a kid's story, that Harry Potter ain't half bad," Rooster said, and gave Tom a friendly whack on the back of the head. "You shoulda told me how good it is. I might have started in to read it myself if I'd known."

"I did tell you." Tom said without rancor, neglecting to add that it hadn't done any good because Rooster had never willingly cracked a book in his life.

His choice of reading material tended toward the tabloids, *People,* the latest issue of the *Prorodeo Sports News,* and, once a year, the swimsuit issue of *Sports Illustrated.* Like most cowboys, he did love a good yarn, though, and was an avid fan of the books on tape that could be rented at one truck stop and returned down the road at another. It hadn't taken him long to discover that having somebody read to him was better still for whiling away the long, dreary hours on the road.

"It is a good story, isn't it?" Roxanne said, turning her head to smile at Rooster over her shoulder.

Tom cast a speculative sideways glance at her, amazed at her patience and good humor, not to mention her skill at reading out loud. Not everyone could do it well, either reading too fast or too slow, or plodding along in a monotone that could render a book boring no matter how talented the writer. She read with verve and animation, bringing the characters to life in a way that suggested she'd had a lot of practice—and making Tom wonder just where she'd acquired the skill.

"You need another sip, Roxy?" Rooster said, none too subtly prodding her to resume reading. "You want me to open you up a cold one so's you can finish the next chapter?"

"No, thanks," she said and, taking the hint, resumed regaling them with the magical adventures of Harry Potter and his friends.

"THERE'S A RODEO someplace in the country almost every day of the year," Tom told her as they sped along the highway between Phoenix and Window Rock, which was seven and a half hours away in the heart of the Navajo reservation in Arizona. "Considerably more, of course, during the summer months," he continued, his voice low to avoid waking Rooster, who slept stretched out on the back seat of the cab because sleeping in the back, inside the camper top, made him carsick. "On weekends, it's not unusual for a cowboy to compete in three or four different rodeos in as many different cities. Two a day, sometimes, if he can squeeze them in. Fourth of July week is especially crazy because of all the festivals and celebrations going on then. A lot of them have rodeos attached."

Roxanne tried, unsuccessfully, to stifle a yawn. "Why?"

Tom slanted her a glance out of the corner of his eye. "Why what?"

"Why would you want to compete in more than one rodeo a day?"

"Points," said Rooster from the back seat, proving he wasn't asleep, after all.

Roxanne started and looked around guiltily, devoutly hoping he'd been asleep thirty minutes ago when she'd distracted Tom from the tedium of the road with a little digital sex.

"Points and money," Rooster said. "Each dollar you earn in winnings counts as a point in the standings. And only the top fifteen cowboys—the top fifteen money winners—in each event go to the finals in Las Vegas. The more rodeos you enter, the more money you earn, the more points you win. See?"

"That's the theory, anyway," Tom said.

"So, how many rodeos does a cowboy have to enter to get the points he needs to make the finals?" Roxanne asked.

"Well, now, that all depends. You ride in a lot of little Podunk rodeos, with Podunk purses, you don't make many points. What you gotta do is hit as many of the big venues as you can, that's where the big money is."

"Big being a relative term," Tom said dryly.

Rooster paid no attention. "Cities like Dallas and Fort Worth. Denver. Phoenix. That's where the big money is. And your big state fairs and festivals, now, there's good money to be had there, too. The Buffalo Bill Rodeo in North Platte. Pike's Peak or Bust in Colorado Springs. Frontier Days in Cheyenne. And Mesquite, a'course. The Mesquite rodeo has become real popular. There's a rodeo going on there purt' near every weekend. Big money there."

"Big being a relative term," Roxanne said, and earned a sly, sidelong grin from the driver.

"NO, ABSOLUTELY NOT. No way." Roxanne slapped at Tom's hands and tried to stifle an excited giggle. "I am absolutely *not* going to have sex in the back of a pickup," she said primly, even though the very thought of it had her juices flowing. "They'll hear us."

"They" were Rooster and two other cowboys who were hitching a ride to the next rodeo. Their car had overheated in the middle of the Arizona desert, causing the engine to freeze up. Since it was on its last legs, anyway, an oil-guzzling junker purchased for a couple of hundred dollars, they simply left it where it was, hefted their gear on their backs, and started walking. Tom picked them up about a hundred miles east of Window Rock, which worked out just fine because it gave them two more drivers on the long haul to Canon City.

"Nobody's going to hear a thing, Slim," Tom wheedled, his voice warm and cajoling. "Rooster's got his George Strait CD turned up full blast. And even if he didn't, what with the road noise and the wind, and us back here all private and cozy under the camper, snug as two bugs in a rug, they wouldn't hear us, anyway. Not unless you scream real loud." He grinned wickedly, and tugged at the placket of the Western-cut shirt she'd bought at the rodeo in Santa Fe, popping the little pearl snaps to expose her leopard-print push-up bra to his avid gaze. "Damn, you wore this on purpose, didn't you?" He ran his hand over her décolletage, tracing the upper curves of her plumped-up breasts with his fingertips. "You know it makes me crazy."

"No," she said, although it was true. "I wore it because it's the last clean one in my suitcase until we can stop at a Laundromat."

He skimmed his hand down over her stomach to the top button on her jeans and popped it open, too. "Are you wearin' those sexy little leopard panties, too?" He pulled the zipper down before she could stop him. "Let me see."

She slapped his hand away again. "I mean it. We're not having sex back here."

He traced a fingertip along the edge of her panties. "How about we just fool around a little bit, then?"

"Absolutely not," she said, and rolled over on her side, away from him. "Go to sleep. You've got to ride in less than eight hours."

"I'd rather ride you right now," he murmured, and kissed her nape.

Roxanne steeled herself against temptation. "Sleep," she said sternly, and closed her own eyes.

"I'm too keyed up to sleep." He slid his hand over her hip and down inside the opened fly of her jeans. His palm was flat on her belly, his long, callused fingers sliding under the edge of her panties to touch the crinkly blond hair that covered her mound. He brushed them back and forth, just above where she was beginning to crave his touch. "I'd probably drop right off to sleep if I was more relaxed."

"Relax yourself," she suggested. But she scooted back, just a little, until the curve of her butt was pressing into his groin and he didn't have to reach quite so far to caress her.

He returned the pressure of her hips, snugging his erection up against her, and inched his fingers a little further down inside her panties. "Didn't your mother ever tell you that relaxing yourself will make you go blind?"

"My mother didn't talk to me about relaxation. She talked about the importance of a diversified stock portfolio and how to hire a good caterer and cleaning ser—" She gasped as his fingers found just exactly the right spot. The gasp turned to a moan, and her hips rolled, moving rhythmically against his clever fingers.

He took advantage of her momentary distraction to ease her loosened jeans down over the curve of her hip, baring her to mid-thigh. His fingers slid deeper between her legs, cupping her, his long index finger sliding in and out of her wet sheath, his thumb riding her clitoris.

She bit back a shriek. "Stop that," she moaned, casting an apprehensive glance toward the cab of the truck.

He started to draw his hand away.

She grabbed at it, keeping it right where it was. "No, don't!"

He chuckled wickedly and popped the buttons on his own fly, freeing his erection. Roxanne arched her back and wriggled her butt against him, her legs parting as far as the restricting jeans would allow. Tom slipped his cock into her from behind and began a slow, leisurely pumping, while his fingers continued manipulating her clitoris from the front.

"Don't scream, now," he whispered, just as she was about to come. "They might hear you."

THEY CHANGED PLACES at the halfway point, the two hitchhiking cowboys stretching out in the back of the truck to catch a little shut-eye, while Tom and Roxanne shifted to the front seat. Rooster, as usual, unfolded himself along the back seat to sleep, unable to stomach the close confines of the camper top. They rolled into Canon City, Colorado, just in time for the afternoon rodeo. Barely.

Tom took first place on the back of a high-rolling bronc named White Lightning, which was enough to nudge him one step up in the standings. Rooster pulled down second, squeezed out of first by the extra two points won by Clay Madison. They packed up as soon as their events were over, pushing hard to make the two and a half hour drive to Elizabeth in time for the evening performance.

Tom drew a respectable ride in his second rodeo of the day, pulling down third on a dun-colored pile driver that hit the ground stiff-legged, snapping Tom's teeth together and sending a jolt up his spine with each buck. Rooster drew the Widow Maker. The animal was a particularly bad-tempered two thousand pound Brahman with a reputation for going after downed cowboys. He was dangerous in the chutes, too, and had been known to rear up and fall over backward on top of the cowboys who tried to ride him. If a cowboy could stick, he'd be sure to pull down a top score. But not many had been able to stick. In the three years the Widow Maker had been on the circuit, two cowboys had died from the injuries he'd inflicted. Countless others wore scars inflicted by his hooves and horns.

Knowing all this, Roxanne paled when she heard the name of the bull Rooster had drawn. Rooster rubbed his hands together and cackled with glee; a ride to the horn on the Widow Maker would earn him a guaranteed first place, and put him ahead of Clay Madison. The crowd roared and stamped their approval when the pairing was announced over the loudspeaker, anticipating a good show in their favorite event.

Bull riding was the most popular event at the rodeo because—in Roxanne's opinion, anyway—it was the bloodiest, most dangerous event, with the most potential for the "wrecks" so beloved by the fans and the camera crews from ESPN and the Nashville Network. As a general rule, it drew the smallest, most compact cowboys as competitors. The late great Lane Frost, who'd been killed by a bull named Taking Care of Business, hadn't been much bigger than a jockey. Ty Murray, the All-Around Cowboy for three years running, was only five feet six inches tall—and that was only, some said, if you measured him with his boots on.

"It all has to do with gravity," Rooster explained earnestly as Roxanne pinned his number on his back and tried to pretend she wasn't the least bit concerned about his safety during the upcoming ride. "A man's center of gravity is in his chest, see? And the closer the center of gravity is to the bull, the easier it is to stay on. That's why you ain't gonna see any six-footers like Tom at the bull ridin' finals. Gravity will do 'em in every time."

It was gravity that did Rooster in at the Elizabeth rodeo. Gravity and a bull named Widow Maker. The animal came out of the chute like a rocket shot off the launching pad at NASA. Its massive body rose straight into the air, twisting as it toppled the cowboy on its back into the dust and rolled over on him.

Roxanne surged to her feet with the rest of the crowd, her hands pressed to her mouth to stifle the scream that rose to her lips. Paralyzed, unable to move, she watched the bullfighters rush in, standing between the downed cowboy and the enraged bull, distracting him before he could do any more damage, driving him out of the arena and into the pens behind it. And then Tom was vaulting over the fence from behind the chutes, beating the paramedics to his fallen friend. Roxanne shook off the paralysis that gripped her and raced down the grandstand steps, fighting her way through the milling crowd, ignoring the shout of the security guard as she ran through the gate that led to the staging area.

Rooster was laid out on an examining table in the medical tent when she got there, his eyes closed, his lips white and compressed, his fingers clutching the rounded edges of the table in a white-knuckled grip while the medics worked over him. His flak jacket had already been removed and lay in a crumpled heap on the floor. The right leg of his chaps had been unbuckled and folded back, the leg of his jeans split and torn open to mid-thigh. One medic poked and prodded his exposed leg, while another took care of checking vital signs. Roxanne approached the head of the table, out of the way of the medical personnel, and reached out, touching Rooster's white, drawn face with a gentle hand.

"Rooster?"

His eyes fluttered open. "Hey, Roxy." He managed a smile for her. "Tom," he said, looking up at the man who stood behind her. "How bad is it, pard?"

"Not too bad," Tom said. "Doesn't look like anything's

broken." He glanced at the medic poking at Rooster's leg for confirmation.

"Nope, nothing broken," the medic said cheerfully. "Nothing bleeding, either, 'cept for a few scrapes. The knee's already swelled up like a balloon though, and it's gonna be badly bruised. Could be just a sprain." He shrugged. "Could be torn ligaments. I can't say for sure without X rays. You're gonna have to take him over to the hospital in town to find that out."

"No hospital," said Rooster. "No time. I gotta ride tomorrow in Fort Collins."

"Rooster!" Roxanne was appalled. "You have to go to the hospital. That bull rolled right over on top of you. All two thousand pounds of him. You might have internal bleeding."

The medic who'd been checking vital signs looked up at that. "Doubt it," he said as he released the blood pressure cuff from around Rooster's arm. "Pressure's normal. If he was bleeding inside it'd be way down."

"There's still his knee," Roxanne insisted. "He needs to get it X-rayed."

"I ain't goin' to no hospital, so just get that thought right out of your head." Rooster struggled to sit up, shifting to swing his legs over the side of the table. His face paled a bit and the breath hissed out from between his teeth but he managed to stay upright without swaying. "Hell, this ain't nothin'. I just twisted the damned thing, is all. I've done worse trippin' over my own feet on the dance floor. 'Sides, there ain't a bull rider in the world who don't have bad knees. It comes with the territory. Just slap some ice on it," he said to the medic, "and give me a coupl'a pain pills and I'll be good as new."

"Good as new! You can't even stand up." Roxanne parked herself in front of him, preventing him from doing just that, and jammed her hands on her hips. "With the condition that knee's in, I doubt you could even crawl." Her voice rose with her agitation, her New England accent becoming crisper and sharper with each syllable. "So just how the *hell* do you think you're going to be in any condition to ride tomorrow?"

Rooster grinned. "Hotter than a firecracker," he said admiringly.

Roxanne folded her arms across her chest, refusing to be charmed.

Rooster sighed. "I don't hafta walk to be able to ride, Roxy." He looked to the man standing behind her for confirmation. "Tell her, Tom."

Roxanne whirled around. "Yes, tell him, Tom," she said. "Make him go to the hospital."

"Rooster knows what he's doing," Tom said. "If he says he doesn't need to go to the hospital, he doesn't need to go. And I'm not about to try and make him."

"Oh, for crying out loud! What is it with you guys?" Roxanne's fulminating glare took in not only Rooster and Tom, but all the other battered and bruised cowboys being tended to in the medical tent. "It's that stupid cowboy tradition, isn't it? It wouldn't be manly to admit you're hurt, would it? No, of course not! You could have six bleeding wounds, two broken ankles and a concussion, but you'd still have to suck it in and cowboy up, just to prove you have real try. God forbid, any of you should admit you're hurt or in pain. The world as we know it might come to an end."

"Tom rode once with a broken collarbone," Rooster said when she paused for breath. "At the Mesquite Rodeo, wasn't it, Tom?"

Tom nodded.

"Did you have a concussion that day, too? Or was it just the collarbone?"

"Just the collarbone," Tom said, his lips quirking up at the outraged expression on Roxanne's face. "The concussion was at the Bowie Rodeo a year ago last May."

"That's right, I remember now." Rooster nodded. "It was just the collarbone that day in Mesquite," he said to Roxanne. "He had to have the bone reset after the last go-round, but it sure was a pretty ride."

"Idiots!" She threw her hands up in exasperation. "You're all idiots. Morons. I wash my hands of you. You can all kill yourselves for all I care," she said, and stomped out of the medical tent with the cowboys' delighted laughter following behind her.

SHE DIDN'T WASH HER HANDS of them, though. Instead, she read the final chapters of Harry Potter to them by flashlight, keeping Tom awake during the long nighttime drive to Fort Collins, keeping Rooster's mind off the throbbing pain in his knee. The next day at the rodeo arena, when his knee had turned ten shades of purple and swollen to the size of a cantaloupe, despite the constant icing, she was right there at his side, offering pain pills and sympathy, ready to help him hobble over to the chutes if that's what he wanted.

It was Tom who convinced him to turn out. "You drew a piss-poor bull, anyway, a real dink, so you probably wouldn't place no matter how good you rode," he said. "And, hell, any cowboy who's ranked in the top ten can afford to take one goddamned day off to rest up."

Rooster insisted on riding in Casper, though. There was good money to be had there, and he'd drawn a decent ride. And young Clay Madison was steadily advancing in the ranks behind him.

During the long frantic Fourth of July weekend, they did Riverton and Hot Springs, Worland and Cody, Billings and Bighorn, and half a dozen other small towns in quick succession, three rodeos a day sometimes, when scheduling and distance made it possible. Somewhere along the way, Roxanne took over the domestic duties for what had become their little family. Mostly out of self-defense against widening thighs and clogged arteries.

"I refuse to eat another greasy hamburger at another greasy truck stop," she said, her arms folded over her chest in a way that her traveling companions knew meant she'd come to the end of her rope—and theirs. "From now on, we eat normal food, like normal people. Vegetables," she elaborated, when they just looked at her. "Fresh fruit. Salads. Whole-wheat bread."

"I had a salad last night with my dinner," Tom said, just to aggravate her. "Vegetables, too."

"Wilted iceberg lettuce with gloppy pink dressing is not a salad." She sniffed disdainfully. "And canned green beans cooked in bacon grease do not qualify as a vegetable in my book."

She took the truck the next day while they were competing and found a Wal-Mart. When it was time to stop for dinner, she demanded they bypass the easy-off, easy-on, fast-food joints and truck stops, directing them, instead, to pull over at the next rest area.

"There's a camp stove in the back of the truck," she said, wrapping the sleeves of one of Tom's shirts around her waist like an apron to protect her last clean pair of pants.

She'd been reduced to wearing a pair of her pre-Roxy khaki slacks. They were conservatively cut, of course, with a pleated front and a cuffed hem. Paired with one of her snug little tank tops and her red boots, with a bandana threaded through the belt loops instead of her shiny alligator belt with the gold buckle, she thought she'd achieved a sort of funky urban-cowgirl-meets-Connecticut-Yankee kind of chic. At least, nobody'd laughed when they'd seen her coming.

"The propane tank is in the back seat next to the cooler," she continued, ordering them to fetch and carry as easily as she did her students. "Utensils and paper plates are in the bag with the groceries. By the time you've washed up, I'll have some veggie sticks ready for you to munch on."

A half an hour later they were dining on skinless, boneless grilled chicken breasts, a green salad with fat-free dressing, and whole-wheat rolls. Rooster grumbled and rolled his eyes when she put the grilled chicken in front of him—"I generally like my chicken fried," he said—but he ate every morsel and asked for seconds.

"Since you were such good boys and cleaned your plates—" she pulled another container out of her magic bag of foodstuffs "—you get dessert." She placed an aluminum tray of frosted brownies between them on the picnic table. "I stopped at a bakery on the way back from the Wal-Mart," she said, delighted with their reaction to her surprise.

It was later, as they were loading the camp stove and supplies back into the truck that she mentioned the laundry. "I didn't get a chance to stop by a Laundromat today. But I will tomorrow while you're competing. If you'll give me your things, I'll wash them at the same time I do mine."

"You want my skivvies?" Rooster said, scandalized.

It was Roxanne's turn to roll her eyes. "I've seen men's underwear before, Rooster. I've got three brothers."

"Yeah, well, you ain't seen mine before."

She put her hands on her hips. "You aren't going to have time to do any of your own laundry in the foreseeable future," she said. "And if you don't do any laundry, then you'll have to wear what you've been wearing for the last two days. And if that happens, you're riding in the back of the truck until you do have time to do it because you're already beginning to smell like one of those bulls you ride." She smiled sweetly. "But it's up to you, of course."

Tom, who wasn't shy about his skivvies and knew a good thing when he saw it, handed over his dirty laundry without a fuss.

THEY STAYED AT A MOTEL after the last rodeo of the weekend in Miles City to ensure a full night's sleep before tack-
ling the nine-hour drive to the one billed as the *Daddy of 'em
All*—Frontier Days in Cheyenne, Wyoming.

Amazingly enough, cowboys considered the *Daddy of 'em
All* to be a vacation of sorts. The event lasted for ten days,
with a rodeo in the same fairground arena every day. As there
was no traveling from venue to venue, the cowboys got to
bed down in the same place for a while, be it in a motel or
a camper parked on the fairgrounds, and eat food that didn't
come from a greasy-spoon truck stop. Those who had families they rarely saw could have them come to Cheyenne and
be assured they'd have long stretches of uninterrupted time
to spend together between the eight-second rides. There was
top-name country-western entertainment nearly every day
after the rodeo, and all the usual fairground attractions, plus
Indian Dancing exhibitions, art shows and a special performance by the United States Air Force Thunderbirds.

"It makes," Tom said, "for a real party atmosphere."

It also had the largest purse in professional rodeo. A cowboy who'd slipped behind in the standings could make it all
up—and then some—in Cheyenne.

None of that mattered to Roxanne, though, as she snuggled down into the crisp, cool sheets of a Motel 6 with a blissful sigh. She'd had a long, leisurely bath, and a real dinner
in a real restaurant with real linens on the table and fresh
salads on the menu and a decent wine list, and now she was
faced with the utterly delicious prospect of a full night's sleep
in an unmoving bed—for the second night in a row!—before
she had to be up to face the craziness of the Frontier Days
celebration.

She could hear Tom rummaging around in the bathroom—showering, shaving, gargling—and then the door
opened and he strolled out with one of the too small motel

towels wrapped around his lean hips. His body was long and lanky, without an excess ounce of fat anywhere. Wide shoulders. Broad chest. Washboard stomach. Tight little cowboy butt. Strong horseman's thighs. A perfect masculine specimen, marred only by the scars of his profession. He'd been stepped on, kicked, punched, battered, bitten and broken, and nearly every part of his body showed silent evidence of it.

There was a crescent-shaped scar on his right tricep where an angry horse had taken a bite out of him, and another one just under his bottom lip where his own teeth had snapped together during a particularly bone-jarring ride. He had a steel pin in his right thigh and a knee that talked to him when the weather changed. Both of his shoulders had been dislocated at least twice, his collarbone had been broken once—at the rodeo in Mesquite—and he'd lost count of all the dislocated fingers, crushed toes, and torn ligaments he'd racked up over the years. And, then, of course, there were the fading yellowish-green bruises that still ran down the length of his left arm, courtesy of a feisty little mare called Hot Sauce. Although he claimed it was fine and didn't bother him at all, he often rubbed it absently, just above his elbow where the bruises had been the worst.

"Tell me again why you do it," Roxanne said as he dropped the towel and crawled into bed beside her.

"Do what?" He wrapped his arms around her, pulling her close, and bent his head to kiss her.

She put a fingertip to his lips, stopping him. "This," she said, tracing the faint white scar under his lip. "And this." She touched the bump on his collarbone where the bones had knit imperfectly. "And this." She ran her hand down the mottled bruises on his arm. "What makes you risk life and limb, over and over again?"

"The sheer glory of being a cowboy," he said without missing a beat.

"No. I'm serious."

"So am I."

"Where's the glory in living like a nomad? Of driving three hundred miles or more every day, just so you can spend eight seconds on the back of some half-wild animal? The pay's lousy, the food's worse—"

"Food's been pretty good lately," he reminded her. "Thanks to you."

"—and the benefits are nonexistent," she said, ignoring the interruption.

"So, I guess the magic's worn off for you, huh?" His tone was teasing, but the look in his eyes was suddenly guarded and wary. "Does that mean you're going to be packing up and heading back to whatever New England state it is you came from?"

"Connecticut," she said. "And, no, it doesn't mean I'm packing up. The magic of the rodeo may have faded—" she cupped his lean cheeks between her hands and smiled up into his face "—but your magic just keeps getting stronger and stronger."

To her delight, he very nearly blushed.

"I intend to hold you to our agreement, Tom Steele. I'm a one-man woman—and vice versa—until the end of the summer."

Which was only six short weeks away.

Roxanne felt a stinging in her eyes at the thought, and a painful tightening in her chest. She blinked once, hard, and willed the feeling away.

They still had six weeks, and she intended to make the most of them.

"But I still want to know why you do it," she said.

"We'll talk about it later," he murmured, and bent his head to take her lips. "Much later."

She sighed and let the magic take her as his lips covered hers. It was a leisurely kiss, soft and sweet and deliciously unhurried. Their lovemaking had always been tempestuous before, frenzied and wild. Now it was indescribably tender.

He took a long time kissing her. Her lips, her cheeks, her eyelids and temples, the soft curving underside of her jaw, the delicate well at the base of her throat, the slope of her shoulder, the bend of her elbow, the pulse beating heavily underneath the pale skin of her wrist, her palms and fingertips. He lavished time and care and infinite attention on all those soft delicate parts of a woman that aren't generally considered erogenous zones, but indisputably are.

She kissed him back the same way, trailing her lips over his eyelids and cheekbones, over his chiseled jaw and the strong curve of his neck where it melded into the swelling strength of his shoulder. She kissed the hair-dusted curve of his pectorals, his sinewy arms, his hard, callused, clever hands.

The fire took a long time to build and when it caught, finally, it was the slow-burning kind that pulsed with a deep incinerating heat, instead of the raging wildfire they were used to generating between them. Their movements were fluid and unhurried, there on the big cool bed in the anonymous motel room. They kissed and caressed and fondled with languorous deliberation, awash in sensation and sensuality. When he slipped into her, it was without haste, without the frantic urge to possess. He gave to her instead, his powerful thrusts deep and gentle and slow. There was no driving need to race to completion, for either of them, no desperately raging desire to have it happen *now, now, now!* The climax, when it came, was as gentle, as devastatingly tender, as deep and pulsating and lingering as what had gone before.

Her body arched up from the bed in a long sensuous curve as her orgasm rolled through her, rippling outward from her vagina and clitoris until every part of her body was tingling with sensation. She said his name, just once, longingly, lovingly, achingly, an inarticulate plea for even more closeness.

He put his hands beneath her back, supporting her, lifting her against him, pressing her tingling body to his chest, holding her close as his own body contracted in a deep, delicious orgasm of utter completion.

"Roxanne," he said, and kissed her.

Magic, indeed.

Chapter Nine

THERE WAS A FREE PANCAKE breakfast in downtown Cheyenne the next morning. It was, of course, packed. No cowboy worth his salt was going to turn down free made-from-scratch pancakes and freshly brewed coffee. Long picnic tables covered with cheerful blue-and-white-checked tablecloths had been set up in the plaza between the shops. Smiling cooks in cowboy hats and white aprons manned the large rectangular griddles—easily four feet by two feet—situated at each end of the dining area. The tantalizing smells of coffee, maple syrup and sizzling pork sausage filled the air. A rodeo clown offered free face painting for the dozens of kids running around. The place was packed.

Roxanne settled into a seat at one of the long picnic tables, saving their places while Tom stood in line. From there she saw a whole different side of the cowboys she'd gradually been coming to know over the past few weeks.

Tug Stiles, one of the wildest, rowdiest cowboys on the circuit, ate his breakfast with a pink-cheeked toddler sitting on his lap and an adoring young wife by his side. Clay Madison sat between his beaming parents, who had driven in from Nebraska to watch their son compete. Even Rooster had a lady friend with him, a sweet-faced waitress from

Laramie who'd taken the day off from work so she could spend it with him.

"Most cowboys have wives and kids, just like everyone else," Tom said, answering the question implicit in her lifted eyebrow as he came back to the table with their breakfast. He pried the lid off of one of the cups of coffee he'd brought and handed it to her—the requisite one-half teaspoon of sugar already stirred into it—then inserted himself into the bench seat beside her. "And those that aren't married have sweethearts." He took an appreciative sip of his own heavily sugared and creamed coffee. "Or parents," he said, with a friendly nod at Mr. and Mrs. Madison. "Frontier Days gives them a chance to spend some time together. Lots of rodeo families make this their annual vacation every year for just that reason."

Sitting there, eating her breakfast of pancakes and little link sausages, watching the cowboys she thought she'd come to know so well interact with their families, she realized she didn't really know them at all. Never in a million years would she have believed those rough-and-ready, devil-may-care loners could look so pathetically happy to have their families close by. It very nearly brought tears to her eyes to see big Tug Stiles bent so attentively over his tiny daughter, feeding her bites of pancake off the end of his fork. Or the way Clay Madison preened and purred under loving attention of his proud parents. She hadn't realized until just this moment how desperately lonely the cowboy life was, for both the cowboys and their families—which made it all the more puzzling to her why anyone would choose to live this way.

What was it about the rodeo that made it so attractive to those men?

"Why do you do it?" she asked Tom again as they strolled hand-in-hand through the carnival midway on their way to the arena. "And don't give me that glory business. I'd like to hear the truth, please."

"That *is* the truth."

She gave him a skeptical look, lips pursed, eyebrows raised, the kind of look she gave her fifth graders back in Connecticut when she thought they were being less than completely forthcoming with their answers.

"Honest," he said, giving her the same earnest look her students did.

"Explain."

"I don't know if I can, exactly."

"You don't have to be exact," she said. "I'm just looking for a little insight, is all."

"Well..." He took a moment or two to gather his thoughts. "I guess what it all boils down to, really, is that for most cowboys the rodeo embodies the myth of the West, the way it used to be. Or—" he slanted a wry glance at her "—the way we *think* it used to be, which amounts to the same thing. Rodeo is John Wayne driving the cattle herd to the railhead in Abilene in *Red River,* or Gary Cooper walking down the middle of the street in *High Noon,* doing the hard thing because it's the right thing. For those eight seconds in the arena, a cowboy gets to live the legend. He gets to *be* the legend, a living, breathing icon of the American West. And not just in his own mind, either, but in the minds of the crowd, too, because we were all brought up on the myth. We all believe it to some extent. Even sophisticated east-coast city girls like you." He slanted another glance at her, wondering if he'd revealed too much of the man under the myth to a woman who saw him only as a summer fling. "Maybe, even, especially sophisticated east-coast city girls."

Roxanne knew exactly what he was getting at. She'd come West looking for a cowboy, looking for the myth, and found her own particular version of it in him. Six feet of lean, well-muscled male in a cowboy hat and tight-fitting jeans. He walked beside her now, the quintessence of every movie cow-

boy she'd ever seen or dreamed about. His bronc saddle was
slung over one broad shoulder, his index finger hooked under
the fork where the saddle horn would be if it had one. He'd
buckled on his chaps and spurs before they left their motel
room instead of carrying them, too. The chaps were made
of battered, natural-colored leather, with a modest fringe and
a widely spaced row of silver conchas down the outside of
each leg. They flapped gently around his long, lean horseman's legs, framing the bulge beneath his fly and his tight
cowboy butt. The little silver jingle-bobs on his spurs sang
a sweet cowboy song with every step. Just looking at him
made her breath catch and her heart beat faster.

Did that make her shallow? Or just susceptible?

"Who said I was from the east coast?" she asked, avoid-
ing, for the moment, the question of her character. "I could
be from Denver. Or Dallas." She laid the accent on extra thick
and fluttered her eyelashes at him. "Or even San Antonio."

"Not with that accent, you couldn't," he said, deadpan.
"Besides, you told me yourself you're from Connecticut."

Well, yes, there was that. "Did it ever fool you?" she said,
getting back to the matter of the accent. She'd thought it had
sounded pretty authentic—when she remembered to use it,
that is. "Even for a minute?"

"Maybe for a minute." He slanted a glance down at her.
"Did you want to fool me?"

She lifted one shoulder in a quasishrug. "Not really," she
admitted, knowing in her heart of hearts that the only one
she'd been trying to fool—was *still* trying to fool—was herself. "I thought it went with the look."

"The look?"

"You know, the yahoo-ride-'em-cowgirl look."

He stopped walking to look down at her. "Are you kidding? You think you look like a cowgirl?"

"Don't I?"

He shook his head. "Madison Avenue's idea of a cowgirl, maybe. In one of those sexy ads for designer jeans."

She looked down at herself. "These jeans are *not* designer," she said indignantly.

"No, they're Levi's," he said, humoring her. "Cowboys—and girls—wear Wrangler. And that hat looks like it just came out of the box. Plus, you're wearing it set back on your head like some greenhorn hayseed." He hefted the saddle from his shoulder with a twist of his wrist and bent at the knees, setting it gently on the ground between them, then reached out and grabbed her hat by the brim with both hands. Flexing the bendable wires in the straw brim, he reshaped it so that the sides flared up a bit and the front and back dipped down, and set it back on her head, making sure it tilted forward. "That's the way you wear a cowboy hat."

"Well, why didn't you tell me before?" she said, wishing she had a mirror so she could see how it looked. "Instead of letting me run around looking like a hayseed?"

"I thought that's the look you were aiming for."

"Ha. Ha." She stuck her tongue out at him. "Any other fashion faux pas you neglected to tell me about?"

"Well, now that you mention it…"

"What?"

"Those boots." He shook his head in mock consternation. "Look around you, Slim. You see anybody else in bright-red cowboy boots?"

"But I got them at Neiman's in Dallas."

"I rest my case," he said, and bent down to retrieve his saddle.

"Tug Stiles's boots are purple with yellow roses on the sides."

"You gonna take fashion cues from a guy who has a lightning bolt sewn on the crotch of his jeans?"

He had a point. "So, what color should I get? Brown?

Black?" She glanced around, checking out the footwear of the other people on the midway. "Or should I just go step in a couple of cow patties and muddy these up a little?"

"You don't need new boots. And you don't need to step in any cow patties."

"But you said—"

"I was just teasing you, Slim." He slung his saddle over his shoulder and reached for her hand, enfolding it in his once again. "And you know how much I love to tease you," he said, giving her a smoldering look and that sexy cowboy grin of his that set her susceptible city girl's heart to beating erratically.

THAT NIGHT after the rodeo there was a free chili cook-off. A cowboy would no more pass up free chili than he would free pancakes, especially when there was a beer tent set up close by and a country-western band providing background music. Roxanne had washed and fluffed her hair, leaving her remodeled cowboy hat back in the motel room to avoid hat head, and changed into her short denim skirt and a sleeveless scoop-necked camisole in anticipation of the dancing that would come later, after dinner.

"You know what they say about why cowboys like chili so much, don't you?" Tom said as they sat down at the wooden picnic tables—covered with red-and-white-checked oilcloth this time instead of the blue—with their favorite picks of the various chili offerings.

"No," she said, playing along. "What do they say?"

"Chili's like sex. When is good, it's great. And when it's bad, it's still pretty good."

Rooster snickered as if he'd never heard the joke before. He'd been swapping stories and slapping backs at the beer tent and was in a jovial mood. "You know who makes good chili?" he said after he'd gotten over his glee. "That Jo Beth over at the Diamond J. That little gal makes a right good chili. Hot enough to sear through the roof of your mouth if you ain't careful. You said so yourself, remember?" He smiled happily at Tom, oblivious to the discouraging scowl on his partner's face. "At the barbecue her folks had last spring when she graduated from A&M? You said she made the best chili you ever tasted. Remember?"

"I remember," Tom said through his teeth.

Rooster might have been oblivious to Tom's displeasure, but Roxanne wasn't. "Who's Jo Beth?" she said, looking back and forth between the two men.

Tom shoveled a spoonful of chili into his mouth.

"Jo Beth Jensen," Rooster supplied, happy to be of service. "Her daddy's spread runs right alongside of the Second Chance. Nice little gal. Sweet as cherry pie and as pretty as a newborn foal. Smart, too. Got herself a degree in— What was it she got her schoolin' in, Tom?"

"Animal science," he muttered, wishing Rooster would shut the hell up about Jo Beth. "How's your chili?"

"Chili's fine," Rooster said, and turned back to Roxanne. "She aims to take over the Diamond J someday. Well, she'll have to, won't she, seein' as how she's her mama and daddy's only chick. Someday, some lucky man's goin' get himself a nice little wife *and* the Diamond J." He waggled his eyebrows suggestively, grinning at Tom through a beery haze. "Ain't that right, pard?"

"I wouldn't know." Tom pushed his bowl away and rose from the table. "Come on, Slim." He grabbed Roxanne's hand, pulling her to her feet. "Let's dance."

THEY CIRCLED the makeshift dance floor a couple of times in silence, their booted feet scuffing along the bare wooden planks, his right hand curved around her neck under her tousled blond hair, her left thumb hooked in the belt loop on the side of his jeans. Their clasped hands were held low at their sides, in classic country style, as he guided her backward around the crowded floor. It was the perfect setting for romance. The air was soft and warm. The twilight sky was just beginning to fill with stars. The band was doing a credible rendition of George Strait's heartfelt cowboy lament "Does Fort Worth Ever Cross Your Mind?" as they moved together over the floor.

Tom danced with his jaw clenched and his gaze fixed firmly on a point somewhere over her right shoulder, wishing he'd never heard the name Jo Beth Jensen, wishing to hell Slim had never heard it, either. Roxanne stared at the faint white scar on his chin and wondered if she should just keep her mouth shut.

What did it matter who Jo Beth Jensen was? And what difference did it make if she was smart and pretty and could make a "right good" bowl of chili? And so what if her daddy's "spread" ran alongside Tom's?

It wasn't as if she—Roxanne—had any real claim on him, or even wanted one, if it came to that. Their affair had very definite limits. To the end of the summer and that was it. That's what they'd agreed to. No fuss. No muss. No strings. Once the summer was over she'd pack up and go back to Connecticut where she belonged, putting her Wild West adventure behind her. And he could go back to his "spread" in wherever Texas and marry his neighbor's horse-faced daughter and raise a whole passel of horse-faced kids, and…

"Are you the lucky man who's going to marry Jo Beth and get himself a nice little wife *and* the Diamond J?" she said snidely, unable to keep her mouth shut, after all. A month of speaking her mind freely had obviously left its mark.

His gaze flickered to hers. "I'm not engaged to her, if that's what you're asking," he said defensively, and looked away again.

"I wouldn't care if you were," she lied. "I was just wondering, is all."

That got his undivided attention. "You wouldn't care if I was engaged?" His expression was indignant and disbelieving. "Are you saying you'd knowingly sleep with a man who was engaged to another woman?"

She wanted to lie again, wanted to shrug it off with a laugh and an insouciant toss of her head, but she couldn't. "Yes, of course, I'd care! I *do* care. And, no, I wouldn't knowingly sleep with a man who was engaged to another woman. In fact, I'd be inclined to *geld* a man who put me in that position." She smiled with saccharine sweetness. "And I'd use the dullest knife I could find to do it."

"You can put your knife away, Slim. I'm not engaged to her."

"Are you going steady?"

"No, we're not going steady. Cowboys don't go steady. We keep company."

"So, are you keeping company with her?"

"No, I'm not keeping company with her. We've never even dated."

"Well, then…" She looked up at him, a puzzled expression in her whiskey-colored eyes. "I don't understand. If you're not involved with her why the guilt trip when Rooster mentioned her name?"

Tom gave it his best shot. "It's against the cowboy code to talk about one woman when he's with another, is all. Bad manners. If Rooster hadn't had a few brews too many he would have been more gentlemanly and not mentioned her."

Roxanne didn't believe that for a minute. She'd been around cowboys long enough to know they'd talk about any woman, any time, anywhere. Just like any other man. "What a load of B.S.," she scoffed.

"That's my story and I'm sticking to it," Tom said, and

twirled her in series of quick spin turns in the hopes she'd get dizzy and forget what they'd been talking about.

But Roxanne was made of sterner stuff. "You've thought about it, though, haven't you?" she said, resuming their conversation right where she'd left off when he brought her back in against his chest again. "That's why you reacted like a kid who'd got caught with his hand in the cookie jar."

"Thought about what?"

"Marrying little miss Texas A&M with the degree in animal science and her daddy's spread as a dowry."

"I wouldn't marry a woman for money," he said, insulted.

"What would you marry her for, then?"

"A life partner," he said instantly, like a man who'd recently given it a lot of thought and didn't have to pick and choose his words now. "Someone who could understand and share my life. Someone to raise a family with. Build a future with. Grow old with."

Someone like you, he thought, surprising himself.

He stumbled and missed a step, causing them to bump shoulders with another pair of dancers. "Beg pardon," he mumbled, wondering where the hell *that* had come from.

She wasn't the kind of woman he had in mind to marry. Not by a long shot. The kind of woman he had in mind to marry was, well…he suddenly wasn't sure exactly what kind of woman he had in mind. He'd thought it had been someone like Jo Beth but, suddenly, someone like Jo Beth seemed kind of tame and uninteresting and dull. Still, a prudent man didn't marry a woman like Slim. She was a good-time girl, a buckle bunny who picked up cowboys in bars and took them back to her motel room for wild raucous sex. Except that she wasn't…quite. He was the only cowboy she'd picked up, after all, and she hadn't so much as smiled at another cowboy with anything like invitation in her eyes, despite that little misunderstanding they'd had about Clay Madison.

No, the way she treated the other cowboys—Clay, in-cluded—was almost, well, motherly. And she'd become like a big sister to Rooster, chiding him about his diet, fretting over his injuries, reading him bedtime stories, for God's sake!

Were those the actions of a die-hard buckle bunny?

But, then, hell, he thought, even if they weren't, what difference did it make, anyway? So what if there was more to her than he'd thought that first night in Lubbock? So what if she was more than sass and sex and sweetness? Forever wasn't part of their deal. He was just a summer fling, a part of her Wild West adventure, and in six weeks she'd be leaving him to go back to her real life. The thought gave him an odd, uneasy feeling in the center of his chest. He didn't think he'd be ready to let her go in six weeks. Not in six months. Hell, maybe not ever...

"And Jo Beth is that someone?" she prodded, unable to let it go.

He gave her a blank look. "Someone who what?" he said, still trying to sort it all out in his mind. He had to let her go, of course. He *would* let her go. That was their deal, and it had been his plan from the get-go. Neither of them was looking for anything permanent...

"Someone you might marry," she said, exasperated.

"Well...ah..." With an effort, he shook off his distraction. "I guess I've sort of considered that she could be," he admitted, wondering how he'd ever thought that possible. He certainly wasn't considering it now.

"Aha!" Roxanne pounced on that like a barn cat on a mouse. "I *knew* it! You *have* thought about marrying her!"

"I haven't thought about marrying her, specifically," he said, backtracking for all he was worth. "I've just been thinking about getting married in a general kind of way. And what with her living right next door, so to speak, Jo Beth was just one of the possibilities."

"Oh, really?" Her eyebrows disappeared into her bangs. Her chin came up in that way that tempted and challenged him. "And just how many other possibilities are there?"

Tom tightened his grip on her right hand and moved in closer, in case she took it into her head to try to sucker punch him again. "For crying out loud, Slim. Do you mean to take everything I say the wrong way?"

"You said Jo Beth was only *one* of the possibilities. How else am I supposed to take it except to mean there are others?" She narrowed her eyes at him. "I don't like being one of a crowd."

"You're not one of a crowd, damn it. You're one of a kind. For which I am profoundly grateful. I don't think the world could handle more than one of you." He was on the hairy edge of exasperation, his tone colored with unwilling amusement, hovering somewhere between frustrated and admiring. "I know I sure as hell couldn't."

Roxanne ignored the exasperation and focused on the admiration. "You think I'm one of a kind?" She leaned into him, all the fight gone out of her, and smiled up into his face. "Really?"

"Really," he said, and gathered her in close, dropping her hand to wrap both arms around her.

She sighed and snuggled into him like a kitten in familiar hands, her own arms lifting to circle his waist, her head on his shoulder, her face nestled into the warm curve of his neck.

They danced without speaking for several long minutes, feet shuffling over the wooden dance floor, bodies swaying under the stars, hearts beating in time to the music and the slow, sweet pulse of unhurried passion, content for the moment merely to hold each other and be. And then he lifted his head, and she lifted hers, and they stared at each other, intently, like lovers staring at each other across the width of a pillow.

"I want you," he said, and wondered if he meant for now, or forever. "So much."

"I know." She touched her lips to his. "I want you, too."

He smiled.

And she smiled.

And without another word they turned and, hand-in-hand, left the dance floor.

They continued to hold hands in the cab of the truck on the way back to the motel. They held hands on the short walk from the truck to their room. They were still holding hands—both hands now when they stood face-to-face beside the bed, palm to palm, fingers intertwined—when he leaned down and kissed her.

It was a soft, sweet kiss, his lips barely brushing across hers...lifting away...coming back for a second taste...a third...the pressure increasing slightly then, but still gently, almost hesitantly, as if it were the first kiss between them, as if he had just discovered the promise of passion in her and was testing its depths. Entranced, Roxanne answered in kind, her kisses as soft, as gentle, as giving as his, until, finally, gentleness wasn't enough and she opened her mouth to him, inviting a deeper possession, a closer communion, a more complete union.

He wrapped his arms around her, bringing her body flush against his, taking their clasped hands to the small of her back, and slanted his mouth across hers, deepening the kiss. He used his tongue now, but still softly, still sweetly, the subtle seducer rather than the bold invader. Roxanne sighed and let herself be seduced.

His kisses trailed from her lips to her jaw to the soft sensitive place behind her ear, slowly—oh, so slowly—sliding down the long, slender column of her neck to the valley between her breasts. As he had once before, he buried his nose there and simply breathed her in, as if the very smell of her intoxicated him.

And, as she had before, Roxanne shuddered in his arms and fell a little bit in love. Not all the way in love, she cautioned herself. Not all the way, but just a little bit. Just enough to make her breath catch and her heart beat faster. Just enough to make her dizzy with need.

"Tom." It was the only word she could think of to say. The only word that made any sense at the moment. "Tom."

He raised his head and stared down into her flushed face. Her lips were slicked and red from his kisses. Her eyes were nearly golden in the dim light, her pupils large and round and focused intently on his face. "You're so damned beautiful," he murmured. "And I want you so damned much."

"Then take me." Her head fell back in surrender. "I'm yours. Take me."

His eyes flared wide, passion and heat and something else warring in their hot blue depths. He let go of her hands and stooped, lifting her into his arms so he could lower her to the bed. She expected him to fall upon her, then, to shove the necessary bits and pieces of clothing out of the way and ride her, wildly, as he had so many times before. Instead, he straightened and began undressing himself. He dropped his clothes where he stood; his hat, his boots, his shirt and jeans and underclothes were all discarded, falling like leaves onto the carpeted floor, as she lay there and watched, mesmerized. When he was naked, he began undressing her.

He removed her boots first, dropping them on the floor at the foot of the bed. He unzipped her little denim skirt and tugged it off her hips and down the length of her bare legs. And then he sat down on the edge of the bed, bypassing her panties, and reached for the first button on her white eyelet camisole.

His gaze locked with hers, something more than passion still burning in his eyes as he slowly unbuttoned her blouse and spread it open. Her underwear was new, purchased on her whirlwind shopping trip to Wal-Mart the week before. The fabric was old-fashioned and sweet, white cotton lace with tiny blue forget-me-nots embroidered on it. The cut was scandalous—brief and unabashedly sexy. The whole was as much a dichotomy as the woman who wore it.

"So beautiful," he said, and bent down, pressing his lips to the plump swell of flesh above the edge of the bra. "I want you."

There was an edge of desperation in his voice, a need she had never heard before, a something that set her blood to racing through her veins, and her mind to weaving impossible fantasies. She lifted her hands up to his head, threading her fingers through his thick dark hair. "I want you, too," she whispered, and brought his mouth down to hers for a searing, openmouthed kiss.

The loving that followed was hot and intense, incredibly wild, impossibly tender. And when he was finally positioned between her silky thighs, on the verge of taking what they both wanted so desperately, their hands were linked, palm to palm, fingers entwined, pressed into the mattress on either side of her head.

"I want you," he said as he thrust into her.

A HOT, SWEATY, tempestuous hour later, they lay, skin to skin, heart to heart, in the middle of the rumpled motel bed.

"I'm sorry about the third degree tonight," Roxanne murmured into the damp curve of his neck.

"I'm not." Tom ran his hand down the length of her bare back to the curve of her equally bare bottom, and gave it a little squeeze. "Every time you throw one of your little hissy fits, we have really hot make-up sex."

Too relaxed to manage a more forceful display of feminine ire for his chauvinistic remark, she bit him lightly on the neck. "No, really, I mean it. I'm sorry." She kissed the place she'd bitten and raised up, crossing her arms over his chest so she could look down into his face. "I have no right to pry into your personal life. What you did before this summer and what you do after it isn't any of my business," she said, as much to remind herself of that fact as to reassure him. "You're only required to be a one-woman man while we're together."

"I reckon I'm pretty much a one-woman man all the time, anyway," he said, wondering if, from now on, that one woman was going to be her. Wondering, too, what the hell he was going to do about it if that were the case. "One at a time is about all I can handle." He grinned at her. "Especially when that one is a tall cool glass of water with a hair-trigger temper and a mean right jab."

"I do not have a hair-trigger temper."

He raised an eyebrow.

"It's your own fault, anyway," she said, and tweaked his chest hairs.

"How do you figure that?"

"You're the only person I've ever hit in my entire life, so it must be your fault."

"Isn't that called blaming the victim?"

"Victim, my ass."

"And it's such a nice ass, too," he said, and pinched it.

She squealed and tweaked his chest hairs again, harder this time so that he yelped in response. "See? You *made* me do that. I'm not normally a violent per—" The last word was muffled against his chest as he surged upward and rolled her beneath him.

A brief but vigorous tussle ensued. They wrestled across the bed like rambunctious children, Roxanne squirming and squealing, Tom trying mostly to keep her from pinching any-thing vital. In his effort to evade her grasping fingers, he rolled too near the edge of the bed and toppled off onto the floor, dragging Roxanne down with him. She snagged a pil-low as she went over and was up on her knees in an instant, pummeling him with it before he had to a chance to catch his breath.

"Dang, woman." He cupped his hands over his privates. "Watch your knee."

"Say uncle." She bashed him in the head with the pillow. "Say it."

"Uncle."

She checked her next blow, surprised by his easy ca-pitulation. That quick, he snatched the pillow out of her hands, tossed it aside, and reversed their positions. Flat on her back on the floor, her arms held down on either side of her head, her chest heaving with exertion, Roxanne went limp. "What now, sugar?" she said, and batted her eyelashes at him.

"Now, we have *really* hot make-up sex," he said, and lowered his mouth to hers.

She bit his lip.

"And you say you're not a violent person," he chided, lust and laughter sparkling in his blue eyes as he stared down at her.

Roxanne stared back, breathless with laughter, flushed with arousal, waiting for what he would do next.

He got a cagey, considering look in his eyes. "You know what happens to violent little girls, don't you?"

"No," she said, her eyes glittering with anticipation. "What happens to them?"

"They get punished." He grinned evilly. "Severely."

There was a long beat of silence as they stared at each other. The air between them was ripe with expectation and excitement, the thrill of the forbidden, the lure of the illicit. It was like that first moment between them at Ed Earl's all over again, that moment when they stared into each other's eyes from a distance of inches, with the sexual energy crackling back and forth like heat lightning, and wondered if they were going to end up spending the night together. And now, as she had then, Roxanne provided exactly the prod he needed to make his move.

"You wouldn't dare," she said, all the while hoping desperately that he would.

Tom not only dared, he did.

Without letting go of her wrists, he heaved himself to his feet, sat down on the edge of the bed and jerked her, face-down, across his lap. She squirmed in excitement and delicious libidinous fear. His hand came down on her bare bottom with a sharp smacking sound. It stung a bit more than she expected it to.

She reared up in surprise. "Hey, that hurt!"

"That was for sucker punching me at the rodeo in Santa Fe," he said, pushing her back down with a hand on the top of her head. He smacked her again, not quite so hard, but still with enough force to make her skin tingle and redden. "And that was for dancing with that clown in the Bare Back Saloon and letting him hold you too damn close. And that—" he smacked her a third time "—was for kissing Clay right under my nose."

"Stop!" She squirmed against his thighs, but made no real effort to get away. She could feel his erection against her stomach, as rock-hard and ready as if they hadn't just made love. Her own body was practically dripping with desire. "Stop it right now."

"Are you going to be good?" He brought his hand down again, lightly this time, caressingly, shaping his palm over the satin skin of her bottom. It was as rosy as the valentine it resembled, as hot as the sun-baked sand of the desert.

"Yes." Instinctively, without conscious thought or design, she arched her back, thrusting her tingling posterior up against the curve of his hand, exposing the glistening pink folds of her sex. "Yes, I'll be good."

"You sure you know how?"

"Yes. Yes, I know how. I'll be good," she said, nearly panting with excitement. "I promise."

He slipped his hand down between her legs. "How good?" he asked, and slid a finger into her.

She nearly came right then and there. Her breath caught in her throat as she tried, and failed, to stifle a whimper.

"How good?" he asked again.

"How good do you want me to be?"

"Only as good as you want to be." He withdrew his hand from between her legs and let her slide to her knees beside him. "How good do you want to be, Slim?"

She put her hands on his thighs and looked up at him from under her lashes. "Good enough to make you beg for mercy."

Tom leaned back on his elbows. "I dare you," he said.

Her gaze locked with his, Roxanne smiled and slowly, inch by excruciating inch, slid her hands up his hair-dusted thighs to his groin. Despite his deliberately relaxed position, she could feel the coiled tension in his long, lanky body, see it in the clenched muscles of his hard thighs and abdomen. His penis was nearly parallel to his stomach, pointing straight up at his navel. It jerked when she touched it.

"Aw, isn't that cute," she said to cover her own nervousness. "He's shy." She curled her hand around his shaft and, very gently, brought it upright. "I'll be gentle," she promised, and bent her head.

She'd never done this but a few times before, and not very successfully, judging by the reaction of her partner at the time. She suspected it was mostly because she hadn't really wanted to do it. Now, she did. And now, she wanted to be very, very good at it. She wanted to make him beg, as he had made her beg.

She began by kissing the round plum-shaped head, tentatively at first and then, as he indicated his pleasure, with more confidence. She progressed to little catlike licks, moved on to long, leisurely swipes with the flat of her tongue until, finally—when he was on his back and clutching the bedspread in his fists—she had pity on him and took him into her mouth.

"Please," he said, when she had tortured him for several minutes. Sweat beaded his upper lip and dampened the dark, crinkly hair on his chest. "Please."

She raised her head. "Please what?"

He reached down and grasped her by the shoulders, pulling her up the length of his body. "Ride me," he said, holding his shaft so she could mount.

She swung her leg over his supine body, straddling him, and impaled herself.

They both closed their eyes against the exquisite pleasure of it, savoring the feeling of unity and oneness. And then she leaned forward, putting her hands on his slick, sweaty chest for balance, and began to move against him, raising and lowering her hips as if she were riding a horse at a rising trot.

She'd only ever done this a few times before, too, because the other half of her former mature adult relationship hadn't favored the woman-on-top position. She found that she liked it very much, indeed. It gave her a freedom she'd never had before, allowing her to control the depth and the speed and the angle of penetration. She experimented, swiveling her hips first one way, then the other…slowing down and speeding up…varying the rhythm until she found the one that made Tom suck in his breath and whimper.

"Sweet Lord in heaven!" He hissed the words out between clenched teeth as his body rose and tightened, exploding in a rapturous climax.

Roxanne had just started to follow him over into bliss when the phone rang.

It wasn't the hotel phone on the bedside table. It was his cell phone, the one he kept clipped to the belt on his jeans, except when he rode. Roxanne had seen him use it to call ahead to the rodeo to find out what horse he'd drawn, or to make a motel reservation when they rolled into town late at night, but she'd never heard it ring before.

"I'm sorry," he said, as he tipped her sideways onto the bed. "I have to answer that."

Chapter Ten

"HOW BAD IS IT?" Tom was sitting on the edge of the bed, the phone tucked awkwardly between his ear and shoulder as he dragged on his underwear and jeans. "What does the doctor say? Surgery? When? Why so soon? No, that's all right, Augie. Don't worry about it. I'll talk to the doctor my-self as soon as I get there. You and the other kids go on back to the ranch and keep on with your regular routine." He pulled on his socks and boots, and stood to fasten his jeans. "Yes, I know, but try. The Padre would want it that way. You know he would." He grabbed his shirt from the floor and shrugged into it, one arm at a time, as he listened to the slightly hysterical voice on the other end of the line. "It's going to be all right, Augie. You and the boys just sit tight and try not to worry. I'll be there as soon as I can and we'll all get through this together. Tell the Padre to hang in there." He flipped the phone closed. "We've got a family emergency," he said to Roxanne as he headed for the door. "I've got to go roust Rooster out of bed and let him know what's going on."

Roxanne jumped up from the middle of the bed where she had been kneeling, watching him throughout the telephone conversation. Grabbing one of the blankets off of the floor to wrap around her naked body, she followed him to the door, wondering what was going on. Augie? The Padre? The other kids? Were they his brothers? His children? The fact that she didn't know brought home to her how little she really knew about him.

"Come on, Rooster." Tom pounded on the door of the adjoining room. "Haul your ass out of bed. We've got trouble."

There was a thumping noise, then a muffled curse, and Rooster appeared at the door. He was blinking and bleary-eyed, his short brown hair sticking up in all directions. He was holding on to his head with both hands. "What's all the racket about?" he demanded querulously. "Where's the fire?"

"I just got a call from home. The Padre's had a heart attack."

"A heart attack?" Rooster scrubbed at his face with both hands as if that would help him absorb the news. "The Padre had a heart attack? When?"

"A couple of hours ago. Augie called me from the hospital."

"How bad?"

"Bad enough, from what Augie said. They almost lost him a couple of times before they got him stabilized, but he's resting comfortably now—whatever the hell that means—and they've got him scheduled for a triple by-pass first thing in the morning."

"Sweet baby Jesus!" Rooster swore softly.

"I'm going to call around, see if I can find some kind of charter flight that will get me home before the surgery. Otherwise I'll take a commercial flight into Dallas and drive from there."

Rooster nodded. "It'll only take me a minute to get my gear together."

"There's no need for you to go, too. No, hear me out," Tom said, as Rooster started to protest. "It only needs one of us to ride herd on the kids and see that everything's running smooth. You've got to be here for the finals on Sunday, and then Wichita the day after that, and Oklahoma City the day after that."

"But—"

"The Padre'll understand. And he isn't going to care much, anyway, about who is or isn't pacing around in the waiting room."

"Maybe you should be the one to stay for the finals," Rooster said, when he could get a word in edgewise. "You've been scorin' good all week. An', hell, I got this bum knee slowin' me down, anyway."

"Not so's anyone would notice," Tom said dryly, seeing through the ploy. Rooster's knee hadn't given him a lick of trouble since they got to Cheyenne; he'd pulled down some of the best scores of his life that week.

"Besides, I got a good five, ten years of rodeoing in me yet," Rooster said. "I don't make it to Vegas this year, there's always next. But this is your last chance an' it's a damned good one. You pull down a winning score in the finals on Sunday and you're in the top fifteen, guaranteed. I should be the one to turn out," he said earnestly. "I know how much it means to you to get to Vegas before you retire."

"Not as much as it means to you," Tom said. "I never wanted it as much as you. Ever. That's why I've been content to be a circuit cowboy all my life. Here—" he handed Rooster the cell phone. "You keep this with you and I'll call you the minute he comes out of surgery." He dug into the pocket of his jeans. "And here's the keys to the truck. I'll expect to see it, and you, in Bowie next week after you kick butt in Oklahoma City. The Padre ought to be back home by then—" he smiled crookedly "—and we'll all be about ready to have a new face around to keep him from driving everybody crazy."

Considering the subject closed, he turned away without waiting for an answer, and headed back to his room.

Roxanne stepped back, out of the way, as he brushed past her, then stood awkwardly, unsure of what to do, watching as he dug the Yellow Pages out of the drawer of the bedside dresser and set about arranging a charter flight to Bowie, Texas.

This was the end, then, she thought forlornly, trying desperately not to cry. He was going to fly home to deal with a family emergency and she was going to— What? Go back to Connecticut? She didn't *want* to go back to Connecticut. Her vacation wasn't over, damn it! She still had a few fantasies she hadn't fulfilled. And she wasn't nearly ready to say goodbye to her good-looking dangerous cowboy.

Not yet.

Maybe not ever, she thought, and realized that the San Antonio barrel racer had been dead on the money; she probably *was* going to get her poor little heart broken—and a lot sooner than she'd anticipated, too.

"You'd better get moving," he said as he hung up the phone. "The plane leaves in less than an hour."

"You want me to come with you?" she said, hardly daring to hope.

"Well, I thought..." But the thing was, he realized as she stood there, staring at him with an incredulous look on her face, he *hadn't* thought. He'd assumed. He wanted her to go with him, ergo she must want it, too. Simple as that. Except why the hell would a woman like her want to fly down to Bowie, Texas, while he nurse-maided a sick old man and rode herd on a bunch of rowdy kids?

On the other hand, he wouldn't be playing nursemaid the entire time and the kids were a self-sufficient bunch, and what was between the two of them was still as hot—hotter— that it had been that first night in Lubbock. Why *wouldn't* she want to go with him?

"I thought we had an agreement," he said, finally, because

he didn't know what else to say. "We've got nearly six weeks to go on it."

"You want me to come with you?" she said again.

"Well, it wouldn't set right on my conscience to leave you by yourself in Cheyenne. And I'm pretty sure you don't want to finish out the season riding shotgun with Rooster. Do you?"

She shook her head.

"And if it turns out you don't like it in Bowie—" he shrugged to show it made no never mind to him "—Dallas is less than a hundred miles away. You can catch a plane to anywhere from there."

"I wouldn't by in the way?"

"Probably," he admitted. "But I want you there, anyway. I haven't near got my fill of you, yet."

And, God help him, he was beginning to think he never would.

THE PLANE that was going to take them to Bowie was a small twin-engine Cessna. They waited on uncomfortable orange plastic seats in a small, glassed-in lounge, watching through the window as the pilot conducted a thorough preflight inspection of the plane under the bright industrial lights shining down from the roof of the metal hangar.

"What did Rooster mean about you wanting to get to Vegas before you retire?" Roxanne said, trying to distract herself from the coming flight. She wasn't an enthusiastic air traveler at the best of times and the sight of the tiny Cessna had her nerves jumping.

Tom smiled distractedly, his gaze on the pilot and the plane, and squeezed her hand. "Vegas is where they hold the rodeo finals," he reminded her.

"I know that. I meant what did he mean about you retiring?"

"This is my last go-round. I'm officially hanging up my saddle at the end of the season."

"Why?"

He looked at her then. "Why does anybody retire? Because it's time."

"But you're only—what—thirty. Isn't that a little young to retire?"

He grinned. "Darlin', That's old for a cowboy. Damned old. And cowboyin' has never been my whole life, anyway. Not like it's been for Rooster. Rodeo's always been more a hobby for me. I've mostly done it weekends, close to home, so's I could fit it in around my regular life as much as possible. Only full-time professional cowboys can rack up enough points to make Vegas."

"And that's what you wanted to do before you retired? Make the finals in Vegas?"

He shrugged. "I thought it'd be fun to give it a shot. Make my last year something to remember. Really go hog wild." His grin flashed again, a little self-deprecating around the edges this time. "Have myself one last fling before I settle down."

"Settle down to what, exactly?"

"Marriage. Kids. All the normal, everyday things a man wants at the end of the day. We've got big plans to enlarge the school at the Second Chance so we can take in more kids. And I've got an experimental breeding program going on with Dan Jensen over at the Diamond J that I want to devote more time to. Can't do all that if I'm running off to the rodeo every weekend. So—" he shrugged "—I decided to give it one last shot. Just me and Rooster, going down the road together, living the footloose and fancy-free life of the professional rodeo cowboy before I packed it in and become entirely respectable."

"We're just about ready to take off, so if either of you folks need to visit the facilities before we head out, now's the time to do it," the pilot said, poking his head into the room before Roxanne could ask if she was part of that footloose and fancy-free life, that final fling.

She didn't really have to ask to know, though. Of course, she was part of it. Wild sexual encounters were always a part of what final flings were all about. She knew that firsthand; wild sexual encounters with a good-looking dangerous cowboy had been an integral part of her own plans for a last fling.

So why did she feel so sad that their plans were so in sync? It was exactly what she wanted. Wasn't it?

"Slim?" Tom nudged her out of her abstraction. "You need to visit the ladies'? It's going to be a long flight and there's no facilities in the Cessna."

Although she didn't really feel the need to go, Roxanne headed for the "ladies'" on the theory that you should never pass up the opportunity to use the facilities. It was a little tidbit of wisdom she'd picked up living on the road; you never knew how far away the next bathroom would be, so it was better to grab every opportunity.

The pilot was already in his seat when she exited the hangar. Tom was standing next to the wing, waiting to hand her in. The plane only had four seats. Roxanne squeezed into the one behind the pilot. Tom put his saddle in the one beside the pilot and climbed into the back next to Roxanne. It was a tight fit, strapped in, noisy and uncomfortable. Because they had to wear headphones to communicate, any private conversation was impossible. All of the questions Roxanne was burning to ask Tom—about the life of respectability he envisioned for himself, about the Padre and the kids, about Jo Beth Jensen and how she fit into his plans—would have to wait until they were on the ground again.

"How long to Bowie?" Tom said, after the plane was safely in the air and the pilot was free to make conversation.

"Eight hours, give or take, depending on the head-winds." The pilot's words crackled through the head-phones. "We should set down around seven, seven-thirty at the latest."

Tom nodded, then reached over, tapping Roxanne on the shoulder. He motioned for her to take off the headphones. "You should try to get some sleep," he said, his lips against her ear. "It's going to be chaos when we get there." He wrapped his arm around her shoulders, silently urging her to lean against him, and stared out the window at the dark-ness, never once closing his eyes during the entire trip.

THEY LANDED AT A SMALL private airstrip about ten miles outside of Bowie. Owned by a group of local ranchers, it con-sisted of two parallel runways and a single barnlike hangar planted smack-dab in the middle of an empty field. There was a light on inside the hangar, despite the warm golden-pink glow of the rising sun, and two pickups parked outside of it. One was a battered blue Dodge with the Second Chance brand painted on the side. The driver was waiting for them when the plane taxied up to the hangar. He rushed to the air-craft as soon as the propellers had stopped spinning and jerked the door open.

"Boy, am I glad to see you," he said, automatically reach-ing for the saddle Tom handed out to him. "The Padre's op-eration is at nine and I was afraid you weren't gonna get here on time. Miz Jenzen is out at the ranch with the kids. The Padre told me to call her to come over. He was talkin' pretty good last night after they got him settled in. He—"

"Hey, whoa, there now, Augie. Slow down, boy." Tom put his hand on the boy's shoulder and gave it a comforting squeeze. "Take a deep breath before you hyperventilate."

Augie smiled sheepishly and sucked in a breath, letting it whoosh out in a gusty sigh. "I sure am glad to see you," he said again. His gaze darted to Roxanne as she stepped out onto the wing of the plane.

Tom turned around to hold out a hand to her and steady her descent. "I'd like you to meet a friend of mine," he said to the boy when she was on the ground beside him. "This is Miz Roxy Archer. Roxy, say hi to Augustine Chavez."

The boy was tall, thin and gangly, more youthful-looking than the sixteen she knew he must be to be driving the pickup truck, with dark curly hair and liquid brown eyes that showed signs of sleeplessness and worry. He had a crudely fashioned tattoo peaking out from under the cuff of his shirt.

"Hello, Augie," she said politely, wondering what the relationship was between him and Tom. Not father and son, certainly, judging by the different last names. And probably not brothers, either, as there wasn't the slightest physical resemblance between them. "It's a pleasure to meet you."

"Ma'am," the boy said, the expression in his eyes wary and assessing.

Roxanne knew what he would see when he looked at her. She was rumpled and travel weary, her hair sticking all up anyhow from sleeping on Tom's shoulder, her lipstick chewed off, her face pale with the faint nausea that came from flying in a small plane. She had Tom's denim jacket slung over her shoulders, hanging down over her snug red tank and city-slicker jeans.

The boy dismissed her with a single disdainful glance and turned his attention back to Tom. "I've got a thermos of coffee and a sack of sausage biscuits in the truck in case you're hungry," he said. "The biscuits are from MacDonald's but Miz Jensen made the coffee." His eyes flickered back to Roxanne for an instant. "Only got one cup, though, from the top of the thermos."

"One cup will do us just fine." Tom said. "Why don't you

go on and stow my saddle in the back of the truck. We'll get the rest of the gear out of the hold and be right behind you."

"I don't think he likes me," Roxanne whispered as the boy headed toward the truck with the saddle slung over his shoulder.

"He's just leery around people he doesn't know," Tom said. "Give him a few days, and he'll be talking your ear off."

He certainly talked Tom's ear off, filling him on the situation as they drove to the hospital. "He was out in the corral with that little sorrel mare, Magpie. You know the one with the freckled nose? She'd snagged her left hock on a nail and he was out there doctorin' her up when he suddenly just keeled over, right there in the corral. He just up and keeled over," Augie said. "Scared the bejesus out of the new kid, Jared. He came runnin' into the barn, all kinda white in the eyes like a horse on loco weed, and said the Padre was havin' some kind of fit, and somebody better call 9-1-1. The ambulance got there right quick and the paramedics used those electric shock things on him. It'd been kinda cool to see if it hadn't been the Padre they were doing it to."

By the time they pulled into the parking lot of the Bowie Community Hospital, Roxanne knew all about the Padre's condition, but nothing about who the Padre was or, more importantly, who he was to Tom.

TOM SAT WITH HIS FOREARMS balanced on his widespread knees, a cup of vending-machine coffee dangling between his hands. He'd just spent twenty grueling minutes with the surgeon, getting the lowdown on the upcoming by-pass operation, and another heart-wrenching ten holding the unresponsive hand of the elderly man who would be undergoing it. He was bone-tired and scared shitless.

Not knowing what else to do, how much he would let her do, Roxanne reached over and rubbed his back lightly. "Talk to me," she said softly, her voice low in deference to Augie, who sat slumped sideways in his chair on the other side of Tom, sleeping off the long night of worry while they waited for the Padre to come out of surgery. "Let me help."

"His name is Hector Menendez," Tom said as if she'd asked. "Everybody calls him Padre, though, because he studied for the priesthood when he was younger." He picked at the rim of the coffee cup with his thumb. "He runs the Second Chance Ranch."

"I thought the Second Chance was your place."

"No. The Second Chance belongs to the Padre. It's where I grew up. Or mostly, anyway." His gaze flickered up to her face and away. "It's a home for delinquent and abandoned boys."

Roxanne's eyes widened. "You were an abandoned child?"

"I was a delinquent child," he corrected. "My mother was barely fifteen when I was born. Unwed. Mostly uneducated. She did her best by me, but—" he shrugged "—her best wasn't very good back then. By the time I was ten, I was already getting into trouble with the police."

"What kind of trouble can a ten-year-old get into with the police?" Roxanne asked, her tone skeptical and disbelieving.

Which proved, he thought, how little experience she'd had with the seamier side of life. "Shoplifting. Vandalism. Truancy. All petty stuff, but the way I was going, I would have been a hardened felon by the time I was twelve if she hadn't turned me over to the Padre."

"She abandoned you?'

"She saved me," he said. "I was too much for her to handle and she knew it. The Padre gave me the kind of structured environment I needed. He gave me chores, taught me self-discipline and self-control, made sure I did my homework and went to school. If it weren't for him, I'd've ended up riding broncs at the Huntsville prison rodeo. Instead, I went on to college, became a teacher, made a decent life for myself."

"And your mother? What happened to her?"

"She moved to Dallas and got a job. Went to night school and got a better job. She's a nurse at Presbyterian Hospital now," he said, pride evident under the weariness in his tone. "Works in ER."

"Did you ever live with her again?"

Tom shook his head. "By the time she got herself together and could've made a home for the both of us, I was already in college."

"And your father? Where is he?"

"The Padre is all the father I've ever had. All the father I've ever needed," he said, and found himself suddenly fighting tears. He blinked them back, refusing to let them fall. Cowboys didn't cry, no matter how much it hurt.

Saying nothing, Roxanne placed her hand over the back of his. Without a word, Tom turned his palm up, twined his fingers with hers, and held on tight.

Two and a half hours later, the surgeon stepped into the waiting room. Tom shot to his feet, dragging Roxanne with him, jostling Augie who sat up and blinked like a sleepy toddler.

"He came through like a champ," the doctor said, answering the question before anyone could ask it. "And no, you can't see him yet," he added, anticipating the next one. "He's still in recovery. He's going to be there for the next little while, until the anesthesia wears off, then we'll take him back to his room. You could probably see him for a few minutes then, but he's still going to be mostly out of it and won't remember whether you were there of not. I'd suggest you all go on home, get some sleep yourselves and come back tonight after supper. He'll be ready for company then."

SEVERAL MILES from the hospital, they turned off the two-lane blacktop onto a long graveled road that was marked only by the tall, gateless arch that spanned its width. The top of the arch bore the same insignia—the Roman numeral II superimposed over a capital C—that decorated the side of the blue pickup. At the end of the road, a quarter mile distance or more, as far as Roxanne could tell, was a copse of trees and what appeared to be several buildings. As they neared the end of the road, Roxanne was able to make out a barn—the largest of the structures—and two smaller buildings, perhaps a bunkhouse and a henhouse or toolshed, she thought. They were set to the side and slightly behind the stand of cottonwoods and oaks that sheltered the ranch house itself.

It was weathered old Victorian, white clapboard with slate-blue shutters. A wide covered porch wrapped around the entire first level. There were dormer windows on the third level—the attic, Roxanne decided—and a pair of rocking chairs on the porch on either side of the front door. A small picket fence enclosed the front door and one side of the house, protecting a struggling green patch of lawn and a thriving vegetable garden from rambunctious boys and livestock. Roxanne thought it could have used a few touches, a new coat of paint on the front door and shutters, some colorful hanging plants on the porch, maybe a flowerbed to soften the foundation, but all in all, it was warm, inviting and utterly charming.

"By Texas standards, it's not all that big a spread," Tom said as they got out of the truck. "But it's home."

It was also as chaotic as Tom had predicted it would be. Nearly a dozen young boys, from ages six to sixteen, came running toward the truck as it rolled down the long driveway and came to a stop in the yard between the gleaming forest-green pickup and the late-model Chevy sedan that sat in the driveway next to the house. All of them were talking a mile a minute, all of them were clamoring for news and attention. The littlest one, tears running down his face, attached himself to Tom's legs and demanded to know if it was true that the Padre was dead.

Tom stooped, snagging the child under his rear end with one arm, and lifted him on to his hip. Placing the thumb and index finger of his free hand against his front teeth, he gave a piercing whistle to settle the rest of them down.

"The Padre is going to be fine," he said into the ensuing silence. "The by-pass operation is over and the doctor said he's resting comfortably."

"Does that mean he's not dead?" blubbered the little boy.

"Yes, Petie, that means he's not dead." He wiped at the little child's cheek with the pad of his thumb in a gesture so natural and tender it made Roxanne's heart turn over in her chest. "After supper tonight, I'll take you to the hospital so you can see for yourself, okay?"

"Can we go, too?" said one of the other boys.

"Not everybody all at once." Tom bent to set Petie back on his own two feet. "That'd be too much for him to handle just yet, and the hospital wouldn't allow so many visitors at one time, anyway. We'll have to go in shifts. A few tonight, a few tomorrow morning, a few more tomorrow night, and so on until it's time for him to come home, That way, we won't tire him out and he'll have plenty of visitors to look forward to while he's there."

"How long's he gonna be there?" another child wanted to know.

"Yeah, Tom, when's he comin' home?'

"He'll be home in a week. Maybe less if he heals up real fast." He swept his gaze over the anxious, eager faces upturned to his, looking for one in particular. "Where's Jared?" he said, when he didn't find it.

"Right here." A young teenager, barely into puberty, stepped away from the rear fender of the pickup where he had been loitering, just outside the circle. Unlike the other boys, who wore cowboy boots and trim Western-cut shirts neatly tucked into their jeans, Jared sported a long-billed baseball cap and a baggy, too large T-shirt that hung over a pair of camouflage pants. His boots looked as if he'd picked them up at an army surplus outlet. He had a little silver ring dangling from the outside corner of his right eyebrow and his attitude was such that Roxanne wouldn't have been surprised to see him put a cigarette between his lips and light it while they watched. She remembered that Augie had referred to him as "the new kid."

Tom smiled and moved toward him through the crowd of kids. "I understand we owe you a real debt of gratitude," he said, and extended his hand.

The boy took it automatically. "Huh?"

"Augie tells me that it's due to your quick thinking that we still have the Padre with us today."

"Huh?"

"I what?" said Augie.

"You're the one who insisted on calling 9-1-1 when the Padre collapsed, aren't you?"

"Well, yeah. Sure." The boy shrugged. "I guess."

"Then you're the hero of the hour," Tom told him. "The surgeon said that if the paramedics had gotten to the Padre even a few minutes later, he probably wouldn't have made it. You saved his life."

"I did?"

"He did?" said Augie.

"You did," Tom said. "And we all owe you our thanks." His steely blue gaze touched each boy in turn. "Don't we?"

Petie, the youngest and most unselfconscious member of the little group, stepped forward and threw his skinny arms around Jared's waist in a show of unfettered appreciation. "Thank you, Jared," he said. "Thankyouthankyouthankyou."

Looking slightly panic-stricken, Jared patted the little boy's shoulder awkwardly. "You're welcome, Petie."

That made the other boys laugh in commiseration—they'd all been the focus of Petie's unbridled enthusiasm at one time or another—and they surged forward, each eager to shake Jared's hand. Tom let the congratulations go on for a few minutes, then stepped into the fray before the backslapping and handshakes could descend into roughhousing.

"Don't you all have chores that need doing?" he said, neatly dispersing them.

"That," Roxanne said, smiling up into his face as the boys hurried off in various directions, "was absolutely masterful. I am in complete and utter awe. You must be a wonderful teacher."

He shrugged, looking as uneasy as young Jared had a few moments before. "It weren't nothin', ma'am," he said, parodying both the accent and attitude of the stereotypical bashful cowboy to hide his own embarrassment at her praise.

"Is she your girlfriend?"

They turned as one to find Petie staring up at them.

"Don't you have chores?" Tom said.

"I already finished feeding the chickens, and I pulled the weeds, too. Is she?"

"Is she what?" Tom said, stalling.

"Is she your girlfriend?'

"Well…" He shot a quick glance at Roxanne to see how she was taking the question. His gut instinct was to answer in the affirmative, but he didn't know how she would feel about that. *Was* she his girlfriend. Did that describe what they were to each other? Or did the word "girlfriend" imply a level of commitment they didn't share?

She looked back at him, her expression bland and non-committal, waiting to hear what he would say.

"Well…" Tom said again, having found no help there. "She's a girl and she's my friend."

"Tom has a girlfriend. Tom has a girlfriend," Petie screeched, and went running off to tell the other boys.

Tom's gaze went back to Roxanne's face. "Should I have told him something else?"

"I don't know what it would be," she said. "I don't think there's actually a word for what we are to each other." The thought that there wasn't tugged uncomfortably at her heart-strings. The lack of a word to describe their relationship made them seem so…temporary. Which they were, of course, but… She shrugged to show it didn't matter one way or the other. "Girlfriend works for me if it works for you."

"It works for me,' he said, his voice and demeanor just as carefully casual as hers had been. He reached out, putting his hand on the small of her back. "Let's get inside. I need to make a couple of phone calls, let Rooster know how things are going," he said, as he ushered her up the wide steps of the ranch house to the wraparound porch. "I probably ought to call Miz Jensen, too, and—"

"Would that be Jo Beth Jensen?" Roxanne said with an arch look.

He grinned. "No, that'd be her mama. She's the one who always gets called when someone here 'bouts needs a neigh-borly hand. I need to call and let her know I'm here so's she doesn't have to be inconvenienced any more than necessary. Then we'll get you settled in and—"

There was a young woman standing at the old-fashioned white enamel sink with a plastic ice cube tray in her hands. She was curvy and petite with long, soft brown hair clipped back at the nape of her neck, and big soft brown eyes. She was wearing an apron over her jeans and nice sensible brown leather cowboy boots with modestly high heels. Her blouse was pale pink, with a narrow row of twining leaves and flowers outlining the Western-cut yoke. There was a pot of something savory simmering on the big six-burner stove, and three fruit pies cooling on trivets on the long wooden kitchen table.

Roxanne suddenly felt like something the cat had dragged in off the street. She'd managed to slip into a bathroom at the hospital and take a few minutes to freshen up, finger-combing her hair into some kind of order and applying a fresh coat of cherry-red lipstick, but she was still wearing the same clothes she'd been wearing all night—the snug red tank top and tight jeans, the high-heeled red boots. Tom's jacket was still slung over her shoulders. She resisted the urge to pull it together in front so she could hide behind it.

"I thought that must be you when I heard the truck pull up outside," the other woman said, smiling at Tom. "I would have been right out, but I had to take my pies out of the oven before they burned. And then I thought I might as well just take a minute and make some more iced tea." She dumped the ice cubes into a glass pitcher as she spoke. "The boys drank the last of it with their dinner and I know how you like your iced tea when you've been outside in the heat." She set the empty ice cube tray in the sink and dried her hands on her apron. "Hello," she said, extending her hand to Roxanne as she crossed the width of the kitchen. "I'm Jo Beth. Jo Beth Jensen. And you are…?"

Chapter Eleven

TOM INTRODUCED HER to Jo Beth as his friend. Not his girl-friend, which they'd both just agreed was as good a designation as any, but simply as his *friend*. He removed his hand from the small of her back and got all distant and formal and tongue-tied—which she knew damn well he wasn't!—and acted as if they were nothing more to each other than mere acquaintances. Casual ones, at that.

Jo Beth was no dummy, of course; Tom wouldn't have considered marrying a stupid woman. She knew something was up, that there was more to their relationship than he was letting on, but she was too polite—or too crafty—to make an issue of it. Instead, she delivered a few instructions about last-minute touches to the pot of chili that was simmering on the stove—"Should I write this down or do you think you can remember it?" she said sweetly to Roxanne—and removed her apron.

"Will you look at the time," she said, as she headed toward the door. "I told Dad I'd be home by three and it's nearly that already. He wants me to go with him to take a look at some breeding stock Matt Thomas—you know, the T Bar ranch just this side of Vashti?—has for sale. He's probably pacing up and down the front porch by now, cussing me out something fierce." She laughed lightly, as if the threat of being cussed out by her father was more amusing than anything else, and went up on tiptoe to plant a quick, friendly kiss on Tom's cheek.

He stood, stiff and uncomfortable and indisputably guilty, his hands at his sides, and didn't kiss her back.

She didn't seem to notice his lack of response.

"Tell the Padre that Mom and I will be over to see him in the next couple of days, hear? We'll sneak him in a piece of cherry pie." She held her hand out to Roxanne again. "It was very nice to meet you," she said pleasantly, although it was patently clear—to Roxanne, at least—that it was nothing of the kind. "Do you think you'll be able to stay long enough for the party?"

"Party?"

"Oh, nothing like you're probably used to," she trilled, somehow making it seem as if the parties Roxanne was probably used to were along the line of drunken orgies. "Nothing fancy. It'll just be a quiet, neighborly little get-together to celebrate when the Padre comes home from the hospital. Like the one we had for Dad—remember?" she looked up at Tom "—after he had *his* by-pass two years ago. And don't worry—" she patted him on the shoulder "—you don't have to do a thing. Mom and I have already got everything all planned except for the date." The screen door squeaked in protest as she opened it. "You ought to squirt a little WD-40 on that before it gets worse," she said, and then the door closed gently behind her—she didn't slam it the way Roxanne wanted to—and she was gone.

Tom and Roxanne stood silently, not looking at each other, listening as Jo Beth started up the engine of the shiny green truck—not revving it the way Roxanne would have—made a Y-turn in the graveled yard, and drove sedately away.

"So. That's little miss Texas A&M with the degree in animal science. Rooster was right. She's very pretty." Roxanne picked up the spoon sitting neatly in the spoon rest on the kitchen counter and dipped it into the pot on the stove. "And she makes great chili, too. I can certainly see why you're thinking of marrying her."

"For the last time, I am *not* thinking of marrying her," he said. And it was the absolute truth. He wasn't thinking of marrying her. Not seriously. Not anymore.

"Really?" The spoon still clutched in her hand, Roxanne turned around to face him. "Well—" She leaned back against the counter, folded her arms over her chest, and crossed one booted ankle over the other. "You'd better start running, then, because she's certainly thinking of marrying you, sugar."

ROXANNE TOLD HERSELF that if she had any pride or self-respect, she'd have left the Second Chance right after Jo Beth did. She'd have demanded the keys to that rattletrap old pickup parked out in the yard, driven herself to the municipal airport and gotten on a plane for Dallas. Instead, there she was, tucked up in one of a narrow pair of twin beds in an attic room with steeply slanted ceilings and a single dormer window overlooking what appeared to be the north forty. The walls were painted pale green, the floors were hardwood, the bedspreads were patchwork quilts, the furniture was rich golden oak, and the bedsteads were painted white iron.

And she was lying in one of them, dressed in nothing but her leopard-print underwear and a dab of Passion behind each knee, waiting for all the kids to go to sleep so Tom could sneak up and join her. She'd obviously become a slave to her hormones. Or a slave to his, she wasn't sure which.

She'd been about to throw the chili spoon at his head— she'd had her hand cocked back, ready to let fly—when he'd started across the room in that slow deliberate way he had, moving with that loose-kneed, hip-rolling, purposeful cowboy swagger of his that always made her mouth water, and curled his fingers around her wrist.

"I swear to God, Slim. There's nothing between Jo Beth and me. I've never given her *any* reason to think there was," he said earnestly.

And then he kissed her. He didn't lean into her, or grind his pelvis against hers. He didn't let his hands wander to her breasts or her butt or between her legs. He just kissed her.

Completely.

Thoroughly.

At length.

Lips and tongue and teeth, all nibbling and licking and nipping at hers, making hot, sweet love to her mouth with nothing but his mouth, the way he had that last night in Cheyenne. She gave in to it without a murmur of protest, coiling her arms around him like a lariat when he let go of her wrist to cup her head and tilt it to a better angle. They didn't break apart until the screen door screeched on its hinges and half a dozen boys of various sizes and shapes trampled into the kitchen like a herd of rambunctious young cattle.

"Tom has a girlfriend. Tom has a girlfriend," little Petie singsonged, making Roxanne wonder if he'd been chanting the words ever since Tom sent him chasing off after the other boys.

Jared hooked an arm around the smaller boy's neck. "Give it a rest, kid," he said, and slapped his hand over Petie's mouth.

A brief tussle ensued, ending with Petie giggling delightedly as he dangled upside down over his new best friend's shoulder. His new best friend, Roxanne noted, who was wearing a battered black cowboy hat in place of his base-

ball cap. She glanced at Tom to see if he'd noticed. His secret smile of satisfaction told her he had.

"I brought your gear in," said Augie, the responsible one,
as he hefted the two bags up on the end of the table. "Where
do you want me to put hers?"

"Please don't bother putting it anywhere," Roxanne said,
mindful that the boy still regarded her with suspicion. "I can
take it myself, if you'll just tell me where."

"We use the dormer room for guests," Augie said. "It's all
the way at the top of the stairs. In the attic."

"It's small, but it's private," Tom added, "and you've got
your own bathroom up there."

"We came in to get something to eat," one of the smaller
boys said, tired of all the adult chitchat.

All eyes turned to the three pies cooling on the table.

"After dinner," Tom said, before they could ask. "If you're
hungry now, have an apple." He grabbed one out of the big
wooden bowl sitting on the tiled kitchen counter and led by
example, biting into the crisp green Granny Smith. "We'll be
out in the barn." He dropped a quick kiss on Roxanne's lips.
"Holler if you need any help figuring out Jo Beth's instructions about the chili," he said, and pushed open the creaky
screen door.

Roxanne *would* have thrown the spoon at him then, except that there were children present and she didn't want to
set a bad example. Instead, she stirred the chili and contented
herself with a hidden smirk over the smear of chili sauce he
wore across the back of his shirt.

She carried her bag upstairs to the dormer room tucked
up under the eaves and unpacked, shaking out her clothing
and hanging it up in the lovely old-fashioned armoire that
graced nearly the whole of one wall. She tidied up in the tiny
but nicely appointed connecting bathroom, then headed back
downstairs to the kitchen.

Since she didn't have anything else to do, anyway, and nothing else to occupy her time, she prepared a large tray of crudités and rolled out a mammoth batch of fluffy made-from-scratch biscuits just to prove that little miss Texas A&M wasn't the only one who could cook. Not that she hadn't proved it already—and quite well, too, she thought—but grilled chicken breasts and salads were a far cry from chili and cherry pies, especially with a bunch of boys. She considered dropping the pies on the floor and calling it an accident, but good sense prevailed when she realized she had neither the time nor the ingredients necessary to whip up one of her famous chocolate-fudge cheesecakes to replace them.

It was then, when she caught herself wondering if chocolate-fudge cheesecake would tip the balance in her favor and make him fall in love with her, that she realized there was no *probably* about getting her heart broken. It was going to happen. It was only a matter of timing. Now, or six weeks from now, it was going to happen.

And *that's* when she should have headed out to the truck and taken off for the airport.

Instead, she was lying in a strange bed under the eaves, listening for the telltale creak of the attic stairs and wondering just how long it took a dozen young boys to fall asleep.

TOM WAS BEGINNING to think the boys would *never* get to sleep. Lord knew, they should all be dead tired. He certainly was. Or would be, if he weren't looking forward to creeping upstairs to the attic bedroom. After supper, he'd taken Petie and two of the other boys to the hospital with him to see the Padre. It had been an emotionally charged experience, with Petie starting in to cry as soon as he saw the Padre in the hospital bed, hooked up to all the various drains and IVs, looking frail and bruised and sick. The other two boys, being nine and eleven respectively, had struggled manfully against their own tears and managed to keep them to a few discreet sniffles, wiped off on their shirtsleeves when they thought no one was looking. Tom wished he'd been blessed with Petie's lack of inhibitions; he would have liked to howl, too, and let the nurse carry him off to get a soda pop out of the vending machine at the end of the hallway.

Instead, he waited until the other two boys trailed Petie and the nurse out into the hall and put his hand over the frail veined one laying so quietly against the sheets and squeezed gently. "How you feeling, Padre?"

"I feel like I've been kicked in the chest by a bad-tempered bronc," the old man grumbled. "How the hell else would I feel?"

Tom felt the tight knot of tension inside him give way. Despite the hospital bed and the tubes and the monitoring machines, the Padre was the same irascible, indomitable, straight-from-the-cuff kind of man he had always been. "You gave everybody quite a scare," Tom said.

"I gave myself quite a scare," the Padre admitted. "Thought for sure I was a goner. If it hadn't been for Jared, yelling for somebody to call 9-1-1, I would have been. You be sure to let the rest of them know I said that, you hear? They've been riding him pretty hard these past few months. Testing the new kid out, just like they always do. Not that he doesn't give it back to them, just as hard as they dish it out, but I've thought for sure, a couple of times, that he was going to rabbit on us. I wouldn't like to lose him."

"I don't think you have to worry about that anymore. Before supper tonight, he was ridin' Petie on his shoulder and wearing Augie's old black hat."

"Oh, that's good. That's real good. He's a good kid, deep down. He's got real potential."

"You think they've all got potential."

"And they all do," he said, with utter conviction. "You've just got to help them find it."

Petie came back into the room then, trailed by the other two boys. He seemed to have regained his equilibrium, and came right up to the edge of the bed, more curious than scared now. "Tom's got a girlfriend," he said, wanting to be the first to impart the news.

"Does he now?" The Padre slanted a glance at Tom. "What's her name?" he asked Petie.

"Roxy."

"Roxy, huh? Is that a new one?"

"Well, I ain't never seen her around before."

"Haven't ever," Tom corrected automatically.

"I haven't ever seen her around before," Petie repeated obediently. "She's kinda skinny, but I like her hair. It's the same color as Goldie's tail." Goldie was a gentle old palomino mare all the Second Chance kids learned to ride on. "And she makes real good biscuits. I had about ten of 'em." He took a sip of his soda pop. "Tom was kissin' her in the kitchen before supper."

The Padre uttered a bark of delighted laughter. It ended in a wheezing cough that had him grasping his chest. "I'm all right," he said, waving Tom back down when he jumped up to summon the nurse. "I'm all right, damn it. It just hurts when I laugh, is all."

Tom summoned the nurse, anyway.

"I think you've had just about enough visiting for tonight, Padre," she said severely. "Say good-night to your guests and we'll get you ready for bed."

"I'll say good-night when I'm damned good and ready to say good-night," he groused, "and not a damned minute sooner." He motioned for Tom to lean closer. "This new girl of yours with the palomino hair, she wouldn't happen to be the little firecracker Rooster told me about, would she?"

"I don't know," Tom hedged. "What did Rooster tell you?"

"Only that you were so smitten you couldn't see straight," he said, and began to wheeze again at the expression on Tom's face. "You bring her to see me, you hear?" he ordered, clutching his chest with one hand and waving the nurse off with the other. "I want to get a look at her."

The nurse stood firm and shooed them all out into the hall.

And now Tom had a word for his feelings about Roxanne. He was smitten, that was all. Besotted. Infatuated. Perhaps even a little bit obsessed. But he was not, thank God, in love. Not love with a capital L, anyway.

SHE WAS ASLEEP when he finally judged it safe to sneak up the stairs. She lay on her side on top of the covers on the narrow bed, in her ridiculously sexy underwear, with her knees drawn up like a child and her hands tucked under her cheek. The bedside lamp cast exotic shadows over her face, giving her a look of mystery that was excitingly at odds with the prim, little-girl position of her body. The ceiling fan turned lazily overhead, causing just enough air movement to ruffle the edges of her tangled blond mop. She was adorable and sexy and inexplicably dear.

He tiptoed across the room, meaning only to turn out the light she'd left on and kiss her good-night before creeping back down the stairs to his own bed, but her eyelids fluttered open at the butterfly brush of his lips against her cheek.

"Hey, cowboy," she whispered, and smiled at him.

"Hey, Slim" he said, and nuzzled her nose with his.

Their lips met briefly, parted, then met again and clung. Without breaking the second kiss, he stretched out beside her and took her into his arms. Their loving was sweet and slow and careful, there on the narrow bed in the tiny attic room, both of them more than a little tired and mindful of the need for discretion with a houseful of children sleeping in the

rooms below them. There was no frantic writhing or muffled screams or graphic words of lustful encouragement and
appreciation. Instead there were soft rustlings, and softer
sighs and softly murmured words. When it was over and con-
tentment had mellowed them both and soothed the jagged
edges of the day, he turned her onto her side and spooned
her from behind, cuddling her close to his heart.

"Did I remember to thank you for dinner?" he whispered
into her hair.

"Yes." She yawned. "I believe you did."

"I was only teasing you about the chili, you know. I didn't
actually expect you to go ahead and make supper for all
those kids."

"Yes, I know," she said, which was partially—okay,
mostly—why she'd done it. To show him that anything Jo
Beth could do, she could do better. Or just as well, anyway.

"Those biscuits were the best I've ever tasted. The boys
liked them, too. Petie told the Padre he ate ten of them."

"It weren't nothin'," she drawled modestly, feeling the
warm glow of his praise wash over her.

She felt his chest move as he chuckled against her back.
"You could have knocked me over with a feather when I
walked in the kitchen and saw those two huge plates of biscuits setting on the table next to Jo Beth's chili. I'd never have
pegged you as the down-home domestic type if I hadn't seen
it with my own eyes."

"Oh, really?" She felt the warm glow fade a little, wondering if he'd suddenly forgotten all those meals she'd cooked
on the road the past couple of weeks. Didn't that count as
domestic? Or were grilled chicken and salads lower on the
domesticity scale than chili and cherry pie? "What type do
you have me pegged as?"

"Oh—" she felt him skim a hand through her hair, lifting it away from her head and letting it fall back "—one of

those pampered trust-fund babies, I guess," he said, basing his assessment on her effortless high-tone polish even in bright-red boots and skintight jeans, and a vaguely re- membered mention of a stock portfolio and household staff. "The kind born with a silver spoon in her mouth, with ser- vants to do the cooking and cleaning. And no need for you to do anything except collect your stock dividends and have a good time."

The warm glow turned into a cold lump in the middle of her chest. Was that really what he thought of her? That she was some useless parasite who spent her life partying? And wasn't that *exactly* what she'd intended him to think when she picked him up at Ed Earl's? That she was a carefree, fast- living, good-time girl? Talk about being hoist on your own petard! She'd played the role so well, he couldn't see through it to the real her.

"Am I close?" he probed, hoping she'd tell him he was way off base, hoping she would say that the woman who'd scolded them about their lousy eating habits, and did their laundry with hers, and read to them on the road was the real her. That the woman who'd competently and cheerfully made dinner for a dozen hungry boys was who she really was under the high-tone polish and sexy exterior.

That woman might actually want to stay and make a life with him on the Second Chance; the trust-fund baby would be gone in six weeks, eager to get back to her life of ease and privilege.

Roxanne knew she could tell him he was wrong, of course. Except that he wasn't, completely. The picture he painted was just true enough—except for the partying part—that she wasn't able to deny it. "Close enough," she said, and man- aged an insouciant little laugh to cover her dismay.

She felt him sigh against her neck, and then, a moment later, he raised himself up on an elbow and leaned over her shoulder. "I'd better get out of here before I fall asleep and blow our cover." He kissed her cheek and slipped out of bed, heading down the stairs to greet the dawn in his own room.

Roxanne lay there after he had gone, staring at the moonlight shining in through the dormer window, and wondered why her heart felt as if it had already started to crack.

"DO WE HAVE TO do this *now?*" Roxanne asked, sounding, even to her own ears, like a whiny little kid. She tried to inject a little adult rationality into her voice. "I mean, really, wouldn't it be better to wait until he's out of the hospital?"

She'd already decided—*almost*—that she'd be gone by then. It would be much better to leave now, before the summer was over, rather than drag it out for the remaining few weeks. They could end it on a high note, leaving each other with happy memories of hot sex, good times, and lots of laughter. If she stayed much longer, she had a sneaking suspicion it would end in tears. On her part, anyway. And that would be a damned undignified end to her Wild West adventure.

"A string of visitors all day long can't be good for a man who's just had a triple by-pass," she said. "And I'm sure he'd rather see one of the boys instead of me, anyway."

"He asked me specifically to bring you in for a visit."

"He *asked* to see me?"

"Actually, it was more of an order." Tom slanted a quick glance at her as he maneuvered the pickup into an empty spot in the parking lot. "He said he wants to get a look at you."

"Get a look at me?" She got a hunted look in her eyes. "Why?"

He grinned evilly, but she was too agitated to notice. "Said he wanted to make sure I hadn't introduced his boys to some loose woman who'd exert a corrupting influence on their developing psyches."

"I'd say it's probably too late to be worried about that,

since we've already been introduced," Roxanne said. The words were nonchalant, but her palms were sweating.

She had a pretty good idea of what the Padre would see when he looked at her. Tight jeans, red boots, a snug little eyelet camisole top with too much cleavage showing for the middle of the day, topped by a deliberately tangled mop of flyaway blond hair. And the nails, she thought, catching sight of them as she rubbed her damp palms up and down her jeans-covered thighs. Let's not forget the man-killer nails. He was going to think she was some kind of Jezebel, for sure.

"You scared?" Tom said.

"Scared? Me?" She lifted her chin. "Of course not."

But she was. Scared to death. She'd built up an image of him in her mind. This saintly man they all called the Padre. This selfless paragon of virtue who had studied for the priesthood, then gave it up to minister to lost boys instead. She kept picturing someone like the late Spencer Tracy in his priestly garb in the movie *Boys Town* or, even scarier, Charlton Heston in any one of his biblical epics, stern and condemning and regal.

Instead, she found a grizzled old lion of a man in a faded green hospital gown, a little plastic bracelet around his left wrist. His hair was thick and dark, heavily sprinkled with gray. His face was brown and leathered with age, sagging a bit at the jowls, but still strong and craggily handsome in a patriarchal kind of way. He looked a little tired, a little frail, even to someone like Roxanne, who was unfamiliar with his normal appearance. He was leaning back against the sharply elevated head of the hospital bed, drinking a Dr Pepper through a straw, and carrying on a quiet conversation with a very attractive woman sitting in the visitor's chair in front of the window.

Tom checked in the doorway, as if in surprise, then dropped Roxanne's hand and hurried forward. "Hello,

Mom," he said, bending down to kiss the woman's smooth cheek. "I didn't realize you were in town. How are you?"

Mom? This lovely, soft-eyed woman, who didn't look more than forty years old, was Tom's mother? What kind of setup was this? Not only was she going to meet the man who was, to all intents and purposes, her lover's father, but now she had to face his mother, too? Was she being checked out? Roxanne wondered, resisting the urge to tug the front of her camisole a little higher on her chest. Were they going to gang up and warn her away before she could corrupt their darling boy? She lifted her chin, determined to brazen it out.

And rather enjoying the prospect, too, she realized. She'd never been warned away before. It made her feel like a dangerous woman. She'd never felt like a dangerous woman before. It was kind of exhilarating.

"I had no idea what had happened until Hector called me himself last night," Tom's mother was saying plaintively. "I wish someone had thought to let me know sooner." She looked up at Tom, her expression gently reproachful. "I would have gotten one of other nurses to take my shift at the hospital and come immediately."

"Now, now, Molly, don't fret," soothed the Padre. "There was no need for you to be here any sooner. There was nothing you could have done, except sit around and wait like everyone else. It's much better that you're here now, so we can visit. And isn't it nice that Tom's brought his new friend so you get a chance to meet her, too?"

He turned suddenly, his gaze pinning Roxanne where she stood, still hovering in the doorway. His eyes were brown and alive and knowing. His teeth, when he smiled at her, were strong and white, more than capable of taking a bite out of anything that got in his way.

"Come on over here, girl," he said, and held out his hand, motioning her forward with an imperious flick of his fingers, reminding her, suddenly, of Charlton Heston at his most imposing biblical best. This man, too, could have parted the Red Sea with a flick of his hand, even lying on his back in a hospital bed. "Let's have a look at you."

Roxanne crossed the room and put her hand in his. His grip was warm and firm. "Well, introduce us," he said to Tom, without taking his eyes off Roxanne.

She held his gaze steadily, without flinching, the same way she'd held Tom's at Ed Earl's in Lubbock. Her chin was elevated, her eyes full of silent challenge and bravado. No way were they going to see her sweat.

The Padre chuckled approvingly.

Tom couldn't hide the surge of pride he felt. "Mom. Padre. I'd like you both to meet Roxy Archer. Roxy, this is my mother, Molly Steele. And this—" the pride showed through, here, too "—is Hector Menendez. Better known as the Padre."

"Ms. Steele," Roxanne said crisply, dipping her head in her best finishing school fashion, as if she were standing there clad in a demure linen shift and graduated pearls instead of blue jeans and dusty red boots. "Mr. Menendez. A pleasure to meet you both."

"No need to stand on ceremony with me, girl. You can call me Padre like everybody else does around here. Sit yourself down—" he tugged on her hand "—right there on the edge of the bed is fine. You won't hurt me—and tell us about yourself. Tom, here, has been pretty scant on the details. How'd you two meet?"

Roxanne flicked a glance at Tom, silently asking for directions.

He smiled back blandly, leaving it up to her.

"I picked him up in Ed Earl's Polynesian Dance Palace in Lubbock after the rodeo," she said, letting them make of it what they would.

Molly Steele pursed her lips disapprovingly.

The Padre looked as if he were turning over her answer in his mind, reserving judgment until he knew more.

"Anything else you'd like to know?" she said to him, with the air of a smart-ass child pretending to be helpful.

"Well—" his dark eyes twinkled "—what do you do with yourself when you're not chasing cowboys?"

Tom smothered a laugh.

"Hector, really! What kind of a question is that?" chided Tom's mother.

"It's a perfectly legitimate question. I want to know what she does. Girl's a grown woman. She must have something that keeps her busy. She can't chase cowboys all day, can she?"

"I'm a teacher," Roxanne said.

"A *teacher!*" That was Tom, expressing his surprise.

"And for the record," she said, ignoring him in favor of addressing her remarks to the man in the hospital bed. "I've only chased one cowboy." She paused for effect. "So far," she said, and batted her lashes flirtatiously, blatantly intimating that she might be persuaded to broaden her horizons for him.

The Padre wheezed out what lately passed for his version of a laugh. "Girl's a real firecracker," he said, slapping his knee through the bedclothes. "Just like Rooster said."

"Where do you teach?" Tom said quietly, drawing her attention back to him.

"St. Catherine's Academy in Stamford, Connecticut. It's a fully accredited private school," she said, in case he doubted it. "Kindergarten through twelfth, both boarders and day students. I teach fifth grade English Lit and Latin."

"That where you're from?" the Padre asked. "Connecticut?"

"Born and raised."

"Got family there?"

"My parents and three brothers. One older and two

younger," she said before he could ask. "A sister-in-law and two nieces, with another on the way."

"Any beaus?"

"Dozens," she lied.

"Then what in blazes are you doing down here in Texas?"

"Why, I thought you knew—" she slipped into her corn-pone-and-molasses accent "—I'm down here chasin' cowboys on my summer vacation." She batted her eyelashes again, tilting her chin down so she could look up at him through her lashes. "You interested, sugar?"

The Padre wheezed delightedly.

ROXANNE WAITED until she and Tom were in the truck and on their way back to the Second Chance before she pounced. "Well, that was a nice little ambush you arranged."

Tom cast a wary glance at her out of the corner of his eye. "Ambush?"

"You didn't tell me your mother was going to be there."

"Because I didn't know she was going to be there."

Roxanne uttered an inelegant little snort. "Uh-huh."

"I swear, it was as much a surprise to me as it was to you. The last time my mother was in Bowie was when I had that concussion a year ago last May."

"Are you saying she only comes to visit when someone is sick?"

"Yeah, I guess that about sums it up," Tom conceded. "Since she left, nothing much less than a medical emergency will get her to set foot in Bowie."

"Not your birthday? Thanksgiving? Christmas?"

"Oh, my birthday, sure, when I was a kid. And holidays, too, sometimes, when she could get off work. After I got old enough to drive, though, I'd usually go to Dallas to see her. It's easier on everybody that way."

"Everybody who?"

"My mother, mostly," he admitted. "Bowie doesn't have a lot of good memories for her."

"It has you," she said, beginning to form a very poor opinion of Tom's mother.

It was one thing to turn him over to the care of someone who could do a better job of raising him. It was quite another to abandon him entirely to that someone else's care, even if that someone was the Padre. A child needed to know his mother loved him.

Tom took his eyes off the road a minute to look at her. "Don't make it into something tragic, Slim. It isn't. She did what she had to do, for her and for me, and we're both okay with that. She just hates it here, is all." He reached over and patted her thigh. "And I'm okay with that, too."

"I'll tell you something else she hates," Roxanne said. "Me."

He flicked another glance at her. "What makes you say a thing like that?"

"Oh, please." Roxanne rolled her eyes. "She thinks I'm a loose woman out to snag her baby boy and she doesn't like it—or me—one little bit."

Tom shook his head. "You must have misunderstood something she said."

"Oh, it wasn't anything she *said*. Not directly. It was more the way she looked at me. As if I had just strolled in off of the street."

He reached sideways and placed his palm on her forehead. "You feverish?"

"I'm serious." She grabbed his hand between both of hers. "Your mother thinks I'm going to corrupt you. So—" she brought his hand to her mouth and sucked his index finger inside, and pulled it out, very slowly "—how am I doing?" she said, and grinned at him.

Chapter Twelve

TWO DAYS LATER—fully three days ahead of schedule and against his doctor's advice—the Padre checked himself out of the hospital and demanded to be taken home. Tom agreed to the plan only if a nurse came with him and stayed for what would have been the remaining three days of a standard hospital stay for a triple by-pass patient. The Padre grumbled, declaring his boys could provide all the care he needed, but Tom was adamant and the nurse and her equipment were bundled into the truck for the ride to Second Chance.

And Roxanne, against all her better judgment and the resolutions she made in the middle of the night after Tom left her to sneak back to his own bed before the boys woke up, was still there. Since it would be churlish to leave before the Padre's welcome home party—planned for three days hence, when he would have returned to the Second Chance had he been inclined to follow doctor's orders—she decided to stay for just that much longer. Besides, Rooster would be there for the party, too, flush with his success in Cheyenne and Wichita and Oklahoma City, and she wanted to say goodbye to him before she left. They'd gotten to be good friends on those long rides between rodeos. She owed him a personal goodbye.

But then she was absolutely, definitely, without a doubt, leaving.

She'd gotten what she came for, after all. She'd found her good-looking dangerous cowboy and had her Wild West adventure. It was time to bow out, to retreat with good grace, while the Welcome mat was still out. She didn't want to wait around until the end, to see him wondering when she was going to pack up and go so he could get on with the nice little life he had planned for himself. She didn't want to wait until he had—God forbid—"gotten his fill of her." She wanted to leave while she could still see the want in his eyes, while that nice little life full of kids and cows—and the wife, let's not forget the wife, she told herself sternly—was still only something he was thinking about as a part of his future.

She wasn't going to be heart-whole when she left—any possibility of that had disappeared somewhere on the road between one rodeo and the next—but she was going to go in style, with her head held high and her dignity intact.

It helped, a little, that the only place for the Padre's nurse to bunk while she was at the Second Chance was up in the little attic room with Roxanne. It cut down considerably on the opportunity for her to dissolve into undignified tears and declare her undying love to a man who, by no stretch of her imagination, wanted to hear those words from the woman who was his "last fling."

She'd come dangerously close a couple of times, up in that little attic room in the middle of the night. The sex was sweeter between them in that room, more gentle and tender. Maybe it was the narrow bed, which limited their more wild sexual antics, or the need to be quiet so as not to alert the boys to what was going on over their heads. Maybe it was the fact that he got up and left her when the loving was over that made her want to cling and cry. Whatever it was, the room was dangerous.

Since the nurse had been sharing it with her, though, they'd had to rely on quickies at odd times and out-of-the-way places, which neatly precluded the trappings of romance that weakened her resolve. Roxanne had approached the lack of privacy with a positive attitude, seeing it as both safeguard against embarrassing confessions and an opportunity to fulfill as many of her remaining sexual fantasies as possible and store up memories for what was sure to be the coming sexual drought.

"WAIT, WAIT—" she was panting and wet, her jeans and panties on the floor of the truck, her blouse and bra pushed up around her neck, trying to maneuver so she could straddle his lap "—the steering wheel is in the way."

Without removing his mouth from her breast, he shifted position, edging over into the passenger side of the cab, and cupped his hands around the backs of her bare thighs to guide her legs to either side of his.

"Now the gearshift is in the way," she moaned.

"That's not the gearshift," he said, and slid into her.

"STOP IT!" She giggled and slapped at his hands, trying to wriggle away as he burrowed down the front of her jeans. Since he had her pressed up against the wall in the tack room, she couldn't wriggle very far. And she wasn't trying very hard. "Stop it right now," she said again, sucking in her stomach to make it easier for him to find what he was searching for. "I think someone's coming."

"That'd be you," he said, as he found the swollen little nubbin between her legs and began to massage it.

"GOOD GOD ALMIGHTY, woman! You're going to get us killed."

She raised her head from his lap, peering up at him through a tangle of hair. "Do you want me to stop?" she asked, and ran her tongue up the length of his rock-hard penis as if it were a great big peppermint stick. "I'll stop if you want me to."

"No, don't stop." He clutched the steering wheel in his fists, struggling manfully to keep his attention on the road while she drove him over the edge with her hot mouth and clever little tongue. "Don't stop."

AND THEN, suddenly, before she was ready for it, the day of the party dawned, bright and hot and sunny, and she realized her Wild West adventure was just about over. Roxanne almost cried, then, as she lay there, staring at the whitewashed ceiling, but the presence of the nurse in the other bed saved her again. She blinked the tears back and got up, determined to enjoy what was going to be her last day with her good-looking dangerous cowboy. One more day—and one more night—that's all she had, all she was going to allow herself.

And she was determined to make it the best night of her life. And his.

THE PROPOSED PARTY had somehow evolved from a simple welcome home potluck supper with a few close friends into a lavish barbecue that apparently included everyone in the entire county, and the kitchen was a beehive of activity when Roxanne finally made her way downstairs. Jo Beth and her mother, as the official hostesses of the event, were already there, overseeing the food preparation. So was Tom's mother, Molly Steele. Apparently, she had decided to lift her ban on Bowie, except in cases of emergency. Although, in Ms. Steele's mind, anyway, Roxanne was pretty sure she qualified as such. So maybe the ban hadn't been lifted, after all.

The three women were working together in the big, old-fashioned kitchen, a companionable trio with no room for a fourth—especially a fourth with man-killer red nails, questionable morals and possible designs on one of the most eligible bachelors in town.

"Can I do anything to help?" Roxanne asked, even though she already knew what the answer would be. There was no way any of the three women was going to allow her to show off whatever culinary expertise she might possess if Tom Steele was anywhere in the vicinity.

"We've about got it covered in here," Mrs. Jensen said. "They might need some help out back, though, getting the picnic tables set up and into position."

Which meant, Roxanne knew, that Tom was either in the front yard, doing whatever needed to be done out there or, more likely, down at main corral, seeing that the arrangements for the junior rodeo were progressing apace. Molly Steele and Jo Beth Jensen weren't the only women who were set on bringing Tom into the Jensen family fold.

Roxanne poured herself a cup of coffee, and pushed open the screen door to the back porch. It screeched loudly.

"Someone really ought to put some WD-40 on that," she heard Jo Beth say to the two older women.

She let it the door slam behind her—a petty gesture, but deeply satisfying—and strolled down the steps and across the struggling patch of lawn to where the Padre sat in a rocking chair under a copse of cottonwood trees, his trusty nurse by his side to make sure he didn't overdo, supervising as Jared and Augie set up the barbecue pit.

An entire side of beef—more raw meat than Roxanne had ever seen in one place before—lay on a tarp on top of one of the picnic tables, waiting to be hoisted onto the spit. She tried not to look at it.

"You ever seen a more beautiful side of beef?" asked the Padre as Roxanne approached. "Raised right here on Second Chance."

"Beautiful," she said admiringly, while privately thinking that she might never eat another steak for as long as she lived.

The Padre caught the flicker of distaste in her eyes. "You're not a vegetarian, are you?" he asked, as if it were a perversion of the worst sort.

"I wasn't," she said dryly.

He laughed and slapped his knee. "A real firecracker," he chortled gleefully.

Roxanne gave in to impulse and bent down to kiss his leathery cheek. "Try not to give your nurse too hard a time today," she said.

He caught her hand as she straightened. "Was that goodbye?"

"No," she said. "That was a deep and abiding appreciation for a good-looking, dangerous man. I'll tell you when it's goodbye."

"Fair enough," he said, and squeezed her hand—just as Molly Steele came out onto the back porch with a pile of bright, checkered tablecloths over her arm.

"Don't you overdo, now, Hector," she called, frowning when she saw the two of them apparently holding hands. "You mind what your nurse says and don't get yourself too excited. And, you—Roxy, isn't it?" She motioned her forward with her free hand. "I'd appreciate it if you would come on over here and help me cover these tables. We can chat a bit while we work and get to know each other."

Roxanne sighed. No way did she want a private tête-á-tête with Tom's disapproving mother. Seeing no way to avoid it, however, she was about to do as she was bid, when she felt the Padre's hand tighten on hers.

"I need Roxy to help me walk down to the barn." The Padre rose to his feet, using the support of Roxanne's arm for leverage.

"That's what the nurse is here for," Molly said. "And you shouldn't be walking that far, anyway. It's not good for you."

"It is, too, good for me. The doc said walking is the best exercise I could do right now. And I want Roxy to walk with me." He waved the nurse away. "You go help Molly cover those tables. I'll call if I need you."

"Thanks," Roxanne said.

"The thing you got to know about Molly," the Padre said, his head bent companionably to hers as they slowly ambled around the side of the house toward the barn, "is that she means well. She's just become kind of narrow in her opinions and strict in her ways, is all. Comes of her background, I guess, just like it does with most folks. She was kind of wild as a girl, with parents who were too busy to be bothered. She took off with the first cowboy who said he loved her when she was barely fifteen and came home six months later with a full belly and no husband."

"Yes, Tom told me some of the story," Roxanne said, and sipped her coffee.

"She tried to make a go of it on her own but, hell, you know the story…a young unmarried girl, no education, no health coverage, no access to good child care, forced to take one minimum-wage job after another to make ends meet. She pulled herself out of it, though. Admitted she couldn't do it on her own, and did what she had to do to make it right for her boy."

"Tom said she saved him when she gave him to you."

"She did. She saved herself, too. She worked hard, got a college education, and a good job. The thing is, though, instead of being proud of how far she's come, she's ashamed of where she's been. She has no sympathy for the girl she once was, and— Can she see us from where she's at?"

Roxanne glanced back over her shoulder. "No, I don't think so."

"Then let's set a spell, shall we?" He indicated the steps leading up to the porch. "I need to catch my breath."

"Are you all right? Should I call the nurse?"

"No. No, don't call the nurse. I'm fine. Just haven't got my stamina back yet, is all. Now—" he settled down onto the top step, under the shadowed overhang of the porch "—where was I?"

"You said Tom's mom hasn't got any sympathy for the girl she once was."

"No, she hasn't. And she's got no tolerance for anyone else who strays from what she considers the straight-and-narrow, either."

Roxanne looked up at him from where she stood at the foot of the stairs. "And I'm about as far off the straight-and-narrow as a woman can get, is that it?"

"That's certainly what Molly thinks." He gave her a sly, knowing smile from under his bushy gray eyebrows. "I have my doubts about that, though. I'll wager Tom does, too."

Roxanne shrugged. "I wouldn't count on that," she mumbled, and buried her nose in her coffee cup just as Petie came roaring around the side of the house, screaming at the top of his lungs.

"Rooster's here! Rooster's here!" He danced past her, heading down to the barbecue pit under the cottonwoods, then spied the Padre sitting on the steps and made a sharp left turn. "Rooster's here, Padre!" he trumpeted in his piercing little-boy voice, and then changed direction again, heading down toward the barn at a dead run. "Tom! Rooster's here, Tom. Come see. Rooster's here!"

"I swear, that little fella has got more energy than ten bucking bulls," Rooster said to no one in particular as he came around the side of the house. "Plum wears me out to watch him."

He came to a dead stop when he saw Roxanne, a wide smile

lighting up his plain, honest face at the sight of her. "Hey, Roxy." He reached out as if to hug her, then stepped back indecisively, a little red around his ears at his presumption.

Roxanne set her empty coffee cup down on the porch step and solved his problem for him by stepping forward and wrapping her arms around his neck. "Hey, pardner." She gave him a good, hard hug. "Congratulations on the big win in Cheyenne," she said, and planted a big, noisy kiss on his cheek.

Rooster blushed to the roots of his hair.

"If you're givin' out your kisses for winnin' rides, I'd just like to say, I beat his score in Wichita *and* Oklahoma City."

Roxanne looked past Rooster's shoulder to the man standing a few feet behind him. "My goodness," she said, her accent as thick and sweet as honey. "Clay Madison. What are you doing here, sugar?"

Rooster gestured toward the young cowboy with a jerk of his thumb. "Clay's my new travelin' partner."

"So," Clay said. "Do I get that kiss?"

Roxy grinned and went into his arms. "That's for Wichita," she said, and kissed him on one cheek. "And that's for Oklahoma City." She kissed him on the other.

It seemed to be her day for kissing cowboys.

Unfortunately, the only one she hadn't kissed yet chose that particular moment to make his appearance.

"You want to unhand that woman," Tom said, "or do I have to rearrange your pretty face for you?"

Clay grinned and tightened his hold on Roxanne, keeping her from stepping away from him. "You're welcome to try," he invited. "Any place. Any time."

"If you don't let go of me, *I'll* rearrange your face for you," Roxanne said, and jabbed him in the gut. She was in too close to do much damage, but it was enough to surprise him into letting her go.

Clay stood there, a half smile on his handsome face, his

hand on his abused stomach, watching her as she walked back to the porch and retrieved her coffee cup.

Tom watched Clay watch her, and contemplated the possible satisfaction to be gained in carrying out his threat.

Roxanne sashayed up the porch steps, and sat down on the porch steps next to the Padre to finish her coffee, pointedly ignoring them both. Or pretending to.

"You boys may as well stop pawing at the ground," the Padre said. "She isn't impressed. And we haven't got time for it now, anyway. We've got company comin' up the drive."

THE PARTY was in full swing by noon. The long gravel driveway was lined with pickup trucks and dusty ranch cars. The kitchen counters were groaning under the platters of fried chicken and baked ham, the fresh corn tamales and enchiladas, the molded gelatin salads and layer cakes and homemade pies that had been brought by the ranchers wives to supplement the side of beef that was slowly roasting to perfection on the spit outside. There was a wild game of tag going on in the backyard and an impromptu horseshoe tournament being waged in the specially constructed horseshoe pits beyond the cottonwood trees. The Padre was sitting on the back porch, where he could keep an eye on the barbecue, playing a fiercely competitive game of checkers with the surgeon who had done his by-pass operation. There were fiddlers on the front porch for those who cared to dance or to just listen. And down in the main corral, out by the barn, the junior rodeo was in full swing under the careful supervision of Tom and Rooster.

Roxanne took it all in, enjoying it to the full, wandering from activity to activity like a child at a county fair, storing up memories in defense against the not-to-distant future when she would be back in her narrow, boring little life in Connecticut. She tossed horseshoes with a jovial white-

haired man who turned out to be a county judge, offered un-
solicited advice to the checkers players, cheered on the bud-
ding rodeo stars, ate more barbecue than she intended to, and
danced with anyone who asked.

At the end of the evening, after the fires in the barbecue
pit had been carefully banked, and the mothers had gathered up their sleepy children, and the fiddlers had packed
up their bows, and the Padre had gone to bed, exhausted
after the long day, and Molly Steele had gotten into her little blue Honda and headed back to Dallas, Roxanne found
herself right where she wanted to be—alone in the moonlight with Tom.

She leaned back, resting her elbows on the step behind her,
and looked up at the stars.

"Tired?" he said.

"Peaceful," she countered, and turned her head to smile
at him. "Do you think everybody's actually gone home?"

"I sure as hell hope so. It's coming up on one o'clock."

"And everybody in the house is asleep?"

"It appears that way."

"Then, do you think, if we got a blanket and went out to
the barn, we'd be alone?"

He gave her a slow, sweetly wicked smile. "I can guarantee it."

She leaned over and kissed him. "Meet in the tack room
in fifteen minutes," she said, and disappeared into the house.

DETERMINED TO SET the scene for romance, Tom used his
fifteen minutes to excellent advantage. It only took a few
carefully selected props. A bale of hay spread out over the
wooden floor for atmosphere, a pair of quilts on top of that
for comfort. An electric lantern turned down low to provide
the necessary candle glow. A bouquet of sweet peas in a jelly
jar to show her that he cared.

"It should be roses," he said when she stepped into the small cozy room, "but we don't have any in the garden."

Roxanne felt the sting of quick, foolish tears and blinked them back, determined not to ruin her last night with him. "Roses would be overkill," she said, and kissed him.

It was soft and sweet and utterly romantic.

"Would you do something for me?" she whispered.

"Anything."

"Would you take off your shirt?"

"Just my shirt?"

"Just your shirt." She smiled. "For now." She slipped her fingers inside the front placket, beneath the pearl snaps. "I'll help you," she said, and gave a little tug, popping them open in one quick motion.

He stripped off the shirt and draped it over one of the saddles on the rack. "Now what?"

"Now you just stand there and let me seduce you."

"You've already done that, Slim. All you have to do is look at me like you're doing right now and I'm putty in your hands."

She arched an eyebrow. "Putty?" she said, and cupped her hand over the fly of his jeans. "It doesn't feel like putty to me."

"Really hard putty," he amended. "Cement." He pressed his hand to the back of hers, molding her fingers to the solid shape of him. "Concrete."

"I'm going to make you harder. I'm going to make you so hard you hurt." She slid her hand out from under his and backed away. "But no touching."

Tom was already being to ache. "No touching?"

She shook her head. "Not until I tell you. Until I tell you, all you can do is stand there like this—" she took his hands and placed them at his sides, palms flat against his thighs "—and watch." She backed up, well out of reach, and flicked open the top button on her vest. "And want."

He realized then that she'd used her fifteen minutes to change clothes. She was not longer wearing the jeans and tank top she'd had on all afternoon. She'd changed into her ruffled white-eyelet skirt and denim vest.

"Do you remember that night at the Bare Back Saloon, Tom?" She flicked open the second button. "The night when you made me keep my hands against the wall and wouldn't let me touch you?" She worked the third button loose. "Wouldn't let me move until I was nearly crazy with desire?" She lingered on the fourth and final button, playing with it. "Do you remember that night?"

As if he could forget it! "Yes," he said, and licked his lips to ease the dryness.

"Now it's your turn," she said, and slipped the last button from its buttonhole.

The denim parted slightly, revealing a thin slice of flesh between her breasts. She ran her fingertips up and down the opening, those long, red, man-killer nails of hers brushing against her skin, driving him crazy.

"Do you want me to open my vest?"

"Yes."

"Yes, what?"

"Yes...please?"

She smiled in approval and edged the vest open a mere inch, then two, revealing the inner curves of her breasts and the sleek flat line of her stomach.

"More?"

"Yes. Please."

She peeled the two halves of fabric all the way back, slowly, tucking them beneath her arms to display her breasts. And then she cupped her hands over them and began massaging herself, making little circles around her areola, drawing her fingers together to pluck at her own nipples.

"Would you like to touch me like this?"

"Yes, please."

She tilted her head, looking at him from beneath the tangle of her overlong bangs. "No," she said, and smiled when his fingers flexed against his thighs. "Well…" she made a little moue, a suggestion of a pout "…maybe I can come up with something else." She sauntered within reach. "No touching," she warned him, and leaned in, rubbing the very tips of her breasts to his chest. "Do you like that?"

"Yes."

"Tell me."

"I like it very much," he said. "Come closer."

She leaned into him a bit, flattening her breasts against his bare chest.

"Closer," he said.

She shook her head and backed away.

"Have mercy, Slim. You're killing me here."

She tilted her head, considering that. "Sit down," she said. "There." She pointed at a squat wooden stool.

He sat. It put him nearly at eye level with her bare breasts.

"You can't touch them with your hands." She came closer, putting her breasts within reach of his mouth. Barely. "But you can kiss them."

He strained forward, closing his lips around one tempting nipple, and sucked.

Hard.

She moaned and leaned into him, giving him more, turning her body slightly to subtly direct him to the other breast. He took the hint and transferred his attention, giving it the same treatment. She moaned again, and he could feel her shudder. Her hands came up to his head, her fingers raked through his hair.

"Enough!" she said, and jerked his head away.

He nearly howled in frustration.

She stood there for a moment, panting, her breasts quivering with every shuddering breath. Her cheeks were flushed. Her eyes were bright with arousal, and the knowledge of her own seductive powers.

"Would you like to see something else?" she said.

"Yes, please."

She backed away a bit so he would get the full effect, placed her hands on her thighs, and began gathering the fabric of her skirt into her palms. The hem rose, inch by excruciating inch, revealing the tops of her bright red boots, the lacy white stockings that sheathed her slender legs, the stocking tops…

"Aw, Slim!" he groaned. "Don't stop now."

"Remember, the last time, when you tore my panties off?"

The skirt rose a half inch higher, revealing a slice of bare skin above the top of the stockings.

He started to sweat. "Yes. I remember."

"This time you won't have to do that."

"I won't?" he croaked.

The skirt rose another scant inch.

Two.

"Do you know why you won't have to rip my panties off?"

"No," he said, but he could guess.

"Because—" she lifted the skirt to the top of her pubic mound "—I'm not wearing any."

He came up off the stool in a rush and lunged at her like a maddened bull.

"No touching," she hollered, but it was too late.

He grabbed her by the waist and spun her around, bending her over one of the saddles on the rack, and flipped her skirt up over her head. Holding her there with a hand on the back of her neck, he used the other to rip open his jeans and free his erection, then inserted one foot between her booted ankles and swept it from side-to-side in two quick, convulsive movements, widening her stance. Grasping her hips in his hands, he stepped forward and thrust into her, burying himself to the hilt.

She shrieked in mindless ecstasy and pressed back against him, increasing the pressure. He thrust once...twice...a third time...and they both came in a blind, cataclysmic explosion of raw passion.

They were both so exhausted, so wrung out by what had just passed between them, that they hung there for a moment or two, both of them bent over the saddle, both of them panting and weak and filled with churning emotions.

Roxanne felt an overwhelming exhilaration, a fierce kind of joy that was almost painful in its intensity. He wouldn't forget her now. No matter what happened, no matter who he married or what his life became, he wouldn't ever forget her.

Tom was swamped with an unnerving, almost brutal tenderness. He'd taken her like an animal, driven to possess her in the most basic, elemental way, and yet there he stood, curled over her body, his overriding instinct to cherish and protect what he had just ravaged.

It wasn't how he had meant for this night to go. He'd planned on romance. He'd planned to shower her with flower petals and kisses. Planned to woo her with soft seductive words, and softer caresses.

He'd planned to tell her how he felt.

But the time to tell a woman you were in love with her wasn't after you'd just mounted her like a stallion in rut and ridden her to exhaustion. Especially when you weren't more than half sure she wouldn't laugh in your face. Falling in love hadn't been part of their bargain, and she hadn't given any indication that she wanted that bargain changed. She had a life up there in Connecticut. A family. Friends. A job. And he knew damned good and well she was used to better than he could give her. She came from cultured, sophisticated people and—despite his fancy college education—he was just a cowboy.

And he really wouldn't want to be anything else.

Not even for her.

The declaration of his feelings would have to wait.

He straightened, lifting her against him with an arm around her waist. She sagged against him, as boneless as a rag doll.

"Are you all right, Slim?"

"I think so." Her voice was soft. Hesitant. Faint. "I'm just so…tired," she managed.

He turned her in his arms and bent slightly, slipping an arm under her knees so he could lift her. Staggering slightly, his own strength curiously lacking, he stumbled to the makeshift bed of hay and quilts, and sank down into the welcoming softness. She lolled against him, already sound asleep. Cuddling her in his arms, he closed his eyes and joined her.

Chapter Thirteen

ROXANNE WOKE at first light, disturbed by the prickly, uncomfortable feel of straw poking into her bare thigh, and the urgent need to relieve her bladder. She wasn't sure, in that first waking moment, of exactly where she was. And then she became aware of the heat of the body beside her, the weight of his arm over her waist, the soft rush of his warm breath against her shoulder, and it all came flooding back.

Last night.

It had been earthy and magical. Elemental and ethereal. A transcendental experience on a rawly physical plane. And it had made her transformation from good-girl Roxanne to good-time girl Roxy complete.

She'd touched herself like a wanton, tantalizing and teasing her dangerous, good-looking cowboy until he was driven to take her like a beast. And she had reveled in it! There wasn't the slightest sting of embarrassment, not the faintest trace of shame. None of the unspoken taboos and conventions she'd been brought up with had intruded to mar the experience in any way. Her overriding feeling about the night just past was one of supreme satisfaction.

She'd satisfied him.

Utterly.

He'd satisfied her.

Completely.

She'd accomplished what she'd wanted to when she'd set out to seduce him out of his mind. She'd met all her own expectations. Fulfilled every fantasy, except one. And that one hadn't been part of the original bargain. It wasn't fair to change the rules now and ask him to give her something he hadn't bargained for.

It was time for her to go home.

Thankful that he was a heavy sleeper, who always woke slowly, in stages, she picked up his wrist in both hands and gently lifted it off her waist, placing it by his side. Still moving slowly, she sat up and rose to her knees, carefully working her rumpled skirt out from under his thigh. And then she paused and smiled, looking down into his face, wishing, for one fleeting moment, that it had been different. That she had met him under other circumstances, in another place. That she hadn't made the promises she'd made. No muss. No fuss. No strings. And no looking back.

Particularly no looking back!

That was the one she had to remember.

From now on, she would only look forward.

Looking back would hurt too much.

She leaned down and kissed him softly. "Goodbye, sugar," she said.

Rising to her feet, she tiptoed from the tack room.

ROXANNE HAD THE LITTLE attic room to herself. The nurse had gone home after the party last night, her duties at an end, leaving Roxanne free to indulge in a long hot bath and a good hard cry—after which she had to lie down on the bed with a cold washcloth over her eyes for nearly half an hour to soothe the resulting redness away. When she went downstairs, there must be no trace of tears. No evidence of sadness or regret. Good-time girl Roxy had to be completely in charge. It was the only way for good-girl Roxanne to get through the coming goodbyes with her dignity intact.

She did her makeup carefully, using concealer and shadows to camouflage any lingering signs of weepiness, and bright red lipstick to draw attention to the smile she intended to have plastered to her face. Although she tried to linger over the task, she was dressed in a few minutes. Boots and jeans and one of her little sleeveless eyelet blouses didn't lend themselves to a lot of sartorial fusing. Her packing only took another minute or two—she only had the one bag—and before she was really ready, she was heading downstairs to face the music.

Her chin high, her boot heels clicking on the bare wooden treads, she headed for the kitchen as if she were happy to be leaving.

Although there were signs that breakfast had recently been prepared and consumed, the kitchen was empty. Roxanne set her bag on the end of the table and headed for the coffee pot. After pouring herself a cup—and adding the requisite one-half teaspoon of sugar—she plucked the bag off of the table and pushed through the squeaky screened door onto the porch.

It was a beautiful morning, not too hot, yet, although all the signs promised it would be a scorcher. She could hear cattle bawling somewhere off in the near distance. Chickens pecked around the yard under the cottonwood trees, picking up scraps of food dropped in the grass the night before. Off somewhere near the barn, beyond her field of vision, she heard the boisterous sounds of barking dogs and boys at work and play. A child's laugh—Petie's—drifted out from an upstairs window.

It was paradise, and she had to leave.

The blue Chevy truck—Rooster's ride now that he'd returned the black monster to Tom—was sitting in the yard, the bed already packed with his and Clay's gear. They were headed for the Mesquite rodeo; she planned to ride with them as far as the Dallas-Fort Worth airport. She looked around, wondering where they had gotten to and how long it would be before they were ready to go. She didn't want to drag out her goodbyes. She walked down the wooden stairs, crossed to the truck, and heaved her bag over the side, determined to be ready to leave the minute they were.

The rhythmic squeak of the rocker against the wooden planks of the porch had her turning her head toward the sound. The Padre sat, exactly where he had sat the day before playing checkers with his surgeon, and watched her over his own cup of coffee. She sighed and moved back up the steps and across the width of the porch to his side. Bending down, she kissed him on the cheek.

"That's goodbye," she said.

"I figured it was." He took a sip of his coffee. "What I didn't figure is that you'd turn out to be such a coward."

"A coward?" she said carefully.

The Padre shook his grizzled head. "I never would have expected it of a firecracker like you."

"Expected what?"

"You running out on him."

She didn't pretend not to know who he was talking about. There was only one *him,* and they both knew it. "I'm not out running out on him. I'm going home. Back to Connecticut were I belong."

"You're running," he said.

"All right, yes, I am. I admit it." Her tone hinted that she was humoring an old man's fancy. "I'm running back home before I get my poor little heart broke," she said, laying on the cornpone accent to show she wasn't serious.

"Have you ever thought that by doing that, you might be breaking his instead?"

"That's impossible."

"Not if he's in love with you."

Roxanne felt her heart leap at the thought. She shook her head. "He's in lust with me," she said. "It's not the same thing."

"No, it's not," the Padre said. "And I'm not saying he doesn't have a healthy case of lust where you're concerned. But he also happens to be in love with you."

Roxanne looked him square in the eyes. "I wasn't joking about how we met," she said. "I picked him up in a bar in Lubbock, just exactly like I told you. I went there *specifically* to pick him up. And then I took him back to my motel room and had sex with him six ways from Sunday before he even knew my name."

"And your point would be?"

"For crying out loud, Padre! I'm his summer fling. His last hurrah before he retires from the rodeo for good. And he was my walk on the wild side. My study subject for "What I Did On My Summer Vacation." That's all it was ever meant to be between us. That's all it can be."

"It may have started out that way, but that's not how it ended." He gave her a level look. "For either of you."

"And your point would be?" she said, firing his words back at him.

"Don't you think you owe it to him—and yourself—to tell him how you feel? Even if I'm wrong and he isn't in love with you, don't you think you should at least be honest about your *own* feelings?"

"We had an agreement. No muss. No fuss. No strings. When it was over, it was over. And it's over." She could feel the hot tears prickling the backs of her eyes. She clenched her hands around her coffee cup and held on, refusing to let them fall. "I'm not about to change the rules at this stage of the game. It wouldn't be fair to expect more from him now."

"Not only a coward, but a liar, too."

"I haven't lied," she said, incensed. "I never lied to Tom."

"To yourself, Slim," the Padre said, using Tom's pet name for her. "You're lying to yourself."

She ducked her head, dashing at her cheek with the back of her hand. "How do you figure that?"

"It's not his feelings you're worried about, it's your own. No, don't go throwing that chin up at me. I'm too old to be taken in by it." He reached out and grabbed her wrist, holding her by his side when she would have turned away. "How's it going to hurt Tom to know you're in love with him? Hmm? If he loves you back, well, that's fine, then, and everybody's happy. If he doesn't, he'll be a mite embarrassed to hear you admit to feelings he doesn't share, but it isn't going to hurt him any. It's your own pride you're worried about. You're so afraid of looking like a fool for falling in love with a man who might not love you, that you're willing to break your own heart over a possibility rather than face the truth of what is."

Roxanne went absolutely still as the reality of the Padre's words sunk in. He was right. It was *her* pride she was worried about. *Her* dignity.

And that was good-girl Roxanne thinking.

She was the one who worried about looking like a fool. She was the one who always pretended to be cool and unconcerned in case anyone thought she cared too much. She was the one who buried everything inside for the sake of good manners and good breeding and not making a messy, emotional scene.

Good-time girl Roxy wasn't anything like that. She believed in letting it all hang out and letting the chips fall where they may. She believed in letting 'er rip, and to hell with worrying about whether her emotions and her needs were dignified or proper.

What good were dignity and pride when your whole future happiness was at stake?

She got a calculating look in her eyes. "Is he still out in the barn?"

"Yep."

"Hold this." She thrust her coffee cup into his free hand, then leaned down and kissed him again, full on the mouth. "That's thank you," she said, and marched on down the stairs and toward the barn with a sassy hip-swinging stride.

"You go get 'em, Roxy," he said, and chortled gleefully.

SHE FOUND HIM in the tack room, right where she'd left him. Or, almost. He'd obviously been up for a while. The quilts they'd slept on were neatly folded on top of the squat little stool. The lantern was back in its accustomed place. The jelly jar of sweet peas was empty and sitting on a shelf next to other jelly jars full of bits and pieces that were used in maintaining and repairing saddles and other tack. He had his shirt on, but it was hanging open over his chest, the collar wet from where he'd either dunked his head in the water trough or held it under a faucet. He was forking up the hay that had been piled on the tack room floor, dumping it into a wheelbarrow by the door.

He barely glanced up as she came into the room. "I thought we said our goodbyes last night," he said without pausing in his work.

"Our goodbyes?"

"That's what you're here for, isn't it? To make it official?"

"Official?" she said, confused by the cold, dispassionate look in his eyes. He'd never looked at her that way before, with no emotion, no feeling.

She began to wonder if the Padre had been wrong.

"Rooster told me you were leaving with him and Clay this morning," he said. "That you arranged it last night. Before you came out here with me."

"Yes," she admitted. "I did."

"So last night was—what? Your final performance? Give the cowboy one last thrill before you packed up and headed out?"

She wanted to lie, wanted to say it wasn't like that at all, but she couldn't. "Something like that," she said. "But the thrill was for my benefit, not yours. I wanted one more memory to take with me."

"Well, you got it."

"Yes, I did."

"So what do you want from me now? Another go-round? One for the road?" He knew he was being a jackass, knew he sounded like a petulant fool, but he'd been ready to declare his love last night. Ready to offer his heart and his hand, and she'd been using him for cheap thrills. It was worse than having her laugh at him. He stabbed another pitchforkful of hay and heaved it toward the wheelbarrow. Some of it fluttered down over the toes of her boots. "I'm afraid I'm too busy right now to accommodate you." He looked her right in the eyes and delivered his killing shot. "Maybe you can get Clay to oblige you."

It took about three seconds for his meaning to sink in. Three seconds in which her fabulous whiskey-colored eyes widened with shock, glistened with hurt, and narrowed in fury.

"That was a really shitty thing to say," she said, fighting to keep the tears out of her voice.

"It was a shitty thing to do."

"What? What did I do? I haven't slept with Clay, and you know it. I haven't ever *wanted* to sleep with Clay. And you know that, too."

"I wasn't talking about Clay. I was talking about last night."

"Last night?" she repeated, at a loss. "Last night was— It was wonderful. It was thrilling. What was so bad about last night?"

"I don't like being used."

"But I wasn't using you. I wouldn't use you. I—" She put her hand on his bare chest, needing the connection.

He stood, quivering beneath her palm like a stallion awaiting the bit, but he didn't move away.

She took encouragement from that. "Do you care for—"

No, that was the wrong way to go about it. It was her feelings she had to be concerned about. Her feelings she had to own up to. She took a deep breath, prepared to make a fool of herself if that's what it took, and plunged in with both feet.

"I love you," she said. "I know it wasn't part of our agreement. I know I promised no strings and no looking back. And I meant it. I still do. If you want me to leave, I'll leave. But I can't go without telling you how I feel. You don't have to do anything about it. You don't have to love me back. I just wanted you to know. I love you. You can take it or leave it, whichever you want. It's up to you."

His eyes heated as he listened to her heartfelt confession. His lips curved. His whole life took a decidedly upward turn, and the world was suddenly bright and shining. He put his hands on her shoulders. "I'll take it," he said, and yanked her against his chest.

Their kiss was long and liquid and leisurely, a silent affirmation of their feelings for each other. She could feel his heart pounding against the palm of her hand, counterpoint to her own wildly beating heart. She smiled up into his eyes as he drew back to look down at her.

"Does that mean you love me, too?" she said, wanting to hear the words.

He bumped his groin against hers. "What do you think, Slim?"

"I think we should skip the preliminaries—" she slipped the toe of her boot behind his ankle and shoved, hard, against his chest, pushing him backward into the mound of hay on the floor "—and get right to it."

He hooked an arm around her knees and brought her down on top of him. "Damn, I like a woman with sass!" he said, and rolled her over, pressing her down into the hay beneath him. His expression sobered as he stared down into her glowing eyes.

"I love you, Slim," he said, giving her the words she needed to hear, the words he needed to say. "I want you for my partner. I want you to share my life and have my babies, and grow old with me. I want you to marry me, Slim. What do you say?"

"I say yes, cowboy."

Epilogue

IT WAS SUNDAY AFTERNOON, the final day of the National Prorodeo finals. Down in the arena, country star Randy Travis had finished singing the national anthem, and the Grand Entry parade was well under way. The state flags of every cowboy in the rodeo were unfurled, carried around the ring by riders mounted on the backs of gleaming palominos. The rodeo queens and their courts rode by, sparkling in sequin-studded Western shirts and elaborately studded jeans, waving and smiling at the stomping and cheering crowd.

Across the strip, in a suite at the Grand Bellagio Hotel and Casino, Roxanne watched the first event on the television screen as she did her hair and makeup, and tried not to listen as the mothers of both the bride and groom bemoaned the tackiness of a Las Vegas wedding. Amazingly, the two women were in perfect accord.

"They could have had a lovely wedding in the front parlor at the Second Chance," Molly Steele said. "The room has an alcove that would have been perfect for a wedding bower. But Tom wouldn't even consider it. He wanted to have the wedding here, in Las Vegas—" she said the name as if it were synonymous with Sodom "—during the rodeo finals."

"I'd always hoped Roxanne would get married in the garden at our country house. In June, of course, when the roses are in bloom and everything is looking its very best." Charlotte Archer sighed at the incomprehensibility of her daughter's choice of locations for her nuptials. "She used to be such a considerate, biddable girl. Never gave her father and me a moment's trouble. And then she turned thirty, and I don't know what happened. I blame it on those awful boots."

Both women looked toward the offending footwear. The red boots sat, gleaming with fresh polish, at the foot of the bed, an affront to good taste and moderation.

"She wanted a pair when she was nine years old," Charlotte confided, "but I refused to buy them for her. I felt bad about it then. I mean, I thought, really, what harm could one pair of boots do? Now we see the results," she said, and gestured toward her daughter. "Unbridled excess."

Roxanne grinned at her mother in the mirror. "Don't you mean *bridaled* excess, Mom?" she said, and struck a pose, feet primly together, eyes downcast, hands in front of her waist as if she were carrying a bouquet.

She was dressed all in white, as befitting a bride. A white satin corset embroidered with pale-pink rosebuds nipped in her already-slender waist and plumped up her breasts, tiny white bikini panties barely spanned her hips, white lace garters held up gossamer-white silk stockings. Considering the way she was dressed—or rather, undressed—the pose was just the tiniest bit salacious. She planned to strike the same pose for Tom later that night before she let him unhook her corset.

A knock sounded on the connecting door, causing all three women to jump and look toward it.

"It's me. Tom. You about ready in there?"

Roxanne started for the door, but her mother grabbed her firmly by the arm. "It's bad luck for the groom to see the bride before the ceremony," she warned.

"Especially when she's still in her underwear," Molly said reprovingly as she got up to answer the door. She opened it a crack, so he couldn't peek around the edge and glimpse his bride. "What do you want?" she demanded of her son.

"The bull riding is going to start in less than a hour. We need to get this show on the road if we're going to get it done before then. Everything's ready in here. All we need is the bride."

"Roxanne is just putting her dress on now. She'll be out in a minute," Molly said, and started to shut the door.

Tom put his hand on it, stopping her. "Wait a minute, Mom," he said, suddenly looking as nervous as a schoolboy. "Give this to her for me, will you?" He slipped a flat jeweler's box through the crack. "And tell her I love her with all my heart."

"She heard you," Molly said dryly, but she was smiling when she turned away from the door and carried the box to her soon-to-be daughter-in-law.

Roxanne accepted it with trembling fingers. He'd already given her an engagement ring. It sparkled on the ring finger of her left hand, an antique square cut ruby that matched her ruby-red nail polish. She hadn't expected anything else. The box contained a necklace in the same gleaming silver metal as the setting for her ring. It was as delicately wrought as cobweb, the chain nearly invisible, with a tiny number seven suspended from it. Her eyes clouded up with emotion. Seven had been the number on the door of her motel room that first night in Lubbock.

"Lucky number seven," she murmured, remembering the way he had carried her to the room that night. And what had happened after.

"Don't get all blubbery now," her mother said. "We haven't got time for you to redo your makeup." She took the necklace from Roxanne's fingers and fastened it around her neck. The tiny number seven nestled in the soft hollow at the base of her throat, in the spot that Tom liked to kiss when he was feeling especially tender and romantic.

"Be careful now," Molly said, as they maneuvered the dress over her head. "Try not to mess up your hair."

"As if you could tell with that mop," Charlotte said, but she was smiling.

Unlike the risqué underwear, the dress was elegant and demurely ladylike. Made of matte satin with a dull sheen, it had a simple sweetheart neckline that merely hinted at the presence of cleavage. The illusion sleeves were long and narrow, ending in a flat satin cuff at her wrists. The skirt flared slightly from the natural waist, ending a few inches above her ankles to show off the red cowboy boots she intended to wear with it.

Both of the mothers sighed when Roxanne stomped into them, but neither one of them said anything. Roxanne was as adamant about the boots as she had been about the location.

They helped her fasten on her veil and handed her the bouquet—sweet peas and baby's breath—and suddenly, she was ready. There was no more to do, no more preparations to make.

Molly opened the door into the main room of the suite, signaling Roxanne's father. There was a rustling and a bit of chatter, and then everyone was settled in their places, congregating on either side of the room to leave a path for the bride. The organist began to play softly, signaling the bride's entrance. Roxanne took a deep breath, slipped her hand into the crook of her father's elbow, and stepped into the flower-bedecked living room of the suite.

Her eyes found Tom's immediately and she focused on him, her gaze never wavering as she made her way through the throng of people crowded into the room. All the Second Chance boys were in attendance, from Petie on up to Jared and Augie. Rooster and his new traveling partner and fellow bull riding finalist Clay were there, decked out in their fanciest rodeo shirts. The Padre waited beside Tom, ready to offer his support as best man and maid of honor combined.

Tom held his hand out as she approached. She let go of her father's arm and reached out, laying her fingers in his. He brought them to his lips for a brief butterfly kiss and then, together, as one, they turned to the justice of the peace.

"Everyone please remove your hats," he intoned severely, and then, when everyone had done as he requested, "Dearly beloved," he began.

Five minutes later, the new Mr. and Mrs. Steele were gazing at each other, dewy eyed with love, identical smiles of blissful delight on their faces.

Forty minutes later, they were at the rodeo finals—still in their wedding finery—watching Rooster ride to the winning score on the back of the Widow Maker. Rooster stood in the center of the arena as the announcer broadcast his name and score over the loudspeaker, a wide grin on his face, his arms raised overhead in triumph. Roxanne gave a loud, raucous, unladylike whoop of joy and tossed her bridal bouquet into the ring in tribute.

And then she tossed herself into her husband's waiting arms.